John Harding is the author of two previous novels, the bestselling *What We Did On Our Holiday*, which was shortlisted for the WH Smith New Talent Award, and the acclaimed *While the Sun Shines*.

Also by John Harding

What We Did on Our Holiday
While the Sun Shines

and published by Black Swan

ONE BIG DAMN PUZZLER

John Harding

BLACK SWAN

ONE BIG DAMN PUZZLER
A BLACK SWAN BOOK : 0552999806
9780552999809

Originally published in Great Britain by Doubleday,
a division of Transworld Publishers

PRINTING HISTORY
Doubleday edition published 2005
Black Swan edition published 2006

1 3 5 7 9 10 8 6 4 2

Set in 10.5/12.5pt Bembo by
Falcon Oast Graphic Art Ltd.

Black Swan Books are published by Transworld Publishers,
61–63 Uxbridge Road, London W5 5SA,
a division of The Random House Group Ltd,
in Australia by Random House Australia (Pty) Ltd,
20 Alfred Street, Milsons Point, Sydney, NSW 2061, Australia,
in New Zealand by Random House New Zealand Ltd,
18 Poland Road, Glenfield, Auckland 10, New Zealand
and in South Africa by Random House (Pty) Ltd,
Isle of Houghton, Corner of Boundary Road & Carse O'Gowrie,
Houghton 2198, South Africa.

Printed and bound in Great Britain by
Cox & Wyman Ltd, Reading, Berkshire.

Papers used by Transworld Publishers are natural, recyclable
products made from wood grown in sustainable forests. The
manufacturing processes conform to the environmental
regulations of the country of origin.

For Catherine Sutton and Simon Taylor

'There is nothing either good or bad,
but thinking makes it so.'
Hamlet

1995

ONE

The day the plane brought the white man was an important one for Managua. He was, as usual, occupied by his translation of *Hamlet* into language the rest of the tribe would understand, and he could have done without the interruption because this was the day he had set aside to work on the famous soliloquy. As the only islander who could even read, let alone write, Managua felt the burden of his culture upon his shoulders the way he imagined an old turtle bore the weight of its carapace upon its back: it was certainly a secure home, a comfort and a blessing, but at times like this, when he had a tricky scene to write, it was plenty damn heavy too.

Although he later swore about the coming of the white man and the disruption to his work that the resultant excitement caused – not to mention the anxiety to him personally – if truth be told, long before the whirring of the plane's three propellers stirred the torpid island air, his task was already suffering insufferable disturbances from his wife Lamua who once again had gotten herself into one big sweat about the pig.

Is be or is be not, is be one big damn puzzler

he had written. He read it over again, allowing his lips to move so he could get the feel of how the words would sound, although he dared not permit even a whisper to escape him. The way Lamua was bustling about the hut, moving this and that (as though she might find the pig here! as if you could conceal even a bantam pig in this single, sparsely furnished room!), any sound from him would be jumped upon like a snake by *koku-koku* and taken as an invitation to conversation.

'I is tell you now,' she muttered. 'I is eat that pig if is be last thing I is do.'

Managua adjusted his spectacles and peered more intently at his *Complete Shakespeare*, partly by way of showing Lamua that he was ignoring her but also because the print was so bloody damn small. He must see Miss Lucy about some new reading glasses. This pair seemed to be losing all their strength, but then again that was only to be expected; he had had them for a couple of years and they were second-hand when he got them, or rather *second-eye*, he told himself. He smiled, congratulating himself on his little joke. It was the kind of joke Shakespeare made all the time, which just showed the benefit of reading the great man, and why it would do the islanders good to see *Hamlet*.

'You is better not laugh at me now, man,' snapped Lamua, catching him a cuff round the head as she passed his mat. 'I is tell you, that bloody pig you is be so fond of is be good as dead.'

Managua squinted at the next line.

'*Whether 'tis nobler in the mind to suffer*' was how Shakespeare had got it. Managua had looked up *nobler* in the dictionary and realized right away that it was one hard word to translate. The island didn't have any nobles. There wasn't even a chief, like he'd heard tell some islands possessed. When something needed to be decided on all the men just crawled into the *kassa* house and talked it over until everyone was agreed. If it was some little thing they indulged in some *kassa* first, which generally meant the matter got decided on pretty damn quick since no-one was usually in a mind to argue. If it was something important then they refrained from *kassa* on the grounds that they needed to think clearly. But if people were thinking clearly in different directions then they might grind a few *kassa* seeds, mix up the paste and keep spooning it down until they were all so out of their heads that no-one cared enough to argue

about what they decided and just wanted to settle the thing plenty
fast so they could really get stuck into the *kassa. Kassa* pretty much
ruled out any necessity for nobles.

Lamua was sweeping now and a more disputatious person than
Managua might have felt that a disproportionate amount of dust
from the hard earth floor was ending up on his books, but he
simply brushed it away and got on with his work. Another meaning of noble was 'lofty' and cross-referencing in the dictionary told
him this meant high or tall. So for the second line Managua had:

Is you be bigger man for put up with

It seemed to him that was what Shakespeare had in mind. And it
would be understood, too. Managua was exceptional in height as
well as in literary ability; the islanders were not generally big, but
rather of small stature, and slim. Bigness impressed them, in body
or in mind.

'I is go enjoy slaughter that pig. I is go drink she blood like
Coca-Cola, oh yes,' Lamua was saying, as though to herself.
Although he knew this was just for his benefit, Managua couldn't
help flinching. But then his mind drifted, as he had observed the
mind usually will, away from the unpalatable to something
pleasurable, in this case the other image conjured up by his wife's
words. Coca-Cola. He hadn't felt the harsh tickle of its ice-cold
bubbles against his throat for some sixteen years, not since the
Americans left, all that time ago. It presented a more powerful, as
well as a more pleasing picture, than the one of his wife drinking
Cordelia's blood.

'*The slings and arrows of outrageous fortune*'

Well this was sure another damn difficult one. The islanders
didn't use slings or bows and arrows and had no knowledge of
these things. It was only through his extensive reading that
Managua understood what they were. Here they used blowpipes
and poison darts – although not at all since the Americans had
come and destroyed the only other big village, which had been on
the northern end of the island, rendering it permanently un-
inhabitable by establishing their firing range there and leaving it

riddled with mines and unexploded shells when they departed; the
sorry remnants of its inhabitants had had no option but to trek
south and amalgamate with Managua's village, or disperse themselves among the various smaller settlements and hamlets scattered
across the island, leaving Managua's people with no-one to fight.
He sighed at the thought of it.

'I is hear you!' shrilled Lamua. 'I is hear you make they lovesick
sounds for you old pig. What you is think of? You is dream of sneak
off and make *fug-a-fug* with you little pet again?'

'I is think about Americans,' said Managua. 'About how there is
be two big villages before they is come.'

This was the wrong thing to say, especially in so wistful a tone.
As a child, Lamua had come from the northern village at the time
of its evacuation. She lashed out with her broom, knocking
his books from the upturned plastic crate Managua used as a
desk.

'I is see you is like they times back. You is like you wife at other
end of earth so you is never meet she and you is free for make
fug-a-fug with pigs. Oh yes, I is see right through you. You is be thin
as water, not thick like Coca-Cola.'

Pleased with this last simile she threw the broom triumphantly
into the corner where it normally resided and stormed from the
hut.

The trouble was, thought Managua, as he rescued the books
from the floor and restored them to his desk top, that while you
could suffer, or put up with, slings and arrows, however painful, the
same could not be said of poison darts of which the tips had been
dipped in the venom of the *terrada*, the green shoestring snake.
Once it was in your bloodstream, you had approximately thirty
seconds to live. There was no known antidote. It wasn't something
you endured, exactly. Enduring had to last more than half a
minute. And why would anyone want to fire an *unpoisoned* dart at
someone? What would be the point? It was scarcely likely to do
any damage without the venom. In a way, this was what Managua
liked about translating Shakespeare. The Bard set you a problem

and the pleasure was in pitting your mind against his to find a way around it.

He thought about other weapons the islanders used. Until the coming of the black bantam pigs, imported by the British shortly after World War II, they had not been hunters. Their main source of protein was fish which they caught with nets. You couldn't suffer from nets. Other than fish they ate the fruit and nuts that grew plentifully on the island and the maize, yams and vegetables they cultivated in their gardens. Of course if they came across a stranded turtle or a snake they would eat that too, and the occasional water-fowl, which they caught with snares, but other than these there was nothing worth hunting. It was taboo to kill any of the island's fourteen species of monkey, their resemblance to the islanders being considered too close for comfort. Eating them would have seemed like cannibalism, something else the islanders eschewed.

The black bantam pigs, which were no larger than a small to medium-sized dog, had been brought by the British from another island or group of islands, New Guinea perhaps, Managua couldn't now recall. The idea had been to domesticate them to save the British having to import quite so much meat. The pigs were known to survive well in jungle conditions, they would eat any-thing and their flesh was succulent. Unfortunately the British had neglected to ask themselves why the pigs had not been domesti-cated wherever it was they came from. The answer to that unasked question was soon made clear. The pigs were not only vicious, with a tendency to bite with their surprisingly sharp teeth anyone who came near them, they were also adept escapers. It was impossible to keep them contained. They gnawed through bamboo fences or burrowed under them. When barbed wire was tried, they simply walked through it, their tough hides impervious to the barbs.

The British left, their fifty years of intermittent attempts to establish a base upon the island abandoned. They bequeathed the islanders their language, which various missionaries had taught the natives, and the black bantam pigs. They couldn't have taken the pigs even if they'd wanted to, as the animals had all long ago escaped and turned feral, if, that is, they could ever have been said to be anything *but* feral. So the islanders had taken to hunting them. At first they had used the only deadly weapons they were familiar with, poison darts. The flaw with this soon became obvious when a number of islanders died after feasting upon the kills. The *terrada* venom had spread throughout the pigs' bodies and was so potent that even a small piece of pig meat proved fatal. Thereafter the natives dug pits and filled the bottoms of them with pointed bamboo stakes. Any pigs that weren't killed by being impaled on the stakes were finished off with wooden clubs. After he had ruminated on this for some time, all the while ignoring the excited shouts blown along to the village on the breeze from the landing beach, Managua finally settled on the line:

Clubs and bamboo pits of real damn bad luck

He wasn't quite happy with this. *Bamboo pits* ought to come first. After all, you didn't use the clubs until *after* the pig had fallen into the pit. But the trouble was it just didn't sound as good the other way round. Never mind, it would have to do for now. He could go back to it later.

The cries were getting louder, as though people were running along the shore from the landing beach, a mile or so away, to the village. He hoped there wasn't going to be a lot of shouting here. It was bound to be over something trivial. Maybe the agent had sent them a case of Coca-Cola. People had gone berserk the last time that had happened, a year or so ago. It was all anyone could talk about although the stuff had got itself drunk pretty fast; Managua certainly hadn't seen any of it.

'*Or to take arms against a sea of troubles*'

Now this was, in Managua's opinion, a rare example of a piece of poor writing by Shakespeare. For how could you take arms against a sea? What, attack the ocean with poison darts? Or even slings and arrows? Club it to death? The image was ridiculous. Shakespeare must have been having an uncharacteristic bad moment. Maybe he had lost his concentration because his wife was looking for a pig. The idea of fighting against the sea reminded Managua of that mad

British king who had ordered the tide to turn. Typical
loony British! Worse than their homicidal pigs! You couldn't fight
the sea, as Managua well knew. It was eating up the island and
would eventually swallow them all but there was nothing anyone
could do about it. And then, somehow, as it always did when he
was writing, if he just kept faith and trusted the process, the answer
came to him ready-made and he hastened to scrawl the end of the
paragraph.

He read through what he'd got so far, trying to blot out the cries
that were growing closer.

> *Is be, or is be not, is be one big damn puzzler:*
> *Is you be bigger man for put up with*
> *Clubs and bamboo pits of real damn bad luck,*
> *Or, is take blowpipes for fight herd of pigs*
> *And is by use of snakebite, end they?*

It worried him a little that he had used the word *damn* twice,
but on the other hand it was a good word and it was surely better
to use a good word twice than substitute one use with a bad one.
He was just mulling this over when Tigua burst into the hut,
running so fast he was almost unable to stop and only just
managed to avoid colliding with Managua's desk.

Tigua was so out of breath he could scarcely speak. 'Managua,
Managua,' he panted out at last, 'you is must come landing beach.
Plane is bring white man!'

Even Managua, who liked to pretend he was above the petty
excitements of the rest of the tribe, was startled by this. 'White
man?'

'Yes,' said Tigua, fiddling with his false breasts and reaching
under his dress to adjust the shoulder strap of his bra. 'White face
and yellow hair. He is stand in door of plane for wait boat. I is see
he plain as I is see you. You is must come. Everyone is say come get
you.'

Managua stirred himself. 'Bring me my leg.'

Tigua fetched the artificial leg that was leaning against the wall of the hut and waited anxiously while Managua strapped it to his stump.

'Help me up,' said Managua.

'Of course,' said Tigua, bending low and offering his shoulder for Managua to pull himself up by.

Managua limped towards the door of the hut, then realized Tigua hadn't moved. 'Come on then, you is say there is be big damn hurry. What you is wait for?'

'I is just wonder,' said Tigua, 'you is happen for know where Lamua is keep she lip paint?'

TWO

William Hardt stepped gingerly across the threshold of the flying boat's door. Even though the plane had landed a fair distance out into the bay, way beyond where the big rollers formed and broke, there was still a significant swell to the sea, rocking the keel of the aircraft so that it was difficult to keep his balance without holding onto the door jambs. The pilot had hooked some steps over the bottom lip of the doorway and down the side of the plane. William stood on the top step. Below, tossing about in the waves, he could see a large dugout canoe, with a single outrigger float to one side. All around, the ocean was alive with dozens of other craft – dugouts and canoes of all sizes, some with outriggers, others with sails, some with both, some with neither. The whole population of the island seemed to have turned out to meet him, and indeed this wasn't far from the truth, although they were not there to meet him since they hadn't had any idea he was coming; the monthly visit of the plane was enough in itself. The first thing he noticed was that they were all almost naked, the mass of light brown flesh scarcely dotted with clothing. The women were in short grass skirts, their bare breasts bobbing around with the movement of the boats in which they sat or, more commonly, stood, the better to get a look at him, he supposed. The men wore only what appeared to be a piece of leaf, held over their genitals by a string which travelled between their legs and buttocks to another around the waist, like a stripper's G-string. They were of every age, old men and women, small children, teenage boys and young women whose nipples peeped between the *leis*, the garlands of richly coloured flowers of welcome they wore around their necks, presumably for the pilot as they couldn't be for him. All seemed to be pointing up to him and saying the same thing: '*Gwanga, gwanga*', chattering away like the monkeys whose lives they so respected, although of course William Hardt knew nothing of that yet. He had done his research on the island, but none of it had had to do with the culture or customs of its people. His interest in the place lay elsewhere.

As the whine of the plane's motors ceased and its propellers gradually stopped turning, the hubbub swelled until it seemed to fill all the space in William's head so that he had no room to think.

'*Gwanga! Gwanga!* Is make jump!' He looked down and saw a young man, probably in his late teens, looking back up at him from the large dugout which was now alongside the plane, level with the door, its outrigger perilously close to the plane's port wing float. The man was holding a hand up to him. Fortunately William had the presence of mind to remember his suitcase. He reached inside the plane and somehow hefted it over the rusty metal lip of the door. He turned and looked at the native.

'Is please chuck bag, *gwanga*,' yelled the youth, struggling to make himself heard over the din.

The dugout was lurching up and down in such a way that William hesitated. He caught himself squeezing the handle of the bag with first one hand and then the other. His anxiety level was high. It would be a disaster if his bag missed the boat and plunged into the sea. Even supposing it was possible for it to be recovered, everything inside, the papers, his books and the tape machine, would be destroyed and his whole mission aborted before it had even begun.

'Just drop it, Mr Hardt,' said a voice behind him, and he turned to see the Australian pilot who had flown him here. 'They'll catch it before it can sink.'

William let go the case which landed in the outstretched arms of the youth who made a sound like air escaping from a punctured tyre, as it knocked the breath out of him and he collapsed under its weight into the waist of the boat, where he lay flattened beneath it while his fellow boatmen dropped their oars and struggled to lift it from him.

'Come on Mr Hardt, I don't have all day,' said the pilot. 'I got to get back before nightfall. Here, jump!' And with that, he gave William a firm push between the shoulder blades. William's arms wheeled through the air as he flew down and he shut his eyes, anticipating the splash as he hit the water, but was pleasantly surprised to feel solid wood beneath his feet. He almost toppled over but several pairs of hands grasped him and a moment later he was sitting in the stern of the boat facing the nodding and smiling faces of the eight oarsmen and feeling stupid as he nodded and smiled back. Somehow the boat was already well stacked with wooden crates and cardboard boxes from the plane and the rowers were pulling for the shore. Behind him, he could hear the aircraft's engines spluttering once more into life.

'*Gwanga*,' said the boy who had caught his case.

William shook his head and put on a puzzled expression to show he hadn't understood.

'*Gwanga*,' said the boy again, dragging his fingers through his short black hair and nodding at William. He frowned when he saw that William still didn't get it. He repeated the gesture with hand and hair and William wondered whether this was simply an idle movement or had some relevance to what he was saying.

'*Gwanga. Gwanga.*'

Again William shook his head. 'What is *gwanga*?' he asked, not knowing if he would be understood.

'*Gwanga*?' said the boy. 'You is not know? *You* is be *gwanga*! You! Ha ha! You is not know *gwanga* and you *is be gwanga*!' He roared with laughter and turned to his comrades. '*Gwanga* is not know what *gwanga* is. Is you can believe that? He is be *gwanga* and is not know it!' They all collapsed laughing over their oars and one man

let go of his and had to be held by his legs by his comrades while
he stretched out over the rocking side of the boat to reclaim it.
After that they settled back into their rowing, but their steady
rhythm was none the less punctuated from time to time by many
cries of '*Gwanga!*' and a great deal of laughter during the fifteen
minutes it took to row to shore. William laughed too, it seemed
only polite, and as they appeared to like this he even ventured to
tap himself on the chest a couple of times and say '*Gwanga!*' which
made them all roll about and the boat pitch so violently that had
it not been for the outrigger it would have capsized.

Between bouts of laughter William raised his eyes to look at the
place that was to be his home for the next month. After a border
of bright yellow sand fringed with the white of the surf, brooding
emerald hills rose in the centre. A solitary white cloud hung above
the island as if put there to emphasize how blue was the rest of the
sky. A travel agent's paradise, thought William, except it was three
hundred miles from anywhere that wasn't another nowhere, had
no landing strip and was reachable only by sea plane and was
rumoured to be well short of modern conveniences. Still, at least
there was a hotel, as far as William had been able to see from the
old British map he'd dug up. Assuming it was still there. He
certainly hoped so. After three days of travelling, he was ready to
wallow in a long, hot bath.

As the boat came close to shore William realized that the men
had ceased laughing in order to put all their energy into their
rowing. He could tell from their strained expressions that the going
was getting harder all the time and he deduced that this was
because of an undertow. The now fairly big waves broke upon a
wall of coral that ringed the shore, and bounced back out from it,
so that for every ten feet the men rowed the boat was hurled back
five. At times it even seemed as if they were thrown back further
than they had rowed since the last time, but this must not have
been the case as finally they managed to get past the undertow and
were riding on the crest of a huge breaker, the oarsmen paddling
frantically to steer the craft through a gap in the coral reef, and

surfing in on a cauldron of white spray which finally spat the boat out onto a sickle-shaped sandy beach. For a moment the men rested over their oars, panting.

'Are you all right?' William ventured, as after a couple of minutes not a single one of them had moved from this posture of exhaustion. 'That seems to have been an exceptionally hard row.'

'Hard row?' gasped his youth. 'Not bloody damn likely. Too much damn *kassa* last night.'

As William disembarked into the foaming water swirling around the boat he cursed himself for wearing his loafers. His white tropical suit too. Anyone with any sense would have known to have worn something waterproof. Sea boots or plastic flip-flops most likely. He went to reach his bag out of the boat but the boy said to him, 'No *gwanga*, I is fetch!'

While the oarsmen unloaded the boat, putting the contents higher up the beach where the sand was dry, then pushing the vessel's lightened keel out of reach of the waves, William was surrounded by natives. The crowd parted to allow a trio of smiling young women, each wearing an exotic *lei* around her neck, to step forward. Once in front of him they removed the *leis* and placed them over William's head. He peered over multicoloured petals at six bare, brown-nippled breasts. He was conscious that he ought not to stare at them, but on the other hand, breasts seemed to be everywhere he looked. Fortunately the problem was solved by the crowd closing up and engulfing him again. Now he felt bare breasts pressed against him, but at least they were too close for him to be caught looking at them.

'*Gwanga! Gwanga!*' the people were calling. 'Welcome, *gwanga!*'

The air was close and oppressive and William was starting to feel claustrophobic when the pressure of bodies against his own eased and the crowd parted once more, forming two lines facing one another and making a kind of walkway – rather like crowds of people waiting outside a film premiere, William couldn't help thinking – and he found himself staring at two people at its opposite end.

They were a bizarre couple. One was an old man, maybe around sixty, wearing only the ubiquitous pubic leaf and sporting below his right thigh an artificial limb attached by leather straps that ran all the way up to a belt around his waist. Beside him, breasts covered by a proper dress, a smart, pale green, Western cocktail dress – and, it appeared from their shape, encased in a bra underneath – was the strangest-looking woman. She had big bushy eyebrows and a five o'clock shadow. William presumed he was looking at the island's chief and his wife.

He decided the proper thing to do would be to walk towards them, but when he lifted his suitcase he remembered how heavy it was. He had to use both hands and shuffle along the gauntlet of smiling natives, the bag banging against his shins. The chief and his wife walked towards him. William was about to speak but the chief held up his hand in the manner of a policeman stopping traffic. Strange, thought William, how some gestures are universal to the human race, wherever we live, whatever our culture. Then again, it occurred to him, he was just assuming that the guy was telling him not to speak. What if the gesture *didn't* have the same meaning here? What if, for example, it meant, Hey everybody, give it half a minute then grab this *gwanga* and cut his dick off? But wait, the old guy was clearing his throat and starting to say something.

'Sir, I invite your Highness and your train to my poor cell, where you shall take your rest for this one night; which part of it, I'll waste with such discourse as, I not doubt, shall make it go quick away.'

William knew immediately that his dick was safe. This was definitely a welcome speech, and more than that, even though he could make neither head nor tail of it, it had a certain elegance about it that suggested the old guy was intelligent and cultured. Had William been more cultured himself he would have recognized it as Prospero's offer of hospitality to the shipwrecked Alonso in *The Tempest*, but he wasn't and he didn't and so was confused by the look of puzzled disappointment that flickered across the old guy's face. Instead of replying with an apt titbit of Jacobean verse, then, William did things the American way: he stretched out his hand to shake. This had the effect of making the old man appear even more puzzled. He studied the hand for a moment, as though it were an object divorced from the rest of William and then looked him in the face and smiled.

'Come!' he said imperiously.

William went to pick up his case but before he could do so, the chief's wife beat him to it and grabbed the handle. Although she was only young – William would have guessed, seeing her close up now, that she was no more than sixteen or seventeen – only a girl really and of slight build, her shoulders were surprisingly muscular. She hefted the heavy bag as though it weighed nothing at all.

'I is take,' she said in a gruff voice.

'Are you sure?' asked William. 'It's very heavy.'

'For you, *gwanga*, mebbe, not for me. I is carry fish catch.'

William considered this for a few steps. Interesting that the chief's wife engaged in menial labour. It was hard figuring out the pecking order here.

The chief watched his wife struggling with the case for a moment then said to William, 'Bag is be plenty heavy.'

'Yes,' said William.

'What you is have in there?' asked the old man. William didn't know quite how to reply to this. On the one hand he didn't want to be rude. On the other, he didn't want to divulge too much too soon of his reason for being here.

He shrugged nonchalantly. 'Oh, this and that.'

'This and that,' murmured the old man slowly, as though chewing it over. 'Is must be heavy this and that.' And then suddenly, 'Books is be heavy. You is have books?'

William wondered for a moment if they had somehow got wind of his visit, but then dismissed the thought as absurd. 'Yes, one or two,' he said.

'One or two,' said the chief, nodding to himself. Beside him the butch girl clutching the case had broken into a sweat and was looking daggers at the old guy, obviously willing him to get a move on. The chief suddenly stuck his face into William's. 'Any Shakespeare? *Complete Works* by any chance?'

William shook his head.

'Not even *Hamlet*? Not even *Hamlet* on he own?'

'Sorry, not even *Hamlet*.'

'Bugger!' said the old boy and turned and limped off. The girl panted after him. William felt abashed at his own lack of gallantry and tried to grasp the case's handle to take it from her, but she pushed him off with such a surprisingly strong arm that he realized she was better equipped to carry it than he. Maybe I should try hauling fishing nets as a method of body-building when I get back to the States, he thought.

They moved slowly, following a pace behind the old man's laboured limp, William assumed as a matter of protocol (although actually it was because Tigua found the case a good deal heavier than he'd let on). The gaggle of islanders surrounded them every step of the way, some of them reaching out occasionally to touch William, as if he were a religious statue perhaps, tentatively, as though full of awe.

It struck William as strange that, given the island boasted all the desirable young women who had waggled their breasts at him, the chief should have chosen this butch specimen as his partner. Unless of course William had got it wrong and she wasn't his wife, but perhaps his daughter. That would make more sense, given their relative ages. William decided he had to get a handle on things. He remembered the travelling salesman's line when a housewife opened the door to him in the old days: 'Excuse me, miss, is your mother home?' and decided to go at the matter from the same angle.

'Forgive me asking, but are you the chief's daughter?'

Tigua burst out laughing.

'What?' said William. 'Have I said something funny? You're not his daughter, you're the chief's—'

Before he could get any further the old man turned and said. 'I is be Managua. I is not be chief.'

'You're not the chief?' repeated William. 'I'm sorry, I assumed . . .'

'We is have no nobles here,' said Managua in a stately voice.

'Nobles?' said William.

'Chiefs,' explained Managua. 'We is have no chiefs. I is come meet you because I is speak English good. Most good of anyone on island. I is speak language of Shakespeare. Now I is take you village.'

As Managua resumed walking, William went beside him to take full advantage of the opportunity for conversation that had opened up, leaving Tigua lugging the suitcase a pace behind still.

'On the subject of language,' he said, 'perhaps you can tell me. What does it mean, *gwanga*?'

Managua stopped again and turned to face him, eyes twinkling. '*Gwanga*? Is mean white man with yellow hair who is drop from sky with heavy bag,' he said.

'That's what *gwanga* means? Just one word means all that?'

Managua resumed walking. 'Is be *one* of things *gwanga* is mean. Is mean many other things too. Is be very thrifty language we is have here. Is not waste words with they is mean just one thing.'

THREE

While all this was going on there was one islander who hadn't joined in the bustle to meet the plane and the procession back with William Hardt. As soon as Lamua saw Managua hurrying off with Tigua (if that man could ever be said to hurry anywhere. Come to think of it, she'd heard tell he hadn't been exactly fast even before his right leg was blown off), she decided to pass up the chance to go to meet the plane. This was not an easy decision to make. The plane came once a month to collect the various things the islanders produced: mainly fruit, fresh fish and wood carvings, for the agent on the big island; and to bring the things they had requested in return, chiefly cloth and tools, plus whatever the agent saw fit to throw in of his own accord. Sometimes there would be a case of Coca-Cola, which meant twenty-four cans. It was the nature of the islanders to share such bounty, but their sharing was indiscriminate: someone would break open the cardboard box and toss cans into the waiting crowd. If you weren't there to catch it, the Coke wouldn't be around by the time you were. So Lamua was passing up the possibility of Coke – although twenty-four into five hundred meant that it wasn't that much of a forfeit – and whatever else might turn up. But then she had good reason. Managua's rare absence from the hut and his damn Shakespeare, and even rarer absence from the village, gave her the perfect opportunity to search for the pig.

She figured she had at least an hour. It would take the old bastard that long to hobble along to the landing beach and back again,
not to mention what time it might take to deal with whatever it
was that had occasioned Tigua's urgent request for him. Thinking
about that, her curiosity as to what could have needed Managua's
presence so urgently almost got the better of her, but only for a
moment. There was nothing she wanted more than to find the pig.

Lamua hated herself for being jealous of something as despicable
as a pig. Someone with experience of ordinary pigs might have
added especially a black bantam pig, but Lamua knew no other
kind and therefore had no idea just how insulted she should feel.
But the pig had somehow come to embody all her feelings about
how Managua had ceased caring for her, how distant he had
become as a result of his obsession with Shakespeare. Even when
you spoke to him he replied as if in a trance, not hearing what you
said, like a man after an evening in the *kassa* hut, seeing still only
the dreams and visions he had experienced there.

The pig had come into their lives like this: the black bantam pigs
had been hunted for enough years to know to stay out of the way
of humans. They tended to keep deep in the jungle, where they
were more or less safe. None of the islanders could be bothered to
shift themselves and go on a pig hunt there. What with the having
to make spears for themselves which had no other use than pig
killing, and crawl through dense undergrowth with the constant
risk of stepping on a bright green shoestring and maybe not even
knowing anything about it until half a minute later when you were
dead, and then still not necessarily – indeed probably not – catching a pig, well, why would you bother, unless it was for a wedding
or a funeral, or some other special occasion? After all, the islanders
had lived for millions of years without the taste of pork and it
always seemed to most of them that they could go without it
another day or two at least. But every so often the pigs would
come out of the deep jungle in search of the orange fungi that
grew around the bases of the trees in the various clearings the
natives had made. The fungi wouldn't grow where there was dense

undergrowth, but where it got thinner, they were everywhere. The amazing thing about the fungi was that they were poisonous. Just as deadly as a shoestring bite if you ate them, although not as fast-acting. This made being poisoned by them both a better and a worse way to die. You were in terrible agony for twenty-four hours from stomach cramps and your arse exploded with hot crap that seared the skin off it, but on the other hand, at least you got time to say – or rather, scream – goodbye to your friends and neighbours. Why would anyone eat the orange fungi? Well, they looked just like a species of light red fungi that were the sweetest most succulent thing you ever tasted, and some people, well, some people just never learn. But anyway, the amazing thing about the fungi was that they were poisonous to humans, but when the pigs ate them, they didn't kill the pigs. Not only that but, unlike when the natives had fired poison darts at the pigs and then eaten them and died, when you ate a pig that had eaten the fungi, it didn't harm you either. This was very convenient. After all, you knew when you'd fired a poison dart at a pig, but you couldn't ask it what it had been eating.

Although, thought Lamua, Managua might. Managua talked to his pig. Managua's pig even had a name, Cordelia. How all this had come about was that a boy had been out looking for red fungi when he came across a larger than average black bantam sow grazing in the same area. It was fortunate for the boy and his family that he did see the pig because he'd been about to pick the fungi when the pig came along and started eating them. Lucky escape! The fungi were, of course, the orange kind; the pigs never touched the reds, which only tasted so good after they were cooked.

The boy forgot all about fungi and raced back and told his father what he'd seen and that the pig was big and extremely fat. His father called a few other guys and as no-one could be bothered to sit down and make a spear they grabbed the clubs they used to finish off bamboo pit pigs and ran as fast as they could to the place.

The pig was long gone, black bantams having an instinct about such things as human kids running off yelling about them, but there were enough orange fungi – at least they *looked* like orange fungi and no-one was going to test them to find out – to convince the men the pig would most likely return and that it was worth digging a bamboo pit, so that's exactly what they did. Then they sat down, sharpened some bamboo stakes, stuck them in the bottom, put a few palm leaves over the hole to cover it and went home to carry on with their lives. Everyone knew of course that a watched bamboo pit would never produce a pig, the animals were too canny for that. The best thing was to go away and forget all about it until you heard a pig squeal. Unless you were very unlucky and the bamboo stakes got the pig right away it would probably only be severely wounded and it would squeal loud enough to wake the dead, not that the dead were actually asleep, not according to the islanders' mythology, that is, but that's something else.

It so happened that the big sow wandered back on the very day that the plane came in. This was six months ago and, as usual, everyone in the village had gone down to the landing beach to meet it. Only Managua was left, poring over *Hamlet* and trying to work out the central enigma of the play, the reason for the hero's inability to act. This was especially difficult for him because his *Complete Shakespeare* didn't actually live up to its title. It *had* been complete, at some time in its life, but when Managua acquired it, when he was picking over some things the British had left at the Captain Cook Hotel, it had been missing a few pages. There were two gone from *Hamlet*, just before the end of Act III, and they were important ones because Polonius somehow got himself killed in them. Their absence meant that Managua just couldn't figure out the play; if Hamlet could kill Polonius so precipitately and seemingly with virtually no provocation, why wouldn't he take a sling or a bow and arrow and finish Claudius right at the start? What was it that prevented him from acting? To Managua it beggared belief that a genius like Shakespeare had written such a great play – Managua considered it his very best – that just didn't add up. He became convinced that the answer to the riddle must lie in those missing two pages. If only he had those, all would be explained! And *that* was why, seeing from Tigua's struggle to carry it, the weight of William Hardt's suitcase, he would become excited at the idea that it might contain a *Complete* – a truly complete – *Shakespeare*, or if not, then a *Hamlet*. After all, what kind of man would carry his own weight in books around with him and *not* have *Hamlet*? Anyone who had so many books would know to have that one.

Be that as it may, on this previous occasion of the plane's visit, this day six months earlier, Managua had been fretting over this perennial problem when he was shaken from his reverie by what he at first thought was a child being tortured. Of course he realized almost right away that it couldn't be a child. The islanders never even smacked their children let alone tortured them. It had to be a pig caught in a bamboo pit.

Managua crawled across the floor of his hut and found his leg. He had to crawl because Lamua was down at the landing beach and not there to hand it to him. He hadn't expected to be going anywhere. He knew of course about the new bamboo pit, although he wasn't sure where it was, but that didn't matter because all he had to do was follow the death screams of the pig.

Sound travels strangely in the jungle. It cannot move in straight lines because of the dense vegetation so it must meander around trees, push aside gigantic leaves, disturb the petals of exotic flowers as it threads its way through them and dodge between immovable shrubs. Consequently it took Managua some time to locate the bamboo pit and even longer to get there because his progress was slow on account of his artificial leg, the only advantage of which was that it reduced by 50 per cent his chances of being bitten by a green shoestring should he happen to step on one.

Eventually Managua reached the pit and was dismayed by the pitiful sight that greeted him, not to mention the noise which was like a thousand parrots screeching at once. The pig had evidently fallen straight down, her legs splayed out on either side so her stomach was impaled by the bamboo stakes, several of which protruded through her back.

For a moment Managua was helpless. The screaming of the pig was such that he couldn't think. Then he realized the pig was looking at him with something that could only be supplication in its small black eyes. It was actually asking him to finish it off. 'Come on, get on with it,' those eyes seemed to say. 'Where's your club?'

It was a good question. Where *was* his club? Stupidly Managua had not had the foresight to bring one and it was too late to go back for one now. By the time he returned here with it the pig would be dead anyway, having suffered the most unspeakable agony in the meantime. Anyone else might have run back for a club but not someone with Managua's prosthetic limb. Not for the first time he cursed it for its uselessness but even as he was doing so an idea blossomed in his brain. Perhaps his Achilles heel − or rather his whole bloody damn Achilles leg − could also be his strength.

'All right, all right, calm youself,' he said to the pig, and for a moment it did indeed stop screaming, as though listening to what he was saying. He eased himself down onto the ground beside the edge of the pit, as close to the pig's head as he could manage. Then he reached down to his knee and unfastened the leather straps that held on the leg. It was not of the latest design where the lightest metals are shaped in such a way as to give them disproportionate strength. In fact it was second-hand, second-*leg*, Managua told himself, although perhaps that should be third, since would not the original owner have been using it as a second leg to replace the one that he had lost? or even fourth because Managua was also using it for that purpose . . . ?

Whatever, this was not the time to think about it. Suffice to say, the leg was plenty damn heavy, as anyone who had tried walking with it would tell you. Having removed it, Managua turned it around and took the foot − not that you could actually call it that, it ended in just a rounded tip − in his fingers. He hefted it in his hand, getting the feel of it. Then he rolled over so that he was on his front, and shutting his eyes because he couldn't bear to look at the pig while he did it, he swung with all his might. There was a surprisingly soft thud and an immediate cessation of the screams. Managua opened his eyes and found the lifeless eyes of the pig staring back at him. He'd killed the pig at the very first attempt. Kneed it to death with a single blow.

He was just heaving a sigh that was a mixture of satisfaction and relief when the screaming from the pit started up again. It was such a shock Managua almost dropped his leg into the pit. Thinking the pig must have recovered and cursing himself for being so smug, Managua peered down into the pit again. The same lifeless eyes returned his gaze.

At this Managua began fumbling with his prosthetic limb once more. He had but one thought – to get away from there fast, or at least as fast as a man with an antiquely overweight artificial leg could. Like all the islanders Managua knew that nothing really died and that the spirits of his ancestors were all around, as any regular visitor to the *kassa* house understood. And it went without saying that the same thing applied to animals, for how could the dead live in a world without them? But it was one thing to believe all that and another to be stuck in the jungle with a dead pig, one you had just killed, and hear it carry right on screaming just as if it were still alive.

Managua could hardly manage to do his leg straps up. He was so scared his fingers just wouldn't work. But fortunately, the time it took him to turn his leg back from a murder weapon to its original purpose also allowed him to think and to notice that the screaming wasn't quite the same. It was higher, more shrill, less powerful. And then it occurred to him to wonder *why* a dead pig should go on screaming. If it was dead it couldn't be in pain any more. Why, he'd seen people who had died in terrible agony from eating orange fungi walking around afterwards with big smiles on their faces. What in the name of *fug-a-fug* did the pig have to scream about now?

Carefully, ready to roll back at any moment, he lifted his

shoulders and turned his head to peep into the pit. The pig was as lifeless as before. He'd caught it a good one with his knee – especially for a first attempt – and this was one pig that wasn't going to get up again, at least not in this life.

And then he saw it move. Or rather he didn't, but he thought he did. Its backside seemed to be twitching. He looked at the front end of the pig. Dead as dead could be. He looked at the back end. Definitely twitching. Then, without any warning, a bit of the pig's arse seemed to detach itself and start moving towards the pig's head. Not only that, but this bit of the pig's arse was what was doing all the screaming.

Managua was afraid to breathe. This sort of thing just could not happen, at least not without *kassa*. It was only when the bit of arse reached the pig's face and its screaming subsided into what Managua could only call a whimper that he at last realized what was going on. It wasn't a bit of pig's arse after all. He was looking at a baby pig. It must have been walking along with its mother and fallen into the pit with her when what they'd thought was the ground suddenly gave way beneath them. The baby pig was no bigger than a man's hand and right now it was standing beside its dead mother's head and licking her lifeless snout.

Then and there Managua knew that he would never eat pig again. It was surely as unnatural as eating monkeys. A vile habit the British had introduced and perverted his people with. He was at once glad that he had put the mother pig out of her agony and sick at the memory of the actual execution of his act of mercy. The little pig's continuing screams made him feel guilt at having orphaned it and he felt compelled to explain himself. 'I is must do,' he said softly. 'You *mamu* is suffer real damn bad. There is be no other way.'

When he spoke the pig stopped screaming, not so much with the air of listening to him but more as if from fear that he might be about to produce an artificial leg and bash its brains out. Managua resolved he would do his best to make it up to the piglet. It was too young to survive in the jungle alone. He would take it home and care for it.

And that's what happened. When everyone came back from the landing beach and heard the little pig's cries, they found Managua had climbed down into the pit and was cradling the shrieking animal in his arms. Of course he couldn't get back out of the pit again, not with one leg useless for climbing and both arms occupied by pig, so he'd been there all afternoon. And everyone agreed he'd earned the right to keep the pig for enduring its screams for so long. No-one else wanted it anyway; it was too noisy and it was too small to eat.

And now Lamua couldn't bear to think about how Managua had nurtured the pig and fallen in love with it and out of love with her. She didn't want to go over and over in her mind that it was all somehow connected with her failure to provide him with children. It was a double disappointment for him, she knew. He was unlucky in his choice of wives. Although his first wife had managed to produce a baby it hadn't given Managua a family because soon afterwards mother and child had died. As for Lamua, she knew there was something wrong with her. The floating babies never sought her out to be their mother.

She felt a tear prick her eye, and hastily wiped it away before it could get going. She told herself that she had done too much crying over that, and that anyway, there was no time for this today. She had to put all these thoughts out of her mind for now and concentrate on finding the pig.

She spent a few fruitless minutes searching the hut. She flicked idly through the papers on Managua's desk, as though he might have left some clue there, but then she realized what she was doing and laughed at herself. After all, what was she searching for? A picture of a pig and the place where it was hidden? Like everyone on the island apart from Managua and, of course, Miss Lucy, Lamua couldn't read. And if she had been able to, her understanding of English probably meant she wasn't up to reading it. The islanders' indigenous language had no written form and was so limited in vocabulary that after the arrival of the British they had relied more and more on a mixture of it and English to express themselves. English had all but replaced the old words, but when Managua read aloud to her from his *Shakespeare* there always seemed to be plenty of words Lamua didn't know.

Earlier efforts to follow Managua when he went out and she suspected he was sneaking off to feed the pig had ended in failure. The old *gamada* had a way of knowing you were following him and once or twice he'd limped all over the island for a whole afternoon just to annoy her, although it must have been much harder work and more exhausting for him than for her. He was that kind of man; he would put up with a great deal of discomfort to cause her a little.

So today Lamua had decided to follow his tracks. It was quite easy at first, trailing the combination of bare footprint and round indentation left by the end of his artificial limb. She was able to make out where it left their hut and walked across the open space that was the centre of the village. But then she began to have problems. The trouble was so many of the islanders had artificial legs that it was difficult to make out which indentations belonged to Managua and which to someone else. And to confuse matters even further there were the almost identical marks made by the high heels that Tigua and his she-boy friends usually wore.

In the end Lamua decided there was nothing for it but to trust to instinct, to her intuition for which was Managua's artificial leg dent, and this was what she did. After the open space in the village centre, where it seemed to linger, taking a small pace back or forward here and there, mingling with the she-boys, crossing another couple of dents that were surely different and smaller, made by a child's prosthetic foot most likely, the trail suddenly struck off into the jungle. Once there it followed a solitary course. At one point another similar trail crossed it, but when Lamua ignored that and carried on following her original path it turned out that this *was* the other trail circling back to cross itself.

Pushing an *adula* frond out of her way she fumed at the thought that Managua might have deliberately doubled back to show her he knew she would be trailing him. The old bastard! Crafty as a *koku-koku*. But Lamua was a woman spurned and was not to be so easily put off. She stuck with the trail and followed it for some considerable distance, until she had circled around in the jungle so many times she had no idea where she was.

Then she heard the soft moan of the waves and realized she was close to the ocean. Here the tracks made an abrupt right turn and plunged through a line of trees and Lamua found herself out on the beach. The breeze was off the water today and told her immediately which beach she was on. The shitting beach! No more than a couple of hundred paces from the village where she'd started out.

Gingerly, treading carefully to avoid stepping in anything unpleasant, as the tide hadn't been in since the morning, Lamua followed the trail, the footprint now accompanied by a small hole where Managua's stump had drilled into the soft dry sand. Lamua found herself walking in her husband's footsteps, or foot-and-stumpsteps, to avoid the faeces all around.

It occurred to her that Managua must have come this way this morning, or the footsteps would have been erased by last night's high tide, but this would not have been first thing, when he came to shit, for he had not been gone long enough then to take such a circuitous route through the jungle to get here. It was one big damn puzzler! But it was about to get bigger, for the trail continued towards the sea, keeping on until it reached the first wavelets of the still-outgoing tide. If Managua had been going to feed the pig then the animal must surely have drowned, for her husband had walked straight into the sea.

FOUR

FROM 'THE OTHER SIDE OF PARADISE: THE SEXUAL LIFE
AND CUSTOMS OF AN UNSPOILED PEOPLE' BY L. TIBBUT
(UNPUBLISHED MANUSCRIPT)

The whole way of life of the islanders, their social, sexual
and domestic relationships, their morals, their religious
beliefs, and the manner in which these things differ from
our own, stem from a single – and in my experience of
nearly a decade of studying primitive peoples in this region,
singular – gap in their understanding. It is this: the
islanders have never made the connection between sexual
intercourse and conception; they appear to have no awareness of physiological paternity. They believe that women
are solely responsible for the production of babies and that
men play no role in the process.

Quite how this misconception about conception came
about is difficult to explain. Their burial practices, which
involve the exhumation and dismemberment of the corpse
of the deceased, have given them an extensive knowledge of
human anatomy. They recognize and have names for the
major organs of the body. Among these they value
especially the eyes, which they believe to be the principal
means of sexual arousal; the heart, which they see as the
seat of strength and character, and the kidneys. These
latter are the organs they associate with sex.

Having traced the path of the urethra from the kidneys

to the sex organs they believe this is the route of the fluids released by both male and female during lovemaking. They make no distinction between vaginal fluid and semen, believing both to have the same purpose, namely lubrication during the sex act. My suggestion to a group of male islanders, as we sat together outside Managua's hut one evening discussing these things, that it might be the testes, not the kidneys, that produced the male fluid, was greeted with astonishment followed by somewhat derisive laughter. 'What, then, are the testes for?' I asked, when eventually they quietened down.

'Why,' said the man Purnu, the one who is said to be the island's most powerful sorcerer and who always takes most delight in making fun of Western beliefs, 'for decoration. They is make you *pwili* look beautiful. Think how silly *pwili* is look without balls for rest upon.'

A discussion followed in which one after the other they averred that it was necessary to have two objects behind the single phallus to give it a balanced appearance. They cited the eyes on either side of the nose as corroboration for this arrangement.

I then suggested that, whatever its origins, the male fluid might be essential for procreation. Again, I was greeted by raucous laughter. Even Managua showed none of the keen intellectual interest with which he is usually wont to address any remark of mine challenging his knowledge or beliefs. He appeared astounded at the idea of anyone thinking men had anything to do with conception.

I mentioned that they must surely have noticed that adolescent girls on the island only became pregnant after they began having intercourse.

Managua dismissed this as nonsense. Children on the island began their sexual activity as soon as they reached puberty. But none of them produced babies until several years after this. There was obviously no connection.

'So it follows that a virgin can produce a child, then?' I countered in my turn.

'Is not you own Jesus be born from virgin?' asked Purnu and the whole gathering dissolved into noisy mirth.

'Yes,' I replied. 'But that's a special case. It's because we know it's not normally possible that we worship him. And anyway, it's a story.' They blanked on this. Only the literate Managua understands the concept of fiction. For the rest, magic and myths are part of everyday reality.

Managua, sitting stately as a carved Buddha, waited for the laughter to subside and raised a hand to silence the last dribbles of it. He himself was sensitive enough to my feelings to make do with a wry smile. When he had quiet he addressed me with an air of patient condescension, as when a kindly parent explains something he considers obvious to a small child.

'Virgin is not have baby,' he explained, 'because if way is not be clear, how is baby get out? Is necessary woman is make *fug-a-fug* for clear entrance of womb. But *fug-a-fug* is not be necessary for make baby.'

'So a virgin birth is possible?' I urged. 'Assuming the way is made clear by some other means?'

'Of course, but is not usually happen because all girls is make *fug-a-fug* from pretty early time and way is be clear from that.'

Here the man Purnu interrupted. 'Is be many example of womans is have babies without make *fug-a-fug*. How you is explain that one?'

'I would say that it is impossible. That if a woman has a baby and says she has not made *fug-a-fug* then she is not telling the truth.'

Purnu smiled in that superior way of his. 'That is where you is be wrong.' He turned to the others. 'She is never meet Gawaloa.'

Several of them exploded into great guffaws at this. I was puzzled and must have looked it. Purnu turned back to me. 'Gawaloa is be one ugly sow,' he said. 'She is be so ugly no man is want for put he *pwili* any place near she.'

'She is be more ugly than sow,' interjected another. 'Is insult sow for compare they.' At this the laughter became even more raucous.

'She is be so ugly is hurt eyes for look upon she,' said another. More laughter.

'Even pig is not want for put he *pwili* near that one,' said yet another.

'If you is have *pwili* like big strong stick' – and here Purnu sketched a massive erection with his hands – 'and you is see Gawaloa, *pwili* is become liana,' and he mimed the drooping of the penis as if it were a dangling vine.

'Is shrink you *pwili* plenty worse than cold sea,' said one of his cronies.

'Man, that sow is be ugly,' said someone else. And they all whistled and nodded their heads as though thinking about the poor woman and contemplating in their minds' eyes her awfulness. I imagined that at that moment, were they all to remove their pubic leaves, I would find a collection of shrivelled *koks* with not a single erection among them. It would have been impossible to confirm this, of course. The natives' natural modesty and taboo against public sexual display, especially before a member of the opposite sex, renders such an idea unthinkable.

'I get the idea,' I said. 'Gawaloa is not considered a beauty.'

'No, you is not get *all* idea,' said Managua, who, with his superior intelligence, was, as might be expected, the one to return the discussion to its starting point. 'Gawaloa is not only be most ugly woman on island, so ugly no man is bear look for upon she. She is be also mother of five children. Explain me that.'

I made an attempt to insist that in spite of what everyone
said of this poor individual, not all the men on the island
could think it because someone had certainly impregnated
her at least five times.

The discussion was then sidetracked from this important
central point by some talk about how arousal was produced
in the kidneys by virtue of them receiving messages from
the eyes, and that intercourse would therefore be impossible with a woman so ugly. She was simply incapable of
arousing a man.

'So you cannot make *fug-a-fug* in the dark?' I asked
mischievously.

One of them replied that of course this was possible. But
only with someone who had already been observed in the
light whence came a visual memory sufficient to accomplish
arousal.

It was also pointed out to me that unmarried girls freely
indulged in sex with many partners from an early age, yet
there were very few unmarried pregnancies, virtually
none, in fact. How could this be if pregnancy was a result
of *fug-a-fug*?

I had to admit I had no opposing answer. My researches
to date lead me to believe that unmarried pregnancies occur
at most in only 1 per cent of all island pregnancies, yet I
am entirely satisfied the natives practise no form of contra-
ception, not even coitus interruptus. Of course infanticide is
another possibility, or it may be that babies are born
secretly and then given up for adoption. Either would be
logical since there is a great taboo against unmarried
motherhood. This taboo has nothing to do with sexual
morality. How could it, if sex has nothing to do with the
production of babies? It is another wonderful example to be
put among the many I have discovered over the years
among primitive peoples of how taboos contribute to a
desired social order. In our society we had, until recently,

a taboo against unmarried sex as a means of enforcing monogamy and hence social stability. Western society is paternalistic. Our sexual morality is about one man preventing other men from impregnating his woman and inserting their genes into his family. But not having made the connection between sex and paternity, and having no taboo against unmarried and promiscuous sex, these natives have nevertheless instituted a taboo to accomplish the same end.

Be that as it may, it remains that I am at a loss to explain the apparent absence of unmarried pregnancies and it is an area to which I intend to concentrate my further researches, the results of which I hope to include in a later publication.

Although the natives do not acknowledge physiological paternity, their children are not fatherless. Far from it. The father of a child is considered the husband of its mother. Indeed their word for father is *tama* which means, literally, mother's husband. He takes responsibility for the care and upbringing of her children and bonds with them from an early age. This is demonstrated by the fact that while division of labour is along wholly traditional lines seen throughout the wide world – he hunts, fishes, makes tools, etc., she sews, cooks and cleans the hut – there is one striking exception. One of the husband's tasks is to fondle the baby. He dandles it on his knee and keeps it clean from excrement.

Here, in a society which may not have changed in many thousands of years, we have then a precursor of the new man. In spite of believing himself to have no physical link with his children, the father cares for them in the most basic and intimate way. This would seem to be their means of ensuring that, despite the absence of a physical connection, the father bonds emotionally with his children. This is certainly the result, since the islanders are fiercely proud

of their wives' offspring and boast unremittingly about all
their petty achievements, just as much as if they could take
some genetic credit for them.

FIVE

William Hardt sat cross-legged on the floor of Managua's hut where he had just been introduced to Managua's real wife. She was certainly a step up from the butch girl Tigua, who stood peeping in through the doorway, William thought. Lamua was beautiful, a woman who might have stepped out of a Gauguin. Black hair hung to her waist and through it, as she served him a coconut bowl of spicy stew, peeped a pair of hard brown nipples. Her skin was the colour of honey and her lips exceedingly red and full. He would have found the sight of such a woman arousing, especially the now-you-see-them-now-you-don't breasts as she moved her head and with it her curtain of hair this way and that, except that she smelled of, well, crap. He couldn't help noticing the brown stains on the soles of her feet as she sat opposite him. Managua was beside her and present as well were half a dozen of the island's menfolk. Some kind of elders, William had at first assumed, although in fact they were just the ones who'd managed to squeeze in before Lamua had refused entry to anyone else because she didn't want them messing up her hut, which was rich, coming from her, William thought now, seeing as she was the one with shit-stained feet. Then again, maybe having shit all over your feet was pretty normal here and perhaps had been the basis of Lamua's objections: she wanted to keep the numbers down because she didn't want *more* shit being walked around her home.

Managua had shredded some dried leaves and was packing them into the end of a long-stemmed wooden pipe. Around him one or two of the men kept sniffing the air.

'What is be that stink, Managua?' It was a scrawny little man with a sour face, sitting on the other side of Lamua, who asked. 'You is be sure this *kassa* is be fresh?'

'I is pick myself last day and is dry overnight by fire. How much fresher you is can get?' Managua reached behind him where there was a pile of books on an upturned plastic crate. From among them he pulled a US dollar bill. William was astonished to see him roll it up into a narrow tube and thrust it into the fire. When it was burning, he stuck it into the bowl of the pipe and began sucking on the stem to fire it up.

'Um, excuse me?' said William. 'But isn't that a US dollar you have there?'

Managua ignored him for a moment, obviously fearful the fragile beginnings of a light for his pipe would go out. Once it was fired up he took a puff or two, then handed the pipe to the sour-faced man. 'Here, Purnu, now you is tell me this is not be fresh.'

Purnu took a drag, held it in, nodded, then took another. 'Is be fresh all right, but is still smell bad. Is smell like shit.'

William tried not to look at Lamua's feet. She was sitting right next to Purnu. He didn't want to give her away. He looked at the soles of everyone else's feet. They were all covered in dust, but none of them in shit.

William decided to change the subject by putting his question again. 'I said, did you know you just lit your pipe from a dollar bill?'

Managua looked at the half-burned money still smouldering in his hand. He tossed it contemptuously into the fire. 'Dollar, yes, is good for light pipe. Is not burn too fast. Is give plenty time for light *kassa*.'

William chuckled. 'You mean you got money to burn?'

'Money?' said Managua.

'Yes, dollars. You could have bought something with that dollar.'

'Bought?' said Managua. 'What you is mean, bought?'

William felt a surge of excitement within his breast. In all his planning for the visit it had never occurred to him that the society he would encounter would be pre-cash, presumably a barter economy.

His immediate thought was that this was charming, the idea of a whole people unsullied by money. His next was that it must mean they had little contact with civilization.

'There *are* other white men on the island . . . ?' he ventured.

Managua took a moment to reply, then shook his head. 'No, is be no other white mans, not for many years.' He'd paused a moment to consider the correct answer to William's question and then responded truthfully. If William had said 'white *people*' he would have said yes, because there was Miss Lucy. But William had only asked about men.

'You can exchange dollars for something else,' William continued. 'For example the dollar you just burned might have been changed for . . . oh, I don't know . . . say a can of Coca-Cola.'

'Coca-Cola?' said Managua. 'Man, you is be crazy. Who is go give you Coca-Cola for piece of paper? Why, you is not can write on this paper. I is know, I is try. What use is be?'

William was puzzled. There was something that didn't add up here. Managua had mentioned Shakespeare. Surely if he'd read Shakespeare he'd know about money?

Before he could work it out, his thoughts were interrupted. Purnu said something William didn't catch but he had a good idea of what it must have been as Purnu lifted one cheek of his behind from his mat and made a butt-wiping motion with his hand. Everybody laughed.

'For white mans,' said Managua, who had been initiated into Western lavatorial purposes during his stay in the hospital on the big island. 'But here everyone is know sea is be better.'

After Purnu had tried the pipe and affirmed the fitness of the *kassa* leaves it was passed to William as guest of honour. Before he could stop himself, he wiped the stem of the pipe on his shirt and then had to smile an apology when he looked up and found all the natives staring uncomprehendingly at him. His first drag inhaled hot sparks into his lungs and resulted in a dramatic fit of coughing. Lamua leaped up and came back with a half coconut shell filled with water, which William drank. His need for water was so urgent that it overcame the troubling thought of where this water had come from, and who else might have been drinking from this coconut shell. When he'd just about recovered, fighting back tears, he looked again at the natives. Their faces were a mixture of concern and disbelief that someone should make such a big deal out of smoking a bit of *kassa*. Managua lifted his hand to indicate that William should try again. This time he was ready for it and took a light pull on it. This time it wasn't harsh and the taste was sweet and perhaps a little sickly. He was relieved to hand the pipe to the person next to him.

Of course, William knew nothing about *kassa*. He didn't know that the leaves of the *kassa* tree contain the same active chemical compound as the seeds, but in a slightly different form, which, along with taking it through the lungs rather than the stomach, gives a different effect. Smoked, *kassa* has none of the hallucinogenic properties of when it's eaten, rather it produces a mild relaxant effect, not unlike that obtained from cannabis. But while it was certainly true that William's body seemed pleasantly weightless, his mind remained its usual seething mass of anxiety, untouched. Not only was he not relaxed, he was suddenly fearful. It was as though the *kassa* had enabled him to step outside his own body and see the potentially dangerous situation he had put himself in. He was alone, the only white man, so far as he could tell, on an island populated by natives who were so primitive they didn't even know what money was. Their earlier contact with Americans had been disastrous and they used poison darts.

It was now that he noticed that Managua was winking at him, first with one eye and then the other, and his heart sank another foot closer to the hut's dirt floor. Another Westerner might have assumed Managua's alternate winking was part of some ancient ritual, perhaps to welcome him. But William knew instantly it was no such thing, Managua could only be winking at him because *he* was winking at Managua. William had hoped that coming here, to a land that had sounded like some sort of tropical paradise, a slow and peaceful place, and moreover coming here to help people and thereby ease his constant unfocused guilt, would overcome or at least diminish all that, but here it was already, and he hadn't even known he was doing it until he saw it reflected by Managua.

William's problem was Obsessive Compulsive Disorder, a mental disorder with behaviour patterns that vary considerably from one individual to another. The way it worked for William was that he was plagued by unwanted thoughts that filled him with overwhelming anxiety that could only be alleviated by certain comforting rituals the practise of which would somehow – magically and illogically – ward off the things he feared. At the same time William knew, as all OCD sufferers know – indeed it is a requirement for a diagnosis of OCD that they know – that both the unwanted thoughts and the idea that the rituals might protect him were illogical and ludicrous. In fact sometimes the rituals themselves became so demanding and frustrating that they had the opposite effect to the one desired and actually *increased* his anxiety levels and upped the frequency of the intrusive thoughts.

William's first intrusive thoughts had been about death. As a five-year-old child he would be lying in bed and suddenly have the idea that he was in a coffin and that the coffin was in a grave. He could feel the wooden sides of the coffin hemming him in, he sensed how cold was the earth beyond them. He would pass a cemetery and have the feeling that if he looked at a particular headstone he would find his own name upon it, as one day he surely would – or rather not him but someone else, he wouldn't be looking at the headstone, he'd be under it, weighted down for eternity. In time it got so the trigger required to set him off down this melancholy trail would be something as insignificant as the mention of the word 'death', as in a phrase such as 'I'm tired to death'. It might be an offhand remark used by a teacher in class, or another child in the playground. By the time he was nine or ten the fear and the rituals had begun to play a bigger and bigger part in his life. They were choking up his schoolwork; they were cutting him off from his friends.

Although William guarded his fears and his rituals fiercely because he felt the very worst thing he could do would be to reveal them to other people and so make them real, he couldn't hide his lack of friends from his parents. They were thoughtful, kindly people and his father, especially, adored his only son. When William was eleven, in an effort to help his social life they invited one of his classmates at the upstate boarding school William attended on a weekend home with him. Not only did the plan not work, it was such a disaster it actually accomplished the very opposite of what the Hardts had intended. It earned William the nickname of 'Wanker' and made him even more of a social pariah.

It happened like this. William's parents had invited the boys to spend the weekend at their holiday home on the Long Island shore. It was a pretty place – clapboard and shingles and a porch overlooking the beach – but it wasn't very practical because it was so small. The Hardts had been given it as a wedding present by Mrs Hardt's parents and although they should by now have upgraded to something more suitable for a family with children and their guests (William's older sister Ruth had a friend along that week-end too), they just hadn't any spare money for anything bigger. Besides, the place held too many happy memories of their early married life for them to be able to do it. There were only three bedrooms, his parents had one, of course, so William and his friend had to double up and Ruth and her friend did too. For all these people, there was just one bathroom.

The only friend the Hardts had been able to get to come stay with William was of course another social pariah, but more understandably so than William, who was a nice boy but just a little odd. In contrast, the guest had everything against him a kid could have. He was small and weedy, he wore glasses and he had ginger hair. He was half Jewish which wasn't the best thing to be in a WASP boarding school and on top of everything else he had the potential

for a silly nickname. His name was Aaron Beach, which, with his
hair, naturally meant everybody called him Sandy. With all this
against him you'd have thought Sandy Beach would have made
more effort to get people to like him, but as well as all the things
he *couldn't* help he had a horrible personality too. He was a real
pain in the butt. His parents had never expected anybody to invite
him for a weekend and practically wept with gratitude when the
Hardts phoned up to ask. Mind you, after Sandy Beach had left,
William's dad had said they were probably crying with relief at
getting shot of him for a couple of days.

On this particular day, he and William were playing a game of
chess in the bedroom they shared. William was a much better
player but was forced to let Sandy Beach win because the brat
would cut up rough if he didn't and that would get William into
trouble. Even when he was let win Sandy Beach was still a pain.
What did it for William was when Beach said, 'That's your queen
gone – prepare yourself for an early grave, my friend.' Even the way
he talked was irritating but it wasn't what William noticed here. It
was the word grave. It so paralysed him he moved a rook without
thinking and blundered it. Unlike all the other pieces he'd lost, he
hadn't actually meant to lose the rook. Suddenly he felt suffocated
by the heat in the bedroom. It was raining outside and the sea
looked morose and threatening. William imagined himself dying
and then came a sudden awareness of the inevitability of it all. He *was*
going to die. There was absolutely nothing he could do about it.
There was no way anybody was going to grant him everlasting life,
not even if he offered to spend eternity with Sandy Beach, which he
would have done. *That's* how terrified he was.

As Sandy Beach made the move that he hoped was his
penultimate before checkmate, William scrambled up from the
floor and made for the door. 'I have to go to the bathroom,' he said.

In the bathroom William locked the door and took a deep
breath. Calm down, he told himself, it's going to be all right.
The bathroom was spartan – it wasn't big enough for any
furniture – and, on this day, cold, and there wasn't a deal of

incentive to hang around in there, but William had a lot to do.

If he stood with his back to the door, the lavatory bowl was against the opposite wall, to his left, and the washbasin was fixed to the same wall and immediately in front of him. The bath ran along the wall to his right, the taps at the end further away from the door. The floor was covered with black and white check linoleum which at this moment had the unpleasant effect of reminding William of his chess game and *that* had the effect of reminding him of what Sandy Beach had said. The linoleum had been laid in two strips with the join roughly down the centre of the room, running from the door to the washbasin.

If William closed the door behind him, took a couple of steps into the room and stood with his feet apart, astride the join, and kept his head perfectly erect, he could look left and see into the lavatory bowl, but without bending he couldn't see the water at the bottom. If he looked to his right he could see into the bath, but he couldn't see down as far as the plughole. But by leaning to his left, he could see the water in the toilet bowl. And by leaning to his right, he could see the plughole. With a weary sigh at the unavoidability of it all he took up this familiar position. He leaned slightly left and saw the water. To even things up he returned to the vertical and then inclined a little bit right. He could see the plughole in the bath. But he couldn't leave it at that; things still weren't even. The lavatory had, of course, been favoured, by dint of going first. To square this he made a second run at the whole thing. He leaned to his right, took in the plughole and then leaned to his left, lavatory pan.

For a brief moment he enjoyed a sense of equilibrium and calm. His anxiety subsided for a nanosecond. But of course, only a fool – and William was no fool – would have been satisfied with this simulacrum of balance. For when he put the two sets of movement together, he had a sequence that went – WATER-PLUGHOLE-PLUGHOLE-WATER. In other words a sequence of four movements where two waters were bracketed around two plug-holes. Water not only now went first but had the satisfaction of

rounding the whole thing off and of also going *last*. This was so
patently unfair it had to be rectified. So William put in another four
movements, which were, naturally: PLUGHOLE-WATER-
WATER-PLUGHOLE. He paused at the vertical, took a deep
breath and felt a few seconds of peace. The anxiety was subsiding, he
was going to get over this, everything would be OK.

It was at this moment that Sandy Beach pounded on the door.
Sandy Beach had not only got tired of waiting for William to come
back and get checkmated, he'd also got so excited at the prospect
of beating William, the best chess player in the whole of their class,
that he was nearly peeing himself. He was desperate to pee and
then he was desperate to do the checkmate.

'Hurry up in there, I need to pee!' he shouted.

'OK, OK, go away, I won't be long!' William called back. Sandy
Beach's interruption did nothing for William's anxiety level
which now began to rise again after the brief remission granted by
the second sequence. He made himself concentrate. He didn't
want to forget where he was up to and have to start all over
again. What he had now were two groups of four, the first
beginning and ending with water, the second with plughole.
Although perhaps less uneven than his single initial glance in
either direction, it was still worryingly askew. He had now to add
another two sequences to match things up a bit. So he threw in
another PLUGHOLE-WATER-WATER-PLUGHOLE and then
a second WATER- PLUGHOLE-PLUGHOLE-WATER. What
he had now was WATER-PLUGHOLE-PLUGHOLE-WATER;
PLUGHOLE-WATER-WATER-PLUGHOLE; PLUGHOLE-
WATER-WATER-PLUGHOLE;WATER-PLUGHOLE-PLUG-
HOLE-WATER. It might have ended there if Sandy Beach
hadn't called out, 'If I don't get in there this minute I'm going to
pee myself!'

In a moment of uncharacteristic irritability, brought about by
the extreme pressure he was under, William made the mistake of
shouting, 'You do and I'll tell the whole class.' He didn't mean it.
William would never have done anything as mean as that, but

Sandy Beach, who *would*, didn't know that and that was why the
remark would later cost William so dearly.

Even then everything might have been OK had not Ruth heard
the ruckus and come to investigate and then join in.

'You come on out of there right this moment, William Hardt!'
she yelled, rattling the doorknob. 'You've no call to be in there so
long.'

Unlike Sandy Beach, Ruth didn't need to pee at that moment.
What she wanted was *access* to the bathroom. Ruth was thirteen
and hadn't started her periods yet, although most of the girls in her
class had. Amy Fowler who was spending the weekend with her
and had now followed her out onto the landing had recently
begun her periods and had made a big show of placing some
sanitary towels in her bedside chest when she unpacked the night
before. Ruth was ahead of Amy Fowler in everything else at school
and this made her sure she was going to get her first period any
time now and what worried her was that when it came there
wouldn't be any warning. It would just happen and when it did
she was going to need to get into the bathroom urgently. She had
to stop William blocking up the bathroom now. She couldn't
wait to fight that battle then. The alternative was just too horrible
to contemplate.

This wasn't the only reason she wanted him out of there. Ruth
was supporting evidence for research that indicates OCD may
have a genetic factor since she had a few obsessions of her own.
One was with bodily hygiene. She had a horror of bodily fluids
which was why being able to get into the bathroom when her first
period occurred was so vital. It also meant she was horrified at
what William was up to behind that door. He was spending more
and more time in the bathroom and she didn't even want to think
about why. She'd seen photographs of sperm swimming in biology
textbooks – nasty little tadpole things – and it could drive her
crazy worrying about it if she let herself. How long could they
survive on a lavatory seat, for example? Did that sort of homing
instinct they were said to possess work outside the womb? Did

bleach kill them the way it did other microscopic organisms? And if not, what if the stuff ended up on the floor? Could it crawl across linoleum? Could you get pregnant even though you hadn't had your first period? It was all too gruesome to contemplate and Ruth fought to keep it out of her head.

'God,' she said, turning to Amy Fowler, 'that room is going to be *drenched* in sperm.'

'Do you think so?' said Sandy Beach, overhearing her. 'Do you really think so? Is *that* what he's doing in there?'

Ruth turned and looked at him as if he were a sample of spermatozoa himself. It wasn't a subject she wanted to discuss with a boy, especially one who looked like Sandy Beach. She turned on her heel, followed by Amy Fowler who lingered only long enough to say to Sandy Beach, 'Men are just so disgusting!'

In the bathroom panic was rising up William's oesophagus like bile. He was finding it hard to catch his breath. He quickly began a new sequence of four fours, beginning PLUGHOLE-WATER-WATER-PLUGHOLE. By the time Sandy Beach rattled the door again he had: WATER-PLUGHOLE-PLUG-HOLE-WATER; PLUGHOLE-WATER-WATER-PLUGHOLE; PLUGHOLE-WATER-WATER-PLUGHOLE; WATER-PLUG-HOLE-PLUGHOLE-WATER; PLUGHOLE-WATER-WATER-PLUGHOLE; WATER-PLUGHOLE-PLUGHOLE-WATER; WATER-PLUGHOLE-PLUGHOLE-WATER; PLUGHOLE-WATER-WATER-PLUGHOLE.

The door rattled again. 'Come on out, I know you're pulling your dick off in there!' screamed Sandy Beach. 'I'm going to tell the whole class.' Sandy Beach wasn't too nice to do this and *that* is how William ended up with his nickname.

WATER-PLUGHOLE-PLUGHOLE-WATER;   PLUG-HOLE-WATER-WATER-PLUGHOLE;   PLUGHOLE-WATER-WATER-PLUGHOLE;   WATER-PLUGHOLE-PLUGHOLE-WATER;   PLUGHOLE-WATER-WATER-PLUGHOLE;   WATER-PLUGHOLE-PLUGHOLE-WATER;

WATER-PLUGHOLE-PLUG-HOLE-WATER; PLUGHOLE-
W A T E R - W A T E R - P L U G H O L E ;
PLUGHOLE-WATER-WATER-PLUGHOLE;   WATER-
P L U G H O L E - P L U G H O L E - W A T E R ;
WATER-PLUGHOLE-PLUGHOLE-WATER; PLUGHOLE-
W A T E R - W A T E R - P L U G H O L E ;
WATER-PLUGHOLE-PLUGHOLE-WATER; PLUGHOLE-
W A T E R - W A T E R - P L U G H O L E ;
PLUGHOLE-WATER-WATER-PLUGHOLE;   WATER-
PLUGHOLE-PLUGHOLE-WATER.

It wasn't enough, but it would have to do. Each new round had
at least reduced the unevenness to a smaller percentage of the
whole, making it that much more bearable. And it was getting to
the stage where it was counterproductive; having to do it, just having
to *remember* it all, what with all the pressure from Ruth and Sandy
Beach outside, would actually increase his anxiety levels if he didn't
stop now.

'OK, OK,' said William. 'Gimme a minute, won't you?' He
pulled his pants and shorts down and sat on the lavatory. After all,
he was an eleven-year-old boy alone in a bathroom. He *still* had to
masturbate.

Thanks to Sandy Beach, when they returned to school William
soon became known as Wanker, a British term meaning 'complusive
masturbator' that Beach had somehow unearthed and that he
smugly explained to their schoolmates had the auxiliary humiliating
connotation of 'total loser'. It was already difficult for William to
disappear somewhere by himself – boys' boarding schools offer few
opportunities for privacy – and this new sobriquet didn't help. So he
devised other coping strategies for his OCD that could be done
more or less in public. The first of these involved the alternate
clenching and unclenching of his fists while they were concealed in
his pants' pockets. The trouble with this was that Sandy Beach
spotted it and, in an attempt to ingratiate himself with the rest of the
class, pointed it out in his own inimical fashion.

'Wanker's playing pocket pool!' he chanted and William was caught, well, if not red-handed, then with his hands in his trouser pockets. After that he settled for blinking his eyes alternately. Of course when he did it really frenetically people couldn't help noticing but they thought it was just a tic and nothing worse than another thing to think him odd for. Its big advantage was that it could bring him instant relief from intrusive thoughts, even in the middle of a class. The downside was that his kindly father noticed him – as he assumed – squinting and thought the boy must have strained his eyes. He insisted on William wearing glasses even though the ophthalmologist said they weren't at all necessary. And the result of that was that Sandy Beach used this as the ocular proof of William's onanism, gloating, 'I told you you'd go blind if you kept beating your meat.'

Now, here, in Managua's hut, William forced himself to stare. It made him look like a police mug shot of a serial killer but not blinking at all was the only way he could guarantee he wasn't doing it alternately. He was brought out of his reverie about the past by the realization that Managua was speaking to him. It was the question he had been hoping wouldn't come up, at least not yet.

'What for you is come here?' asked Managua.

All eyes in the hut were on William. The natives were prepared to be astonished by his answer. The only person to come to the island in recent times and not affect it adversely was Miss Lucy. Before that, over a period of half a century, they had been visited sporadically by the British en masse and most of the islanders were still confused over what *that* had all been about. The British had introduced the black bantam pigs, built half a hotel and then left. Besides that, the only other newcomers in the last fifty years, during one of the lapses in British interest nearly two decades ago, had been the Americans, who were mad in a different way from the British. Instead of building something – *half*-building something – the Americans had more or less destroyed the northern village. Then they'd gone away leaving behind not black bantam pigs, but something far more deadly.

William smiled. 'I have a job to do here,' he said, and looked around as though that might take care of it. He was pleased to see all the natives were smiling back. He didn't know that they had no idea what he was talking about because they hadn't encountered the Western concept of work. The nearest they came to it was catching fish or picking fruit and those were just things you did, for your own immediate needs, as natural as breathing or taking a shit every morning. It wasn't something you thought of as work.

'Job?' said Managua, as puzzled as the rest of them. Then he became aware that all the others were looking at him, expecting him to understand. Managua didn't want to admit he didn't know what the word meant either. He especially didn't want to admit it in front of Purnu. The two of them were rivals. Purnu was jealous of Managua's ability to read. Managua sensed he was desperate to learn himself, although Purnu pretended the opposite was the case and never ceased mocking Managua for all his book-learning. But sometimes he'd come to his hut and look over Managua's shoulder as he was writing and point to a word and say in an overly casual way, 'What is be this word?'

Managua would tell him and Purnu would nod sagely. Managua would continue writing and a couple of minutes later Purnu would indicate another word and say, 'I is just wonder what is be that one?' and Managua would tell him that one too.

It made Managua laugh. The bloody damn fool thought that if he asked what every word was he'd eventually know them all and be able to read, whereas of course that wasn't the way it worked, you had to learn the sounds the letters made together. Sometimes when Managua was feeling particularly annoyed with Purnu he would reply to a question, 'Is be so-and-so, I is already tell you that one,' even if the word wasn't what he said it was and he hadn't ever told it to Purnu before, because the other man would never know and would be forced to dissimulate and would nod and say, 'Ah yes, of course, I is see now. You is not write so good this time, I is not recognize.'

Managua's one big fear was that Purnu would one day go to Miss Lucy and ask her to teach him to read, the way one of the nurses had taught him when he was hospitalized on the big island. Managua felt that if Purnu ever learned to read it would take something away from him, Managua. He knew this feeling to be envy and that it was bad but at the same time he realized it was Purnu's problem, not his. It was because Purnu was an envious person that he could make Managua feel it. Envy was virtually unknown on the island. The islanders had nothing to covet, except occasionally one another's wives, and maybe yams which they used instead of currency, and then if you were really worked up about someone having more yams than you you could just work your damn arse off and grow some more, although of course no-one ever was or did. Managua's ability to read was the only thing on the island that no-one else had.

So now Managua corrected himself. 'Ah yes, job, of course,' he said knowingly. He turned and bent low, peering through the doorway. 'Is be late,' he said. 'You is be tired after you journey, is want for go sleep, I is think? I is show you *bukumatula* house, where you is sleep.'

William thought about it. He didn't want to stay in the village if he could help it. For one thing it was all so primitive. For another he remembered reading about an especially deadly snake that inhabited the island and he thought he'd be more likely to encounter one on the dirt floor of a native hut than the polished tiles of a modern hotel. And for a third, he wanted a base where he could work away from the prying eyes of the natives.

'I was thinking maybe I could stay at the hotel, you know, the Captain Cook?'

At first this suggestion was met by complete silence. The natives looked at one another, pulling faces. In spite of the cultural differences between them and him, William could recognize the signals. Raised eyebrows, widening eyes, shaking of the head, in short, total incredulity. Then the man Purnu began to chuckle. His neighbour took up the sound and a ripple of laughter ran around the hut, increasing in volume until you might have described it as hearty. There was much knee-slapping, and people pushed one another's shoulders, practically knocking each other over, as they fought to outdo themselves in ridiculing what William had just said. Finally Managua wiped his eyes, and, with the help of the girl Tigua, pulled himself to his feet.

'You is come, *gwanga*,' he said. 'Captain Cook is not be possible.'

'You is must wait till is be finish!' said Purnu, and again the whole room erupted with ribald laughter.

'Come,' said Managua, suppressing a smile and speaking kindly, 'I is take you *bukumatula* house.'

SIX

'What exactly is the *bukumatula* house?' William asked Managua as they walked the path between the two concentric circles of wooden huts that made up the village. Managua had earlier explained to him that those around the outside were the homes of the people, while the inner circle consisted of workshops and storehouses, and also, apparently, the various *bukumatula* houses.

'You is say bachelor,' replied Managua. 'Is be hut for unmarried boys. When boys is be small and father is make *fug-a-fug* with mother parents is just say, "Go sleep! Is not watch!" and children is obey. But when is get bigger, is become young man, is have too big interest. Is make difficult for parents. Audience is be for play like *Hamlet*. Is not be for make *fug-a-fug*.'

'So they go and live in the *bukumatula* house?'

'Not live, is just sleep there. Is satisfy curiosity theyselves.'

William wasn't quite sure what this meant, but he had no opportunity to ask because Managua had stopped in front of a large hut, at least three times the size of his own. He ducked his head into the doorway and shouted something. A moment later a teenage boy emerged. 'Ah, *gwanga*!' the boy said and William recognized him as the leader of the rowers from the boat, the one who had complained of a *kassa* hangover, presumably from smoking the stuff William had just tried.

'Tr'boa is look after you now,' said Managua. 'We is talk again next day.'

'Yes,' replied William. 'Thanks.'

Managua frowned and stood staring at him with such obvious displeasure that William wondered what he had done wrong. It occurred to him that his gratitude might have seemed somewhat peremptory. There was probably some elaborate ritual form it should take.

'I really am most grateful to you for all the kind assistance you have given me,' said William, hoping that sounded formal enough.

Managua's frown deepened and he shook his head, much as a European might have done at something that amazed and annoyed him. Without a word he spun around on the tip of his artificial limb and stomped off.

William turned to Tr'boa. 'Did I say something wrong?'

Tr'boa laughed. 'Is you say something wrong? You is thank he. Is be plenty big insult for thank someone who is show you hospitality. Is seem like they is just welcome you for get thanks and is not do from real kindness.'

'Oh,' said William. 'Thanks.'

Tr'boa frowned.

'Oh, God!' exclaimed William. 'I didn't mean that, sorry.'

The boy broke into a big smile. 'Is be OK. I is only make joke of you. Is be all right for say thanks except for hospitality. But next day you is not thank me for welcome you into *bukumatula* house.'

'OK,' said William. 'Thanks.'

Inside the hut, William was surprised to see how sparsely furnished it was, even compared to Managua's. Mostly it seemed to consist of a dozen or so bunks against the walls. There were no tools or kitchen implements lying around, and there had been no fire or cooking pot outside. When he questioned Tr'boa he was told that the boys slept here, but took their meals at home with their parents. 'Is be same for girls, they is not eat here either.'

'Girls?' said William. 'What would girls be doing in a bachelor hut?'

Tr'boa raised an eyebrow. 'You is not know?'

'Oh,' said William, 'of course. Yes, silly me. What else.'

Tr'boa showed William to a bunk. It consisted of a raised wooden platform built against the side of the hut, with a straw mattress and a blanket of woven vegetable matter to cover himself.

William set his case down by the bed, climbed onto it and pulled the blanket over him. It was already growing dark and with the fading of the light came the sounds of the jungle, the throaty rasp of frogs from afar, the whooping of some bird, the hum of insects.

William was weary as weary could be after his long journey and was almost asleep when he heard voices. Opening his eyes he saw two dim shapes moving like ghosts across the room in the dying light, a boy and a girl, both teenagers. The boy whispered something and the girl giggled. They climbed onto a bunk against the opposite wall. Immediately there were more voices and other couples came in and made their way to their bunks. The hut was alive with their whispering. It was too dark to see now but there were rustling sounds that William imagined were grass skirts being discarded and dropped discreetly onto the dusty floor.

He shut his eyes and tried to sleep. He was suddenly aware that he was grinding his teeth, rotating hard the molars of first one side of his jaw and then the other in his old right-left-left-right combination. He told himself that this was understandable. His anxiety levels were high. He'd come halfway around the world to a remote place, peopled by savages who had strange customs and might still intend to slaughter him; the landscape was elemental too; there were no skyscrapers here to blot out the enormity of the sky, no TV to mask the relentless pounding of the waves that spoke to him threats of eternity. He was full of his old free-floating fear, which he had hoped to lose here, away from the stresses of modern life, but which at heart he suddenly felt he would never shake off because at its root was that one unanswerable fear, of his own inevitable extinction.

He was glad when a sudden gasp interrupted the way these

thoughts were heading. He heard the rhythmic rustling of a blanket, the old familiar beat of two people making love, but it was the first time he'd heard it when he wasn't one of them. Although the couple were obviously trying to be discreet – he could sense the girl biting her lip in an effort to hold back the increasingly frequent gasps of delight as she accelerated towards orgasm – their lust overrode this discretion. They could not conceal the quickening frenzy of their breathing.

Then, in syncopation came another set of breaths, more gasps of surprise and pleasure, and then a third pair joined in the orchestration and a fourth. William had no way of knowing that the youngsters around him really were trying to spare his feelings, that in the *bukumatula* house they abandoned their normal practice of the man kneeling between the woman's raised thighs to make love and settled for the quieter if less satisfying position of lying side by side, the woman's top leg over the man. As far as William was concerned there was no restraint in their performance; he found himself trapped in a wild delirium of surround-sound lovemaking.

He put his fingers in his ears in a futile attempt to block it out but without success. Besides, the air was thick with the scent of human sweat, vaginas and semen. There was no place to hide. One girl was shrieking with pleasure now, her squeals suddenly becoming muffled which William imagined was the effect of her partner putting his hand over her mouth. He imagined her bright white teeth seizing the hand and playfully biting it. Elsewhere a boy was grunting – ugh! ugh! ugh!, getting faster and faster ugh!ugh!ugh!ugh!ugh!ugh! The noises seemed to go on for hours.

Just when it began to grow quiet there would be a faint rustle of blanket and a giggle or two and it would start up again and that would wake someone else and they would begin and wake up another couple and so on until the whole hut was at it. Except William of course. At first he wondered at the natives' sexual prowess, but then remembered they were teenagers and how he had been at their age, wanting sex over and over again, although, of course, not usually able to have it, at least not with anyone other than himself.

As the long night wore on, William decided he could stand it no longer. As quietly as possible – more to spare his own embarrassment than for fear of waking anyone else, since they all seemed to be awake and pounding away at one another hammer and tongs anyway – he picked up his bag and struggled out with it.

He was probably committing some heinous breach of the etiquette of hospitality, but he didn't care. He had to get some sleep. Outside the silver light of a crescent moon showed him the way to the shore. He struggled with his bag along the strand. It seemed that even a couple of hundred yards from the village he could still hear the desperate sounds of teenagers humping, but he knew that couldn't be so. The waves that crashed on the shore eclipsed any other noise.

He set down his bag to rest for a moment and surveyed the endless expanse of ocean. He picked up a pebble or two and flung them as far as he could into the water. He was reminded of how Isaac Newton had surveyed his life and likened himself to a small boy playing on the seashore while the whole vast ocean of truth lay unexplored before him. If Newton, whose mark still remained upon the world centuries later, felt his achievements dwarfed by eternity, then how could William believe he had any significance when measured against this sea, which had beaten these same shores for aeon after aeon and would continue to be here long after the island itself, let alone he, was gone?

He thought of the first creatures crawling out of the water and the millions of years it had taken them to grow legs and then again to stand up on those legs, and the still more millions of years until they were able to invent landmines to blow off the legs; the vast time to make the whole unlikely passage from their watery beginnings to him. How could he take comfort in the idea that man had come from the ocean and would ultimately return there? How could he, as he knew some people did, find repose in the idea of his identity dissolving and vanishing into this mass before him, never to emerge again?

He picked up his case and staggered on, head bowed, shoulders slumped, desperate for sleep. He had no idea where he was going except for a vague recollection that the hotel, the Captain Cook, had been marked on his map as not far from the village in this direction. Just when he began to think his arms were going to break from the weight of the case, he saw a low concrete building, only two storeys, set back from the shore in front of him. He dragged the case through the sand to it.

The back of the hotel faced the beach. There was a veranda running around it. William crossed it and walked through an open doorway. He noted that there were no doors. Inside, he realized this was because the hotel was half-finished. The building itself seemed more or less complete, but the concrete walls were mostly not plastered. There were shutters on the windows, but no glass in them. A wooden staircase in front of him seemed half-rotted and he decided not to risk it.

He went through a doorway to his right. The room was almost dark except for a little moonlight filtered through gaps in the shuttering. As his eyes grew accustomed to the obscurity he realized it had been intended as some kind of dining room. There was a wooden bar built in the shape of half the hull of a boat against one wall. The centre of the room was occupied by an enormous long table, a solid black shape in the dim light. It was covered in dust. Something scuttled past William's feet. A lizard perhaps. He looked around for somewhere to sleep, but there was no other furniture. He didn't fancy the floor and whatever might be crawling around down there. He brushed his arm along a section of the table to clear it of dust, climbed onto it, lay down and, despite the hardness of his bed, was soon asleep.

SEVEN

Sandy Beach was rattling the bathroom door and shouting, 'Wanker! Wanker! You is come now pretty damn quick! Is be time!'

William opened his eyes and realized he had been dreaming. He was not an eleven-year-old boy any more but a man, twenty years older, twenty years closer to the day he most feared, the day he would cease to be anything.

He blinked – eyes synchronized this time – and began to look around. He appeared to be lying on a long table made of what looked like mahogany. For a moment he thought he must have been drinking heavily in some bar last night and collapsed here, but then he remembered his journey to the island and dimly recalled trudging to all that was left – or rather all that had been started – of the Captain Cook Hotel.

It had been but dimly moonlit when he'd arrived earlier this morning and it was only now he was able to take in his surroundings properly. The room was large and pretty much empty, except for the dining table, although he hadn't noticed before that there were a couple of matching chairs and a grand piano in one corner. At the opposite end was a built-in bar in the shape of a boat. He vaguely recalled that. What he hadn't seen last night, on the wall behind the bar, was a large mural. Peering at it William discerned the figure of a man in historic naval uniform, stumbling as a group of naked brown-skinned natives clubbed him to death on a tropical beach. It took his weary muddled head a moment or two to realize he was witnessing the murder of the eponymous Captain Cook on Hawaii. He shivered as he recalled his own situation.

Not wishing to dwell on this unhappy parallel he turned to contemplate his bleak surroundings. Spartan they might be but at least he had managed to get some rest, well away from the aural sex of the *bukumatula* house. And he needed his privacy; here, ten minutes' walk along the shoreline from the village, he'd be away from the villagers' prying eyes. Managua appeared a nice enough guy but he had seemed overly interested in finding out what William was here for.

He'd scarcely had this thought when the banging started up again and the shout of '*Gwanga! Gwanga!*' and he realized it had been no dream and that the voice belonged not to Sandy Beach but to the man he'd just been thinking about, Managua.

He hauled himself off the table and over to the window where the shutters were being rattled. After a moment's struggle he managed to release the rusty catch holding them closed and was nearly knocked over as they burst inwards. Managua stood outside, framed in the window aperture, looking furious.

'What you is do here? I is must track you here from *bukumatula* house.'

'Sorry,' said William. 'I just couldn't get any sleep there. I didn't mean to cause you any trouble.'

'Is not be trouble once I is figure out you is pull bag after you. Before then I is not see any tracks. I is think you is fly away.'

'Just like Superman, eh?' said William.

'Superman?' said Managua.

'Forget it,' said William. 'I'm just a little groggy.'

'What you is be is late,' said Managua. 'You is wait one moment. I is find door.'

William straightened his clothes while Managua hobbled round the veranda and came into the dining room.

'You is better hurry,' said Managua. 'I is need shit.'

'Where's the toilet?' William asked. He knew the hotel was

unfinished, but he had no idea exactly how unfinished it was.

'No toilet,' came the reply.

'No toilet?' said William in disbelief.

'Come,' said Managua and stomped off through another door beside the bar. William followed him into what had obviously been intended as the men's room. There was the usual symbol of a forked and unaccommodated man on the door, and inside there were toilet stalls and urinals. The urinals were unconnected; there were no pipes emanating from beneath them. The stalls were empty. Against one wall was a pile of smashed lavatory bowls.

'Is never be finish,' said Managua. 'British is come for build hotel plenty year ago. Big ship is go come. Is go bring people for stay in hotel. Then big ship is say is not come. So British is not bother for finish build hotel. Is go away.' He smiled. 'Plenty good riddance. British is be plenty stupid. Americans is be evil, but British is be plenty damn stupid.'

'So what do I do for a toilet?' said William, letting the insult to his countrymen pass because his bowels were rumbling from the spicy stew he'd eaten as Managua's dinner guest the night before.

'Use beach,' said Managua. 'I is show you. But you is must hurry.'

'You use the beach?' said William. 'You just, um, shit on the beach?'

Managua studied him as one might a child who was having difficulty grasping something simple. 'Listen, in America, you is use this?' He indicated the pile of smashed lavatories.

'Yes,' said William.

'Tell me, where shit is go?'

'Well, it goes into a pipe.'

'And then?'

'Well, I guess then it goes to a treatment plant.'

'Yes,' said Managua, 'but after that. Where shit is end up?'

'Um, well, in the sea I guess.'

Managua shrugged. 'So what for is need all this? Is be crazy. Is much smarter if you is just shit on beach in first place. Now you is come quick, we is be plenty damn late. Too much talk, not enough shit.'

William found his shoes and squeezed into them with some difficulty. They were still wet from the sea yesterday. As Managua limped outside, William reached into his suitcase and grabbed a wad of toilet tissue. The gurgling in his stomach told him he could not afford to hang around. The urgency only increased at the thought that not only would he not be able to have it in his own bathroom at home, nor in his temporary residence, the Captain Cook, but would be forced to evacuate himself on an open beach. He consoled himself that at least he would be unmolested by the bacteria that lurked in other people's bathrooms. That was what mattered.

Outside Managua was moving faster than the day before and William had to almost run to catch up with him. Managua's jaw had a purposeful set to it. He looked like a man with a mission.

'Where exactly are we going?' asked William.

'Shitting beach,' said Managua. 'I is take you make shit.'

The rim of the sun was only just edging above the line where ocean met sky. The light was as yet grey and objects indistinct. They headed along the shore in the direction of the village. Soon William could see the roofs of its huts through the trees. Through the pale light dozens of silhouetted ghosts were visible on the beach.

'We is be here, this is be shitting beach,' said Managua, heading now across the sand.

'Here?' said William, appalled. 'You shit on the beach right next to the village?'

Managua nodded and limped on.

'B–but how can you do that? How can you pollute your own beach? What happens if you want to swim?'

Managua stopped walking and turned to him. 'If you is want swim, you is can walk next beach. If you is need shit, you is want beach near.'

He turned away and strode on. William hurried after him. The sun was half up now and the ghosts on the beach had fleshed out into real people. There must have been upwards of two hundred men and boys, all squatting with one hand holding their pubic leaf strings away from their bare buttocks.

As they passed, these hunched fingers lifted their free hands in greeting, smiled and called out, 'Moning! Moning Managua! Moning *gwanga*!'

Managua waved back cheerily and William did his best to smile as he tagged along after the old boy. The beach was so crowded it was practically impossible to see a place where you could squat and not be shitting on somebody. William was beginning to understand Managua's haste.

He felt his toe stub against something soft and realized he hadn't been looking where he was going. He'd stuck his foot into a colossal mound of faeces. He paused and looked around. Everywhere there were similar mountains of the stuff, all steaming in the cool morning air.

William couldn't believe that anything smaller than an elephant could pass so much shit in one go. He didn't know that as a result of their low-fat, high-fibre diet of fruit and vegetables the average islander's dump was two kilos, compared to an eighth of that for the average Westerner's bowel movement.

He was appalled at the way the islanders simply dumped and walked away without cleaning themselves afterwards. He didn't know that the minimal amounts of fat in their diet (except on the rare occasions when they ate pig) meant their faeces were smooth rather than sticky and simply slipped out without fouling their behinds.

Managua stopped so abruptly that William almost collided with him. In a bizarre parody of a Westerner looking for a bare patch of sand on which to sunbathe at a resort beach, the old man had been searching for, and at last found, a people-free, shit-free area.

'We is be late this morning,' he said, squatting with surprising ease for a man with an artificial leg and pulling aside his pubic leaf string. 'You is take long time for wake up. You is need get here early for find best place. Nevermind, nevermind, this is be OK.'

William smiled weakly and made to walk on.

Managua half rose from his squatting position, his face clouded with bewilderment. He seemed hurt. 'Where you is go?' he asked. 'You is not want shit with me?'

'I er, I think I see a bigger space there. Wouldn't want to crowd you,' said William. He hurried off before Managua had chance to reply.

He trudged on until the crowd thinned and found a reasonably private spot, although when he turned he could still see Managua watching him from a hundred yards or so away. He looked at the people around, trying to make sure they were all male.

He had never before had a dump in front of another human being, not since early childhood, anyhow, and he couldn't remember that. He could just about manage this, but he knew he couldn't shit with a woman watching. And he did need to shit.

Having satisfied himself there were no women present (although you never could tell, the genders here seemed blurred, to say the least. A couple of the girls yesterday had looked butch enough to be guys) he realized the men around him were all look-ing at him. He recognized one of the squatting figures as the man Purnu from Managua's hut yesterday. They were all smiling and waving and he returned their greetings in what he hoped was a nonchalant fashion. At the same time he felt embarrassed at other people not only seeing him shit, but also seeing *his* shit. And he was appalled at them leaving their excrement in the open on the beach. For one thing, with the breeze coming in off the sea, the stench was sickening.

He decided the civilized thing would be to dig a hole to bury his shit, the way cats did. Still smiling, and staring out to sea as though admiring the view, he began poking around in the sand with his right loafer. Soon he had a reasonably sized hole – at least by the standards of what he intended to put in it, although totally inadequate for the islanders' portions, of course – and dropped his trousers and shorts and squatted over it. This in itself was difficult.

It was OK for the islanders, they weren't hobbled when they were shitting. William was not only not used to squatting, the breeze blowing up his butt, without a lavatory to support him, making him worry that if he could manage a dump in this position he might overbalance and fall back onto it; he was also fearful that he might crap on his clothes.

He shut his eyes and concentrated. In the background he could hear the fall of the waves and above that a descant of grunts and sighs as men all around him registered successful bowel movements. Eventually, just when he thought his calf muscles were going to give out from the strain, William managed a dump.

He opened his eyes to find a circle of natives around him, standing looking from him to the hole beneath him that contained his shit. Embarrassed, he reached down, pulled the tissue from his trouser pocket, hurriedly wiped himself and pulled up his clothes.

He found himself face to face with Purnu who was looking at him suspiciously. 'What for you is dig hole?'

'Yes,' said the man next to him. 'You is go bury you shit, is not be so? What for you is bury you shit?'

Another man pushed through the throng and peered into the hole where William's meagre effort lay steaming. He looked from it to William. 'What you is hide?' he demanded. 'What is be wrong with you shit?'

William found himself edged out of the way as the focus and centre of the throng became not him, but the dump he'd just done. About twenty men were now jostling one another trying to get a look at it. One man came rushing up with a bamboo stick and the crowd parted to let him through. As William fled along the beach in the direction he'd come from, he suffered the indignity of seeing the man poking the stick into the hole while everyone around it chattered excitedly.

Managua was waiting for him. 'What all fuss is be about?' he asked.

'I don't know,' William lied. 'I think they must have found a dead fish.'

Managua turned to walk back towards the village.

'Good shit?' he asked.

'It was OK,' replied William. 'I've had better.'

EIGHT

You'd have thought that after Sandy Beach's disastrous weekend with the Hardts nobody would be in much of a hurry to repeat the experience. But just the opposite happened. Incredible though it may be, he became a frequent visitor to the Hardts' shore house.

The prime mover in this was William's father who was, as we know, a kindly man. Joe Hardt hadn't been involved all his life in civil rights cases against major American companies and the US government without getting to know a real prick when he saw one; he had no illusions about Sandy Beach. But his son needed a friend and if Sandy Beach was that boy then Joe would do everything in his power to facilitate the friendship. In this his wife concurred. Such was her sense of guilt at having reared a boy who had difficulty in forming social relationships she was desperate for one pal, any pal, to assuage it.

That's all very well, you might say, but then why didn't William just come clean and tell them he couldn't stand the little shit? Why did he let them go on thinking he actually liked him and so condemn himself to countless extra hours in Sandy Beach's company, besides those he already had to endure at school?

The reason was that William could see the pleasure it gave his old man to do something for his son, especially something that involved so much suffering for Joe himself; he was making a sacrifice to help his son, he was putting up with Sandy Beach! It would have broken William's heart to disappoint his father. He already felt he'd let his father down by being such a geeky, unpopular child. The least he could do was put up with Sandy Beach for his father so that his father could put up with Sandy Beach for him.

If the weekends and – misery! – whole vacation weeks Sandy Beach spent with the Hardts were something to be got through, and they were, especially with Ruth's constant sniping at the visitor on account of the fact that his physical appearance coincided almost exactly with her idea of what a prodigious masturbator would look like, then the reciprocal visits William had to make to the Beaches were worse.

They lived in a small town upstate. The first visit, Sandy Beach's father met them at the railroad station and, in the back of the car on the way to the house, Beach whispered to William, 'There's uh something I forgot to mention. You might find our house a little um messy. I mean, don't get me wrong, we like it. We find it kind of relaxed and comfortable, but I guess you might say it's not exactly to everybody's taste.'

Now William's mother was exceptionally tidy. And she did have something of a thing about germs. These twin aspects of her personality would, in later years, cause William to speculate whether therein might lie the origins – either environmental or genetic – of his OCD and of Ruth's phobia about spermatozoa. But even allowing for that, even if that hadn't been the case and his home had been as sloppy and germ-ridden as the next person's, he would still have almost flatlined from the shock of stepping into Sandy Beach's.

William knew the Beaches were not rich, certainly not by the standards of most of the families who had kids at his expensive school. William's own parents were far from wealthy, because Joe had elected to put helping poor black people above making a buck, and the school was only possible because a rich relative on his mother's side had left money for the express purpose of sending William there.

But the Beaches were known to be really poor. Sandy Beach always wore uniform from the school thrift shop, usually stuff that was the cheapest because it was so worn out that no-one else would let their children be seen in it. On top of that his mother made sure he got his wear out of it, by buying it when it was two sizes too big and making Sandy wear it until it was two sizes too small. So his clothes were almost always either too big or too small for him. There was only ever a comparatively brief period during the transition from one to the other when they were just right, and then it didn't usually happen that they were all just right at the same time; he might have pants that fitted perfectly, but you didn't really notice that because they were concealed by the blazer that came down to his knees.

And his parents couldn't afford to pay for a decent orthodontist, so that, to add to his other problems, Sandy Beach had crooked teeth. The Beaches had no spare money to put into improving Sandy's appearance, a project that, let's face it, could have proved a bottomless money pit. They had scrimped and saved every last dime to pay for Sandy's education. He had so many disadvantages that they realized he had to have at least one plus to get him launched in life and education was going to be it.

Joe Hardt had a different take on it. 'Well, you would scrimp and save if you were them,' he remarked to his wife when she told him all this. 'Anything to get that kid into a boarding school and away from home. Jesus, I'd rob banks if he was my kid.'

'I can't imagine you robbing a bank,' said Mrs Hardt with a smile. 'You wouldn't take the risk.'

'There wouldn't be any risk,' said Joe. 'It would be a no-lose situation. You get clear with the money, he goes to boarding school; you get caught you go to jail and only have to see him on visitors' day. Why wouldn't you rob banks?'

Mr Beach parked his beaten-up old Ford in the drive at the side of the house and they went in through the back door where they found Mrs Beach at work in the kitchen.

At least William *thought* it was the kitchen. It wasn't that easy to tell for sure. Whatever the room's original purpose, it was now given over to the keeping of stuff. Every surface, every counter, every chair, the table — if that's what was under the central pile — was covered with stuff: piles of old newspapers and magazines, boxes of household equipment, like a cardboard crate of furniture polish concealing itself under a layer of dust, tins of food, packets of dried soup, and a tool box that was probably empty in that various tools — a hammer, a chisel, a set of screwdrivers — lay around in different locations in the room, and that was now paying for its keep as the supporter of a laundry basket loaded with dirty washing.

There were two washing machines, one of them disconnected and in the centre of the room, both piled high with boxes of light bulbs, packets of firelighters, plastic toddlers' toys (although Sandy was an only child, his parents having wisely stopped after having him. 'They probably became celibate after him,' Joe Hardt told his wife. 'Would you trust any form of birth control if there was the remotest statistical possibility of another kid like that?'), unwashed dishes, washed dishes, rusting saucepans, cardboard boxes full of empty supermarket plastic bags with half-eaten bowls of cat food perched precariously on the very top.

The drainer by the sink was similarly afflicted with several stacks of books supporting an old TV with a cracked screen. Even the windowsill was occupied by dirty coffee cups and a few browned apple cores.

'Why, hello William,' said Sandy Beach's mother. She was a large woman with wild hair that stuck out from her head as though she'd just had an electric shock, which was more than possible, given the disarray that surrounded her. 'You'll have to take us as you find us, I'm afraid.' With a sweep of her hands she alluded to the chaos all around. 'I didn't have time to tidy up today.'

She turned and William saw she was cooking food on something he hadn't realized was a stove. Only one hot plate was in use, the one on which she had a skillet in which she was pushing something around. The other three were concealed beneath various piles of clutter. 'If you'll just excuse me a moment, supper's almost ready,' she said. 'Take a seat.'

William stood and helplessly surveyed the room. He was trying to work out which of the piles of stuff might have as its foundation a chair.

'Here, let me help,' said Mr Beach, coming through the back door with William's case. He went to set it down, but there wasn't a bit of floor space to put it on, save for the narrow corridor that led from the back door to the rest of the house between the wavering cliffs of rubbish. Having realized this, Mr Beach opened the back door and set the case down on the porch. 'We'll get that later,' he said. 'Here, hold your arms out.'

William did as requested and Mr Beach began demolishing one of the towers. Onto William's outstretched arms he placed a plastic carton of shredded paper labelled 'Hamster bedding', a few dozen magazines, a case of beer ('Ah, so that's where that got to,' said Mr Beach enthusiastically. 'I just knew I hadn't drunk it all!'), a can of fly spray and a pile of towels that looked clean, but might well not have been.

Clean was rapidly becoming a relative word here to William. Indeed he was not too worried about the possible effects of germs, which, even if fatal, would probably entail a slow kind of death. He was thinking that this was exactly the kind of low-life dysfunctional household that real-crime TV shows revealed to be a breeding ground not just for bacteria, but for serial killers too. The Beaches could have had any number of murdered children concealed about the place and nobody would ever have been able to find them.

Mrs Beach was a large woman. Actually she was morbidly obese, even fatter than a woman whose photograph would later cause William so much trouble, but he wasn't even aware of the term back then. You didn't see so many super-fat people in those days.

Anyhow, eventually Mr Beach excavated a chair. 'Take a seat,' he repeated, indicating it with a bold sweep of his hand that seemed to reveal no small amount of pride in having proved himself to be the owner of one.

Then he saw that the oscillating pile of stuff William was holding wouldn't permit him to move, let alone sit down. 'We'll just,
uh, get rid of this,' he said and began removing things from
William's pile and redistributing them between the various piles
around the room. He was only a little guy and had to stretch to
place a towel or a can of beans on the tottering towers. It was like
watching a circus act. You kept waiting for the object that would
be the last straw and bring a tower down. There was even the
possibility of a domino effect and the whole kitchen disappearing
for ever under stuff.

Eventually William sat down and Mr Beach repeated the whole
exercise so that Sandy could sit beside him. 'Supper's ready!'
announced Mrs Beach. She looked around at the various towers
until she spotted a couple of dinner plates halfway down one.
Slowly and with surprising delicacy for such a large woman, she
slid them out, one by one, without disturbing the rest of the pile,
although it was hearts in mouths for a moment or two while the
whole thing swayed threateningly.

She had to move sideways through the stacks of stuff because the
gangway was too narrow to take her full on. Mr Beach followed
her, like one of those little cleaner fish that hang out with whales,
steadying wobbling stacks that she had brushed against. Having
placed the plates on the table she returned to the stove and came
back with the skillet and turned its contents onto them.

William gazed at the congealing, greasy mess before him. It was
impossible to identify it. There was something yellow in there that
he hoped was egg because he didn't even want to think about
what it might be if it wasn't. There was something black and
cylindrical that he prayed was a charred sausage. Other bits
and pieces defied analysis.

'Don't wait for us!' said Mrs Beach. 'We'll eat later.'

'Yes, we'll have two sittings,' said Mr Beach. 'Kids first, adults
after.'

Indeed, looking around the room, it would have been impossible for them to do anything else. Even one sitting had been a

major achievement. But in spite of everything, William couldn't help feeling sorry for Mr Beach. The way he said 'kids' with such enthusiasm. You couldn't help knowing that it was the first time he'd been able to use the word in the plural in this house. His happiness made William feel uncommonly sad. He knew then he wouldn't have the heart to refuse to come back to this awful place. There was nothing for it; he was going to have to spend a big part of his childhood here.

He began pushing his food around his plate, reasoning that as soon as the Beaches turned their backs it would be pretty easy to conceal the meal around the room. Nobody was going to notice it wherever he put it.

But Mrs Beach was watching him like a hawk. 'Come on now, William,' she said, 'even if you aren't especially hungry, at least eat your vegetables.'

Afterwards William was given a tour of the house by Mr Beach. In some places the alleys between stacks of stuff were so narrow that William thought they must be no-go areas for Sandy's mom. At one point Mr Beach proudly pointed out a glass extension to the side of the property. 'The sun room wasn't here when we bought the place,' he explained. 'We had it put on. I don't know how we managed without it. It's very useful for storing more stuff.'

Now William was not given to any great psychological insights and he was only eleven years old. But his own mental disorder made him empathetic to the psychological problems of others and he had a sense that all the rubbish hoarded in the house was a manifestation of the Beaches' depression (he could imagine his dad saying to his mom, 'Well, heck, I'd be depressed if I had a kid like that!') and he started to feel sorry for Sandy. This didn't mean he liked him any more. Quite the reverse. The more contact he had with the little prick, the more he despised him. But it helped him be a bit kinder to the kid. You had to pity someone who lived in a house that was so cramped there wasn't even elbow room to have a decent wank.

NINE

After the shitting Managua invited William for breakfast. He would have liked to refuse, because he wanted to unpack his things and start on a plan of action, but although his experiences on the shitting beach had made him temporarily nauseous, as soon as he was away from it he realized he was famished. Moreover, he had no food. He had expected to get his meals at the hotel, but there was of course no possibility of that. Not only that but he had nothing to exchange for food since it was obvious the locals had no use for money, let alone credit cards. From the conversation last night he had worked out that yams were a kind of currency, but he had no idea of how to get any or even what they were. Some type of root vegetable, he suspected.

So he accepted Managua's invitation while at the same time wondering how far he could take advantage of his hospitality and, perhaps more importantly, how he could keep himself from thanking him for it in the meantime.

A fire was burning outside the entrance to Managua's hut and on it was a steaming cauldron.

'Lamua!' called Managua, ducking his head through the doorway. There was no reply. 'Now where is be that damn woman?' said Managua, pulling his head out. He looked worried. 'Where she is go poke damn nose today?'

He saw William looking at him and made a show of

brightening. 'You is have wife at home, *gwanga*?' he asked, indicating that William should sit himself down by the fire.

'Ex-wife,' said William, and seeing that Managua looked puzzled, he elaborated. 'I don't have her any more.'

'Ah, I is be sorry for hear that.' Managua sighed. 'Same here. I is have ex-wife too. She is be blow up along with my leg. I is lose both together. Now I is only see she in *kassa* house.'

This speech was completely baffling to William. On the one hand Managua appeared to be telling him that his wife had been killed in an accident; on the other, that after all she was still alive and presumably had left him, perhaps on account of his having lost a limb, but that he still maintained some sort of relationship with her, in this *kassa* house, whatever that was. Whatever the explanation, this was not the time to ask for it.

Managua lowered himself to the ground and unstrapped his leg. He placed it behind him as if fearful it might roll into the fire and began rubbing the tip of his stump. 'Is hurt like damn sow,' he explained, seeing William's surprise. 'Is rub against leg plenty damn bad. Is be some other fella's leg and is be too long for me, that is be problem.'

'You lost your leg because you stepped on a mine?' said William.

'Yes. My leg, my wife and my baby. All is go in one bang. We is see Americans plant mines. Then they is leave. People is wait and wait and nothing is grow, so people is think mebbe they is dig they up for find out what they is be. Big mistake. Then nobody is be hurt for long time, so we is think mebbe all bombs is already be step on. Second big mistake.'

William pulled a notebook and pencil from his back pocket and scribbled something. Managua watched with interest as he took a ladle and spooned thick stew from the pot into a couple of wooden bowls. He handed one to William.

'You is like Shakespeare, *gwanga*?'

'Shakespeare, well yes, I guess. I suppose most people do. Not that I've seen a lot of his stuff.'

Managua almost dropped his bowl. 'You is *see* Shakespeare, *gwanga*? You is see *Hamlet*?'

'Yes, of course, leastwise, I think so.'

Managua shook his head as if in wonderment, though whether at someone seeing the play or at someone seeing it and not remembering, William couldn't be sure. The old man lifted his bowl to his lips. William copied him. The stew had a rooty flavour that William thought would be the way old sweaty socks would taste if you boiled them up. But he was too famished to let that put him off. And besides, anyone who had eaten at Sandy Beach's house, as William had, had tasted far worse than sweaty socks.

William put the bowl down and picked up his notebook again. 'What's your surname, Managua?'

'Surname? What is be, surname?'

'Last name. You know, like a family name.'

'Family name?'

'Yes, the name that comes after Managua.'

'I is have no other name. Nothing is come after Managua. Name is stop there. Nothing is come before, nothing is come after. Is just be Managua.'

'But you must have another name. Everybody does.'

'Not we. We is have only one name. What for you is need two? Is be American thing, always have more than you is need. If you is have more than one name you is just have more you is must say.' He took another mouthful of stew and appeared to be deep in thought as he chewed it. 'Suppose you is be in jungle and you is must call someone come pretty damn quick for catch pig. If you is must call extra name this additional bit is mebbe take just time pig is need for get away. What is be point of have more than one name?'

'Well, to tell one person from another. You get two people with the same name, how does anyone know who you're talking about?'

'No-one is have same name. Is belong me only. There is be one Managua.' He tapped his chest proudly. 'Is be me.'

'But you might not be the only one. Suppose someone else

chose the same name. Or your father called you after himself. It would get confusing.'

'No, you is be one who is get heself confuse. No-one here is have same name. Each person is be born is be new person, so is have new name. Same name is not be use twice.'

'Not ever? You wouldn't even give a child the name of a dead relative?'

'No, no, no. That is be confuse. You is get muddle when you is talk with dead person in *kassa* house. Nobody is ever have same name as nobody else. Not since island is first rise out of sea. Each person is have own name. Each name is be just for one person.'

'How do you keep finding new names?' asked William.

'Is be pretty damn hard, one time,' said Managua. 'But not now, since I is learn for read. Woman is have baby now is come Managua and is ask for name. I is just look in *Complete Shakespeare*. Last new boy is be call Falstaff. Next girl is be call Titania.'

Managua took the ladle from the pot and refilled their bowls. There was silence for a couple of minutes while both men ate, Managua slowly as though savouring every mouthful, William quickly, partly because he was hungry and partly because he *didn't* want to taste every mouthful. Eventually his stomach had enough in it for him to concentrate on something else.

'Well, if everyone has only one name it shouldn't be too hard to track down the person I want to see,' said William. 'I thought it was going to be tricky because I only had the one name, but I guess it's not going to be as difficult as I thought, if every name here is different.'

'You is come here for see one special person?' Managua asked. He didn't see how this could be. How would William know the name of anybody on the island? He was starting to have a bad feeling about this.

'Yes,' said William. 'It's a woman. She'd be around thirty-five years old. Her name is, well, was' – he consulted his notebook – 'Pilua.'

Looking up from the notebook, William found Managua staring

down into his bowl as though he'd suddenly discovered something interesting there.

'Well,' said William, 'do you know her? According to my information, some seventeen years ago she was living in this village.'

Managua took his time to reply. 'Of course I is know this woman. Is be my wife.'

'Your wife? Who was blown up?'

'Yes. I is already tell you all 'bout her.'

Managua studied his bowl again, though William realized now that it was empty. It was as though Managua were reading tea leaves, he thought. Finally the old man lifted his gaze and stared into William's eyes without blinking, either alternately or simultaneously.

'Well then, it's you I need to talk to. I'd like to ask you questions about her death, exactly how it happened.'

'I is already tell you. Is be nothing more for say.'

'And there's something else. I hate to bring this up, but there was a – a – an incident with some American military personnel.'

Managua reached for his leg and began strapping it on. 'Is best you is not ask about that, *gwanga*. We is say here, "You is put you foot on sleeping *terrada*." You is know what is mean *terrada*?'

'No.'

'Is be green shoestring snake. You is step on one you is be dead just about same time you is know you is step on he.' Managua hauled himself upright.

William scrambled to his feet too. 'Look, I understand how painful this might be for you. But couldn't someone else talk to me about it? Would you have a problem with that?'

Managua gave him a steely stare. 'I is already tell you, is be no point. Is be my wife. Is not be something you is need concern youself for.'

'But I—'

'My wife is be dead, *gwanga*. Is be end of talk.'

This time Managua did not meet William's gaze. Maybe that was

why William had the feeling the old man was lying. Or if not
actually lying, then at least hiding something. William could think
of nothing to counter the man's refusal to talk. Even the best legal
argument has no power against a stone wall.

Managua finally looked up and William saw that while he'd
been looking away he'd put a mask on. Now his face wore a smile
as though to indicate the subject of the argument was as dead and
buried as his late wife. 'And now, if you is not mind, *gwanga*, I is
must deal with that damn fool Polonius who is talk too damn
much. I is send girl Tigua Captain Cook for bring you food. And
tonight I is take you *kassa* house.'

'Thank you,' said William, somewhat mollified.

Managua received his gratitude with an exasperated scowl, and
as he had the night before, swivelled on the ball of his artificial leg
and disappeared through the doorway of his hut.

Shit! thought William. I can't believe I did that. I thanked the
old bastard again.

TEN

Is not give for while or take for while for give back,
Thing you is give or is take is get lost and then friend is go same way,
All this give and take is make man not so sharp for look after things.
But this most important: is not not talk tru for you self
And is then follow, like sun-down is be after sun-up
You is must talk tru for any other fella too.

This Hamlet is be plenty damn hard, Managua told himself. He was starting to think it was not worth it. When he looked at the islanders they were like heedless children. The young ones ran around making *fug-a-fug* with everyone and everybody – and he wasn't criticizing it, he had done the same when he was young, before he was married – they picked fruit, they fished, they settled down, had children, they died and then they returned to the *kassa* house. Those were the parameters of their lives and deaths.

They never thought about why they were here, they had no appreciation of the finer things the human mind was capable of, the part of man that could rise above food and *kassa* and the animal way one body fitted into another.

What he was attempting was so damned hard, he wondered if it was actually possible. Even if he had the meaning right, and he was not certain that he had, he wasn't sure the islanders had the cultural references to understand Shakespeare's world view. Even supposing that his translation of Polonius's farewell speech to Laertes was accurate, what could it possibly convey to people who had no idea of their grown-up children going any further than a new hut next door? The longest anyone was ever separated from his parents was when he went fishing or on a pig hunt without them. A matter of a few hours. It didn't require any homilies about how to treat your fellow man.

And all the stuff about borrowing and lending. The islanders had no real concept of personal possessions. If you asked an islander to lend you something the very idea would be so alien he would insist upon giving it to you. If you asked him for one fish, he was likely to press upon you two. If you asked him for a pubic leaf, he'd offer you his ceremonial skirt as well. For keeps. He wouldn't expect to get it back. The very idea of asking someone to give you something and then insisting on returning it would be seen rather as an insult. As far as the islanders were concerned, everything had been put here for everyone to use. There was enough for them all. If at a particular moment you had something in your hands that someone else wanted or needed, and they had no yams to trade for it, why would you not give it to them?

But then, *Hamlet* was such a wonderful play that Managua longed to see it performed. The only trouble was that his version might so bowdlerize the ideas it contained as to render it, if not meaningless, then ordinary. It was possible that in converting it to an island version it might be unavoidable that he destroyed what had made it great in the first place.

Then there were some parts of it even he didn't understand, in spite of all his reading. He would have to ask the *gwanga* about them; after all, the *gwanga* had actually seen *Hamlet*. There must be many things that were puzzling when you just read them in the *Complete Shakespeare* that would become clear when you saw the play performed.

Managua tossed his pencil angrily across the room. That damned *gwanga*! It was his fault that Managua had got so little done all morning, his fault that he could not concentrate, he realized that now when the image of the white man swam to the surface of his mind. He'd been there all day, lurking beneath his thoughts, tugging at him like the undertow at the landing beach, pulling him down from the nobler – the loftier – thoughts of Shakespeare.

Managua bent and picked up his leg and strapped it on. It was no good, he couldn't work with all this on his mind. It was no use ignoring this Pilua business. If he didn't do something about it, the *gwanga* would start asking around. Questions whose answers could lead to something that would destroy the island for ever. But what could he, Managua, do?

Perhaps he should consult Miss Lucy. After all, she understood how the islanders' beliefs underpinned their whole way of life and had always gone out of her way to respect them, apart of course from the silly mistake she'd made over the business of the dresses, and then, of course, she had meant well.

Then again, if he asked her advice, would he not have to lay the whole damn thing out before her? What if she betrayed him to the *gwanga*? He did not think that she would, but who knew if she would feel obliged to side with another white person?

He would take a walk, maybe talk it over with Cordelia, if his wife wasn't watching him too closely. Of course the pig couldn't understand him, but he often found expressing his thoughts aloud to her helped him find out what they were.

Just as Managua was getting to his feet, or rather foot, Lamua came in. She had a guilty air about her and he knew at once that she had been looking for the pig. But she didn't look guilty enough to make him think she'd found Cordelia and harmed her, so he didn't bother to get into a big row about that. The important thing was that he not act suspiciously. It was bad enough this business with the pig, without adding Pilua to the problems between him and his wife.

Lamua began tidying his desk which Managua interpreted as a declaration of hostility because she was angry at not finding the pig. He declined the gauntlet and limped out.

He crossed the central space in front of the *kassa* hut and saw

Tigua and her two she-boy pals larking about. They were playing some kind of game, trying to walk along an old log wearing those damn high heels Miss Lucy had given them. Tigua could do it easily, but the big girl, Lintoa, had a real problem. She was sowing and complaining about her feet hurting, which was not surprising when you thought she was wearing an old pair of Miss Lucy's shoes. Even with new bigger straps they were still far too small.

Their silliness annoyed Managua. There were two old women in the village who had lost a foot and one who had lost both. The she-boys ought to be helping them, doing the things girls were supposed to do, cooking, cleaning, making clothes. But these young people today thought only of having fun. It used not to be this way.

He caught himself thinking this and told himself he was getting old and intolerant. He liked young people. He didn't want to be one of those old folk who went on about how things were better when they were young. Besides, it probably wasn't true. Nothing ever really changed on the island. It had always remained the same – despite the meddling of the British and the murderous impact of the Americans, both of which it had survived intact, well, almost, apart from his own leg and a few other missing limbs – and always would. Provided, of course, that he could stop this *gwanga* from interfering.

Tigua's high-pitched giggle broke into his thoughts. She was one silly girl! He regretted having offered her the part of Ophelia, if and when his *Hamlet* was performed. He worried that she lacked the seriousness for the part. He didn't see Ophelia as much of a giggler. Sussua was the prettiest of the three, but she was so shy you couldn't give her a major role. And Lintoa would never impress anyone as a female lead. Lintoa was just too big. As it was she would have to play Gertrude, which in itself might stretch the audience's credulity. It would be difficult to believe that Lintoa had got one man to marry her, let alone two – and one of them to murder the other for her into the bargain.

Looking at them now, Managua wondered, not for the first

time, if he should have done *Macbeth* instead. They would have been perfect for the three weird sisters. Seeing them now in their Westerners' dresses, with their *susus* strapped up in the devices underneath, tottering around on their high heels, he thought they were certainly weird all right.

Ah well! He would just have to work with what he'd got. It was no different from the way Shakespeare had done it. They didn't have women actors in his day. All his female characters had been she-boys too.

He remembered he hadn't asked Tigua to take the food for the *gwanga* to the Captain Cook and limped towards the she-boys. 'Tigua!' he shouted. It came out rather more angrily than he'd intended, but then the way the three of them were behaving was beyond tolerance and he knew it was Tigua who was the ring-leader. She was the most imaginative and resourceful of the three.

Tigua twisted to see who had called and fell over because of the high heels. At the sight of Managua she removed them, pulled herself to her feet and hurried over, one hand behind her back, obviously holding and concealing the shoes.

Managua didn't mention them. This was not the time to be getting into that; the three of them knew what he thought about the dresses.

'I is want you is go take food for *gwanga* at Captain Cook,' he said.

Tigua's face brightened. A little with relief at the shoes being ignored by Managua for once, but mainly at her good fortune in being the one selected to go see the *gwanga*. Just wait till Lintoa found out.

ELEVEN

'What for British is want for come here?' Tigua paused for a moment to straighten the heavy basket which seemed in danger of slipping off her head.

'Here, let me,' said William gallantly reaching for it, but Tigua neatly sidestepped him and continued along the beach. William shrugged and followed the girl. It didn't seem right allowing a woman to carry all his stuff, but somehow Tigua's insistence on doing it made him feel rude and ungrateful for even offering to shoulder the load himself.

The basket was full of minoa root bread, cakes, fruit, rice, vegetables and turtle eggs. After he'd taken a look around the village, observing the various tasks the natives were engaged in and trying to assess the increased difficulty caused by having only one hand, or arm or leg, William had met up with Tigua on the way back to the hotel and the girl had explained she was bringing food to him.

'What for they is want for build this?' insisted Tigua, indicating the concrete shell of the hotel which now hove into view as they rounded the headland into the next bay.

'To come on vacation,' said William. 'For holidays.'

'What this is be, holiday?'

'It means taking a break from work.' William saw Tigua's brow pleat with puzzlement and remembered that the islanders had at best a hazy concept of work. 'It's a change from your normal life, a rest, do something different.'

'Man, that is be crazy. What for anyone is want for change life? What for is want for anything is be different?'

William took in the horseshoe bay they were entering as they rounded the headland. The sea shimmered in the afternoon sun, the white horses of the breakers galloped in to collapse upon the golden shore, the wind tickled the leaves of the palm trees. Why would you, if you were Tigua, want more? What was there better than this?

'Don't you ever want anything different?' he asked. 'Don't you sometimes wish for something else?'

Tigua screwed up her eyes in concentration. 'No. Yes. Mebbe new dress, is all. Is not want for be anywhere different. Is not want for go another island.'

'And you think that's the same for everyone here? Your friends feel the same way?'

'Yes. Except mebbe Lintoa, she is mebbe like for be boy.'

William remembered the one they called Lintoa from the walk back from the landing beach yesterday. He could understand the poor girl having some gender confusion. She was halfway to being a guy already. Mind you, Tigua, for all her girlishness, was not exactly feminine. He decided to avoid the subject. 'You see, not everywhere is like this. In Britain it's often cold and raining. It would be very pleasant for British people to leave all that behind and come here and sit on the beach.'

'Huh! Come all way across sea just for shit on beach! What is be so great 'bout that? What is be so bad 'bout shit on own beach, even if is make rain there?'

William sighed. He couldn't be bothered pointing out that Tigua had misheard 'shit' for 'sit'. The concept of anyone just wanting to sit on a beach and do nothing was too alien, he suspected, for Tigua to ever encompass it and would seem more eccentric to her, probably, than the idea of travelling halfway round the world to defecate in a different place.

They walked up the broken wooden steps separating the beach from the hotel terrace which opened into the lobby that led into the bar and dining room which William had decided to keep as his bedroom.

Tigua put the basket down. 'Well, thank you,' said William, turning to face the young woman, intending this as a signal that they should part here and Tigua go home. Tigua ignored him and brushed past him into the building, looking around all the time.

'Man, this is be one big place. I is not come here before. People is say bad spirit is live here.' She gave him a simpering look. 'But I is not be frighten with you.'

William felt himself blush with embarrassment. He was used to girls flinging themselves at him because they wanted to protect him, not the other way round. He wished Tigua would go. But you couldn't be annoyed with her. She had a vivaciousness and interest in things that he might have found attractive had she just not been so damned butch-looking.

Together they explored the building. Behind the bar was a room obviously intended as some kind of library or reading room. The walls were lined with bookshelves from floor to ceiling, but there were no books.

'Managua is take books,' explained Tigua. 'No-one else is want; no-one else is can read. Managua is not can read when he is take, but is keep till he is learn.'

Behind the library was a long corridor with doors on the other side of it. There were some ten doors but when they opened them they found they only gave on to the jungle. The front of the hotel had never been built. At one end there was what William at first thought was another bar, but then realized was a reception desk, with a couple of dozen pigeon-holes behind it, optimistically numbered for the guest rooms. Beside the reception desk was the wooden staircase, its treads rotten and holed in places. He started up it but Tigua grabbed his arm.

'No, *gwanga*, Managua is say I is tell you you is must not go up steps. He is say steps is be dangerous. Termites is eat they all. Managua is not want for you is have accident.'

William was going to challenge this because he thought the steps looked solid enough on the side flanked by the wall, but seeing the anxiety in Tigua's face decided he ought not to get the girl into trouble with Managua. Besides, the old guy probably knew what he was talking about and what was the point of risking it? There would be nothing to see up there anyway.

He returned to the dining room and began unpacking his case, taking out the books and positioning them on the opposite end of the dining table from the one he used as a bed. He took out his cell phone too, although he already knew it to be useless. Once his battery ran down he had no means of recharging it. Anyway, there was no mast on or near the island so even if he'd been able to power it up, it wouldn't have worked. He wished he'd done his homework better and prepared for all this.

'Is be plenty books,' said Tigua. 'Is be more than Managua is have. You is read all they books?'

'Well, not exactly. I mean, maybe, over the years a bit here and a bit there, but they're not the kind of books you sit down and read right through. More books to refer to, check things in.'

'All I is say is you is not let Managua is see they books. That man is go crazy for books.'

William pulled up a chair, sat down and opened one of the books. He took out his notebook and began writing in it. He didn't look up. Eventually Tigua cleared her throat.

'Well, *gwanga*, if you is not want anything more, I is go now.'

William looked up and smiled. 'OK Tigua. And thank you for your assistance, my dear.'

Tigua dismissed this with a wave of her hand. 'Is be nothing. You is want anything you is just ask me. You is not go Lintoa, is understand? Lintoa is be one big sow, is throw she weight around all time.'

'I understand. If I need anything, and I'm sure I will, you'll be the first person I come to.'

He was surprised when Tigua gave him a thumbs-up sign. Where had she got that from? 'Sure thing, *gwanga*. I is see you next day at shitting!'

'Yes,' said William. Although to himself he added, not if I see you first. He still couldn't get his head round the idea of a woman watching him take a dump. He didn't know that the she-boys used a separate part of the beach and that Tigua had merely meant he'd see him before or after they visited their respective areas.

TWELVE

Although OCD made his life difficult in lots of ways, it also – as is the case for many sufferers – helped William to be successful in his chosen profession. It made him a good lawyer. The rituals he engaged in required him to pay great attention to minute details, to learn extreme patience and to be painstaking in matters of accuracy. Like many obsessive-compulsives, he exhibited a creative streak. This didn't surprise him. How could anyone come up with the idea of standing astride a linoleum join and rocking from side to side to view different aspects of bathroom fittings as a way to ward off ill fortune and *not* be creative?

OCD people view the world as a place where magic exists, where evil events occur randomly but can – illogically – be prevented by seemingly unconnected practices. In this respect William had more in common with the people of the island than their more obvious cultural differences might have suggested.

These are some of the ways in which William's OCD affected him: he could not sit comfortably in a room in which there was a door open, not even a cupboard door. Nor could he sit with his back to the main entrance of a room. When people noticed this, for instance when he lunched in a restaurant with someone and was forced to jockey in an unavoidably noticeable way for a position facing the door, he would always joke it was on account of what happened to Wild Bill Hickock, that he didn't want to be shot in the back.

He could not bear to have an inappropriate object on the ground within his peripheral vision. For example, if he was sitting with a book at a table at a pavement café and another patron's paper napkin blew onto the ground beside him, his anticipated pleasure of an hour's quiet reading would be ruined.

In such an event a number of courses of action were open to him. First, he could attempt to continue with his book and hope another gust of wind might carry the napkin further away, completely outside his line of vision.

If this did not then happen he'd have to consider his other options. One was to move his chair so that he could no longer see the offending piece of paper, but this didn't really work. He would remain too agitated to enjoy his book. He might not be able to *see* the napkin, but he would still *know* it was there.

He could get up and pick up the napkin, and that was always tempting, but he almost never did it because it would undoubtedly make him appear an oddball in front of the rest of the café's clientele and its waiters. And then there was the problem of where to put the napkin. He had a horror – another aspect of OCD, in which fear of germs and compulsive hand-washing often feature – of other people's litter and would not want it in his pocket or briefcase. Besides, if he did pick up the napkin, what would he do if another one blew from another table and replaced it? Pick that up too? What was he supposed to do, pick up litter all afternoon? His quiet time would still be ruined.

Another possibility was to point out the napkin to one of the waiters, but this seemed not only bossy but also presumptuous. After all, it was their café, their pavement area, who was he to tell them to keep it tidy? If it didn't bother the rest of their customers, why should it bother him? Why should the waiters run around after one freak?

The final option, of course, was simply to put away his book, gulp down the remainder of his coffee and leave, to abort his period of quiet relaxation entirely. And that was what he almost always did. Having a cup of coffee out of doors on a breezy day was not really an option for William, unless it was so windy that any errant napkins got themselves blown right away.

On sidewalks William either had to tread on the cracks between paving stones or avoid them altogether. It didn't particularly matter which, except that having started on a course of action he had to carry on the same way. He couldn't step on a crack and then avoid one with his next step.

He was a tall man whose stride was longer than one paving stone but not as long as two. This meant he had to foreshorten his stride, walking in little steps, like Madame Butterfly, or alternatively, lengthen it to the extent that he looked like a goose-stepping Nazi storm trooper.

It was OK when he was alone but if he was walking with an associate from the office he'd notice his companion looking at him strangely. If they'd been for an alfresco coffee and it was a breezy – but not too breezy – day, then it meant yet another person he worked with would have him down as an oddball.

William liked things to be symmetrical. He could not tolerate a picture hung slightly askew. If he spotted one in someone else's home (well, actually he didn't usually have to spot them, they leaped alarmingly to his attention, they practically shouted at him) he would hope that his host would leave him alone so that he could adjust it. He might even ask for a glass of water or something else that would require the person to leave the room so he could do it.

If that was impossible because there were several people in the room, he made a feature of adjusting the picture. He would pretend to admire it, leaning his head to one side like a bird and squinting at it in an appreciative manner, and then, as part of this process, as a *natural* part of this process he hoped, he would openly reach out and make the adjustment, as though he couldn't care less who saw him.

This sometimes difficult and on one occasion had catastrophic consequences. The offending picture was a photograph, in the home of his then boss, of an obese middle-aged woman. This was when William was still married to his wife, Lola, before his compulsive behaviour had driven her mad and away, and indeed this incident was the last straw that broke the back of her tolerance and led to her leaving.

His boss had invited William and Lola round for dinner. There were two other couples present as well. They were all sitting around having a cocktail before it was time to eat. William spotted the photo only when he sat down on a couch and looked up to see it on the wall above the mantelpiece. It was a regular-size photo, one of three, but its frame was at least a couple of centimetres off true. He couldn't believe his hosts hadn't noticed it. And, assuming they had, how could they live with a thing like that! It made you wonder what sort of people you were getting in with, coming round here for dinner and all.

'*William!*' he heard Lola say and felt the sharp pain of her elbow in his ribs. He came out of his contemplation of the picture and realized he'd been hogging the salted peanuts in the silver dish on the coffee table in front of him. Everyone was staring at him, he'd been eating them so frantically. He'd been working out a strategy, trying to think of an excuse to duck back in here alone when they all went through to the dining room for dinner and put the thing right. He couldn't stand the idea that coffee might be served in here after the meal and he'd have to sit trying not to look at the thing for another hour.

In the end, he could bear it no longer. He got up and asked for the bathroom. Inside it he ran the cold tap and splashed water over his face. He was hot and sweaty from the stress of the situation. He resolved to act rather than endure an evening of misery. Even the meal would be ruined for him, knowing he had to go back in there and look at *that*.

He strode purposefully out of the bathroom and into the room where everyone else was sitting, except for his host's wife who was occupied in the kitchen for the moment. Instead of returning to his seat, William sauntered over to the fireplace and stood in front of the picture. He did the usual peering at it this way and that.

'That's interesting . . .' William began, and then paused. He couldn't think of an appropriate comment because this was not a beautiful oil painting or a delicate watercolour but a photograph of an extremely fat woman. Morbidly obese. Bigger even than Sandy Beach's mother. A real whale. He was suddenly aware of someone standing at his shoulder and half turned his head to find his hostess there. Immediately he recognized her resemblance to the woman in the photograph. She too was plump, although not morbidly obese, not yet, anyway, but you could see she was going to get there. William guessed that the woman's mother was the subject of the photograph, and look at her!

'What's so interesting about it?' his boss's wife asked.

William stared at the photograph searching desperately for any-thing worthy of comment. The picture frame was nondescript; there was no help there. The photograph had been cropped right in on the fat woman, indeed she was so gross there was no space for any background around her, no scenery could have been squeezed in that might have enabled him to say, for example, 'Why, that looks like Lake Tahoe, we spent our honeymoon there!'

'It's my mother, you know,' said his boss's wife.

'Yes,' William agreed. Right away he realized it was the wrong thing to say.

'So, what's so interesting about her? What do *you* find so inter-esting about her?' William remembered that this woman was also a lawyer and was said to be the most brilliant in her whole firm at cross-exam.

'Well . . .' William stared at the photo. Its subject was wearing a lurid pink pant suit that made her look like a barrage balloon with legs or maybe a house-size inflatable rubber pig. He could think of nothing to say.

'I'll tell you,' snapped the woman at his elbow. 'You find it interesting that my mom is fat, don't you? And why it's interesting is because you think I'm fat too? Is that or is that not the case?'

'Well, no, not exactly . . .' In truth William had nothing against fat people. He felt sorry for them if their size made them unhappy and that it was their business if it did not.

'Well, what *is* interesting about this picture then? Come on, answer.'

Her voice was growing ever more strident. It had the ring of a prosecutor going for the death penalty. The hum of conversation in the room died; people picked up their glasses carefully so as to avoid making the slightest sound.

'Answer me!' screamed the woman.

William appealed to the room. He tried to produce a smile. 'Hey,' he said, with what was meant to be a nonchalant shrug, 'can I take the fifth on that?'

He expected another onslaught but it didn't come. The woman seemed to crumple as if her shoulders had just become too heavy for her. She burst into tears. 'My poor mom!' she wailed. 'My poor mom who had a glandular problem and who never did anyone any harm in her whole life!'

The other women in the room – including, he noticed, Lola – were out of their seats and had their arms about her like a shot. Everyone huddled round her trying to comfort her. William was appalled at what he had done, but not so appalled that he couldn't think clearly. While they were all distracted, he reached out and adjusted the picture.

The hysterical woman went on sobbing for a good half hour. Everyone was so concerned for her they all forgot about the dinner which was burned and completely ruined. When the woman finally stopped crying about the photograph she found out about the dinner and started crying all over again about that. By the time she stopped crying once more, her distress had given her a terrible migraine. The party broke up in disarray. As William and Lola left, his boss said meaningfully, 'I'll see you at the office.'

Outside the other two couples bade them a frosty goodnight and made off in a cab together. They were obviously going to a restaurant to eat but they didn't invite William and Lola. In their own cab home William and Lola stared straight ahead to avoid eye contact. All William could think was, if I'd known the party was going to finish so early, I wouldn't have been so bothered about the damn photograph.

William's rituals cost him dear, they cost him Lola for one thing, but he couldn't stop them. They were his security against his fears. Death was still the big one and William saw the abyss opening up at his feet at any one of a number of triggers: a clear night in the countryside when the canopy of stars reminded him of the vastness of space, the infinite number of its worlds and thus his own insignificance; a funeral cortège passing him in the street; the mention of the date of some future event — for example the submerging of various Pacific islands beneath the ocean as a result of global warming caused by Americans using their cars too much — that he would no longer be around to witness.

But death was joined now by another terror. Interestingly, it too concerned the annihilation of his individual personality. William didn't regard his fear of death as illogical. After all, he *was* going to die some day, so it wasn't unreasonable to be afraid of it. What was illogical was allowing the fear to so dominate his life that he could take no pleasure in it and at times might as well be dead anyway. If he wasn't enjoying life, what was so bad about being dead?

This new fear had a less logical basis because it wasn't inevitable. William agonized that one day he might have Alzheimer's disease, which neatly encompassed his principal fear too, since Alzheimer's was always fatal. The reason he was so afraid of it was that his father had died of it and this increased his own chance of contracting it. The statistics weren't as bad as death, where the odds were 100 per cent that it was likely to happen, but William had seen enough of the illness first-hand to know that, whatever the odds, this wasn't the way he wanted to go. About the only thing to be said in its favour was that you lost so much of your mind that you probably stopped worrying about death a long time before it happened.

William knew that although Alzheimer's was considered a disease of the elderly, it was possible for young people to suffer from it too. You could have it in your thirties, and, at thirty-one, he found himself already in the danger zone.

He began daily to check himself for early symptoms. His father had started with aphasia, the inability to remember certain words, especially nouns.

William's father, Joe, was, as we know, a lawyer too, specializing in civil rights cases. Many of his clients were black people who were being discriminated against at work. It didn't worry him that he didn't make a great deal of money, certainly not for a lawyer. He said that law had no business being about making money and he encouraged William to see it as a caring profession, like medicine or social work.

Joe Hardt had an office in his home and when he was there on vacation from law school it was William's habit to wander in while his old man was working (he wasn't that old, only mid-fifties), pull a law tome from a shelf and settle himself in what his dad called the customer's chair to go through a few cases.

William never spoke first. He knew not to disturb his father when he was working. But sometimes his father would speak right away and they'd discuss the case he was on at the moment or whatever it was William had been looking up in the book.

Other times, when his father was busy he would just keep on writing. He'd continue for however long the work took and after maybe an hour, William would quietly slip the book back in its slot on the shelf and retreat from the room.

Then there were occasions on which the old man would finish at last, put down his pen, look up with a warm smile and say, 'Now, how are things with you, my boy?'

Or he might carry on working but speak to William anyhow. He might ask him something. 'Just pass me *Billings Contract Law* would you?' Or, 'Please could you fetch me a cup of tea?' and William would be only too happy to oblige. He knew what his father was doing was important. He was helping other people and it was good that William was able to help him do that, even in such minor ways.

One day his father looked up and said, 'William, would you please bring me a – a—' and then stopped.

'Yes?' said William, thinking his father had been momentarily distracted by another thought about the case he was engaged on.

'A – a – a, you know, a thing of tea?'

'Cup?' said William. 'A cup of tea?'

'No,' said his father, 'not a cup. A – a – you know the thing you put it into the cup from?'

'A pot of tea,' said William getting up and making for the door.

'That's it.' His father was shaking his head. 'Darndest thing, couldn't think of the damned word. Guess I'm either getting old or working too hard.'

In the early stages this was the accepted explanation. And the aphasia wasn't too much of a problem. You could usually work out what William's dad was talking about. He could point at the object or refer to its use – 'the things I put on my hands to keep them warm', 'the stuff I wash my hair with'.

The problem came when the condition moved on and there was more than one unknown in a sentence. 'Where's the darned thing I need to remove the other thing with?' or 'Did I leave that thing on the thing in the thing?' Often nobody had a clue what he was talking about.

It could no longer be denied that there was something seriously wrong and a diagnosis swiftly followed. Once the thing that was happening to him had a name, once it was called Alzheimer's, it was able to get on with its progress much better. Now his father forgot not only the names of things, but the names of people too. And then, not only their names, but who they were. At first he couldn't recall William's name, but he knew he was his . . . his . . . his . . . thing. Then he forgot everything about him. He simply didn't recognize him any more.

Paranoia followed fast. Because he didn't recognize you he assumed the stranger you'd become meant to do him harm. In the street he would pull away from you and scream to passers-by, 'Help! Get the police! I'm being kidnapped!'

There was a stage at which he was ill enough to believe this but not so obviously ill that he couldn't convince strangers – *real* strangers – that it was true. A trip to the park could often involve several incidents in which lengthy dialogues were needed to prove that you weren't abducting him.

When things got so bad nobody could manage him any more, Joe went into a nursing home. The cost ate heavily into William's parents' small savings, but neither Ruth nor he could help out much; she had a young family and he was earning next to nothing as a rookie lawyer helping injured workers get their rightful compensation for industrial accidents.

One day William got a call from his mother, who was laid up with influenza. 'The home just telephoned. You need to get there right away. Your dad's been asking for you.'

It was only with difficulty that William persuaded his mother to stay in bed. The news was so exciting. Joe hadn't recognized anybody for months. William could hardly remember the last time his father had called him by name.

He rushed to the nursing home and was met by an enthusiastic nurse. 'Don't get too excited, you know it won't last, but it will give you a chance to say goodbye to him,' she said. 'It doesn't happen often that they recover any lucidity, not even temporarily. Make the most of it.'

In his father's room the old man was propped up on his pillows. William was appalled at how much weight he'd lost in the week since he'd last seen him. His head seemed to have shrunk. The flesh looked dead. You could almost smell it putrefying. Only the eyes showed any sign of life, glimmering with mad intent. They fixed on William with a desperate intensity.

'Will! Will!' the old man croaked.

'You see, he knows you,' said the nurse. 'It's a small miracle.'

'No, it's not,' said William, biting his tongue so he didn't snap at the woman. 'It's not me he's talking about. He's never in his life called me anything but William.'

'But surely—'

William went and stood by the bed and the nurse took up her position on the other side of it. The old man's frightened eyes flickered from one to the other. 'Will,' he muttered. 'Will.' His tone didn't alter whether he said it to his son or the nurse. It was obvious he wasn't talking to William. His father suddenly started trying to lever himself up, and William bent and lifted him. He weighed less than a ten-year-old child and it took no effort to get him sitting up against the pillows. He seemed to be struggling with something, making a supreme effort. He grasped William's wrist with a skinny claw and pulled him closer. 'I'll cut them all off without a penny!' he whispered hoarsely.

He sank back onto the pillow exhausted, still muttering, 'Will, will,' and William withdrew his hand. The nurse shot him a questioning look.

'My guess would be he's talking about his last will and testament,' he told her. 'He wanted to make some changes to it, but I suppose he'll get over that.'

The nurse nodded. Neither of them stated the obvious. That Joe Hardt would never again be involved with a legal document, least of all his own last will and testament. There was no way this featherweight of a man was of sound mind.

Two days later Ruth called William and told him their father was dead. He'd gone peacefully in his sleep. She was at their mother's comforting her. They had just gotten back from seeing the body at the nursing home. The undertakers weren't coming until the afternoon, so there was time for William to stop off at the home on his way to his mother's if he wanted to say goodbye to his dad.

On the freeway, William debated with himself what to do. He had never seen a dead human being. He didn't know if he could carry the image of a dead person, especially the one he had loved most in all his life, around in his head for the rest of it. On the other hand he couldn't bear never to see his father again, to miss this opportunity to tell him how he had loved him and about the size of the hole his gradual disappearance had left in his own existence.

But then again, there was the idea of a corpse and he didn't think he could take that. He was almost past the exit for the nursing home on the freeway when on an impulse he swung the wheel right and made the last-minute turn.

He told the receptionist he wanted to see his father. She was flustered for a moment and he realized she thought he didn't know his father was dead and didn't want to be the one to tell him. He felt sorry to have upset her. She was only a young girl. 'I mean his – his body,' he stammered. It was the first time that his father was not him any more but a body.

Following a nurse down the corridor, where the only sound was the squeak of her rubber-soled shoes on the shiny floor, William comforted himself with the thought that at least his father had died peacefully in his sleep. Maybe it would help him overcome his fear, a visual image of death as something peaceful, a release from pain and confusion, some kind of blessing. The nurse stopped at the door of his father's room and opened it for him. 'Just take the sheet off and stay as long as you like. Put the sheet back when you leave, would you?' She spoke softly, her face full of sympathy. William stepped inside and heard the door click shut behind him.

The room had been emptied of anything pertaining to his father. Ruth and his mother must have taken away his father's things. How could they have been so practical? He realized he was trying not to look at the bed. The sheet might have concealed anything. A sleeping person, a sack of potatoes, a couple of pillows like in those old stories where a child puts them there so he can fool his parents that he's still fast asleep in bed while he goes off on an adventure. Halfway down something was poking up, just on the right-hand side and William couldn't imagine what it could be. At the top the single thin sheet clung to his father's head.

He pulled up a chair and sat down. He wasn't sure he would be able to lift the sheet. He felt a moment's bitterness that he was even expected to. It should surely not have been his responsibility.

The shape on the bed was now unmistakably a corpse. William

had a sudden horror that he would remove the covering and find his father alive. It was hard to believe he wouldn't. He stood up and took hold of the top of the sheet and peeled it slightly back. He saw the dried-out remnants of his father's hair, there was no mistaking it. He began to cry. Until now, he realized, he had never quite believed in death, his own or that of those who belonged to him. He had never expected it to have a reality, like this, to be here on a particular day, in a particular room. He couldn't bear the tension. With one hand across his eyes, shielding them, he unfurled the sheet in a single quick movement, like a magician revealing a bunch of flowers or a rabbit, and then he peered through the latticework of his fingers like a child cheating at hide and seek and looked at the body.

His father's eyes were three-quarters open, that was the first shock, staring up at something at the foot of the bed. His mouth was open, too, the lips peeled back over the skeletal teeth, as though in a scream. William's eyes skimmed his father's naked, emaciated form, the wizened shrimp of his cock in its nest of grizzled hair. He saw what the strange point beneath the sheet had been, his father's right arm was raised up, fingers pointing, stiff now from rigor mortis.

His father's face, his whole countenance, was one of terror at something, somebody real or imagined, that had come for him in the early hours. Whatever else it had been, this had not been a peaceful death. William stretched out a tentative finger and brushed his father's cheek. Ice-cold. He stroked his hair. The forehead was clammy. Why had he never done this when his father was alive? He sat down, suddenly exhausted, and stared at the thing before him. Undoubtedly his father's body, but empty now, the soul, whatever that was, clearly fled. Leaving behind this shell, frozen for all eternity in the last moment of terror. The skin pale and shiny as fine china. He thought of his father's tanned flesh, all those summers at the beach house, and for no accountable reason he thought of the first weekend Sandy Beach had come, and how his kindly father couldn't stand the boy but had tolerated him in the mistaken belief he was doing something for his own child. It all seemed so long ago.

He must have been there an hour when there was a knock at the door. William rose from his chair and pulled up the sheet, pausing for one last look before he let it fall on his father's face. It was not an image he would ever be able to cover in his imagination. It would be there the rest of his days.

THIRTEEN

'Miss Lucy, you is think pink or purple is look better for me?' asked Tigua.

They were having a girls' night in – that's what Miss Lucy called it – in Miss Lucy's house, a few hundred yards along the shore from the village in the opposite direction from the Captain Cook. They were busy pampering themselves with different beauty treatments and trying out new clothes and looks. In addition to Miss Lucy and Tigua there were the latter's two she-boy pals, Sussua and Lintoa, although Lintoa had protested that he didn't want to come. What Lintoa would have liked was to spend the evening in the *kassa* house, although, as Tigua had pointed out, and not for the first time, it was, as the big she-boy well knew, impossible. Girls weren't allowed in. Besides, even if you didn't like make-up and experimenting with hairdos, Miss Lucy's wasn't a bad substitute. She would give you a can from the crate of beer the plane always brought her.

Lucy studied Tigua's outstretched right hand. The index finger-nail was painted with pink nail varnish; the nail of the middle finger, purple. 'Hmm, it's a difficult one to call. I wouldn't like to choose. Why not have both?'

'Both?' said Tigua. 'How is be possible?'

'Why not do them alternately pink and purple? You know like these two, purple for the thumb, pink for the ring finger and then purple for the, well, purple for the pinkie.'

Tigua was delighted. 'Is be good idea. I is like. But I is must start again. *Pinkie* is must be pink.' He reached for the bottle of polish remover, tipped some onto a cotton pad and began scrubbing the painted nails.

'What you is think, Lintoa, you is go have you nails like this?'

Lintoa grunted. 'Nails different colour is just look one big damn mess.' He shifted his huge bulk, stretching one of his great paws behind him and fiddling with the upper part of his dress.

'Huh, you is just be grouch like you is always be when you is drink beer,' said Tigua, who had picked up a lot of vocabulary from Miss Lucy. 'Beer is never make you is feel good, just grouch.'

'You is be grouch too if you bra strap is dig in you shoulder like mine.'

You couldn't argue with that. Bras *were* getting to be a problem. All four people in the room were wearing the same size of bra which was ridiculous when you compared the slim form of Miss Lucy to the burgeoning bulk of Lintoa. The reason they all had the same size was that all the bras were Miss Lucy's. She'd given Tigua, Sussua and Lintoa her old ones. The difficulty was that while all four of them had the same size breasts – the A cups being filled respectively with Miss Lucy's own small pert breasts and in the case of the other three with old rags she'd given them – their backs were of dramatically different dimensions. Even Sussua, who was lightly built for a sixteen-year-old boy, had had to stitch a piece of liana between the strap ends because they wouldn't meet in the middle any more.

'I is tell you, pretty damn soon I is go take this damn bra off and is walk around bare chest,' said Lintoa. 'I is just not care no more.'

Lucy patted his hand. Poor Lintoa had grown up and most of him didn't want to be a girl any more. Not for the first time, she told herself that she hadn't helped matters. It had seemed such a kind thing to do at the time, giving them all bras. But you had to be so careful, in her line of work, where even a badly phrased question could destroy for ever the very thing you were asking about, let alone introducing an alien concept like the bra. She just hadn't thought it through. The same with the dresses. Tigua had been fascinated by Lucy's clothes and by the fashion pictures he'd come across in Lucy's magazines. So Lucy had given them some dresses. The three boys were always complaining that growing their hair long like women's, wearing grass skirts instead of pubic leaves and putting on make-up was all very well, but how could they really look like girls when their bare breasts confirmed them as flat-chested boys? So she'd given them the bras.

Not that Lucy herself was much less boyishly chested than they were. You could tell the kind of person Lucy was from her breasts. They were, as we already know, small and pert; challenging little tits, pointy and fierce, as were her nose and chin, although the latter were not so much so as to render her unattractive. All these things, breasts, nose, chin, combined with something sharp about her blue eyes to speak of determination and independence. Here was a woman, they said, who did not give her love easily. Her breasts were the sort to make a man long to reach out and grab them and at the same time cause him to be afraid and want to run away and hide. They were enough to scare the hell out of a man like William Hardt.

Lucy regretted the Western clothes, and would not have done it again, but she excused herself on the grounds that any damage was temporary and would be corrected in a couple of years when the she-boys became boys, and also because it had given so much pleasure to them. Although maybe not to Lintoa.

'I is have good mind for throw away this dress and this damn pinchy bra,' repeated Lintoa.

'You is can burn you bra,' said Tigua, who'd learned about the phenomenon from Miss Lucy ('What waste!' he'd said. 'All they bras!'), 'but they is still not let you in *kassa* house. You is born be girl and is much better you is just get on with be one.'

'Just because I is be born girl, I is not must stay this way. I is have choice,' growled Lintoa.

'That's true,' said Miss Lucy, stroking his arm. 'You can be whatever you want to be.'

'You is can be pig if you is like,' said Tigua. 'You is be one damn sow already.'

By 'sow' Tigua meant the same as 'bitch', a word that had no meaning on the island as there weren't any dogs. Fortunately, at least from a linguistic point of view, the female black bantam pigs had a reputation for viciousness and backbiting that more than matched up to their canine counterparts, so 'sow' meant more or less the same thing.

'Well, soon as is be my time for choose,' muttered Lintoa, 'I is go be boy. I is go hunt pigs, I is go *kassa* house and make *fug-a-fug* with girls.'

'Well I is stay girl, so mebbe you is make *fug-a-fug* with me,' said Tigua. He wore his usual big smile as he said it, but no-one laughed. It was no secret that Tigua worshipped Lintoa. It was why he needled him, like a toddler seeking his mother's attention.

'You is make bloody damn joke,' said Lintoa. 'As if I is make *fug-a-fug* with sow like you.'

Tigua ignored the jibe. It was too easy for him to score points off Lintoa. He didn't need it all the time. If he pushed things too far, he'd turn the big boy off him. It was the last thing he wanted to do. He turned to Sussua, who was the quiet one of the three. 'How 'bout you, Sussua? What you is choose when is come you time?'

Sussua paused in painting his toenails. 'I is not be sure. I is really like for be boy. Do all things Lintoa is say. Is like for be *papu*, for have children. But . . .' He paused to push a pebble between two toes to keep them apart while he painted the nails in different colours.

'But?' said Tigua. 'What is mean that but?'

'But there is be so many pretty dress in Miss Lucy catalogue. Is seem shame for give all they up.'

There was silence, the kind of quiet where everyone is thinking his or her own thoughts and all of them melancholy. Lucy rose from the floor and walked over to the ancient mahogany side-board. She cranked up the gramophone and put a record on it. Caruso's voice soared through the crackle and hiss of the old shellac. 'Celeste Aida'. Lucy was aware of the measure of selfishness in her friendship for the she-boys that had led her to compromise the purity of her involvement. She had courted their friendship and moulded them into ersatz girlfriends because, well, because sometimes it got so damn lonely being the only Westerner on the island. A tear forced its way from her right eye and slid down her cheek. She wiped it off quickly with the back of her hand and looked at the three boys to see if any of them had noticed. They were all studying their nails so assiduously she knew that they had.

She cleared her throat. 'Tell me about the white man?' she said. 'What's he like?'

'He is be *gwanga*,' said Lintoa, studying a bottle of black nail polish. The other two giggled. 'He is have hair colour of sun, same as you hair is be, and he is wear eye glasses like Managua.'

'He is have one heavy bag,' said Tigua. 'I is nearly break back when I is carry damn thing. Is be mostly full of books.'

'How you is know that?' said Lintoa, who never missed a chance to challenge Tigua. 'You is see inside bag?'

'No, but I is see he is take out books. Also what else is weigh so heavy? Clothes?'

'Mebbe,' said Lintoa. 'He is go need plenty clothes if he is go swim in they.'

'He went swimming in his clothes?' asked Lucy.

'No, Lintoa is just make mischief,' said Tigua. 'He is walk through water in suit. Is get pretty damn wet.'

'He is still drip when he is reach village,' said Lintoa. They all laughed again.

'Is he British?' asked Lucy.

'No, I is not think so,' said Tigua. 'He is not talk like you. And he is do funny thing with eyes.' He imitated William Hardt's alternate blinking. 'He is be American, I is think. I is be pretty damn sure that eye thing is be American.'

'If he is be American then most likely suitcase is be full of bombs,' said Lintoa. 'Bombs is be plenty heavy.'

'But what about him?' said Lucy. 'Wasn't there anything else you noticed about him?'

Sussua looked down at her lap, studying her nails which were alternately painted green and purple. 'He is be plenty damn pretty,' she said. 'He is be *gwanga* and he is do funny eye thing but he is be plenty damn pretty.'

FOURTEEN

'What for he is be allow in *kassa* hut when I is not?' William was surprised to see the sturdy young woman thrust her big mannish face into Managua's. She looked pretty threatening for a teenage girl, he couldn't help thinking. And there was something scary about the way her fingernails were painted, alternate red and black. She reminded him of the kind of people you worried might commit random acts of violence when you encountered them on the subway. 'He is be *gwanga*, he is not belong here. I is be islander. I is have more right.'

Managua's serene expression was fractured. He looked both angry and embarrassed, like a parent who has been shown up by a naughty child.

'You is be quiet!' he hissed. 'You is show respect for guest.'

The girl pushed her shoulder up against Managua's and for a moment it looked like she might hit the old man, but Tigua shoved her way between them. 'You is come away now Lintoa, you is not get panties in tangle.'

'Is be all right for you, stupid sow,' Lintoa replied as she allowed herself to be led away. 'You is be happy for be girl. Me, I is spend all life want for be boy.'

Managua and William watched them go, Tigua's mincing little steps contrasting with Lintoa's heavy, masculine flat-footed tread, which William somehow thought was due as much to personality as to the fact the former was wearing high-heel shoes and the latter was barefoot. Managua shrugged. 'I is be sorry. They is drink beer tonight. I is smell in Lintoa's mouth. Sometimes young people today is not know how for behave. Is be difficult age for girl.'

'Yes,' said William, thinking, especially for a girl like Lintoa.

It was twilight and the incident had made them late. Already men were dropping to the ground and slipping into the long bamboo entrance tunnel of the *kassa* house. This large hut dominated the centre of the village. It was the only round structure and curiously low, the walls a couple of feet shorter than those of the huts circling it.

'Come,' said Managua. He lowered himself carefully onto his good knee, stretching his artificial leg out behind him, and thence onto his belly. He ducked into the tunnel and William followed, dragging himself along by his elbows, the tunnel roof being too low to permit one to crawl properly.

It was pitch-dark and William experienced a frisson of fear, a sudden panic that he might be letting himself in for something terrible, a set-up the villagers were tricking him into, a snake pit, perhaps, full of green shoestrings. He became aware of someone behind him in the tunnel and a wave of claustrophobia washed over him. For a second he couldn't move. Then he felt the hands of the person behind touch his feet and heard a voice.

'If you is plan for make fart,' it said, 'I is advise you is not or I is punch you plenty damn good when we is get inside.'

William had no idea who was speaking or why the man should suspect him of wanting to fart at him but having to deal with this immediate problem brought temporary respite from his fear. He worked his elbows furiously and scrabbled his way forward. There was no obstacle in front to prevent him. Managua was long gone.

In a few seconds he was through the tunnel. Shakily he stood up and was able to draw himself to his full height. At first he couldn't see a thing and thought he was in darkness but gradually his eyes grew accustomed to the situation and he saw a fire in the centre of the room that gave a soft red glow to everything.

Shadowy figures were moving about, finding places to sit against the walls, making a large circle around the fire.

'You is take time for get here, *gwanga*.' It was Managua. The older man's hand gripped him around the upper arm and steered him towards the wall where there was a small gap between two of the men sitting there. They shuffled either way and Managua eased himself down between them, indicating that William should do the same.

The circle around the wall of the hut was now complete. Only a couple of men remained standing, dim figures in the firelight. William saw that one was the sour-faced man, Purnu. He and his companion were struggling to roll a large round boulder across the entrance to the tunnel, sealing it off. Again William experienced a moment of panic. He wasn't sure he could stay in here. As if sensing this, Managua leaned over and whispered, 'You is not worry, is be for stop spirits escape.'

William didn't find this particularly reassuring.

Purnu and the other man went to the centre of the room and began tipping something from a big wicker basket into a large iron cauldron which sat on the fire. William guessed it must be the *kassa* seeds Managua had told him about. When the basket was empty, Purnu took a piece of wood approximately the size and shape of a baseball bat and began stirring the pot. The hut was filled with an expectant buzz of whispered conversation. It made William think of the moments before a symphony concert when the orchestra is tuning up while the audience chatters in excited anticipation.

After about ten minutes Purnu produced a ladle and began to dredge solid matter from the pot, turning the contents of the ladle into a large wooden bowl. Meanwhile the other man took the wooden club and, using it like a pestle, started grinding away at the stuff as it was added to the bowl. Eventually Purnu seemed satisfied he'd got all the *kassa* mash. He picked up an earthenware pot and emptied a thick liquid from it into the wooden bowl and the other man used his club to stir it in.

'Honey,' whispered Managua. 'If you is not add honey, *kassa* is taste like shit.' William noticed the old man was licking his lips in anticipation, a child watching his ice cream being anointed with chocolate sauce.

Purnu put the little pot down, took a wooden spoon, dipped it in the mix and tasted it. He paused a moment or two. Everyone stopped talking. He nodded and smiled and a cheer went round the room. It was as if someone had just bagged his first deer of the season.

The two men carried the large bowl to the edge of the room and held it before one of the seated men. He took the spoon, dipped it into the bowl and then put it into his mouth. When he was done, the two bowl bearers moved clockwise around the room to the next guy. There was complete silence. William went to say something but before he could get a syllable out Managua put a finger on his lips. 'Ssh,' said the old man. William understood this was a rule. Talking was not allowed.

Eventually the bowl worked its way around to Managua who helped himself and then indicated that William was to follow suit. What William got on the end of the spoon was a small helping of thick red paste. He paused with it between pot and lips. What if this is all some elaborate trick? he asked himself. What if it's just a ruse to feed me some of those orange fungi they were talking about? But then, that was silly. Hadn't he just seen Managua take some? And wasn't Managua his friend?

The two men were jerking the bowl towards him, urging him to get on with it, so they could have the spoon back and move on to the next guy. Gingerly William raised the spoon to his lips, shut his eyes, stuck it into his mouth and sucked the bulbous gob of red stuff from the end. It tasted a bit like something from his childhood. The nutmeg his mother always used to grate into rice pudding, perhaps. But very sweet too, almost cloyingly so. The kind of sweet that makes your throat sore so you long for water.

He replaced the spoon in the bowl which continued its journey around the hut. All of a sudden William felt very tired. He experienced a dull, pleasurable ache that began at the tips of his toes and

gradually worked its way up his body. After a few minutes he
realized he could no longer feel his legs, but this was not a matter
of great concern to him. Rather, he found himself thinking it must
be wonderful for Managua not to be able to feel his legs, to be no
longer aware of the contrast in sensation from the leg he still had
and the artificial one that had replaced the one he didn't, to have
no more absence of feeling than anyone else in the room.

William's head sank back. His whole body was weighed down
by the tiredness now. He was exaggeratedly conscious of his
own breath, the rise and fall of his chest. The in-and-out bellows
of his lungs seemed immense, the noise like the waves crashing on
the beach a few hundred yards away. Apart from his lungs, and his
heart which seemed to have slowed and diminished to a distant
sporadic drumbeat, the only parts of him that still worked were his
eyes.

He became aware of a mist emanating from the fire, as when a
magician at a children's party throws some magic powder onto
naked flames. From the mist pale figures were emerging. They
grew from the flames right in front of his eyes and then stepped
out of the haze and went around the hut, calling out softly. 'Purnu,
Purnu, you is here?' 'Funtua, Funtua, where you is?' and other
names, all of them searching for someone. Soon the figures were
everywhere, a whole mêlée of them moving silently this way and
that, whispering in high, reedy voices. There were both men and
women, islanders dressed in their pubic leaves and grass skirts but
pale and insubstantial. And then, in the flames, another figure,
unlike all the others, arose. It was taller than its companions and
had the pale skin of a white man and it was fully clothed, in chinos
and a red plaid shirt. It came towards William.

'William? William is that you?' it said, bending over and peering
through the gloom, the mist and the smoke, at him.

'Dad? Dad?' William tried to scramble to his feet but found he
couldn't move any more than if he'd been tied down. He *was* tied
down. Or at least, there seemed to be a thick rope of something
wrapped around his ribcage, squeezing him, as though trying to

keep his heart battened down, as it threatened to leap, like a salmon, from his chest.

His dad didn't look as he had the last time William had seen him alive, and he certainly wasn't the nightmare figure who had haunted his dreams, the startled corpse, caught by surprise by death. He was the way William remembered him at the time he was at college, when the Alzheimer's was there, but hadn't yet kicked in enough to be diagnosed.

'Where are we?' his father said, looking around, his expression one of awe. 'It looks like some kind of a – a – damn, what is the word?'

'Hut?' offered William.

'Hut,' echoed the old man. 'It seems to be full of – of – of—'

'Natives.'

'Primitive people.'

Indeed it was. There must have been dozens of phantoms occupying the hut's meagre space now. But somehow it wasn't crowded. These were not solid people, William observed. His father was kind of transparent. You could see right through him, in his plaid shirt and chinos. It wasn't like an X-ray, you couldn't see his internal organs, there were no kidneys or lungs on display. But other people were visible through him and sometimes one would walk right through him and he didn't seem to notice it.

'Dad, I want to tell you something,' William began.

'I know, my boy, you want to tell me you love me. You always wanted to say it and you never could until it was too late and I was lying there with my hand up in the air and seemed to be no longer there to hear it.'

'You remember your hand up in the air, like you were pointing?'

'I remember a fine day on the beach when you were five years old and I turned to your mom and said, Can you get one of your prayers in quick – because you know, I never did go in for the religion thing – Can you get one of your prayers in real quick, I said to her, and ask Him to make time stop? Can you get Him to

just freeze it all here, with the children the age they are now and
no more growing up to be done? Can you do that? I said similar
things lots of times over the years that followed, every year at the
beach house when you and Ruthie were growing bigger and
bigger, and you know what?' He paused, as though struggling to
speak. 'You know what? She never could.'

'But the hand. You were pointing—'

'I know. I remember watching you pull back that sheet. I *hated*
you seeing me like that. How could they just leave you to draw
back the sheet and see what I'd left behind? It was monstrous.'

'But Dad, what were you pointing at?'

His father put his hand to his chin and stroked it thoughtfully.
His forehead furrowed as though he were confused. 'Pointing . . . ?
I don't . . . I don't rightly know. I don't remember the moment I
died. I only remember when you came afterwards. I remember you
bending over me and seeing your mouth against mine. I remember
how blue my lips looked. What a cold kiss that must have been!'

William could hardly see his father now. The mist in the hut
seemed to have grown much thicker. Then he felt moisture on his
upper cheek and realized it wasn't the mist at all, it was his own
eyes filling up with tears. He went to raise his hand to brush them
away, but it was heavy as a rock, it wouldn't move.

He hardly recognized his own voice when he finally got it out.
It was hoarse and full of pain, like an old man's. 'Wh—where are
you now, Dad?'

Again his father looked confused. 'Why, I'm right here, in this –
this – this—'

'Hut,' said William, in spite of himself.

'Hut,' repeated his father, looking around him. A couple of
phantoms passed through him and he watched them go, curiously
unalarmed. 'I'm right here in this hut, with you, my boy.'

'Yes, I know, but when you aren't here . . . ?'

'Well, I guess, I guess . . .' His voice faded, the way it often used
to as his illness progressed, as if he'd just run out of words.

'Try Dad, try to remember.'

Joe Hardt screwed up his face, working on the puzzle, concentrating hard. 'I remember . . . I remember . . .'

'Yes? Go on, Dad, try!'

'I remember that little bastard Sandy Beach!' It was the first time William could recall hearing his father use strong language. 'I remember him coming to stay with us at the shore.' He shook his head, smiling to himself, seeing it all before him. 'What you were doing with that little prick for a friend—'

'He wasn't my friend. Mom said I *had* to invite *someone*.'

'I remember it perfectly. Some things I don't recall too well. I remember how that kid locked himself in the bathroom and wouldn't come out. Do you remember that?'

William wanted to say how it wasn't like that, how it was he who had been locked in the bathroom and that Sandy Beach was the one outside banging on the door, but he couldn't bring himself to do it. There was no point, it would only be to set the record straight, and his old man . . . his old man seemed so pleased to have recalled this incident, so reassured to have it as a sign that his memory was still working all right. William closed his eyes to try to think. It didn't seem right that you could suffer from a degenerative illness in the afterlife. It didn't *fit* that someone who had passed on to a higher plane had an imperfect memory. William decided he would change the subject. He would try to get his dad focused on the here and now. He opened his eyes and was about to speak but the space before him was empty, his dad was gone.

FIFTEEN

From 'The Other Side of Paradise: the sexual life
and customs of an unspoiled people' by L. Tibbut
(unpublished manuscript)

We have already seen how the natives believe the eyes are
the instruments of erotic arousal. It follows that physical
attractiveness occupies a place of great importance in their
erotic relationships. They have, as is only to be expected,
their own concept of beauty, especially in women; size and
strength matter more in a man, where a face that radiates
powerfulness and character is considered more attractive
than one that is merely handsome. In passing it is worth
noting that great stress is placed upon the importance of a
large penis or *pwili* (although of course a woman would be
unlikely to discover this until already committed to a sexual
liaison, there being a strong taboo against public display of
the penis). The fact that size does matter is demonstrated
by one of the women's working songs that goes

> *Wokanika rao au nisapuni naydowala*
> *Naydowuri, wuri*
> *Palapa pasaluya rururi*

which roughly translates as 'Men, your pubic leaf strings
are too short. Strings so short will not persuade us to lie
down with you.' Since the pubic string connects the bottom

tip of the pubic leaf to the back of the waistbelt, a short
string would imply there wasn't much filling the leaf at the
front. The singers are saying they won't make love with
men with small penises.

A woman whose skin is very dark is not considered good-
looking and light skin is always to be preferred. She should
be tall and slim, although the latter factor is almost *hors de
combat* since virtually none of the islanders is at all overweight and obesity is almost unknown and when it does
occur is only because of some rare medical condition. Her
forehead should not be low or projecting over the eyes. They
consider such a forehead to express a lack of intelligence,
as perhaps we Westerners would too. The lips should be full,
rather than thin, but not overmuch so.

Breasts, which, of course, are on display, should not be
small, but neither should they be too large as this tends to
droopiness. What the men prefer is women to have *granoa
tubu*, 'a good handful', and for the breasts to be firm and
pert.

The nose must on no account be aquiline but neither
should it be flattened against the face, rather it should have a
wide but raised bridge. Nose pegs, which used to be considered
an essential for attractiveness, are now going out of fashion
with both sexes, possibly as the result of the influence of
missionaries from Britain during the years of its interest in
the island. (Thankfully this is about the only lasting effect of
the missionaries, that and the use of English as a more
flexible and practical language. Christianity appears to have
altered social and sexual practices not a jot, nor native
mythology and religious belief.)

A woman's hair should be thick and is always worn long.
Hair that curls, rather than waves, is considered ugly. Eyes
should be large and rounded. The islanders have a horror
of oriental eyes which may be due to a visit from the
Japanese during World War II as this extreme reaction

resides largely in the older members of the population. The young seem to find slitted eyes merely unattractive per se.

Having listed all these preferences, the result of many hours of interviews especially with the young men and women of the main village, it has to be said that despite the enormous cultural differences between the natives and ourselves, their tastes and ours are actually not dissimilar. It is as if human beings have an innate feel for what is and is not attractive, no matter where on this globe they live or from what culture they originate.

Invariably when I asked the young men what they thought about a girl I privately considered unattractive or positively ugly they proved to be of the same opinion. When I asked them whom they thought pretty, or whom they fancied, they all – even though interviewed separately to prevent collusion – chose the girls I myself thought attractive and would have expected Western men to pick.

There was complete agreement as to the most attractive female on the island, and it is an opinion I wholeheartedly endorse. This is a girl named Kiroa, who has features that I am sure any Westerner would describe as stunning. She is tall, exceptionally so among the women of her tribe, and slim, and her walk has a most marvellous grace so that to see her progress through the tall grass is to watch the wind pass through it; it seems to give way before her as if it too wishes to acknowledge her beauty. Her features are perfectly symmetrical, and her eyes and mouth both large. She has a winning smile and a flirtatious, but not vulgar, expression in her eyes. Anywhere, any place on Earth, she would be considered what she is, a great beauty, a wonderfully sexy girl.

The irony is that her father is the man Purnu, an ugly brute if ever I saw one. In fact, so incredible did it strike me that this radiant beauty could spring from such a father that I remarked to her, in front of him, that 'you obviously get your looks from your mother'.

At this the poor girl looked as stricken as if I had slapped her, burst into tears (which has the same significance among them as it does with us), covered her face with her hands and rushed away. Purnu looked at me with a face black as thunder.

I was somewhat alarmed about this as he has a reputation as one of the island's most powerful sorcerers and it is said that at least two men who crossed him suffered fatal accidents soon afterwards. So I was at pains to apologize for upsetting his daughter. It was no use. He stomped off. The other men present sat shaking their heads and looking at me as though I had committed a great crime. I held out my hands in a gesture of innocence. 'What?' I said. 'What did I do wrong?'

Managua then explained to me that it is considered a great insult to tell someone that they resemble their mother or any of their mother's relatives. That would have been bad enough but I had so phrased my observation as to commit another, even bigger, insult, namely to imply that Kiroa did not look like her father. It transpires that it is thought a great compliment to say someone resembles his or her father and is something in which the father takes enormous pride.

'But how can that be?' I demanded. 'How can anyone resemble their father if, as you say, the mother gives birth without any physical contribution from him?'

At this everyone pitched in as though I had just evinced the greatest stupidity imaginable. A child grows to look like its father when he is caring for it as a baby, they insisted. When he handles it all the time, he moulds it. Over and over again they used the word 'mould' and I found this an interesting example of how deeply they are convinced of the absence of physiological paternity, that they prefer this roundabout explanation to the more obvious one, i.e. that it is sperm that makes babies.

The fallout from this incident was considerable. I was terrified of upsetting Purnu who certainly has it in his power to turn many of the natives against me which would greatly hinder, if not altogether prevent, my work. Many of them fear his ability in the dark arts. It is said that he dotes on his daughter and has given her the most powerful love potion ever devised – the natives believe that sexual liaisons are only ever accomplished with the aid of magic and always consult sorcerers or witches before attempting to embark on an affair – and that it is this that has bewitched all the local men. Myself, I think it may be more to do with her stature, that come hither look in her eyes, and the slight bounce of those pert breasts as she walks.

Certainly my one hope of reconciliation with Purnu was that he hungers for Western material objects in a way quite unusual here. After Managua had a talk with him on my behalf, I was able to appease him, at least so I think, by the gift of a pocket calculator. It is no great loss to me and he is earning many yams by renting it out to all the young men who spend hours playing with it.

We must now come to a consideration of erotic play among the natives. Since this is an intimate act, committed in privacy by two people, that he cannot witness, especially in a society which frowns upon public sexual display, it poses particular problems for the ethnographer who must rely on interviews alone rather than personal experience. It is worth noting, in passing, that the latter is not only un-ethical but impossible because there is a taboo against sexual intercourse with foreigners, one that is strictly observed. Fortunately there is no injunction against talking about sexual relations and both men and women spoke freely to me about their intimate practices, enabling me to arrive at what I think is a reasonably accurate picture of island love-play. Typically, when a boy and girl have reached an understanding, they will repair into the bush, or perhaps the *bukumatula* house, if it is daytime and the hut is unoccupied and privacy assured for this first erotic encounter. There, love-play commences with talking and the exchange of endearments.

Always the boy presents the girl with a gift. No girl will consider giving herself to a man unless she is given a reasonable present first. This may sound to Western ears like some primitive kind of prostitution, but it is rather the opposite. The girl is not actually interested in the present for itself, for its material value or usefulness. It is as a mark of respect and affection that she esteems it.

After the giving of the gift and a little chatting the couple will move on to inspecting one another's hair for lice. Any that are found are then eaten by the finder. When considered objectively, there is nothing disgusting about this. Anyone who has seen apes performing the same act will have noticed how gentle they are with one another. Here, it becomes an act of great tenderness and intimacy.

Next the couple will move to stroking and caressing one another and it's likely that at this time the grass skirt and pubic leaf will be removed. The couple will then admire one another's bodies, great store being set upon the visual role in arousal. Then they may rub noses gently. They kiss as we do, and as well one will sometimes take the other's lower lip in his or her mouth and suck on it and then bite it, nearly always drawing blood. Indeed a well-bloodied lip is seen as evidence of successful lovemaking. After this it is customary to move up the face and gently nibble the partner's eyelashes, a part of the body not considered attractive here, unlike among ourselves, where long eyelashes are thought desirable in both sexes. From there matters proceed much as in any other culture: next comes play with the nipples, caressing of the genitals and, finally, full intercourse.

SIXTEEN

'What is he interested in Pilua for? What is there to know about her that would be so bad if he found it out?'

It was very early the morning after the *kassa* house. Managua had stomped his way over to Miss Lucy's at first light, long before shitting time. She'd taken an age to open the door to his knock and was bleary-eyed when she did. She invited him in with a reluctance that was against all the laws of hospitality for which she normally exhibited the utmost respect. Looking around her hut, Managua could understand why. The place was one plenty big mess. Several empty beer cans were left to roll around on the floor, where they could easily cause an injury, should someone step on one, especially someone with an artificial leg. There were little coloured jars and plastic tubes all over the place, and bits of cloth stained with the stuff Western women wore on their faces. He guessed she'd had a party with the she-boys. He'd already suspected as much from Lintoa's breath last night; this was the only place on the island you could get beer, which Miss Lucy kept in a gas fridge, and he'd figured they'd been playing with make-up. He'd noticed last night the desecration done to Tigua's nails. Still this was not the time to think about all that. He turned his attention back to Miss Lucy's question and sighed.

'If he is find out 'bout Pilua then everything is be change. All we traditions, all we is believe, all way we is live. All is go. All is vanish like smoke in sky.' His eyes swept the disarray. 'But mebbe you is not think is matter.'

Lucy began scurrying round the room, picking up make-up debris. She dumped it into a plastic bin and drew her robe tight around her before facing him. 'I've told you before, I'm sorry about the dresses and the – the—'

'Chest straps.'

'Bras. It was a big mistake and I shouldn't have done it. I just wanted them to have fun. I wasn't thinking clearly. I meant to be kind.'

He held up his hand. 'Is be OK, they dress is not be big thing. Shoes is break in end and dress is wear out. Is be unfortunate but is not be end of world.' He limped away from her across the room. At the far wall he turned and there was the glint of moisture in his eyes. 'But this – this *gwanga*, this is be end of world. End of we world. All is be destroy. What is I must do?'

'I wish you'd tell me why the American finding Pilua would be such a disaster.' He shook his head. 'Well, in that case, does anyone else know she's still alive?'

He shook his head again. 'No, I is only tell you now because I is not know what for do. But people is always be suspicious 'bout way she is suppose for die. And now, *gwanga* is take me by surprise. I is think he is suspect something.'

'And is it possible for the American to find her without your help?'

'Sure is be possible. That fool Purnu is help he you is can be certain. He is want get plenty thing from America. He is be one greedy fool. But he is be one powerful sorcerer too.'

They sat in silence for a while.

'So what is I go do?' Managua said at last.

'Do you know how long the American intends to stay?'

'I is think only one moon, until plane is come again.'

Lucy was chewing her fingernail and Managua hoped this would help her think, because if it didn't it sure was one dirty habit. It was almost as bad as what he'd learned at the hospital on the big island, that white people wiped shit off their arses with their hands.

'You must stop showing him your opposition, pretend to help him, but you must make things very difficult for him, so he gets tired and becomes discouraged. He'll get fed up and stop trying, then he'll run out of time, the plane will come and he will go.'

Managua nodded slowly. 'Is not be bad plan, no is not be bad at all.'

'The she-boys will help you if I ask them to.'

'That is be good. I is need some help.' He paced around the room again, deep in thought, a painfully slow process on account of his artificial limb. After a few minutes he stopped. The frown he'd brought with him collapsed into a smile. 'Miss Lucy, you plan, I is already have idea . . .'

'An idea? What is it?'

The smile widened from ear to ear. 'Miss Lucy,' he said, 'is you ever read *The Tempest*?'

SEVENTEEN

All normal families are alike but every abnormal family is abnormal in its own way. Sandy Beach's family was overrun by stuff. And William's included a too-tidy mother, a sister who was terrified of spermatozoa and William himself, of course, who walked around in the shadow of death blinking alternately.

No-one should be surprised at Lucy's willingness to indulge in a little skulduggery with Managua, because at the age of eleven Lucy had murdered her mother.

It happened like this. The person who made Lucy's family abnormal was her mother. When William sought advice from a psychotherapist in a last-ditch attempt to save his doomed marriage to Lola, he was told that in selecting a partner we are often searching for what we feel to be the missing piece of ourselves. That might have been a load of hogwash, but if not, then it explains the seeming incompatibility of Lucy's parents.

Her father was relentlessly sociable. He struck up conversations with total strangers in the street; he knew everyone in the small fenland village where they lived; when Lucy went to the nearest town, Ely, with him, he seemed to be acquainted with everyone there too.

Her mother, on the other hand, was fearful not only of strangers but also of people she knew. Even her friends, if you can be said to have friends when you never let anyone inside your house. She exhibited some symptoms of agoraphobia, a condition that is often mistakenly described as a fear of wide-open spaces, an erroneous attribution of the classical root of the word to *ager*, the Latin for field, when actually it derives from the Greek *agora*, the market place, making agoraphobia a fear of crowds. In truth, Lucy never noticed her mother being too concerned about crowds or market places if there were bargains to be had. She never missed the Ely bus on Thursdays, enduring greetings from fellow passengers to elbow her way into the thick of the action with the rest of them, pushing and barging in the hunt for a snip.

No, Lucy's mother's particular fear wasn't of people per se, but of *people coming to the house*. She lived in terror of unexpected visitors, well, all visitors really. There were no expected ones because she never invited anybody round. Her reaction to them reminded Lucy of an old film she'd seen on TV, a Clark Gable war film set in a submarine entitled *Run Silent Run Deep*. When Lucy and her two older sisters heard the crunch of a footstep upon the gravel front path of their small council house, or were surprised by the sudden shock of a fist upon the front door, it was as though their mother had screamed, 'Dive! Dive! Dive!' Indeed Lucy, always the most audacious of the three, once uttered those very words only to earn from her mother a quicksilver slap on the cheek. Not for her levity, you understand, but purely because of the practical risk of her tipping off the caller that the family was in.

Lucy's mother never shouted 'Dive! Dive! Dive!' because she would never have shouted anything. What she did was hiss, *sotto voce*, 'Get down!' The effect was the same. As soon as she spoke, Lucy and her sisters hit the floor. Their mother was not long in following, pausing only to close the curtains, switch off the radio and kill any lights that were on. She lived in fear not only that the family might be heard, but that a person so intrusive as to go calling on people would have no compunction about trolling around outside the house, peering into the windows and listening for the radio, refusing to accept the family's apparent absence.

In some cases, Lucy's mother's fears were only too well realized.

This might occur when someone really did need to see her or her husband urgently.

Or it might be that someone felt annoyed by Lucy's mother's perceived rudeness (as opposed to psychological disorder) and was determined to catch her out. Or rather, in.

Take the Reverend Mr Diggle, the local minister, when he came collecting for various manifestations of the poor. You could always tell it was him. He was over six feet tall and his silhouette through the upper frosted-glass half of the front door was enough to block the light. The Reverend Mr Diggle had an uncompromising, Come out, come out, wherever you are! knock that made the door shake in its frame. This was the signal for Mum to order, 'Get down,' and they'd all hit the deck as though someone had hurled in a hand grenade.

If the TV was on, the person nearest was expected to crawl across the floor and turn the off switch. And then, as the set was visible to someone peering through the front window – but only someone over six feet and standing on tiptoe (as well as on the pansies in the flower-bed beneath the window) – the same person would have to roll three or four times across the floor to the sheltering safety of the settee, as though evading enemy gunfire.

That is the prelude to how Lucy came to kill her mother. The actual event took place one afternoon in Cambridge when the eleven-year-old Lucy was waiting for the bus home from the girls' high school. She was the only girl in the village who attended the high school because she was the only one to have passed the 11-plus. Everyone else, including her sisters, went to the comprehensive.

Lucy had only been at the school for a term, a short enough time for her to still feel awe and terror at the sight of a prefect. So when she saw Christine Bexley approaching her, she tried her best to make herself small in the hope that Bexley wouldn't see her. Bexley was the worst prefect in the school, bar none. If you caught her attention you were certain to get a punishment from her.

Lucy looked at her feet, knowing that, as with a dangerous dog, eye contact was the last thing you wanted. After a minute or so of staring down she raised her eyes and found Bexley standing over her.

'Put your beret on straight, you little tart,' snapped Bexley.

Lucy reached up and made the necessary adjustment. Bexley walked around her like a sergeant major inspecting a new recruit.

'Your blazer is undone, do it up.'

'I can't,' said Lucy miserably. 'The button came off.'

'Then you'd better get your mummy to sew it back on,' sneered Bexley. The way she said *mummy* made it an insult implying that Lucy was a little kid who would still call her mum that. The high school was posher than the comprehensive, but not so posh that the girls called their mothers mummy instead of mum.

This was what induced Lucy to matricide. Even as the words slipped from her mouth, she sensed that the ambiguity in them was not an accident. At some deep and mysterious level, she meant them to be misconstrued. 'I haven't got one,' she said in a tiny voice.

Bexley coloured. 'Oh, I'm . . . er, well, sorry. I um didn't know.'

'That's OK,' said Lucy magnanimously. She didn't feel dishonest, well, not totally. Technically, they could still be talking about the button, although it would probably be stretching it to suggest that Bexley would be so apologetic about a missing button.

'Well, just get one put back on by . . . uh . . . someone,' said Bexley. 'We don't want you catching cold now, do we?' This was followed by a smile. It was the first time in recorded history that Bexley had ever smiled. You could tell from the awkwardness of how the smile looked on her face, the way that it was conscious it didn't really belong there, that she wasn't used to doing it.

At that point Lucy's bus came. She boarded it grateful that its intervention had prevented any interrogation as to the circumstances of her mother's passing. She was also thankful that she had escaped punishment. But that night, lying in bed, she felt the guilt and fear of detection that all murderers, except for psychopaths, experience. From this time on, she began to dread a knock on the door almost as much as her mother ever did.

EIGHTEEN

The little girl's leg sparkled in the morning light. Quite a bit of the flesh-pink paint had got itself rubbed off and the bright sunshine picked out silver grazes. The kid couldn't have been more than five or six years old. She'd had the leg some time, William could see that by the way in which she walked on it. She was fast and competent, running into the clearing at the centre of the village which indicated she'd long become used to it, but for all its speed her gait showed a pronounced limp, meaning she'd already all but outgrown the prosthetic limb. It wasn't her big round eyes that brought the lump to William's face, as he watched her lower herself awkwardly to the ground, suddenly ungainly, the way a swan loses all its grace when it leaves the water and tries to get airborne. It was the big smile, her easy acceptance of the blow fate, or rather his murderous countrymen, had dealt her. You don't have to just take it, he said to her silently. We can do something about this.

William counted thirty-seven of them. They ranged from the small girl to an old man who looked all of eighty. What they had in common was that most of them had lost a limb, or part of a limb. The little girl was missing all of her right leg. It was understandable. The blast from a landmine would do more damage to a smaller person. A boy next to her, maybe seven years old, had lost his left arm from the elbow down. He didn't have an artificial limb. His arm just came to a stop in a neat round stump. The old man was missing his left leg below the knee. The stump of his thigh was encased in a white plastic sheath that slotted into his artificial knee, which comprised a small wheel connecting to the metal stick that made up his tibia which ended in a large black leather boot. A couple of other men had lost whole arms. One man appeared to be blinded. Only two people were uninjured: Purnu and another man, who were there because their wives had bled to death after being injured by mines. The most common injury as far as William could see, and it was exactly what he'd expected to encounter because he'd done his research on anti-personnel landmines, was a missing foot or foot and lower leg.

What made the whole thing so grotesque was the natives' lack of clothes, the men wearing only the pubic leaf and the women their short grass skirts. This exposed the plastic and metal prosthetic limbs they had been fitted with. Those with artificial limbs which had a close resemblance to human flesh looked odd because the fake skin of their prosthetics was either a pale pink, meant to ape a white person's, or deep black, probably designed for Afro-Americans in the US and just as incongruous as white next to the natives' honey-coloured skin.

The older prosthetics displayed chunks of shiny metal – hinge mechanisms to replace knees or elbows – that made the wearer look like some robot in a sci-fi movie whose plastic skin covering has been partially destroyed. Where only a foot had been lost the artificial one that replaced it took the form of a boot. This looked ludicrous at the end of a bare leg, reminding William of the clumpy shoes that terminated Mickey Mouse's stick-like legs, only here rendered even more incongruous by being partnered by a naked foot.

Everywhere the harnesses that attached the artificial limbs, which in a Westerner would have been hidden beneath clothes, were exposed. It somehow made the degradation of their condition that much worse, symbolizing as it did what had happened to them, the purity and innocence of their naked flesh perverted by technology.

There was a hum of excited chatter as William bent over his notebook, waiting for a couple of stragglers to limp over to the others and sit down.

When everyone was seated, Managua clapped his hands as a signal for silence. It was he who had called the people together at William's behest. When William had asked for his assistance, Managua had immediately bristled with suspicion, which, William decided, was a vital part of his make-up. But William had refused to be drawn by his questions. 'It's to help them,' was all he would say.

'Help?' said Managua. 'You is mean we is get better new legs and arms?'

'Well, among other things, yes.'

'What is be they other things?'

'Managua, I can't tell you just yet. Call the meeting, will you, and all will be revealed.'

Now William faced his audience with a certain amount of anxiety. It was not going to be easy, explaining an alien concept to an audience of savages. On the other hand, he was used to having to explain alien concepts of justice, fair play and responsibility to bunches of corporate lawyers. How much harder could this be?

He cleared his throat. 'Thank you for coming, everyone. My name is William Hardt. I am a lawyer from New York City, in America. I have come here to bring you justice, for the injuries you have suffered as a result of US military ordnance, a justice that will punish the people who did this to you and help you to make the best of your lives in spite of it. I have come to bring you compensation.'

There was an immediate renewal of conversation, everyone talking to his neighbour, all of them jabbering at once. Finally Managua held up his hand. A man in the front row, sporting one black boot, continued talking. 'Silence!' barked Managua.

The man recoiled as though struck by a blow, then recovered and stared defiantly at Managua. 'I is not understand,' he said. 'What is be this compensation. Is be thing we is eat?'

Managua stared back, a look you might imagine him giving to an insect crawling on a piece of dung. But even that didn't shut the man up. 'Well, you is know?'

Managua shook his head. 'You is be one plenty big fool, N'roa,' he said. 'I is have enough sense for keep quiet. Is let *gwanga* talk.'

William resumed. 'It's a good question.' N'roa glared triumphantly at Managua. 'In the United States we have laws to protect people from the actions of other people, from large corporations and even from the government itself, and of course its agencies, which includes the military.'

N'roa turned to his neighbour and said loudly, 'What language he is speak now?'

William ignored him. 'If someone causes you injury then they have to compensate you. They have to make amends, to pay you for the loss, suffering, hardship and inconvenience they have caused. It helps you get on with your life; it makes them less likely to do it again to someone else. I am here to try to get this compensation for all of you who have been damaged by the actions of the US military.'

N'roa raised his arm exactly like a child in class, although he could have had no example of that, William mused.

'I is must be stupid,' he said, which was greeted by a large chorus of agreement from the rest of the crowd. 'But I is *still* not understand. What we is go get?'

William had decided that jumping straight on in and mentioning money would get him nowhere. He had already established that the natives had no concept of it. But he had learned that they had a currency of their own, yams.

'It's like this,' he said. 'Suppose I break your arm. I would give you some yams to make up for it.'

N'roa looked puzzled. 'What for you is want for do that? Is be better you is not break arm in first place. Keep yams.'

'I don't mean I would break your arm deliberately,' William said.

'Ah, so is be accident?'

'Sort of.'

'But if is be accident, what for you is give me yams?'

'Well,' said William, trying to think how to explain, 'it's not as straightforward as that. I may not have intended to hurt you, but I did something that damaged you because I was careless.'

'Ah, like G'woa here. He canoe is hit mine because he is not look where he is go. I is fall out, is bang head on outrigger.'

'Yes, exactly,' said William. 'He didn't mean to do it, but it wouldn't have happened if he had been more careful.'

N'roa turned to the man next to him. 'G'woa, you is give me yams,' he said.

'What for is I give you yams? You is paddle you canoe straight across my bow. How is I suppose *not* hit you? You is smash front end of my boat. *You* is give *me* yams.' He turned to William. 'Is not be so, *gwanga*?'

'Well, I'm not sure,' said William. 'I'd rather not get into this right now.' He didn't want to get sidetracked. He was heartened by the fact that they were getting the idea. They'd already grasped the concept of claim and counterclaim.

N'roa turned back to William. 'How many yams America is give for my leg?'

'Well, they won't be giving you yams. They'll pay money. US dollars.'

He tried to say something more but it was drowned out by the loud laughter of everyone else present. Only Managua, he noticed, was not joining in.

'What for we is want that?' N'roa protested as the laughter subsided. 'We is already have dollars. Is use for light pipes.'

'But you can buy things with dollars. You can use them just the same way you use yams.' There was more laughter and much slapping of flesh. Finally it subsided and N'roa said, 'But you is can eat yams. Unless I is make plenty big mistake, you is not get very big meal from US dollars. Guts is stay plenty empty.'

'You could use your dollars to buy yams. You give the dollars to the man next to you, he gives you some yams.'

'That is be all very well,' said N'roa, warming to the argument. 'But then what he is go do with dollars?'

'Well, he could buy more yams and eat them,' said William. 'And the man he buys them from can use the dollars to buy more yams from someone else.'

N'roa let William an exasperated look. 'Yes, but you is not see problem with this dollar business. Sooner or later someone is go end up with dollars. He is not have any yams.'

'That's not the way it works,' said William. 'The dollars keep going round and round. They stay in circulation. You keep buying yams.'

N'roa let out a sigh of exasperation. 'But then what for you is bother with dollars at all? What for is not just use yams?'

'I was using yams for an example. You can buy lots of things with dollars. For example, if you built a fine canoe, I might give you lots of dollars for it. Then you could use the dollars to buy a necklace for your wife maybe.'

'I is can do that with yams. Dollars is be same as yams, 'cept you is can eat yams but you is not can eat dollars and you is can light pipe with dollar but not with yam. Is not be so?'

'But dollars will mean you can buy things from off the island. Lots of things. People will take your dollars and give you things in exchange.'

'What sort of things?'

'Well, foodstuff, I guess, clothes, medicine.'

'Coca-Cola?' someone shouted.

'Yes, Coca-Cola,' William said and everyone laughed and cheered loudly. 'But more important things. You could build a hospital. You could have an airstrip, run planes to the big island. You could have a road. Vehicles if you wanted. Motorboats to help you fish.'

'America is give we all this?'

'Not *give*, pay you as compensation to improve your lives to make up for making them worse. To try to put things right.'

Until now, Managua had kept silent, but William had noticed

the old man shaking his head. He struggled to his feet, breathing hard, though whether from the effort or anger, William couldn't tell. It could have been either. He stood waiting for silence and gradually the talking stopped as the natives realized he was on his feet. He spoke, quietly and with great authority. 'We is not need dollars, *gwanga*. We is not need planes and motor cars and boats. We is not need they . . . they . . . *things*. We is have food, we is have sun, we is have rain. We is not want Coca-Cola.'

'You is speak for youself, Managua,' someone shouted. Others chorused, 'We is want Coca-Cola plenty damn much,' and similar endorsements.

Again Managua waited for them to be quiet, standing still and dignified as a statue. He was trying to contain himself. He was remembering what Miss Lucy had said about pretending to go along with the white man. But this was too damn much. When he spoke it was with barely controlled anger. 'I is have dollar I is use for light pipe. We is not need dollar for any other thing. We is not need what dollar is buy. You is give me dollar I is not buy airplane. I is use for light pipe.'

'Well, you might be right,' said William. 'One dollar alone wouldn't be much use. You'd need rather more to buy an airplane.'

'How many dollars America is give we?' called someone.

'Millions,' replied William. 'I shall be seeking several million.'

'What is be million?'

'A million is a thousand thousand.' They all looked baffled. 'Or to put it another way,' he said, with a flash of inspiration. 'A million is plenty damn lot.'

As William sat taking notes of the names of the injured and details of where and how their injuries had occurred, while at the same time attempting to fight off the crowd of people clustering around him, trying to persuade them to form an orderly queue, he suddenly looked up and saw Managua limping off into the jungle, his back bent, his gait stiff and full of pain. There was something so full of sorrow in the stoop of his shoulders that William wanted to run after him and say, 'Hey, listen old man, it's OK. You deserve this. It's going to make your life a whole lot better. Trust me.' But then his attention was taken by a man elbowing another out of his way to thrust his face into William's.

'I is be call Maboa,' he said. 'You is put me down for one new airplane.'

NINETEEN

William trudged wearily along the beach towards the Captain Cook. After his evening in the *kassa* hut, he'd slept in but still woken exhausted. He'd almost been too late for the shitting beach, arriving as everyone else was leaving and tearing down his trousers in a hurry, like a man with diarrhoea. After his meeting with the people he mentally referred to as 'the limbless' – although of course they weren't, all of them had at least two limbs remaining and most of them three – all he wanted to do was get back to bed. Or table. He hadn't yet managed to find anywhere more comfortable to sleep than on the hotel's dining table. No matter, he was too tired to worry about it now.

Arriving at the hotel, he paused only to slip off his battered loafers, then hauled himself up onto the table. No sooner had his head touched the mahogany than he was fast asleep.

It could have been ten minutes later, it could have been an hour (he would never know because he was to lose consciousness again before he had chance to check his watch), when he was awoken by a noise above him. A faint sporadic tapping. Then it ceased. He lay perfectly still, holding his breath, waiting for it to begin once more. A minute must have ticked by. Two. Five. He was breathing quietly and was just about to relax and stop listening when he heard it again. This time it continued long enough to coalesce into something recognizable. Footsteps, surely, though very light, a child's perhaps, or maybe . . . a ghost's. The idea made him recall what Tigua had told him, that there were spirits in the abandoned building.

William eased himself slowly off the table and tiptoed across the concrete floor, glad now that he'd found the energy to remove his shoes before lying down. In the lobby outside the dining room, standing at the foot of the decrepit staircase, he again held his breath and once more heard the noise. A drop of sweat fell from his face onto the rotting first tread of the staircase with the sound, it seemed to William, of a kettledrum. Every noise he made was amplified partly by the echoing resonance of the empty old building and partly by his own fear, though in what proportions he could not have said.

He wiped his face on the bottom of his T-shirt. He didn't know whether he was sweating more than usual from anxiety or if the humidity was even worse than ever today.

He set a foot on the first tread of the stair, moving his weight onto it as he lifted his other foot to the second, expecting all the while the first to creak. No noise. He paused. There it was again, those same light steps. But although William was frightened, he wasn't a coward. He was going up those stairs. For what if Tigua was right? What if this building were a repository for the spirits of the dead? He'd seen his father in the *kassa* house; what if he were here now? For a whole minute he couldn't move. The idea had him rooted to this precarious spot. His mouth was dry and his heart palpitated with a peculiar beat; something prickled all along his spine. The very thought of his father being, not alive exactly, you couldn't say that, but, well, just being . . .

He took another step and then another. He had to keep close to the wall of the stairwell; as he went higher only the narrowest segment remained of many of the treads, just enough for him to set a foot upon. The centres had long ago given out, eaten through, probably, by dry rot or termites (whatever they were, some kind of monstrous ant, he imagined). The bits of intact step left on the side against the wall seemed fairly solid. He assumed they were supported by something beneath that held the treads to the wall. In places the fragments of stair that were left were so narrow they could only accommodate half the width of his foot. There was no banister for him to grip. He leaned into the wall, trying not to look down. And then, all at once, fear of falling ceased to be a problem, replaced by another that made him all but forget it. When his right foot touched the wall it was with the little toe. With his left, it was the big toe. His anxiety focused upon this lack of symmetry. It seemed the worst thing he had to cope with. Eyelids, fingers, teeth, all were maniacally doing their right-left-left-right thing. Dropping into the abyss beside him would almost be a relief. He took a deep breath and tried to collect himself.

He might have stayed like that for hours but then, there they were again, the footsteps. It was enough to drive him on. Gritting his grinding teeth to push the lack of symmetry from his thoughts he forced himself to put foot in front of foot and took the remainder of the stairs in a crazy, near-suicidal run. He was blinking so fast that instead of offering any calm it was making him dizzy, would have made him dizzy even without the drop to help it. But no matter, his mad dash carried him up and seconds later, with a sense of relief and triumph he placed his foot upon the final step, which was more or less intact. It creaked! Not only that, it creaked loud enough to wake the dead, except, William thought, that they seemed to be awake already here. He listened. There was a skittering sound like a quick scamper of feet and then silence. So total and absolute, save of course for the ever-present jungle sounds, parrots and insects from outside, that William knew any movement he made must shatter it and announce his presence. He sensed that whoever – *whatever* – it was, was waiting and listening, trying to tell if he or she or it had heard something.

He decided to wait it out. A minute went by. Five. Ten. There was no sound. There were two possibilities. Whatever it was had somehow fled. Perhaps it had jumped. The hotel was a low building and the upper floor wasn't that high from the ground. Presumably ghosts could fling themselves from great heights without any great harm coming to them. Maybe it had been no more than a monkey. Or maybe it was still there and listening for him as he was listening for it. If that were so, decided William, he would take it by surprise. He stepped briskly into the room facing the top of the stairs. An empty concrete shell. He turned out of it and into the upstairs corridor. He marched swiftly along it, bare feet silent on the concrete floor. He looked into the first room on the right. Empty. He peered through the opposite doorway on his left and found nothing. Not just nothing in the room, but nothing at all. No room. It was simply an empty door frame opening on to the jungle. Of course! The builders had never finished the front of the hotel.

William peered out at the mass of greenery below considering whether anyone might have jumped down. Too late he heard a jingling sound behind him. Too late he began to turn his head. All he saw was a blur of movement and then something came crashing down on his head and he was falling through the air. 'I'm flying!' he had time to think. 'Just like Superboy!' Before he hit the ground, even as he was crashing through the lower branches of a tree, everything went black.

TWENTY

While it was true that obsessive compulsive disorder brought Lola
to William – she noticed his alternate eye blinking at a party, mistakenly assumed he was winking at her and thought this an
intriguing come-on – it also took her away. She left him soon after
the incident with his boss's wife and after her loss he realized it was
time he did something about his condition.

Like many OCD sufferers William was burdened with an
exaggerated sense of responsibility. When bad things happened in
the world he felt he ought to have done something to prevent
them. Even if the event were a major disaster, such as a train wreck
or a terrorist outrage, something there was never any possibility of
his averting.

Faced with this helplessness and the guilt it engendered, William
had compensated by choosing a caring profession. In his case it was
natural to follow his father in seeking reparation for poor people
injured by multinational organizations or the US government.
OCD had shaped William's life: he was successful at what he did
because OCD made him careful and meticulous; he did what he
did because it had made him a carer.

So it was natural that when William decided to fight the condition, the effect of it upon him would influence the way he went
about tackling it. It was not in his nature to selfishly seek help for
himself alone. He wanted his own salvation to be achieved through

that of other people and theirs through his. He decided to start a self-help group.

He advertised in the *New York Times* for other sufferers to join him in an introductory weekend at a house on the Long Island shore he rented for the purpose. It was a stone's throw from his parents' weekend cottage. It had five bedrooms, and, with some doubling up, William reckoned it would do for the group of seven people, including himself, whom he selected as the group's founder members.

He'd reluctantly rejected several hundred applicants, some because they had problems that would make their attendance at the introductory weekend impossible – a woman who had been unable to leave her house for twenty-three years, a man who spent all his weekends clearing litter from subway platforms, a girl who could not travel in anything with wheels – and others simply because they wrote in block capitals and angry green ink, and arrived at six other people whom he thought capable of being helped and who seemed from their letters to be intelligent and insightful enough to help him and the rest of the group.

He also tried to get a good cross section of the most common OCD types. There were a couple of checkers, people whose lives were being seriously inconvenienced by their having to keep checking that they had done things. One of them, Steve, wrote movingly of his daily difficulty in getting out of the house. After he had gotten himself ready to leave for work (he was an accountant, at the office he spent his whole day – what was left of it once he got there – checking other people's figures), he was unable to exit his apartment until he had made a number of safety checks. First he went round and made sure all the windows were securely locked. They nearly always were, for the simple reason that he almost never opened them. Never mind that his apartment reeked of sweaty socks and stale underpants and that he had had to install air conditioning against the hot summers, the bottom line was that there couldn't be a window open. Except, of course, that sometimes Steve would open one just so he could go through the process of closing it and locking it so he'd know for sure it was locked. Then he could never be certain that he *had* actually locked it so would have to check each and every window each and every time he left the apartment. Besides checking the security, he also had to make sure he had switched off every single electrical appliance in the place (except for the burglar alarm, of course, which he had to make sure he'd switched *on*). Sometimes he couldn't be sure he'd switched something off, so he'd have to switch it on, see it light up and then switch it off so he would have the memory of the light going out that would let him know he had turned it off. But then, of course, he was never quite sure that the memory was a real one; it might instead be an anticipated memory, something he'd foreseen happening but which had not really occurred because he had not actually carried out the necessary procedure, or it might be a real memory, but from the day before, or from a previous aborted round of checking that same day. Steve's checking routine took so long he was regularly late for work and had consequently acquired a reputation as a high-liver, someone who was out at clubs every night and probably doing all kinds of drink and drugs so that he was too tired to get up on time in the mornings. The opposite was true, of course. Steve was actually getting up earlier and earlier so as to have time to fit in his ever more elaborate checking procedure before leaving for work. The idea of staying out late in the evenings or of drinking alcohol or taking drugs was ludicrous to him. He'd never have been in a fit state to do all his checking if he'd had a hangover. But he did nothing to challenge this impression of himself. He'd rather people thought him a dissolute reprobate, which somehow seemed kind of cool, than let them know he had a mental disorder, which did not.

The other checker was also a man, Sam. His dysfunction was not yet as serious as Steve's, being mainly limited to his car. Sam had to perform a series of checks before getting into his automobile. He had to measure the tread on his tyres and make sure all the rear lights – direction flashers, reversing lights and brake lights – were

working before he could drive off. When he parked the car some-
place he had to return to it several times to confirm it was locked,
that the alarm was engaged and that the emergency brake was on.

William was able to sympathize with both these men because he
was something of a checker himself. He wasn't as extreme as either
Sam or Steve, but he would never have left his apartment without
checking everything two or three times and he never got beyond
the edge of a car park before having to return to his car to
check the doors and the emergency brake at least once.

Two of the three women on the weekend were obsessive
cleaners. They had remarkably similar OCD profiles which was
hardly surprising as ritual cleaning is one of the most common
ways in which the disorder manifests itself.

Both Sheena and Rhoda spent most of their free time cleaning
their homes. Sheena, who was in her mid-twenties, lived alone in
an apartment. Rhoda, who was forty-something, had two teenage
children whom she drove crazy by her excessive tidiness. It had
also years ago driven her husband to leave her.

Sheena had been unable to hold down a job because her need
to clean her apartment often made her late for work and she was
always getting fired. Then one day she saw an advertisement on a
card in a shop window for a cleaning woman. She rang up right
away and got the job. She reasoned that as she spent most of her
life cleaning anyhow, she might as well get paid for it. At first the
family who engaged her to clean for them two mornings a week
were delighted by her. Their house had never looked so clean.
Both days Sheena worked not only the morning they had asked
her to work, but until suppertime. The house sparkled like a new
pin. The family happily paid her for the extra hours she'd put in.
Seeing how clean the house was now made them realize how dirty
it had been before. It had needed those extra hours.

Sheena was happy too. She put a card in the shop window herself, advertising as 'SHEENA THE CLEANER' and within days
had lined up a number of clients. The first week she was out all
hours because the houses she had signed up to clean were way

below her exacting standards of cleanliness. They looked like they
hadn't been treated to a thorough going over for years. And she
was still working whole days for the first family who'd employed
her. It was round about the fourth week that trouble hit. The first
woman to employ her took her aside and gently explained that
they would have to let her go.

'Why?' asked Sheena. 'Isn't my cleaning any good?' Even as she
was talking she was looking around for fingermarks on light
switches or dust on the glass top of a coffee table.

The woman shook her head. 'My dear, if anything, your cleaning is *too* good. You clean everything so thoroughly that it takes
you two whole days a week. We can't afford to pay you for that,
we only wanted two mornings.'

'I'll speed up,' Sheena promised her.

The next time Sheena worked there she was still cleaning at
suppertime. As the woman finally ushered her out the door, she said,
'It's no good, you see, you work too slowly. We can't afford you.'

Sheena put her hand on the door to prevent the woman closing
it on her. 'Listen,' she said. 'Just pay me for the hours you wanted
me for. If I go over time I won't ask for any extra.'

'Oh no, I couldn't possibly,' said the woman. 'It wouldn't be fair.
Your hourly rate would be less than minimum wage. I'm a
Democrat.'

'I wouldn't care,' Sheena insisted. 'You see, cleaning's my passion.
It's what I'd be doing if I was home.'

Reluctantly the woman agreed. But other clients were less
understanding. One by one they dwindled away. Some felt too
guilty to adopt a similar arrangement to the one she had with her
first client. Others weren't happy with it because they couldn't
stand Sheena being around the house all hours.

'People want a cleaner to be in and out without them noticing,
except in the results,' she explained to the rest of the group at their
Friday evening get-together session. 'They wanted me to work two
or three hours. I couldn't clean anywhere to my satisfaction in less
than ten.'

So Sheena was virtually unemployed except for her original family who treated her much as one might a pet.

Both Sheena and Rhoda cleaned not only their homes to excess, but themselves too. They would spend hours every day on their personal hygiene, having to go through elaborate rituals, taking two or three showers or baths. Rhoda had so overcleaned her teeth she had worn grooves in the enamel, exposing the dentine which reacted fiercely to hot and cold drinks and sugary snacks. Both said that if their rituals were interrupted for any reason they would have to begin them all over again, a trait common to many OCD victims.

William understood their fetishes as he himself had a bit of a personal hygiene problem. He had a morning ritual which he was unable to vary, no matter how much of a hurry he was in. He always began by brushing his teeth, timing himself for exactly three minutes (he couldn't skimp by even a few seconds, no matter how late he was running), then he'd have a cup of coffee to get his bowels working, take a dump, take a shower, shave and dress in a particular order — shorts, socks, undershirt, shirt, trousers, it never varied. In addition he had a horror of germs in public lavatories and virtually never took a dump anywhere but at home, except when he stayed in a hotel or rented house which then became, temporarily, a surrogate home. He had installed a bidet in his bathroom so that he could wash after every time he defecated. One of the ideas that horrified him was walking around with an unclean butt. He would later find it incredible that he was shitting on a public beach in full view of dozens of other men and then not wiping his butt at all.

His concern with faecal matter also helped him empathize with Lorna, the third woman in the group. Her main concern was with dog shit. She was scarcely able to leave her home because of her fear of treading in it.

At first she had been happy just going out and not stepping in the stuff. But as her condition worsened, she became obsessed with the idea that people who had stepped in dog dirt had then walked on clean areas of pavement, depositing infinitesimal fragments of canine faecal matter on them. And moving on, she worried that other people would walk where they had walked, picking up the dog-shit bacteria and redistributing it elsewhere. She was terrified of anyone bringing the bacteria into her home and insisted on any visitors removing their shoes outside the front door and washing their hands before touching anything.

To prevent herself inadvertently picking up invisible doggie-doo bacteria she covered the soles of her shoes with tin kitchen foil before venturing out. She removed the foil on her doorstep before re-entry. Although William didn't go to such lengths, he knew he too had a problem with canine crap. He would never have touched the soles of his shoes either.

William identified with the final member of the group as well. Frank was a hoarder. He was a middle-aged man who confessed that he had been unable to throw anything other than obvious garbage away for thirty years. The upper floors of his house had had to be reinforced to take the weight of the old newspapers, magazines and books he kept up there. It had never occurred to him to throw them out instead.

Frank had been married for twenty years when one day his wife said to him, 'Either all this junk goes or I do.' Frank had been on his own ever since.

William too was a hoarder. He still possessed all of his childhood toys and comics and found it difficult to dispose of anything to which he had formed a comfortable attachment, for example an old pair of Levi's which had worn through in the crotch. He kept them even though they were beyond wearing any more. But compared to Frank, William was a rank amateur.

One of his secret hopes for the weekend was that Frank might be incited to invite Rhoda and Sheena to his home. William thought that between them they would soon sort Frank out and that having experienced his mess they in turn might realize a certain amount of disorder could be lived with.

Everyone arrived at the farmhouse on Friday evening. They

were all as tired after the journey out from the city where most of them lived as William had expected them to be. They ate an easy meal of pizza which William had ordered in and spent a brief, but relaxed evening introducing themselves to one another and providing brief résumés of their particular problems.

The only sticky moment came when Rhoda fretted about the cleanliness of the kitchens at the pizza restaurant. This led Lorna to construct a theoretical chain of events in which someone who had been in contact with dog dirt had handled the pizza dough. It took some time to reassure her, but William managed to convince her that all the people at the local pizza parlour wore disposable plastic gloves when preparing the food and that while it was possible the motorcycle delivery boy had ridden over a dog dump in the middle of the road, then had a blow out and had to change his wheel and had touched his tyre and then their pizza, it was extremely unlikely. He argued that it was impossible to open a pizza carry-out box without bending the cardboard tab and that he himself had opened the pizza boxes and all the tabs had been intact. Lorna seemed to accept his argument but not her pizza, at least not without a lot of persuasion, so that by the time she was prepared to eat it, it was already too cold for her to do so.

But against Lorna's worry about the pizza, there were signs of the group already beginning to work. William was glad to see that, as he had hoped, Sheena and Rhoda had paired up and were already talking eagerly to one another, although he was not so reassured when he realized they were discussing the relative merits of different cleaning products.

'No, no, you must try my cleaner,' insisted Sheena. 'It's guaranteed to kill 98 per cent of household germs.'

'Well, that's good,' said Rhoda. 'But don't you ever worry about those other two?'

The only person who didn't seem to fit in was Frank, who had arrived with a station wagon full of suitcases and cardboard boxes that he spent most of the evening hauling up to his room.

'It's just stuff,' he explained to William with an apologetic shrug when they met on the stairs. The word reminded William of Mrs Beach who'd used it in just the same way all those years ago. 'I wouldn't feel comfortable not having some of it along with me. I might get homesick.'

William wasn't too bothered about the evening, anyhow. It was just a chance for everyone to settle in and get acquainted. It was next morning that they would really begin exploring their condition and, he hoped, helping one another.

He went to bed happy, already feeling no need to indulge in any alternate blinking, or hand squeezing or molar grinding. He lay on his back listening to the distant sound of the breakers and the quiet but determined noises of windows being opened and closed, doors softly shutting and bolts being driven home as Sam and Steve checked the security before turning in. At what hour they finally came to bed he never knew; he was sound asleep long before the last window catch was screwed down.

Next day though, things began to go wrong right from the start. William woke with a volcanic feeling in his stomach, a hot bubbling accompanied by a griping pain that made him wonder if Rhoda had been right to question the cleanliness of the pizza place. Surely this was just how an infection of *E. coli* would begin? But he didn't have time to lie there and contemplate the situation. He had an urgent need to crap.

He struggled out of bed and tiptoed across the landing to the nearest of the two bathrooms. He tried the door and was surprised to find it locked. After all, it was only 6 a.m. Staying on tiptoe, to avoid waking the other five guests whom he assumed to be still asleep, he made his way along the long upstairs corridor to the other bathroom at the opposite end. But once again the door was locked.

It struck him as a piece of bad luck that both bathrooms should be occupied at the precise moment when he needed a dump and such an urgent one at that, but he consoled himself with the fact that their occupants must have heard him trying the door handles and would soon emerge.

He decided he could hold on a little, in spite of the pain, especially if he were to lie down, reasoning that gravity was making things worse. So he returned to his room, lay on the bed and read through a newsletter from a panic support group that he intended to share with the others at the morning get-together.

After five minutes, though, his mind was too much occupied with his gut to concentrate. It was getting to the stage where if he didn't move soon, he wouldn't be able to get off the bed before he exploded, let alone make it to the bathroom. So he rose and he ventured out again.

Once more the first bathroom was locked. He padded along the corridor barefoot to avoid any slipper slapping on the polished wood floor and tried the door of the second bathroom. Locked! Immediately he wanted to shit even more than before. He locked his buttocks together to keep from doing it then and there. He couldn't believe his luck. His first time back at the shore in years and he found himself in a Sandy Beach situation. Only this time he was Sandy Beach! But unlike his former friend he couldn't bang on the bathroom door. Not on either of them! He didn't want to wake the whole house.

After another five minutes he was desperate. His guts were churning and he knew that his morning dump was on its way, even without coffee. He considered his options. He could stay where he was and make a mess of himself. He could rattle one of the doors, or he could sneak outside and take a dump in the shrubbery.

He rattled the door of the first bathroom.

'I wish you wouldn't keep doing that.' It was Sheena's voice, sounding tetchy. 'That's the second time this morning. Now I'll have to start all over again. Again!'

William realized that Sheena must have gotten up very early in order to complete her washing rituals before anyone else was abroad. Instantly he knew that the other bathroom was occupied by Rhoda and that waiting in the hope that one of them would emerge before he crapped himself was futile.

As he minced downstairs (mince was the only word he could

think of to describe his new tight-assed walk to himself) he consoled himself with the fact that already the weekend was working for him. Here was he, who could never even take a dump in someone else's lavatory, about to have one alfresco in a rented house's garden. That was progress!

He just made it out of the back door and behind a shrub when his bowels finally gave out. He squatted and released what smelled like a toxic flood of bacterially challenged pizza. The relief was so great that he couldn't help celebrating out loud. 'Ahhhhh!' he exclaimed, closing his eyes, as his bowels exploded. 'Ahhhhhhhhhhhhhhhhhh!'

'Hey, William is that you?'

He opened his eyes and saw Sam peering at him from the other side of the garden fence. Fortunately Sam was some twenty feet away which probably meant he could only see William's head. William hastily pulled up his pyjama pants and lowered his dressing gown. His embarrassment at being so surprised was so great that it outweighed his horror at the thought of his besmirched haunches.

He gave Sam a feeble wave. 'Yes, it's me.'

Sam walked over to the fence. As he approached William took a step forward to hide the huge pile of excrement he had produced.

'Whatcha doing crawling around down there?' asked Sam.

'I er, I er heard a noise and I er, I was worried it might be um, burglars. So I er um was hiding behind the fence to check it out. And um . . .' here William gave a silly little laugh, 'I er found it was you.'

To most people his demeanour was so guilty that this explanation might have been greeted with immediate suspicion but Sam had his own embarrassment to hide.

'Yes, I was um, just admiring the er, scenery, you know, enjoying the ocean and all.'

'The car park's probably not the best place to enjoy the ocean from,' said William, realizing now that just as Sam had almost caught him crapping, he had almost caught Sam checking his car. 'For one thing, you can't even see it from here.'

'Well, um, that's true,' said Sam, looking around as if to make sure there wasn't an ocean lurking within view that he hadn't noticed. 'But you can hear it. That's almost as good. And you sure can smell that sea air.' He took a deep, environmentally enthusiastic breath in through his nostrils, but at once the smile vanished from his face. 'Phew! What is that? Smells like dog crap.'

'Er, no, no dogs allowed on the property. Four acres all well fenced,' said William. 'Um, shall we go inside and get ourselves some breakfast?' He was anxious to get Sam away from the incriminating dump. He would have to come back later and bury it, he thought. They walked back towards the rear door of the house, Sam still on the outside of the fence. Halfway to the house Sam paused. He raised a finger in the air in a poor mime of someone who has suddenly remembered something.

'What is it?' asked William.

'Just have to get something from my car,' said Sam, and dashed off back the way he'd come.

'It's OK to say you're going to check,' William called after him. 'That's the whole point of the weekend. You're among friends. You don't have to conceal your disorder. Getting over the guilt may be the first step to managing it better. Controlling it instead of it controlling you.'

Sam stopped, turned and smiled. 'Hey, that's right. I forgot. Well, William, I'm just going to check that I put the emergency brake on.'

He trotted off. 'Sam!' William called after him. 'Could you maybe check my emergency brake too? It's the blue Honda.' William felt sure Sam was the one person he'd ever met who would do a better job of checking his car than he would himself.

He walked through the back door of the house and straight into an argument. Frank was bellowing at Sheena. 'You had no right, bitch!' he screamed. 'That's my room, private.'

Sheena was in tears. 'I know, I know, but you don't have to be so nasty,' she sobbed. 'It was your fault for leaving your door open.'

'Excuse me!' yelled Frank. 'It was *not* my fault. I had to take an urgent dump. My guts were killing me. Jesus, I was in agony. It musta been that pizza we had—'

'I knew it! I knew it!' wittered Lorna. 'I just knew that delivery boy was the sort who'd have been touching his tyres!'

'I bin waiting an hour to get in the friggin' bathroom,' continued Frank. 'When I finally hear the door open I'm not about to hang around to close my door and let some other nut with a cleaning fetish get in that bathroom for another hour and a half while I crap myself.'

'Nut with a cleaning fetish!' sniffed Rhoda who'd just walked in. 'Some support we get from you.'

'Well, listen lady, that's what *she* is,' said Frank pointing at Sheena. 'I'm only out of my room a minute, two at the most, that's how urgent that crap was, and I come back to find *her* in my room and all my stuff moved around.'

'All moved around!' snapped Sheena. 'In two minutes! That's simply not true. I don't work that fast. Ask any of my employers!'

'Thank God I didn't touch that pizza!' Lorna exclaimed, obviously suddenly remembering that she hadn't eaten any of it. 'I could have died. It makes me feel faint just thinking about it.' She put a hand to her forehead and started to sway. Fortunately, at that moment, Sam came in through the back door and caught hold of her.

'Easy does it,' he said.

'Sorry, I just felt faint.'

'You need some fresh air, that sea breeze will soon blow the nausea away,' said Sam kindly. He turned her around and edged her towards the back door.

'No, no,' said Lorna, raising her arms in terror. 'I couldn't possibly. Who knows what dogs have been doing out there?'

'No dogs allowed here, Lorna, it's in the rental literature,' said William.

'But do the dogs around here know that?' she protested. 'They might have come into the garden and – and—'

'It's OK,' said Sam. 'There's a secure dog-proof fence all around the garden. I just walked every inch of it and I um, I er, I happened to notice it was—' He caught William's eye. 'Damn, if I don't keep forgetting,' he said. 'I checked it! There you are, I checked it myself, every inch of the garden fence. Totally secure, Lorna.'

'Well, if you're sure . . .' She allowed Sam to help her through the back door.

'What happened?' asked William, turning back to the combatants. 'Sheena, is it true you went into Frank's room when he wasn't there?'

'Damn right it's—' began Frank but William lifted his hand to silence him. 'I asked Sheena,' he said.

'I – I couldn't help myself,' she said. 'I was going back to my room from the bathroom and when I passed Frank's room the door was open and I – I happened to glance in and I saw all this mess—'

'It isn't mess,' snapped Frank. 'It's my stuff. It's why I'm here, for Christ's sake.'

'OK, OK,' said Sheena. 'Anyway, it was all over the place and I couldn't resist just popping in there and trying to straighten it out a little bit and then he comes in and goes apeshit.'

'Wouldn't you? When I walked back in it *was* a mess. She turned stuff into a mess. She'd rearranged everything so I couldn't find anything.'

'I'd tidied is all.'

'Bitch. Mad bitch!'

Sheena turned and fled up the stairs. William rushed after her but she ducked into the bathroom and slammed the door in his face, drawing the bolt. He heard water running. He knocked on the door. 'Sheena,' he said softly. 'Sheena, please don't do this.'

'Go away,' she said. 'The longer you're there, the longer it will be before I can get started.'

William was halfway down the stairs when he heard a scream, followed by shouting and then hysterical sobbing. He entered the kitchen to find Lorna utterly distraught, crying and flailing her arms hysterically while Sam and Steve tried to restrain her.

'Whatever's happened?' asked William.

'This,' said Rhoda. In her hand she held a woman's shoe, gingerly, between her thumb and index finger.

'Sure is the biggest dog turd I ever see,' said Frank.

'I knew I smelled something out there this morning,' said Sam. 'That's why I checked the fence. I still can't believe a dog could have got in. I must have missed seeing a really small hole in the wire . . .'

'Small hole!' screamed Lorna. 'It wasn't a small dog did that. I don't know what kind of breed could have produced so much stuff, but it must have been the size of an elephant.'

William's eyes were going right–left–left–right so fast that it had an almost stroboscopic effect on his sight. In the brief flashes of vision his OCD ritual afforded him, he caught glimpses of Lorna's shoe, or rather, the top of it. The rest of it was embedded in what was, unquestionably, his own crap.

After this disastrous start to the day things fell apart pretty soon. Steve was the first one to leave. He suddenly didn't remember switching off his electric hob. For that matter he couldn't remember switching it on. Of course, it was possible he hadn't switched it off because it was never on, but on the other hand if it was . . .

This set Sam off to worrying that he didn't remember switching off his hob, either, until he recalled he hadn't got one but then this made him not remember switching on his burglar alarm. There was nothing for it, he'd have to head back home too.

Sheena was so upset about the fight with Frank that when she finally emerged from the bathroom she announced she was leaving. She couldn't stand being in the house and knowing there was all that mess in the room next door to her. Rhoda said if Sheena was going she might as well too. Lorna was so traumatized about the dog shit that there was no question of her staying and so Rhoda offered her a lift but only on condition she dumped her shoes to which Lorna said what kind of person did Rhoda think she was, *of course* she'd dump her shoes, had already dumped them in fact. Frank said he might as well go too. At this, Sheena looked a little guiltily at William and said she could stay a bit if Frank's mess was out of there. Rhoda said she would offer to stay as well if Sheena were but that she'd already promised to take Lorna home. William suggested Frank take Lorna, but Frank had so much stuff to put back in his car he didn't have room for another person which just about summed up what was wrong with his life, Sheena said, which led to another row breaking out. But eventually it all settled down and William was left with Sheena.

'You want me to give you a lift back to the city?' he said. She smiled gratefully. She really had a very attractive smile. 'You could come back to my place for dinner.'

'OK,' she said. 'So long as I get to wash the dishes.'

TWENTY-ONE

The first things William saw when he returned to consciousness after the blow on the head at the Captain Cook were blue eyes staring into his. Well, he thought they were blue eyes, cornflower blue, wasn't that how the paint charts had it? but he couldn't be sure because his own vision seemed to be blurred. The colour of the eyes was not the only thing that was remarkable about them, there was also their number, for there were four of them, arranged in two sets of two that orbited one another, floating around above him. It made him feel dizzy, just watching them all dancing about like that, so he closed his own eyes again. For how long and whether he lost consciousness again, he didn't know, but when he opened them once more the blue eyes were no longer there, replaced by a single pair in brown, framed by Tigua's smiling face.

'Phew! *Gwanga*, you is give we one plenty big scare. We is all say we is dig you bones up in day or two.' This further mystified an already puzzled William who as yet knew nothing of the burial practices of the natives and the ritual exhumation of recently buried corpses. 'I is find you at Captain Cook. I is run and get Lintoa and we is carry you back.'

'*I* is carry you back, *gwanga*, this sow is just hold you hat.' Tigua's even more butch friend appeared behind her. Lintoa's huge box of a head reminded William of one of those Easter Island statues.

'I is be one who is find you, *gwanga*. I is probably save you life,' said Tigua.

'I er I th—'

'Is be OK, *gwanga*,' interrupted Tigua swiftly. 'You is not thank. Is not be proper for thank someone for save life. Thank someone for beer, yes, for save life, no. Anyway, I is not want thanks. Is be I who is thank you. Is be first time I is ever have chance for save someone life.'

Lintoa pulled a face but evidently couldn't be bothered to protest at all this. Instead she turned and called, 'Miss Lucy! You is come quick, *gwanga* is wake up.'

There was the sound of footsteps, shod footsteps on wooden boards, he noticed, not the patter of bare feet on hardened mud, and a slight blonde woman of about his own age appeared. The blue eyes. She smiled. 'I *am* glad to see you awake at last. We were getting quite worried about you. You must have hit your head pretty hard when you fell.' Her accent was British. He noticed she had rather pointy breasts.

'I – I didn't hit it when—' William stopped. Best not say what had happened in front of the two girls; Tigua especially was such a chatterbox. Someone had certainly struck him on the back of the head, but until he found out more it might be politic not to make it public.

'You is hit head,' insisted Lintoa. 'You is have lump size of coconut on back of head. Is look like you is have two heads.'

'Lintoa is exaggerate of course,' chipped in Tigua. 'Mebbe one head and half. Still, is be plenty lucky you is be alive. If I is not find you—'

'You is already say all this,' interrupted Lintoa, giving Tigua a shove on the shoulder which nearly knocked her over.

'No, I is not say. If I is not find you nobody is because nobody else is go near Captain Cook. I is not be afraid of bad spirits because I is already go with you.'

Lintoa shoved her again. This time she slipped out of William's line of vision to be replaced by the white woman.

'Here, take some water,' she said. She slipped her hand beneath his head and cradled it, raising it so he could sip from the glass she proffered in her other hand. An actual glass! The first he'd seen since he'd come to the island.

'Who – who?' he mumbled when he'd finished and she had let his head gently back onto the pillow.

'My name's Lucy Tibbut. I live here.'

'Here? Are we not on the island any more?'

'Of course we are. What makes you think we're not?'

'Managua told me there were no other white people on the island.'

'No, is not be true, *gwanga*,' said Tigua. 'You is ask if is be other white mans on island. Managua is say no. You is not mention white womans.'

Lucy turned to Tigua. 'Listen, he's tired. Why don't you two run along so he can get some rest?'

'How he go is rest when you is talk together all time?' demanded Tigua. 'You is say he is rest for get rid of we so you is can talk.'

Lucy laughed. 'You're absolutely right. So run along now, there's a good girl.'

'I is want for listen.'

'I'm sure you do, but I don't want you to so you have to go. Here, take this.' She walked away from the bed out of William's vision for a moment. Without warning two missiles came hurtling one after the other through the air. Lintoa fielded them as if they were baseballs and tossed one to Tigua. Cans of beer. William was amazed.

'Thanks, Miss Lucy,' said Tigua and the two girls were out of the room in a moment, Lintoa pausing briefly in the doorway to shuck off the slingbacks she was wearing and pick them up.

'Now we've got shot of those two,' said Lucy, 'you can tell me what you're doing here.'

'I could ask you the same question.'

'I'm an ethnographer.' She laughed. 'I'm making a study of the islanders here in their native environment. I'm working on a book about their culture. I've been here almost a year.'

'A woman, on your own?'

'It's perfectly safe. They abandoned poison darts some years ago, they're not cannibals and it's taboo to have sex with non-islanders. You just have to watch out for green shoestring snakes. Your turn, now.'

'Could I have one of those beers?' William wasn't much of a drinker but working on the hair of the dog principle he hoped it might help his *kassa* hangover and the additional ache in his head he'd gained from being hit on it.

'Are you sure you're up to it?'

'Only one way to find out.' He pulled himself up so that his shoulders were resting on the wooden wall of the hut behind him. 'Oooh.'

'Really sure?'

'Yes.'

She returned with a beer, popped the tab and placed it in his hand. 'It's cold,' he said in wonder. 'How come?'

'Gas refrigerator. The only one on the island. It's very small and the only things I keep in it are beer, sun cream and make-up. Mostly beer. My skin's getting used to the sun and I don't have much call for make-up here except when I'm feeling sorry for myself and need cheering up.'

He managed to shuffle himself up a little more so that he was almost in a sitting position, which enabled him to keep the sore part of his head off the wall. He was able to see her better now. She was about his own age, early thirties. Her face was kind of angular, her nose and chin pointy like the sharpened breasts beneath her shirt, but attractive, none the less.

'The plane brings me a crate of beer every month. That's forty-eight cans. One a day plus a few for my friends. Oh, I forgot, I have a bottle or two of white wine in the fridge as well. But you were going to tell me about you.'

As they drank their beer, William explained that he worked for a charity that specialized in providing legal assistance to the victims of American government action. He was here because a former US marine had contacted the organization with a story of atrocities committed against the islanders by American ordnance and military personnel.

Her face clouded as he talked. When she spoke, she was abrupt. 'What does that mean in plain English?'

'I'm here to investigate the possibility of compensation for all the damage done to these people by US landmines. And for at least one victim of rape.' He groaned once more. He'd shifted his position and when the back of his head touched the wall again, it hurt. 'Ouch!' He put his hand on the spot and felt cloth.

'I put a dressing on it. It's a pretty nasty wound. You were lucky, you could have been killed, falling all that way.'

'I didn't hurt myself falling. The trees broke my fall. Somebody hit me on the head and pushed me off the building.'

'Hm, that would be surprising because the people here are a peaceable lot. The worst they'd do to you would be ask one of their sorcerers to put a death spell on you. Are you sure someone hit you? I mean, you're probably concussed, you may not be thinking clearly.'

William stared back at her. The eyes were very blue. 'I know what happened.'

She stood up and walked away. He heard two pops and she returned with two more cans, opened. She seemed lost in thought as she handed one of them to him. 'That's very interesting. I wonder who would want to do that?'

William had no reply to this. He sipped his beer, mulling it over. 'How long are you intending to stay here?'

'Until my work's finished, which it nearly is. There's just one more thing I have to do.'

'What's that?'

'Get into the *kassa* house. It's a bit tricky. Women aren't allowed, it's a strict taboo. I think if I broke that one, I might have to take back what I said about them being peaceable.'

'What's so important about getting in there? Can't you just ask them what goes on? I was there last night, I can tell you.'

Was it a trick of the light, or were her eyes suddenly bright. 'Oh, I have lots of first-hand accounts of it. It's just that it's so fantastic. It's unique. There isn't another place in the world where people claim to commune with their dead friends and relatives. I need to experience it for myself. It will be the making of my book.'

TWENTY-TWO

As William walked home along the beach from Lucy's house, or rather than walked, staggered, because his head was still pounding and his legs shaky from a combination of the blow he'd received, last night's *kassa* and today's beer, his feverish mind teemed with thoughts of the Englishwoman. For the time he had been in her house, a matter of a few hours, that was all it could have been, he'd experienced an unaccustomed sense of security that had made him want to remain there. It wasn't simply that she was attractive, although of course she was, albeit in a sharp sort of way. Actually it was something to do with that very sharpness and the confidence that went with it, the feeling it gave you that if she offered you her protection she would repel all boarders. Indeed she'd suggested he stay at her house rather than put himself in danger any longer at the Captain Cook. She'd told him he'd be very welcome although, for the sake of decency, he'd have to walk to the village at mealtimes and make a point of eating in public. It was all right, she explained, for an un-married man and woman to sleep under the same roof, even sleep together under that roof (when she said this, he blushed; she did not), as long as they didn't share their meals.

'It wouldn't matter if we were fucking each other's brains out,' was how she put it – William winced and hoped it looked like a sudden throb from his wound – 'but eating together here as well would constitute living in sin.'

He found himself thinking about Lucy's height. How would it affect their relationship? Not that they could be said to have a relationship, of course, other than nurse–patient, or white–white on an island otherwise peopled entirely by brown-skinned natives, but suppose they did? He was of above average height for a man whereas she was shorter than the mean woman. The mean woman! His disordered brain picked up on the phrase. It could easily have been applied to Lola who had certainly been mean to him after the incident with the photograph of the obese woman and mean too when it came to their divorce settlement. Lola was of almost exactly average height. But then again, had that brought him happiness? Would their marriage have foundered or, indeed, lasted, if not permanently then at least longer, had she herself been longer? Or shorter? He couldn't think so. On the other hand how would the height difference between him and Lucy affect their sex life? What was he thinking of? They didn't have a sex life! *They* didn't have a *life*. If only she hadn't used that phrase, 'fucking each other's brains out', inciting his obsessive mind to confer upon an innocent meeting a burden of possibility and hope . . .

Suppose he were on top of her, in the missionary position and, well, *inside* her, would they be able to kiss? Certainly not on the upward stroke, when the tip of his chin would barely touch her forehead, but perhaps on the downward one when the not in-considerable length of his penis might mean he could bring his lips close enough to hers while still remaining engaged. No, that would depend on the length of his penis being greater than their differ-ence in height, and he thought that unlikely, the latter measurement surely getting on for nearly a foot.

He stopped dead. What was he thinking of? This was com-pletely over the top! It must be *kassa* and concussion making him imagine himself having sex with a woman who had shown him only kindness and didn't deserve to be given a starring role in his fantasies. Unless of course his back was hunched. Could you make love with your back hunched? He wasn't sure. He'd never seen it in a movie where body parts always seemed to fit perfectly, but then, weren't a lot of leading men – Tom Cruise, Al Pacino – exceptionally short, or at least shorter than average? He resumed walking. If you could hunch then you could kiss. It hadn't been a problem with Lola. Had he instinctively been hunching? Or had it been unnecessary because his penis length was greater than their height difference, something he was pretty sure was true, stopping again now to imagine Lola next to him, assessing where she came up to on him and then attempting to visualize his erect penis standing on top of her head.

It wasn't just sex where relative stature mattered. The height difference between him and Lucy would be most apparent when they were vertical rather than horizontal. How would they look, standing side by side? It wouldn't actually be much of a problem for William himself. How often, after all, did you stand side by side with your partner (partner! it was outrageous, he hardly knew the woman) in front of a mirror? But how would it look to other people? How would the lack of symmetry be to someone else with OCD? Would it be like looking at a picture hanging distressingly askew? The intersection of a thought about fellow OCD sufferers with his musings about relationships immediately brought to mind Sheena who had been tall, almost as tall as he, in fact. Had that had an adverse effect upon their relationship? Maybe so, you could never underestimate the importance of seemingly trivial things. On the other hand the failure of his affair with Sheena was surely due to the obvious fact that they had absolutely nothing in common other than a debilitating mental disorder, probably not the best basis for a romance, when you thought about it.

They had begun with such optimism too, after that first evening when they drove back from the shore to William's apartment and he cooked pasta and afterwards Sheena washed the dishes. Twice. And after that they made love, parts fitting together easily, lips comfortably within kissing range, hunching unnecessary. Next morning Sheena simply stayed on, ostensibly just to tidy up a little, but both of them knew she was moving in. And at first it had been a wonderful liberation for them, the fact they both had OCD. They no longer had to pretend. She didn't have to make up lies or excuses for spending half the weekend in the bathroom. William could openly potter around switching electrical devices on or off as the case might be and rattling doors and windows to ensure the locks were correctly engaged without having to explain himself. He could sit and watch TV with Sheena, blinking alternately to his heart's content, not having to worry about her seeing and thinking him crazy, but rather merely considering him as someone with a mental disorder.

For a while William was able to tell himself that although the OCD self-help group weekend had been a disaster for the rest of those involved, it had succeeded for him and Sheena. Of course he was kidding himself. Meeting Sheena hadn't cured him of his OCD, it had merely legitimized it, allowing him to indulge his irrational urges and, if anything, making them worse.

When one member of a couple has OCD, there are almost certain to be problems. When both have it those problems are not only doubled but they often rub up against one another too. There is almost bound to be friction in a relationship that includes an OCD sufferer with a personal hygiene obsession and an abode with only one bathroom. If both people have the same obsession and an extra bathroom isn't factored in, then you're headed for definite trouble. It doesn't matter that you understand and sympathize with your partner for needing to spend two hours washing if you have to take a dump, and an iron control over your bowels which would permit you to delay it until you get to work is no help because your OCD won't let you do it anywhere else but at home. This is a scenario where sympathy and understanding can go out of the window and intolerance of the other person's obsession creep in.

'But I can't stop washing now,' Sheena wailed one morning from behind the bathroom door in answer to his knock. 'I've been in here two hours. If I come out now that will all be wasted, I'll have to start all over again.'

William caught himself thinking that the two hours were

already wasted since it was totally unnecessary for anyone to spend
that much time washing, especially someone who had done it only
yesterday. But he checked himself before the thought got any
bigger. His own compulsions, he reminded himself, would be just
as extraordinary to other people. He said, 'But if I don't get in there
now I'll be late for work. I mean, I'll be even more late than usual.
I was making good time this morning. I've already got everything
checked. If I could have used the john when I finished checking
this would have been the earliest I've ever been late.'

He heard Sheena sigh. He knew it was a theatrical sigh because
he could hear it even above the sound of running water. 'I can't see
how taking your dump at work would hurt once in a while,' she
said. 'Surely their facilities are adequate?'

The bathroom door remained resolutely locked. William left
and spent an uncomfortable day fighting his body's demands. At
times it was all he could think about and he knew it was affecting his
performance. When a colleague said to him, 'You're full of crap today,'
William could only return a tight-lipped smile of agreement.

But the washing and the dumps problem could have been overcome. They could have worked something out, especially as
William's bowels were so regular and predictable. It was a schedul-
ing problem, when all was said and done. They could maybe even
have moved to a two-bathroom apartment, had the will been
there. But, in the end, it wasn't. What drove them apart wasn't that
they had nothing in common, true though that was. William was
interested in current affairs. He was pretty cultured. OK, we know
that theatre wasn't his thing, so much so that he couldn't even
remember if he'd seen *Hamlet*, but he loved classical music, or he
thought he did, although it was possible that really he only liked
collecting classical music CDs to satisfy his hoarding instinct. He
liked to read novels, good novels, too. Sheena, by contrast, liked to
watch daytime TV. She was actually much too intelligent for it, but
she didn't know that. She had it on all day while she tidied and
cleaned the apartment, which of course didn't bother William
because he was at work. William liked to go to the cinema. He

liked foreign movies whereas Sheena couldn't read the subtitles without spectacles but thought they made her look old-maidish and wouldn't wear them in public even in the dark. Sheena was so gorgeous, with her waist-length blonde hair and her don't-know-when-to-quit legs, that William would have been proud to be seen with her anywhere, spectacled-up or not. He considered just having her on his arm as showing off. But Sheena knew her accent and speech marked her as socially inferior to William's colleagues and friends. She knew that on the rare occasions she accompanied William at social gatherings his friends would be saying, 'Yeah, but what would you talk about with her afterwards?'

None of this would have mattered any more than the conflicting demands of their different OCD problems would. What drove them apart was the OCD problem they had in common, not only with one another, but with millions of their fellow OCD sufferers: it was that they both had to do certain things in a particular way.

For instance, the way they made toast for breakfast: William always put the toast on a dinner plate to spread the butter on it. He did this because any crumbs that were brushed off would end up on the plate not on the kitchen counter. He then transferred the buttered toast to another dinner plate and left the butter-smeared knife on the first dinner plate, ready for another slice later if so desired. He left the butter tub, lid off, in readiness for that event. Sheena, on the other hand, placed her toast on a small side plate to butter it. Well, there was never any hope of keeping crumbs off the counter if you did that! But that didn't bother Sheena. She was going to clean the worktop six or seven times anyhow. What did a few crumbs matter? If anything they improved the situation because they gave her a valid excuse for cleaning the counter. At the same time, she too considered it messy to leave a butter-smeared knife on the counter, but her solution was to always have a sinkful of hot soapy water to hand and to wash the knife and place it on the drying rack. If she decided on more toast, she would dry the knife with a dish towel and reuse it. This drove William mad. To him it introduced an unnecessary task into the proceedings. But Sheena couldn't understand his objection. How could washing something smeared in butter ever be unnecessary to a woman who spent half her life washing things – including herself – that were already clean? Another thing Sheena couldn't stand was to see the butter tub left on the worktop with its lid off where it was bound to attract the attentions of germs. She would replace the lid after each use and return the tub to the refrigerator. It was of course a kind of hell for each of them to suffer the other's way of doing things. Sheena couldn't bear to see that slovenly butter-smeared knife, that plate covered in crumbs, the exposed butter in the unlidded, unreturned-to-the-fridge tub. She just had to wash the plate and knife. William couldn't stand seeing toast sitting on an inadequately sized plate, with all the crumb-spilling that inevitably entailed, and would have to swap the small plate for a large one. If you had taken them aside and said, 'Does any of this really matter?' Or 'Are you really concerned enough about crumbs on counters/butter on knives to jeopardize an otherwise promising relationship or is this just because you've always done things this way?' they would probably have answered 'No', 'No' and 'Yes'. But that didn't mean that they could stop themselves.

On one memorable morning, stressed no doubt by the length of time it had taken to get into the bathroom for his dump, William's tolerance of Sheena's – to him – unreasonable way of doing things snapped. He saw her slice of toast overlapping the little plate it rested upon and he just couldn't take it. He grabbed a dinner plate, seized the side plate, tipped the toast onto the larger one and tossed the small one into the bowl of hot soapy water Sheena had waiting. Sheena, whose back had been momentarily turned washing her butter knife, was alerted by the splash of the flying plate (flying saucer William would have called it because in his lexicon its size hardly qualified it for the description of plate) to what he had done. She immediately washed the small plate three or four times, dried it and reversed William's actions.

'Stop it!' he cried. 'Now look what you've done. You've put crumbs all over the counter.'

'So? I'll wash them off.'

'If you didn't get them on there in the first place you wouldn't have to wash them off.' He was momentarily distracted as his own toast popped up. He took it from the toaster, snatched his dinner plate from Sheena's hand, slammed it on the counter and, holding it with one hand so she couldn't remove it, stretched his other hand to the refrigerator, flipped open the door, took out the butter tub that Sheena had recently replaced there, and then proceeded to butter his toast.

The moment he was finished Sheena grabbed the butter tub. William snatched the lid.

'Give me that!' said Sheena.

'No!' said William.

'I can't put it back in the refrigerator until I have the lid.'

'Then don't put it back in the refrigerator.'

'I have to.'

'No you don't.'

'Yes I do.'

'Why?'

She suddenly crumpled, her tall form folding on itself. Tears jewelled her long eyelashes. 'You know why.'

Instantly, William felt sorry for his behaviour. He took her in his arms. He took her in his arms but he was unable to put down the butter lid. As he held her to him, the buttered lid was pressed against the back of her head.

They kissed for a long time. When their lips parted Sheena gave him a wry little smile. 'Where did you put the butter lid?' she said, coyly.

'I don't remember,' William lied.

'You're holding it,' she said, trying to preserve the mood, to sound teasing, but failing to keep the rising note of anxiety out of her voice.

William held up both his hands to show they were empty. The plastic butter lid was stuck to Sheena's gorgeous blonde hair.

William went off to work and Sheena spent a miserable couple of hours hunting for the butter lid. It was only later in the shower, when she discovered it at her feet, that she realized she and William could not survive.

Every relationship is built upon compromise. It's about being able to make room for the other person in your life. If you always have to do things your own way, then it will never work. In the end it's how you put the spiky differences together that matters. It's not enough that when your sexual organs are fully engaged you see eye to eye and meet perfectly lip to lip. It doesn't mean you fit.

The evening she left, William sat in the dark and listened to one of his favourite recordings, Bruno Walter conducting Mahler's Ninth Symphony in Vienna in 1938 on the eve of the *Anschluss*. The only background noise was the hiss of the ancient recording. There was no sound of scrubbing from the bathroom, no Hoover in the hall. The only discordant notes were those of the music as it struggled to find its beginning; the only distraction the coughs from the audience, which, for an instant, stopped William thinking of Sheena, of the golden shawl of her hair over her naked back when he came upon her in the bath – as, of course, he often had – and made him speculate on whether those same coughers he was hearing were soon to perish in a Nazi death camp, and then to the sad thought that it really didn't matter, that after all these years they would have been dead anyhow. In later days he would notice the absence of Sheena in the presence of dust upon his hoarded, unplayed CDs. He would miss her when he noticed one morning as he washed how dirty and untidy his surroundings were because, anally attentive though he was, he didn't care about the state of the bathroom. For now, he recognized his loss as he listened to his record-ing undisturbed and understood how his human contact was diminished, from the presence of a vibrant, beautiful woman to the plaintive coughing of possibly soon-to-be-gassed Austrian music lovers. The Mahler was wonderful. But somehow, he knew he had gotten a raw deal.

TWENTY-THREE

'I is guess you feet is get damn hot in they,' said Tigua, indicating William's hiking boots with a nod.

'Yes,' said William, 'but at least I won't be getting bitten by any snakes.'

Tigua nodded slowly. 'This is be true.' She studied the boots a moment or two. 'They is make they for womans, you is know?'

'Pah!' Lintoa shook her head in disgust. 'What for they is make for womans, huh? What womans is go in jungle?'

'We is go in jungle, in case you is not remember what you is do today,' spat back Tigua. 'We foots is be naked. They shoes is be damn good for keep off green shoestrings. Girl, you is tread on green shoestring in one of they and *you* is go kill *snake* instead of *snake* is kill *you*. And they is look plenty damn fine too.'

'Well, it so happens they *do* make hiking boots for ladies. I believe you can get them in a number of styles and colours.' Even as he spoke William wondered what on earth had possessed him to go along with Lucy's offer to ask what she called her 'girlfriends' to guide him to the old northern village, taking in Pilua's last known dwelling place en route in the hope of finding evidence that she had not been killed in the bomb blast that amputated half of Managua's leg. It should have been obvious that a couple of silly girls would not be the best jungle trekkers and he already doubted Lucy's assurance of their discretion; Tigua was clearly an incorrigible gossip. But then the thought of Lucy caused a small frisson of excitement along his spine, a shiver in spite of the heat. Was that all there was to it, this expedition, sexual attraction? Had he gone along with the idea simply to get into her pants? Or was it like with his dad and Sandy Beach? Was he simply too kind to deprive someone of the pleasure of helping him, even though he doubted that a hike with the two girls *would* help him in any way? Whatever, he couldn't think about it now. His head still hurt from the blow he'd received a couple of days ago. He didn't want to give it any more to do.

He hauled his backpack onto his shoulders. Lintoa picked up the cloth bag she'd brought along to the Captain Cook and slung it across her back, over one shoulder and under the other. She started walking towards the jungle.

'They is make they boots with heels?' said Tigua.

'Well, I don't rightly know,' replied William, struggling to keep up with Lintoa, who was setting a punishing pace given the already ferocious heat of the sun. They were setting off very early, right after the shitting, before the sun grew too intense.

'What for womans is want heels on boots?' Lintoa tossed over her shoulder. 'How they is go walk through jungle with heels? Is just not make sense.'

'You is have point there,' conceded Tigua. 'Is be first damn sense you is talk all morning.'

'I is talk sense, you is just not hear any.' And Lintoa pushed some *adula* fronds aside and plunged into the jungle.

William followed her. It was the first time he had been in a tropical jungle and it wasn't anything like he'd expected, although those expectations were largely based on the Johnny Weismuller–Maureen O'Sullivan Tarzan movies he'd watched on TV as a kid. For one thing he hadn't appreciated how dark it would be. There were three layers of tree canopy roofing the forest and what light penetrated was filtered through the leaves, giving everything a greenish tinge. It made Lintoa look like the Incredible Hulk in a dress. And then William hadn't expected it to be wet.

Steam rose up from the floor below and condensed on the leaves
above and then dripped back down in heavy globules. It had the
atmosphere you find at an overheated indoor swimming pool. But
the thing that hit him most was the noise. First there was a low-
grade humming or buzzing, which wasn't surprising because the
air – wherever a shaft of sunlight caught it and you could see – was
clouded with insects. Neon-winged dragonflies hovered over pools
of water on the forest floor. Luminous butterflies big as your hand
floated unconcerned before his eyes. Closer inspection of any tree
trunk revealed the bark to be covered by a living tapestry of
beetles, their shiny backs iridescent as they constantly rearranged
themselves. Intersecting the bassline of insect sound every few
seconds was the shriek of some bird, at first glimpsed only now and
then as a flash of purple or orange or blue that flew across their
path, until William's eyes grew accustomed to the light and he was
able to make out parrots and parakeets flaunting their gaudy
plumage from the branches of every tree. Maybe pink high heels
wouldn't be so out of place here, after all. Above the cacophony of
bird and insect noise there was the never-ending, high-pitched
chatter of monkeys. At one point there was a sudden howling and
William stopped so abruptly that Tigua ran into his back. It
sounded like someone being tortured.

Lintoa halted and turned back when she realized the others had
stopped. 'Is be all right, *gwanga*, is not be anything for have shit
about. Is just be howler monkey,' and she pointed up into a tree
ahead where a monkey the size of a cat sat staring down at them.
It had an elfin face fringed with white fur. When it saw Lintoa
pointing, it let out another great howl.

'Is be best you is ignore they,' said Lintoa. 'They is catch you
look they is howl plenty more.'

William felt a sharp pricking in his neck and slapped a
mosquito. It was the third time he'd been bitten already.
He followed Lintoa who, in the time he'd been looking at the
monkey, had driven deeper into the bush and was now almost
out of sight, just the red top of her dress showing against the

green. Behind him William could hear Tigua muttering.

'I is just hope they is do they in pink. Miss Lucy is say pink is be my colour.' She was still talking about the boots, chattering away to herself like one of the monkeys.

The trees were close together. Some of the trunks must have been three feet across at the base. Vines snaked between them and palms that grew to waist height covered most of the floor. William was glad to be under cover, out of the flesh-burning glare of the sun, but he hated the damp. The ground beneath his feet felt spongy and it pulled him down. He found his lungs sucking in the moist air, which was too wet to contain much oxygen. He slapped another mosquito as it bit him. Lintoa had stopped to wait for them.

'Hey, *gwanga*,' she said. 'Tell me, is be true Americans is all believe they is come from monkeys, like Miss Lucy is say?'

William considered. 'Well, I don't know about all Americans, but, yes, it's generally accepted that we're descended from apes.'

Lintoa and Tigua, who'd caught them up, exchanged puzzled expressions.

'I mean, that our ancestors were apes.'

The two girls giggled. Lintoa shook her head in a mixture of disbelief and pity. 'White mans is have some plenty damn crazy thoughts,' she said, turning and pushing through the next bunch of palm fronds. 'I is never go in *kassa* house, but I is not hear tell anyone is see any monkey there.'

'Yes,' said Tigua, 'but how they is can? Is be only white mans who is have monkey for grandfather.'

William would have liked to ask them about what he had seen in the *kassa* hut and whether they knew the visions there to be hallucinations or if they believed them to be actual visitations of the dead. But Tigua and Lintoa had already set off again and he was struggling to keep up. He didn't have a lot of breath left over for less than pressing questions about spiritual beliefs.

Every few paces William would slap himself around the face and neck. The mosquito spray he'd covered himself with that morning had proved completely ineffectual. Already he could feel red swellings all over his neck, face and hands. They itched like hell. After an hour he could stand it no more.

'Wait, you – er – you two.' He had been about to say 'guys', the way he would have done to a couple of American girls, but somehow the word seemed a little insensitive given the lack of feminine grace displayed by his guides. 'I'm being eaten alive here.'

They stopped and regarded him as though he were an interesting specimen of some other species. Neither of them had a single bite and he hadn't heard either one of them slap herself.

'You is be plenty popular with they damn mosquitoes,' said Tigua.

Lintoa put her fingers on William's face, running them across what felt like two huge bumps on his cheek. She whistled. '*Gwanga*, I is be sorry for tell you, but tomorrow you face is go be plenty damn sore.'

'You mean more sore than now? Is that possible?'

Lintoa widened her eyes and nodded. 'Is be possible.'

Tigua said, 'I is not understand why they is keep bite you. Is enough for make anyone think you is not have on any pintoa juice.'

'Pintoa juice?' repeated William, stupidly. He found himself getting angry. 'No, I don't have any damn pintoa juice on.'

The other two looked at one another eyes wide with incredulity. Tigua turned back to him. 'You is come in jungle without pintoa juice? You is be crazy, *gwanga*. What you is think is go happen?'

'I've never heard of pintoa juice!' snapped William, his voice rising in volume. 'How the hell was I supposed to know about it?'

Lintoa shrugged. 'Everybody is know about pintoa juice. Even little child, is can hardly damn walk, is know you is must have pintoa juice on in jungle for keep away mosquitoes. Is know soon as is know how for make talk.'

William glared at her. 'Well, where I come from we don't use it.'

'You is not have mosquitoes in America?' asked Tigua.

'Yes, of course we have mosquitoes,' bellowed William. 'We just don't have pintoa!'

William took off his pack and set it on the ground. He removed his hat, took out his handkerchief and mopped the sweat off his face. Tigua and Lintoa went into a little huddle, leaning their heads together and talking in a low murmur not much different from the ambient insect drone. Eventually Tigua broke away and strolled over to him.

'You is want pintoa juice, *gwanga*?'

'Yes, of course I is want pintoa juice! How the hell can I go on without it? I'm being massacred by those bloody things.'

Tigua recoiled and bit her lip. She looked so like a frightened little girl that William instantly regretted his rudeness. 'I'm sorry, my dear,' he said, 'I didn't mean to get cross with you. It's just that these bites are goddam painful.'

'Is be all right,' said Tigua, 'I is understand. Is not really be me you is get cross with. You is be cross with self for forget pintoa.'

William sighed. 'OK, I guess that's it. So you better let me have some.'

Lintoa again looked astonished. 'We is not have. We is just not think anyone is be such big fool for come in jungle without they is put pintoa juice on first.'

William took the insult like a man. He was just too bitten to argue. 'OK, so let's go get some.'

Tigua cleared her throat nervously. 'There is be just one problem, pintoa is not grow this way. We is must turn off path and is make little trip west for find tree.'

William couldn't help noticing that word 'path'. He hadn't been aware of anything resembling one. To him it looked like they'd been wandering at random in the jungle.

'OK, OK, just get me to the stuff and fast.'

Wearily he pulled on his pack. He felt weak and giddy from the heat. His feet were blistered from where he'd stepped in a stream and got his boots wet. They were covered in mud. Thank God I didn't wear the pink ones! he told himself. The thought made him chuckle hysterically.

'You is not get too happy just yet,' said Tigua as they turned back the way they'd come and branched off to the left. 'We is must go through place where ground is be plenty soft, is be much water.'

'Marsh,' said William.

'No, no, we is not march, that is be plenty foolish,' replied Tigua. 'We is must step very careful or is sink in and is drown. Also is be many mosquitoes there. But then you is get through they and find pintoa.'

They walked for another hour on a route that William calculated was at ninety degrees to their original course. They must be going miles out of their way, he thought. But he didn't really care. He had to have that pintoa. On the way to find it William counted that he was bitten forty-seven times. He'd now been targeted so many times that the mosquitoes were finding it hard to find a place where he hadn't been bitten. Fortunately they seemed to avoid anywhere other mosquitoes had gotten to before them. This meant they spent ages crawling across his flesh first, giving William more chance of swatting them so that his strike rate improved considerably. By the time they reached the pintoa trees, he estimated he was only getting bitten four or five times a minute.

The pintoa fruit turned out to be the size and shape of a mango, with the same green skin turning to red, though not smooth, but dimpled like that of a lemon. Lintoa hoisted her skirt up to her thighs – her very hefty thighs, William couldn't help noticing – shinned up a tree and began throwing them down at Tigua. At, not to. She was trying to hit the smaller girl's head and Tigua was ducking and shouting back at her. 'Stop, you sow! I is go get you for this, girl!'

Eventually Lintoa came down and after Tigua had thrown a few pintoas at her and she'd thrown some more back at Tigua they suddenly ran out of ammunition. Then they realized they'd thrown away everything Lintoa had picked and had to crawl around in the undergrowth till they found some of them again. Lintoa produced a knife and sliced one in half. The inside was red as raw meat and appeared juicy and succulent.

'You is not eat,' Lintoa told William. 'Is be plenty poisonous.'

'Poisonous?'

'Of course. Even mosquitoes is know that. Is what for they is not bite you.'

'Is be OK,' said Tigua. 'Is not be so poisonous as orange fungi. Little bit of juice is not kill you.'

'That's a relief,' said William, as Lintoa squeezed it onto her hands and began rubbing it into his face.

'Yes,' said Tigua. 'Drop or two is not matter. You is only get blind headache and sick guts up. You is not die.'

'Owww!' cried William as the juice made contact with the open sores on his face. It was as if he was being anointed with acid.

But eventually the pain subsided and he realized the bites weren't quite so sore as before. 'It appears to have a soothing effect, is that right?' he asked.

'No,' said Tigua. 'Bites is hurt same as before. Is just they is hurt like hell when you is put pintoa juice on. Then juice is stop hurt and you is not notice how much bites is *already* hurt because pain is not be so strong as pain of juice. Then when little while is pass you is forget how much pintoa juice is make bites hurt and bites is hurt just as damn much as before.'

It didn't take William very long to find out this was true.

Before they set off again, Lintoa popped a few pintoa fruit into her bag. 'Just for be on safer side,' she told William.

Instead of heading the way they had come to rejoin their original path, Lintoa suggested they branch off to the north-east, to intersect with it later on. 'Is for cut short,' she explained.

'Have you been this way before?' asked William.

Lintoa shrugged. 'Mebbe. But is not matter. I is find way. I is have good sense in jungle. Better, mebbe, than boy even.'

William let that one go.

The heat now was oppressive. There was no way of knowing because the jungle canopy was too thick, but he had a sense of the sun being almost overhead. He could feel it pressing down on them. He consulted his watch. In spite of their early start it was now almost noon.

His feet hurt like hell, he was drenched in sweat and his lungs were about to burst. Just when he thought things couldn't get any worse, the ground began to rise. Anywhere else it wouldn't have counted as a big hill; under these conditions it was like going up a mountain.

He became aware of a faint hissing noise. At first he was worried it might be snakes but then he realized it was the sound of water. At once the jungle opened out and for the first time in hours there was clear blue sky above them. In front of them was a torrent of rushing water at least twenty metres wide.

Lintoa stood stock-still, obviously dismayed. William could tell something unexpected had happened. Lintoa held up her right hand and stared at it and then did the same with her left. 'Oh, shit!' she muttered to herself. 'Is this be my right or my left?'

Tigua pushed her face up into the bigger girl's. 'What we is do now, you stupid sow? Is be river.'

'Thank you very much for you information but I is already know that.'

Tigua threw herself down on the river bank. 'Pah! You is know that now. Plenty big deal! We is all know that now. We is all see river. We is not need any jungle expert for tell we that.' She imitated Lintoa's deeper voice, 'I is know jungle better than boy even.'

Lintoa aimed a kick at her, which Tigua just managed to scuffle out of the way of. 'Shut up, sow! I is try for think.'

'What's the problem?' asked William.

'Problem is one plenty big river in front of we,' barked Lintoa, waving a hand at it. 'Is you not can see?'

'Yes, of course. I um meant, what is the problem with the river?'

Lintoa sighed with exasperation. 'Problem is we is be this side of river and we is want for be that side.' She pointed to the opposite bank as though William still might not have got the idea. William saw that there was a sheer cliff-face of some five metres' height down to the water there, with no obvious way up. Apart from this small open patch of river bank, the jungle grew close all along the side they were on making it impossible to walk alongside the river until the opposite bank became lower and more easily assailable.

William sat down, took off his hat and fanned himself with it. Tigua and Lintoa went into a huddle. They appeared to be talking feverishly, and he left the problem to them while he dipped his hat into the rushing water and then emptied the contents over his head. When he looked up he noticed that the two girls were stealing furtive glances at him. He had the idea they were discussing him, rather than their predicament, and were laughing at him. When they saw him watching them, their demeanour immediately grew more serious.

Tigua stood up and strode over to him in a businesslike way. 'Is only one thing for do,' she said, a regretful tone creeping into her voice. 'We is must walk in river until other side is be low enough for we is climb out. Is be necessary for put pack on head.'

William stood up, put on his hat and placed his rucksack on top of that.

Tigua pointed to his boots. 'Is be shame for ruin they.'

William put the pack down again, took off the boots, strung the laces together and hung them round his neck. He put the pack on his head again. Lintoa strode over with her bag balanced effortlessly on top of her square head. She walked easily as though not even aware of it. William found it impossible to keep his load on unless he held it in place with both hands.

They slipped into the fast-flowing water. It was surprisingly cool, given the temperature in the jungle. The bottom was soft and slippery and although the water was only thigh-high, it was hard to make way upstream against its flow. It was murky brown so you couldn't see anything in it. William felt something brush his trouser leg. It might have been a fish or a stick or . . . what? A sudden thought struck him. 'You get any crocodiles around here?'

'Crocodiles? What they is be?' asked Lintoa.

Tigua spoke quickly to her, something William couldn't catch. Lintoa turned and shot William a condescending look. 'You is think I is be in here with something like that? You is must think I is be one crazy girl! Is be no crocodiles here on this island. Snakes, yes. We is have plenty damn snakes.'

'Is be black rope snake,' said Tigua, 'brown *tirobe*, speckle *tirobe*, yellow *tirobe*, yellow speckle *tirobe*, speckle yellow *tirobe*, bush adder, grass adder, tree adder, guinea snake, red *mabuas*, white *mabuas*—'

'Gold *mabuas*,' interjected Lintoa, 'you is must not forget they. Is be one wicked snake.'

'Gold *mabuas*,' repeated Tigua, 'rock snake, river bottom snake . . . you is be lucky, though, no green shoestring, they is not like water, they is not can swim, so is not go in river.'

'Unless one is fall in by accident,' said Lintoa. 'Then he is be plenty damn mad. Most probably he is bite you just because he is be so mad at self for fall in.'

'Like you is be mad at self for forget pintoa. Or if he is not be mad, mebbe he is bite you just for have something for hold on. He is bite you leg for stop water sweep he away.'

'But you is must not worry,' said Lintoa, smiling. 'You is not know anything 'bout that. By time you is feel bite you is already be dead. If green shoestring is get he teeth in you is not matter if he is try for kill you or save he self, we is not see you again till *kassa* house.'

'Except we is not be allow in *kassa* house,' Tigua pointed out.

Lintoa gave William a reassuring stare. 'I is be in *kassa* hut, one day,' she assured him. 'If green shoestring is bite you today, I is see you there one day.'

It must have been an hour later, an hour during which William felt a thousand things flickering around his toes or brushing against his legs and went through a thousand agonized imaginings, that the bank on the other side dipped and they were able to clamber up it. During all this time William had been doing plenty of alternate hand squeezing of his rucksack straps. Now his arms were heavy as lead from holding them above his head so long.

But then his arms were no different from the rest of him. Every bit of him ached. His toes from being bent double as he tried to grip the slippery river bottom, his head from the fierce heat and the weight of the backpack, his calf muscles from struggling against the stream. It was nearly mid-afternoon before the jungle began to thin and later still when eventually the trees stopped altogether. Before them rose the lower slopes of the volcano, its sides strangely devoid of jungle. Immediately in front of them the ground was bare and blackened. For as far as the eye could see, nothing grew. Lintoa put out a hand to restrain him from stepping forward. 'No, *gwanga*. Not unless you is want for hop home on one leg.' She spoke in a whisper as though afraid of evoking the wrath of something powerful and unseen.

'What is this place?' asked William, although even as he spoke, he knew. There was no noise. No insects humming. No parrots shrieking. No monkeys howling. There was nothing living here. A wasteland.

'Is be evil place,' said Lintoa. 'Is be where Americans is come. First they is plant bombs so no-one is can come here. Then helicopters is fly in. Is make white mist on everything. Everything is die. All trees, all plants, all snakes—'

'Black *tirobes*, green *tirobes*, brown river bottom sn—' began Tigua.

Lintoa cut short the other girl's serpent litany. 'All snakes, all monkeys. Even mosquitoes is not can live here. Go ahead, *gwanga*, see what you countrymen is do. Is be very good, you is can walk here without mosquitoes is bite you. You is not need for have any fear of green shoestring.'

'If you is want for blow youself up,' added Tigua.

'And the village,' said William. 'The northern village? Where is that? Can you take me there?'

'We is already do,' said Lintoa. 'This is be northern village. This is be what you Americans is leave behind.'

TWENTY-FOUR

'And you is see he face when we is come out of jungle and is see river and Lintoa is look at she hand and is say, "Oh shit, this is be my right or my left?" I is think *gwanga* is go kill she.'

Tigua took another swig of his beer. Before he had chance to swallow, the beer sprayed back out as he guffawed at the thought of something else. 'We is walk for hours for find pintoa tree and *gwanga* is not know he is walk right past they all time.'

'*Gwanga* is not look up in forest. He is keep eyes on ground for look for green shoestring,' said Lintoa. He bent to Miss Lucy's fridge to get himself another beer, raising an eyebrow to her for permission which she granted by the slightest inclination of her head.

Tigua slapped his knee. 'And then you is say he, "Is best not see green shoestring, *gwanga*, then you is not have time for feel fear before he is bite you. You is just feel bite and you is be dead. Is be much more easy."'

'Oh dear,' said Lucy.

'You is think that is be oh dear, you is must see he when he is get back Captain Cook,' said Tigua. 'He clothes is all be torn and is be so wet with river and sweat is be like when he is walk in sea; he feet is be so sore he is limp like Managua here and he is be cover all over with mosquito bites.'

'Plenty big mosquito bites,' agreed Lintoa, with some satisfaction.

'*Gwanga*'s skin is be all red but I is not know if is be from burn by sun or from mosquito bites,' said Tigua.

'Is be bites,' said Lintoa. 'Face is be just about all bites. Skin is be more bite than not bite.'

'Oh dear,' said Lucy again.

'You is keep say that,' said Tigua. 'So what for you is want we is lead *gwanga* on wild pig chase in first place?'

'Never you mind,' said Lucy. She picked up a loaded plastic carrier bag and handed it to him. 'Here's the rest of the beer I promised you. Now run along.'

She stood in the doorway and watched them as they walked off along the beach, swigging beer and giggling as they went. She turned to the old man. 'I feel a bit bad about setting him up for this now.'

'Is not thing for you is feel bad 'bout,' said Managua. 'Is be my plan. I is be one is think of idea.' His chest seemed to inflate as he said it. 'With little bit of help from Shakespeare.'

'Yes, but I didn't realize quite how he was going to end up,' said Lucy.

Managua turned to her. 'What you is think is go happen? He must get bitten, he is must get wet, he is must have blister and is must tire heself out for put he off search. Now perhaps he is stop look and is go back America.'

'Maybe,' said Lucy. 'I just hope you're right and that we haven't put the poor man through all this for nothing.'

Lucy found William lying on the mahogany table. As the sound of her footsteps echoed in the cavernous dining room of the Captain Cook he shot upright, like a corpse in a horror film, she couldn't help thinking. Mind you, she told herself, didn't he have every reason to be scared? He'd already been attacked here in the hotel. Lucy couldn't imagine who was responsible because the natives were not aggressive by nature. Even though so many of them had been damaged by American landmines their innate friendliness and their tradition of hospitality would prevent them translating any resentment into violence against an individual. She couldn't help worrying that the American might be attacked again. There was something in him that made her feel protective. Even though she wished he had never come, she found she didn't want him to go. She wondered why he refused to entertain the idea of moving from the Captain Cook. It was as if something kept him anchored to this dismal place.

'It's only me.' She said it in a whisper, afraid anything louder might intensify his pain. He let out only a whimper in reply.

She walked over to him and pulled the cool bag off her shoulder. She took out two cans of beer. She pulled the tab on one and handed it to him. Instead of drinking it he put the can against his forehead and rolled it from side to side. He held it against first one cheek and then the other. Finally he took a sip.

'I have a sense of déjà vu,' he said. 'You always seem to be ministering to me when I'm injured . . .'

'Well, you do seem to get into rather a lot of scrapes,' she said.

'How did you know I would need this?'

'There was a rumour going round that you missed shitting this morning. I checked with Tigua and Lintoa and they told me your expedition yesterday wasn't too successful.'

'That's the understatement of the century. Not only did you supply me with a guide who doesn't know right from left so that we never found Pilua's old home, your two girlfriends nearly killed me.'

'I'm sorry. I feel very bad about it.' How bad he would never know. 'Your face looks sore. Are you bitten anywhere else?'

'My chest and back and arms. Pretty much anywhere I have skin. The little bastards took a real shine to me.'

She took a bundle of paper from the cool bag and flung it onto the table. 'I thought if you were bed-bound –' she stopped and smiled, '*table*-bound – you might like something to read.'

'I'm not sure I'll ever be able to read again. The darn things got my eyelids. It's less painful just to keep my eyes shut.' As he said it William thought that at least he might thereby be cured of one of his OCD habits.

'It doesn't matter. It's just the draft manuscript of the book I'm working on. It might help you understand the people a bit better.' As she said it Lucy wondered if giving him her book might be assisting him in what he'd come to do. She was only too aware of how large corporations and governments misused ethnographic research. Still, it was done now. 'I've brought some lotion for the bites.' She took a plastic bottle from the cool bag and began to unbutton his shirt. As she removed it he cried out again. His whole body was a mass of red bumps, some of which he'd lacerated with his fingernails. She applied the cream to her fingers and anointed first his face and then his torso. Neither of them spoke. The touch of someone else's skin beneath her fingertips made Lucy feel it was she who was having some kind of balm applied to her. She had needed it for a long time. William was trying to fight back the soft moans he could not help releasing from time to time as the cream cooled his burning skin. He imagined he sounded like a pathetic little dog, some silly toy breed, a miniature poodle or a chihuahua, perhaps.

'I'm so sorry,' she murmured each time he made a sound.

'It's OK, it's actually the relief that's causing me to cry out. You're making it so much better.' There was more than that, he knew. A slight pressure in his loins told him that.

'Have you a clean shirt?' she asked when she'd covered all of his torso with the cream.

'Over there.' He pointed to a white cotton shirt hanging from a nail in the wall, probably put there to hang a picture, she found herself thinking irrelevantly. She fetched it and, facing him, reached it round behind him and held it out for him while he inserted his arms. Their faces were very close. They looked into one another's eyes. Lucy bent towards him and kissed the biggest boil, which was on the end of his nose. His eyes widened as if he'd been caught off guard, though it was she who would have been surprised to discover how often William had not been the first to act in his sexual liaisons. Women always wanted to comfort him, to take away the fear they saw behind his eyes, to still the nervous juggling eyelids that many of

them noticed. But this time, for the first time, he was taken aback.
He hadn't expected anything from this fierce little woman.

'Ouch!' he said. He meant it; the kiss had hurt.

'Sorry,' she said. She stared at him as though wondering what to
do next. Neither of them smiled. Then she inclined her head again
and kissed him on the cheek. This time she didn't aim for a
mosquito bite but then she didn't have to. His cheeks were so
thoroughly covered in them that pretty much anywhere would
score a direct hit.

'Ouch!' he said, flinching.

'Sorry.' It came out soft and hesitant, the voice reluctant to be
drawn into vocalizing what was happening.

'Ouch!'

'Sorry.'

'Ouch!'

'Sorry.'

'Ouch!'

'Sorry. So sorry.'

'Ouch! Ah . . .'

'Sorry.'

'Ouch!'

'What, even there?'

'Even there. Owwwch!'

'Sorry. Ummm . . .'

'Ouch! Let me—'

'It's OK, I can manage. Oh, sorry.'

'Ow . . . ch.'

'Shh. Sorry. Mmmm.'

'Ow – ahhh.'

'Sorry.' She lifted herself off him and flopped down beside him.
'I really am so sorry.'

'Don't be silly.' He turned to look at her and smiled his vulnerable little smile.

Be careful, she told him mentally, don't get me started again, it's
too much like torture.

'I couldn't help crying out,' he whispered. 'Don't let it make you think I didn't love every moment of it.' He kissed her gently on the cheek.

'No, I mean I'm sorry I let you in for this.' She indicated the massive red sore that was his body. She couldn't tell him just how sorry she was because she couldn't let him know how he had been tricked.

'That's OK, you were only trying to help.' She winced as though someone had just touched a mosquito bite on *her* body and said nothing. 'And I think I can pay you back.'

I hope not, Lucy thought. Not the way I deserve to be paid back. She was asking herself why she had just made love to a man she hardly knew. It wasn't simply her loneliness. It was also a matter of compensation to the American for what she had done to him. She couldn't say anything to enlighten him. Instead she asked, 'Oh, how's that?'

He smiled that little smile of his, less vulnerable this time though, a little bit pleased with itself. 'I've thought of a way to get you into the *kassa* house.'

TWENTY-FIVE

At the time when Lucy liquidated her mother – we're talking the late Seventies here – one-parent families were not yet the norm. Divorce was still rare in a rural backwater like the Fens and it was even more rare for a child to have a parent die. So it was no surprise that Lucy's murder of her mother earned her special consideration. Christine Bexley never punished her again and on one occasion carried this unprecedented kindness even further and gave her a ginger biscuit; she must have spread the word too, because other prefects were just as lenient with her. Lucy's classmates noticed this and often remarked that it wasn't fair, that she could get away with murder. They didn't know she already had.

When she realized word had got through to the teachers too, Lucy felt things had got out of hand. She would have liked to resurrect her mother but of course that was impossible. She took what precautions she could against detection. She took care never to be seen with her mother in Ely, insisting, to her mother's complete bafflement, that her father take her to buy new items of school uniform and other like necessities. She intercepted and destroyed all invitations to school events. Her mother never questioned their absence. Although people coming to the house was her chief phobia, she wasn't too keen on mixing with them anywhere else unless it was to shove them aside to reach a bargain.

All fiction relies on the suspension of disbelief, but why

wouldn't people believe Lucy was a demi-orphan? Who would suspect an eleven-year-old of making up such a thing?

By coincidence – that word that is synonymous with magic to an OCD sufferer – a major event in Lucy's childhood, one that brought her to the brink of exposure, was the result – like William's nickname – of chess. Lucy had been playing for the school team. This was when she was fifteen and had been an un-detected murderess for four years. There had been a match against a side from another school. Lucy had won all three of her games and was in a good mood as she stood alone at a bus stop waiting for the last bus that evening back to her village. Naturally she couldn't have asked her father to pick her up in case someone from school happened to pass and mention mothers or motherless children and how they had a hard time. So, she had to wait for the bus. Lucy's good mood, her winning mood, didn't last long because before the bus arrived an old VW Beetle pulled up. It was Mr Richardson, her history teacher. He leaned over and opened the passenger door.

'Want a lift?' In those days it was still OK for male teachers to be alone in their cars with fifteen-year-old female students. People hadn't yet managed to work out why it wasn't.

'It's OK, the bus will be along in a minute.' She didn't want to be alone with Richardson. The combination of his balding head, his round glasses and the beady eyes behind them reminded her of someone unpleasant but she couldn't think who it was.

'Don't be daft. It's late, it's cold and I have to go through your village. Come on, hop in, I'll take you right to your door.'

That was the last thing Lucy wanted to hear but she could think of no excuse. Reluctantly, she got into the car.

On the way home Mr Richardson attempted to engage Lucy in conversation. He asked her about her family. He didn't mention her mother directly but Lucy deduced he knew she was dead because when she told him about her older sisters he said, 'I expect they look after you.'

Lucy replied that on the contrary they had both left school now and were too busy going out to bother about her. Mr Richardson felt able to take his eyes off the long straight ribbon of road stretching in front through the bleak sugar beet fields to shoot her a sympathetic glance. He had sufficient confidence in his driving to take his left hand off the steering wheel and pat her on the knee. His hand rested there perhaps a second or so too long to give any likelihood to the idea that he might just be being friendly.

They pulled up outside her house. As Mr Richardson switched off the ignition Lucy was able to discern the merest flicker of the front-room curtains and knew her mother had observed them.

'Well,' said Mr Richardson. 'Here we are, then.'

'Yes. Thank you, Sir.' Lucy fiddled with the door handle but was in such a hurry to get out of the car that she couldn't get the hang of it.

'Here, let me,' said Mr Richardson. He reached across and she could smell stale tobacco on his breath as he took hold of the handle. But he didn't open the door. Lucy was pinned to her seat. 'Well,' said Mr Richardson again. Even in Lucy's limited experience it seemed to be the word with which men always chose to begin awkward sentences. 'Well, aren't you going to invite me in? It's normal manners you know. Teacher gives you a lift home, you ask him in for a cup of tea and to meet your parents. Uh parent, I mean.'

'My father won't be in. It's his darts night.'

Mr Richardson released the catch on her door. As she scrambled out he opened his own door and got out of the car too. 'That's OK,' he said. 'You know how to make a cup of tea, don't you?'

It was with some trepidation that Lucy opened the back door (they never used the front one) and Mr Richardson followed her into the kitchen.

'Won't you sit down?' she said. She knew that was what you were supposed to say from films on the TV. He sat down at one end of the kitchen table. Lucy glanced at him and remembered who he reminded her of. She'd seen pictures of Reginald Christie in a series about notorious killers in the *News of the World* a few weeks earlier. Mr Richardson bore a striking resemblance to the necrophiliac mass murderer.

As she stood at the sink to fill the kettle, with her back to him, she felt his eyes upon her. She tugged her skirt hem, trying to pull it lower. She wished she hadn't bamboozled her father into buying her one so short. This was the downside of not shopping with your mother. Nobody else's mums let them get away with anything so brief. At the same time as Lucy cursed her skirt for being so short, she was grateful that the tablecloth was so long, for she knew that her mother would be crouching under the table beneath it.

Lucy wasn't too alarmed at being alone with the spitting image of a serial killer. She knew that if Mr Richardson made a move on her, her mother would come to her rescue. The trouble was, if that happened, it would be she, Lucy, who would be revealed as the murderer. The game would be up. There would be hell to pay at school and her mother would discover that her daughter had simply removed her from existence. What would her mum think of that?

Lucy took the tea things to the table, poured tea for them both, gave the teacher his and took hers to the other end of the table and sat down facing him. 'Goodness, you're awfully far away,' he said. 'It's like Henry VIII and one of his wives at opposite ends of the banqueting table. Why don't I move a little closer?'

He picked up his cup and saucer and sat at the longer side of the table, but right in the corner next to her end. His knee pressed against Lucy's under the table; only the long tablecloth between them prevented actual contact. She would have liked to move her knee away but she was jammed in by the legs of the table and by her mother who had crawled to this end to be as far away as possible from Mr Richardson before he moved.

'I'd be careful if I were you,' Lucy said.

A look of surprise and embarrassment appeared on his face. Maybe if she just confronted him he'd go away and no harm done.

'Prince,' she said. It was the first name that came into her head. It must have been him talking about Henry VIII that had done it. He looked baffled.

'Our dog. He's under the table.'

Mr Richardson went to lift the tablecloth to have a look, but this wasn't easy as it hung almost to the floor. 'I wouldn't disturb him if I were you, he doesn't like strangers.'

'Oh.'

'Yes, he's rather old and crotchety, I'm afraid. He's lovely with children. And women too. But he doesn't like men. Especially strange men.'

The way she said 'strange' would have alerted most people to what she meant by it. But not Mr Richardson. He dropped the tablecloth. 'Oh well, best let sleeping dogs lie, then.'

'He's not asleep.' Lucy gave her Mum a poke with her toe. A baritone growl issued from beneath the table. Lucy was impressed; she hadn't known her mother could growl like that.

They chatted for a few minutes then Mr Richardson said, 'I expect you go out with lots of boys, don't you?'

'Not really,' said Lucy. 'One or two.'

'I bet they try to do things to you, don't they?'

'I don't think that's the kind of question you should be asking me,' said Lucy boldly. She couldn't believe her own nerve.

'It's part of a teacher's job to know things about his pupils. How else can I protect a young girl like you, a *sexy* young girl like you, from being preyed upon by the dirty-minded scum I see around the streets?'

Lucy didn't say anything. She tried to appear calm. She attempted to pour herself some more tea but her hand was shaking so much the spout of the pot rattled against her cup. This was the moment Richardson made his lunge. He reached out and grabbed her right breast. 'I expect they put their hands here, don't they? Well, don't they? I bet you let them, don't you? I bet you love it.'

She rose from her seat to get away but he grabbed her wrist and pulled her towards him. He thrust his hand up her skirt. She clamped her legs together. 'I bet they put their hands up here. I bet they touch your – your—'

There was a loud growl from under the table.

'Mr Richardson, please!' pleaded Lucy, twisting away from him, but not far because he still had her wrist. 'The dog—'

'Oh bugger the dog!' he cried and started to get up himself, but just as he was on his feet he stopped dead. His eyes went wide in surprise. 'Oh, God,' he gasped. 'Oh, sweet Jesus fucking Christ!' He let go of her.

'Mr Richardson, what is it?' said Lucy, at the same time pulling her clothes straight. 'What happened?'

'It bit me! The fucking brute bit me!'

He bent and lifted his right trouser turn-up. Both of them gasped. Blood was flowing from what were undeniably teeth marks. 'Look!' panted Richardson. 'Look what that damn animal has done to me! I'm telling you—'

But before he could say what he was telling her he was interrupted by a long, low growl from beneath the table. He didn't stay to say any more.

As Richardson limped out clutching his bleeding ankle he flung dire imprecations at her about how he was going to the police and would make sure the dog was put down, but Lucy never heard another word about it. At school he greeted her coldly but never again referred to the incident. He went out of his way to avoid her and always gave her strictly accurate grades. Lucy assumed that he must have decided that complaining about the dog would involve the question of why the dog had bitten him. She didn't know that at the emergency department of the RAF Hospital in Ely where he went for a tetanus jab the doctor had assured him the bite mark on his ankle was not of canine origin, but, most definitely, human.

TWENTY-SIX

'*Gwanga! Gwanga!*'

William was just leaving the shitting beach. He turned and saw the man Purnu running after him, lifting his feet high and weaving from side to side as he tried to run and not step in shit at the same time.

'You is make good shit?' asked Purnu when he reached him and stood getting his breath back.

'Yes, thank you,' said William. They both looked back to where the usual crowd had gathered round to inspect William's morning evacuation.

'You is not bury any more?' said Purnu. He looked genuinely interested.

'No,' said William. 'When In Rome.'

'Please, what is mean? What is be Rome?'

'Oh, it doesn't matter. It's too complicated to explain,' said William, turning and moving off, leaving Purnu rubbing his chin, looking puzzled.

'*Gwanga! Gwanga!*' William stopped and sighed. The man was a nuisance. Then again, he was a powerful witch doctor according to Tigua. William put no store in that kind of hokum but he assumed Purnu's reputation for magic commanded a lot of influence among the tribe and he didn't want to cross him.

Purnu caught him up and walked along with him. 'Everyone is

still look at you shit,' he confided. 'They is still want for know what you is want for hide.'

'Only my embarrassment,' said William.

Purnu nodded wisely. 'I is understand. You is not worry. Shit is be shit. We is be friends, no?'

William looked at him keenly. He wondered what went on under that low forehead, behind those beady eyes. He strode on, hoping to lose the little man. Purnu trotted along beside him like an eager terrier though, evidently not wanting to be lost.

'*Gwanga*, I is make you deal.'

William stopped. Deal was a strange word for a man who didn't know what money was, but then again, the islanders did have a kind of currency, yams, so it followed they must have deals.

'You is not have yams. Is be difficult for live on island if you is not have yams. I is give you yams.'

William nodded. 'Well, that could be useful. What do you want?'

'Want?' said Purnu, innocently.

'You mentioned a deal. What do you want for your end of it?'

'Ah, is be nothing.' A coy giggle dribbled from his thin lips. He began drawing idly in the sand with his right big toe, following its doodling, not looking at William. 'Is be foolish thing, is just be silly wish of Purnu.'

'Well, I can't help you if you won't tell me what it is.'

'I is want for you is teach me read,' the little man blurted out. 'You is teach me read, I is give you one basket yams.'

'I'm kind of busy. Why don't you ask Miss Lucy?'

'Miss Lucy is be like this with Managua.' Purnu held up his two hands, the fingers tightly interlocked together. He cast his eyes down. 'I is not want Managua is know. Is be OK?'

William considered. He actually had plenty of slack between interviews with the amputees and writing them up. He was spacing them out; there was only so much misery you could take at a time. It wouldn't do any harm. And it would bring Purnu, the man of influence, onside. Besides, he'd be helping a primitive man towards the delights of civilization.

'Tell you what, I'll make you a different deal. Forget the yams for now. Everyone keeps giving me food. There's nothing else I need, nothing you can get on the island, anyhow.'

'What you is want then?'

'Well, here it is. I'll give you a few lessons, see how we get on. In return, you tell me what you know about Pilua.'

Purnu's eagerness was deflated. 'If I is tell you 'bout Pilua and Managua is find out is be plenty big trouble. I is not dare for take risk.'

'I won't mention a word about it, I promise.' To emphasize this, William laid a hand across his heart. He didn't know that on the island the gesture meant 'I am sorry for your bereavement'. Purnu stared at him, puzzled for a moment, then obviously decided it was another *gwanga* eccentricity.

'I is not be sure.'

'Well, you're trusting me not to tell him about the reading. Why not trust me not to tell him about this?'

'All right, I is agree.' He looked around furtively. 'We is go inside Captain Cook. Is be more private for talk there.'

William sat in one of the mahogany chairs. Purnu spurned the other and squatted at his feet.

'Pilua,' he began, 'is be Managua first wife.'

'I know that. What I don't know is what happened to her.'

Purnu thought carefully before replying. He cleared his throat like someone about to tell a story. 'Many year past, when American soldiers is be here, they is be order by chief soldier for keep they-selves in other end of island. They is be order not mix with island people.'

'No fraternization,' said William.

'I is not know 'bout that, *gwanga*. You is just listen, OK?'

'Sorry.'

'Time is come when Americans is go leave. They work here is be done. They is plant plenty bombs. They is strip all leaves from trees. They is destroy northern settlement. They is decide is be enough. Now, mebbe a week before they is go, this woman Pilua, well is be girl really, mebbe sixteen year, seventeen year, is go water hole alone. Is nobody else is be near.' He paused, looked down into his lap and shook his head from side to side.

'And then?'

'Is be three American. Is all drink plenty beer. They is not even suppose for be in this part of island. They is take Pilua and . . . and . . .'

'And?'

Purnu looked up at him. There were tears in his eyes. 'They is force she make *fug-a-fug*. They is hurt she and force she.' He put his right hand over his eyes and wiped off a tear. William was surprised to see this man, of all the islanders, crying.

The sorcerer let his hand drop and stared at William angrily. 'What for they is make girl do this? This is be how you is do in America? Mans is not be able for have *fug-a-fug* without they is force someone?'

'No, it's not something any man anywhere should do,' said William. He waited a moment while the little man composed himself. 'Tell me one thing, because I need to know, for the compensation. The US military will have clever lawyers, that is men like me, who will try to argue that girls here make *fug-a-fug* freely with lots of partners. Is there any way in which this thing could have happened with Pilua's agreement?'

Purnu stood up and practically spat at him. 'This is be terrible thing you is say! This is be big insult for everybody on island.'

'Calm down, calm down. I'm just telling you what they will say. That she was willing. It will be the word of three men against one girl. Why should anyone believe her?'

For a moment William thought Purnu was either going to hit him, which would have been ridiculous as the man was half his size, or turn him into an insect and step upon him – something which Tigua had told him the sorcerer was capable of – which was only slightly less ludicrous.

'Is be plenty good reasons. First is be taboo against couple make *fug-a-fug* in presence of other people. And is be taboo against make *fug-a-fug* with more than one person at same time. But most of all is be plenty strict taboo say you is not make *fug-a-fug* with foreigner. Is not be possible any island girl is do what these lawyer mans is say.'

'OK,' said William. 'I hear you. I'm sorry I upset you.'

Purnu bristled pulling himself up proudly. 'Upset? I is not be upset. What else you is want for know?'

'Well, what happened to Pilua?'

'She is come tell story in village. Some people is be kind, is look after she. But then other people is say she is be unclean because she is break taboo—'

'But it wasn't her fault. She didn't break it.'

'Is be true. But taboo is still be break and she is be one who is be make unclean. So they is cast she out from village. She is go little way along coast. Is live alone.'

'And then what? Was she never allowed back in?'

'Next thing is be someone is meet she on beach and is see she stomach is grow. She is go have baby. Is be very bad for woman is have baby when she is not have husband.'

'Yes, a fatherless child, bad scene in any society,' muttered William. He didn't know that in island society all children were fatherless, biologically speaking, although they acquired fathers through their mother's marriage.

'Now is be more bad news for Pilua. Is break taboo for have baby without husband. But she is not can have husband because no man is marry woman who is be outcast.'

'Except Managua.'

'Except Managua. He is step up and offer for marry girl. Is be big surprise because Managua is be most strict on all island for observe customs and taboos. No-one is be able for believe he is do this. But you is know what I is think? Managua is not be so big inside as he is look outside. He is have weakness of kidneys. Well, everyone is try for stop he but he is take no notice. He is take girl and is move up north of island.'

William didn't understand the reference to kidneys. He didn't know the islanders believed those organs to be the repository of the emotions, as we the heart. But he got the idea. 'We is have no nobles here,' he murmured. 'He got that wrong.'

'Nobody is see they for mebbe a year. Next thing two boys is hunt pig, is wander north. Is meet Managua and Pilua and she baby. Is greet he and is pass few words but Managua is act very strange with they. Is tell they for go. Is not allow they is look at baby. So they is carry on they hunt. Short time later they is hear big bang. Boom!'

'A landmine?'

'Yes, American bomb. They is hurry after noise. Is find Managua. He is have half leg missing. He is say Pilua is be beside he with baby. They is both be kill.' He shrugged.

'You doubt what Managua said?'

'I is not say anything 'bout that. But is be strange. There is be nothing left of Pilua or she baby. You see, *gwanga*, landmine is not usually kill. There is be no pleasure in that for you Americans. No, mine is blow foot off mostly, sometimes leg. When people is be kill is be like my wife, because they is bleed dead before help is come. Kill by boom is be plenty rare. Even then is be pieces of body all over place. They is not find even one fingernail of Pilua or she baby.'

They sat in silence for a few minutes, each thinking his own thoughts. It was Purnu who finally broke it. 'Now,' he said, his voice a little husky, 'we is start read.'

They sat side by side on mahogany chairs at the dining table. William took paper and pencil from his briefcase and wrote something. He shoved it across to Purnu.

'This is "a",' he said, pronouncing the sound of the letter not its name.

'A,' said Purnu. 'Yes, of course.' He paused. 'What is be "a"?'

'It's a letter,' said William. 'Well, actually the letter is pronounced "ay", as in "day", but the sound it makes is "a".'

'Yes, yes, I is see is be letter,' said Purnu impatiently. 'Any fool is can see that. But what is "a" mean?'

'It's a sound. You put it with the sounds of other letters to make words.'

Purnu let out a frustrated sigh. 'Yes, this is be all plenty good, but I is ask what is "a" mean? Is be animal? Is be plant? Is be kind of fish?'

'No, it's a sound.'

'Is not mean anything?'

It was William's turn to sigh now. 'Well yes, it means "one".'

'If is mean "one", what for you is not just say "one"? What for is complicate with this "a"?' Purnu shoved the paper at William. 'Who is need this "a"?'

'It means one, but it's not quite the same as saying one. You might say, "I see a dog." '

'*You* is might say, *gwanga*, I is not. We is not have dogs on island. How I is go see dog?'

'OK, OK, pig then. "I see a pig." '

Purnu pushed back his chair and leaped to his feet. 'You is see pig? Where you is see pig? You is see pig this day? If you is see pig just now we is not have time for sit here and read. We is must move plenty damn quick, is start dig bamboo pit. Is get clubs.'

'No, no, I didn't see a pig,' said William.

'You is not see pig?'

'No, for Christ's sake, I didn't see a pig.'

Purnu pulled his chair back to the table and lowered himself onto it, all the while staring suspiciously at William. It was the same sort of look he'd awarded William's shit that first morning. 'Then what for you is say you is see pig if you is not?'

'It was an example. I just made it up to show you what "a" means.'

'Ah!' Purnu leaned back in the chair. He put his hands on the arm rests, fondling their smoothness. 'I is see now. You is please carry on.'

'Well, that's how you use "a". "I see a hut." '

'Ah! I know you is not lie this time. You is see hut. I is see you in hut so you is must see hut.'

' "I see a hut." That's when you use "a" to mean one,' William announced triumphantly, but then he saw Purnu shaking his head.

'You is say, "I is see a hut," but I is say, "I is see hut." What for you is need that old "a" for? I is see hut. I is see pig. Is not be necessary. You is teach me something I is not need. What for is want waste breath with this extra word? Go straight for pig. Or hut.'

'Look,' said William, 'I'm not sure this is getting us anywhere. Let's move on to "b". Just remember that this letter here makes the sound "a". You'll be needing it in other words.'

'Well, I is hope so. I is sure not need in front of pigs or huts. I is not go put "a" there; is just be in damn way.'

TWENTY-SEVEN

William spent the night in a state of high anxiety. He thought he heard the tapping noise again. Perhaps it was just the animal the natives referred to as the *koku-koku* which as far as he could make out was something like a mongoose, some kind of rodent thing that was good at killing snakes. Or maybe it was the sound of rats. He'd never heard of a place yet that didn't have rats. He realized that was what Purnu's face reminded him of, a rodent. All of William's old OCD habits were to the fore now, tooth grinding, blinking, removing objects from his peripheral vision. He'd even tried to move the mahogany table because it was not strictly parallel with the walls but it was too heavy. Of course he was frightened to be in the hotel after the blow he'd received and every one of the myriad sounds he heard in the jungle made him jump. But the fear of attack wasn't all of it. William had been deeply disturbed by the vision of his father in the *kassa* house. At moments he could feel exhilarated by the prospect of an afterlife and believe in its existence. At others he felt a sense of disappointment when his logical side told him he was suffering from delusions as a result of ingesting a hallucinogenic drug. But if that were so, then how come Managua and all the rest claimed to see their dead relatives in the *kassa* house too? Could it be some mass hysterical reaction to the drug?

He sat at his table transcribing some of the interviews he'd carried out with the amputees. Their stories were harrowing and

their simple acceptance of their cruel disablement humbled him
and made him ashamed of his country, or rather, even more
ashamed than he already was. He remembered how his childhood
comic-book hero Superman used to fight for 'Truth, Justice and
the American Way'. Well, if you did the first two these days, you
wouldn't be doing the third; they were mutually exclusive. He was
amassing a huge amount of evidence, far more than he had hoped.
It would make a strong case, although he could not help feeling it
would be even stronger with the woman Pilua's testimony. Besides,
he felt a burning desire to obtain justice for this woman, whose
whole life had been ruined because of the American army. Was it
possible she was still alive? Managua had gone out of his way to
help him and be friendly towards him, but could it be that Purnu
was right, that the older man was hiding something?

He heard footsteps and leaped up, grabbing a thick piece of
driftwood he'd found on the beach. The steps were coming his
way. He tiptoed over to the doorway and stood to one side of it,
arm raised ready to get in the first blow this time.

'Hello! Are you here?'

It was Lucy. She came through the door, sensed his presence and
turned to see him with the bit of wood raised above her head. She
dropped the bundle she was carrying under her arm. 'Good God!
You scared the wits out of me.'

'Sorry. It's just because of what happened. It's made me a little
jumpy, I guess.' He lowered his arm and tossed the wood to the
floor.

'Of course. You know, you could just stay in the *bukumatula* hut?'

'You must be joking. If you had any idea what goes on in
there . . .'

'Yes. Well. There's still my place. But remember what I told you.
They don't like people living together if they're not married.'

William grinned. He couldn't get any kind of handle on all the
rules and rituals around here. They seemed so inconsistent. He was
used to a puritan tradition where sex was pretty much always
wrong, not sometimes wrong and sometimes right. 'But they

just wander off into the bush and, well, um, behave promiscuously.'

'Only when they're not married. And they just have sex. They don't have their meals together, that's the point. If a couple had a meal together in the *bukumatula* hut there would be the most frightful scandal and they'd have to get married.'

'But they can go at it hammer and tongs all night and they don't have to? Crazy.'

'No more crazy than some of our daft customs, I should think.' She bent and retrieved the bundle and proffered it to him. 'Anyway, I brought you this.'

He took it and let it unfurl. It was a lightweight sleeping bag. 'I brought it for field trips, but thanks to your compatriots there isn't any use for it here. Nearly all the islanders live in this village. I thought it might make you more comfortable.'

'God yes. It's great. Thanks.' William pushed his glasses up the bridge of his nose and smiled. It was his best Clark Kent smile. You couldn't help liking him when he smiled like that.

Lucy smiled back. 'Just remember to check it for snakes before you get into it.'

'Oh. Right. OK. I will.'

Her smile broadened. 'Would you like to check it now . . . ?'

Afterwards, Lucy's first mistake was not to disentangle her short limbs from the long limbs of William Hardt and to allow herself to fall asleep in his embrace. Her second error was not to make a quick getaway when she woke but to grant herself permission to watch him sleeping. When you watch someone sleeping you discover how you feel about them. If you register the lack of elegance in an open mouth and the absence of anything resembling harmony in their whistling snore then your heart (or kidneys depending on your culture) is probably safe. If, on the other hand, you see a hitherto unsuspected boyishness in the way a man's blond hair flops over his forehead and notice in the unaccustomed stillness of his eyelids an innocent absence of his normal anxiety and find in both these things a vulnerability that makes you want to protect him then you are almost certainly lost. This is what happened to Lucy, only she didn't know it yet. She watched for a while and then she slipped from his arms and out of the sleeping bag and because he was still asleep thought she was safe. Like any woman over thirty who doesn't have a partner, Lucy was a veteran of several failed relationships. She had even been married, briefly. Her marriage had been a big mistake; she knew that now. She had fallen for her husband the instant she first looked into the black pools that were his eyes. One moment she had been free, the next in love. It had happened like magic, looking up from a book in the university library, seeing those eyes and plunging in. Lucy was determined that magic would never again play such a part in her life and that is why, as she hurriedly pulled on her clothes, she turned her back on the unconscious American as if the sleeping bag contained not a single snake, but a whole Gorgon's head of serpents.

TWENTY-EIGHT

FROM 'THE OTHER SIDE OF PARADISE: THE SEXUAL LIFE
AND CUSTOMS OF AN UNSPOILED PEOPLE' BY L. TIBBUT
(UNPUBLISHED MANUSCRIPT)

Magic plays an integral, indispensable part in the lives of
the islanders. They believe, as we have seen, that it alone
is responsible for birth. It determines the weather, the tides,
the number of fish in the sea (and the amount of these that
can be caught), how dark is the night, how bright the sun,
sexual attraction, love and death. No-one dies on the island
except by the ministry of magic.

It follows that they seek to control the magic they find all
around them. There are two ways in which they do this.
The first is by ritual, that is by a set of regulated
actions the strict observance of which they believe will
ward off ambient bad magic and in some cases, they hope,
attract ambient good magic. There are rituals for all the
staging posts of life: birth, coming of age, courtship,
marriage, pregnancy and death, as well as very practical
ones for planting vegetables, catching fish, etc. As with the
rituals of our own Christian church those of the natives
have mainly become a matter of rote. This is not to say they
are not strictly observed, for they are, but rather that the
practitioners have no knowledge of why these particular
sets of actions are necessary. If you ask them what walking around a newly-wed couple's home seven times

clockwise then seven times anticlockwise chanting a pre-
scribed formula of words is for, they will tell you it is to
bring the marriage good magic. If you persist and say, Yes,
but how will walking around the hut help and why seven
times? they simply shrug and say it is what one does. When
I suggested that if seven times brought good magic then
eight times would bring even better, everyone laughed
derisively as if what I'd said was a mixture of ignorance
and stupidity. Perhaps it is! Anyway, enough of these
rituals which are not the subject of the present discussion.
They will be dealt with more fully in a later chapter.

The other method practised to combat or encourage
ambient magic is sorcery which can be used to ensure a
good fishing catch or to cure illness. More than that the aid
of sorcery is enlisted on an individual basis for every
activity of any importance in the islanders' lives. If a boy
wishes to make a certain girl love him, he will visit a
sorcerer. If she rejects him he will not take the snub
personally but will console himself with the knowledge that
a rival has used a more potent spell. If a woman is barren,
she consults a sorcerer. If you have a dispute with a neighbour you may ask a sorcerer to kill him. If he dies then the
magic has worked. If he remains hale and hearty, he has
had recourse to a practitioner of magic superior to yours.
The islanders do not believe that death is something that
simply happens from illness, accident or old age. It is thought
always to have been brought about by the use of magic against
the deceased.

The islanders have no chiefs. The people they listen to
and take notice of are the sorcerers. Some of these have
formidable reputations although it is hard to see why one
should be esteemed above another, other than through a
record of successes brought about by a series of
serendipitous coincidences. Of course, there is the character
of the sorcerer. The reason the man Purnu is held to be the

most powerful sorcerer on the island may have much to do
with his guile. He is a crafty man who can see, for example,
when a boy takes a fancy to a girl and comes to him for a
love potion, what the lovesick boy cannot, that the girl is
already besotted with him, which is often the way with
young people. He performs a spell and lo and behold the
boy's advances are accepted. On the other hand, if he
knows from gossip (he is a great one for gossip!) that the
girl's affections lie elsewhere, he will tell the boy it is impossible she should love him because he has already
performed a spell for his rival. He may even, for all I know,
add something to his spiel about it being unethical for him
to have two clients with conflicting interests.

Managua is respected as a less powerful but nevertheless
extremely effective magician. I suspect this is because he
always talks such good sense and that things others do not
see are obvious to him; this gives him a high success rate
in the matter of predictions. Moreover, since he is the only
islander who can read, Managua has gained enormous
additional kudos from his literacy. The islanders see being
able to make a meaning, or indeed a story, from a jumble
of apparently meaningless symbols on a piece of paper – or
more especially on a Coca-Cola can – as demonstrative of
the highest order of magical prowess. (Incidentally it is not
true to say the natives are wholly illiterate. All of them,
down to the younger children, can recognize the Coca-Cola
logo, even when it is upon a printed page rather than a
can.)

Many special powers are attributed to sorcerers,
although the most superior of these belong only to the
greatest proponents of the magical arts. They can see in
the dark; they can walk through fire; they are prodigious
lovemakers; they can fly.

Purnu once offered to take me on a flight around the
island with him, an offer I declined, although I did ask him

why, if he could fly, he didn't go on a Coca-Cola run to the big island, which is 300 miles away.

'Is be too far,' he told me. 'Is use up too much magic.'

When I asked Managua if he could fly he replied, 'Is not be so easy any more with this damn leg.'

Ludicrous though the idea of men flying seems to Westerners, many of the islanders insist they have observed various sorcerers in flight.

Even magic has its price and sorcerers earn good yams for their spells. Purnu is one of the wealthiest men on the island thanks largely to his reputation and is treated like a good orthodontist; you go to him if you can afford it; if not, you settle for second best.

TWENTY-NINE

After the debacle of the OCD self-help group, William decided he needed professional help. He'd tried many times to discuss his problem with his doctor but the man didn't seem to understand what he was talking about and sent him away with some pills. So William found a therapist who specialized in OCD. Jean said his problem was the result of magical thinking.

'Early in your life you formed the belief that the coincidences which are part and parcel of everyone's life were more than that, that completely separate events had a causal connection,' she told him. They were sitting in comfortable armchairs almost within touching distance in her office, which was in a quiet city street. The walls were a cool pastel shade of blue and on each hung a single painting of a pastoral scene. Not that William actually took in the subjects of the pictures; he was more interested in whether they were hung straight and was relieved that they were. It gave him the feeling he was in the right place. He imagined that Jean made sure her pictures were straight before each consultation.

'For example, suppose, as a child, you were anxious, as is common among small boys, that your father might suffer an early death. Perhaps you might have said to yourself, "If I walk on all the cracks between the paving stones on the way home from school, Daddy will be safe." And you did, and lo and behold your father remained alive and well. That's magical thinking.

'Now of course, most people indulge in such thoughts. We say knock on wood. We avoid walking under ladders. It's part of our primitive make-up to do this. It comes from a time when the world seemed chaotic and uncontrollable. Everywhere there were natural disasters: floods, earthquakes, storms, twisters and so on. It appeared a malevolent magic was at work over which we had no power. For this reason primitive man created his gods. As long as we appeased these higher beings, usually by performing rituals in an established way, they would prevent the natural magic of the world from harming us. You have created your own set of rituals, a system of magic to combat the one that threatens you in the macroworld. You have, for whatever reason, possibly a trauma otherwise too insignificant to worry about, come to disbelieve in coincidence and to see instead cause and effect. You can ward off bad magic by means of practising a certain ritual. Conversely, if you neglect the ritual, the bad thing will happen.'

Afterwards, William realized that she was right. He had always believed in magic. His boyhood hero had been the comic character Superboy, the teenager who would grow up to become Superman. Superboy could fly, was invulnerable to everything except radio-active rocks from his native planet, had super strength and speed, and X-ray vision that enabled him to see through anything except lead. This was as unlike William as it was possible to be, but it was easy for him to identify with Superboy because his hero had an alter ego, a secret identity as an ordinary boy named Clark Kent. Clark appeared to be just like William. He was a geek who wore glasses, which, like William's, were unnecessary. Clark not only had perfect vision, he had super eyesight which could see right out into outer space, and, of course, the already mentioned X-ray vision. William wore glasses to conceal the secret behind his alternate blinking; Superboy wore them so that no-one would recognize him. At one level William knew this was silly, that no-one would fail to be recognized just by putting on glasses; he realized it was a literary convention, as in Shakespeare when a character puts on a cloak to assume another identity and everyone else is fooled. But on another level it was magical. Put the glasses on, you're Clark Kent. Take them off, you're Superboy. By the age of ten William had constructed for himself a complex belief system. He was terrified of death because he feared total annihilation. He didn't believe in life after death, Heaven or God. It wasn't for want of trying to; he was so frightened of nothingness he would have believed in the Devil if he could and would readily have settled for going to Hell when his time came. At least he'd be somewhere. Although William knew that Superboy's powers were owing to him coming to Earth from another solar system, and that he himself wasn't an alien (in spite of what certain of his classmates said about him), he nevertheless cherished a hope that he might one day wake up as Superboy. He would sometimes lie in bed at night and pray to the God he didn't believe in to make him wake next morning to find himself transformed into the Boy of Steel. He would make rash promises of what he would do if this prayer were granted. He would dedicate himself to helping others; he wouldn't use his X-ray vision to look through girls' dresses, or at least, if that proved too difficult to adhere to, not through their underwear as well. It never happened. His integrity was never tested. Every morning when he woke he would stare at the wall in front of him, hoping to see through it to his father shaving in the bathroom next door, but he never ever did. When he got out of bed and tried to spring into flight his body remained resolutely earthbound.

Jean had no time for magic. 'It doesn't exist,' she told him. 'Alter your thinking and you won't have a problem. My therapy will show you that magical thinking is illogical, that catastrophes occur – or not – independently of your actions, that the way to deal with intrusive thoughts is to argue against them, not fight them with silly rituals. We'll start next week by confronting one of your fears. Now, what are you afraid of?'

'Death,' said William.

'Uh-huh. Well, that's a big one to begin with. Have you anything smaller we can tackle? Any cleanliness issues here?'

'Dog poop,' said William.

'Dog poop! Great! I've worked a lot with dog poop.'

William thought she made it sound like a material she used for artistic purposes, the way some people carved statues out of ice or made things out of driftwood. But he resisted the urge to laugh and promised to return for practical therapy.

The following week Jean met William at the door of her office wearing her outdoor coat. 'Come on,' she said, 'let's go find us some dog shit.'

In the lift she smiled at him and said, 'I know a real good area for poop. It's only a couple of blocks from here.'

In the street, as they walked along, Jean's head swivelled from side to side, eyes sweeping the sidewalk. 'There's some!' she suddenly yelled. Sure enough there was a small pile of the stuff fifty feet ahead. Normally William would have crossed the road at this point, but as he stopped dead, Jean linked her arm through his and said, 'Come on, it's OK, I'm with you now. I'm going to get you through it.'

That alarmed William even more until he realized she was talking metaphorically.

'What's your anxiety level out of ten?' she asked as they shuffled towards the shit.

'I guess around five,' he said. 'It's not that big a pile and I've seen it so I know I'm not going to step in it.'

'And what are your thoughts? What exactly is the problem with dog shit?'

'That it might contaminate me. That I might touch it, I guess, and get some horrible disease, you know like the one that makes little kids go blind when they eat it.'

He stopped and retched. 'What's the matter?' said Jean.

'I can't believe I said that, about kids eating dog shit. It's a horrible idea. I'm up to level nine and it's still rising. Is there anything above a ten?'

The pile was on the outside of the sidewalk, next to the kerb. William was glad that Jean was between him and it. Even so he shrank from it, hugging the shop front on the inner side of the sidewalk, as though the kerb were a precipice he might fall off. He also feared a passer-by might accidentally barge into him and send him cannoning into the dog dirt and he anxiously scanned the faces of oncoming pedestrians to check that they were looking where they were going. Fortunately this was before the universal popularity of mobile phones and most of them were. In future years, with everyone phoning on the move, he would speculate about the likelihood of them all walking around in dirty shoes.

Eventually they were past the dog doo and William stopped to mop his brow. 'Well done!' Jean told him and he allowed himself a small congratulatory smile.

'I couldn't have done it without you,' he said.

Next Jean took him to a small park that she said was covered in dog dirt. Indeed, even as they entered it they came across a Dalmatian squatting with raised haunches, straining away in the manner of dogs. William couldn't help wondering if people looked like that when they went to the bathroom. He didn't know that many years later on a beach on the other side of the world he'd have an opportunity to observe several hundred of them in action.

In the centre of the park, where they'd negotiated themselves with enough sidestepping, hopping and skipping to qualify as skilled ballet dancers, Jean halted. She reached into her pocket and pulled out a silk headscarf. She asked William to bend down and tied it around his eyes. He couldn't see a thing. For the first time since his childhood, he longed to have X-ray vision.

'Now you're going to walk back to the park entrance,' she told him. 'I will call out directions to you to make sure you arrive there safely.'

'Does safely mean free of dog poo?' he asked.

'It does not. Dog poo offers no threat to your safety. I will merely be making sure you don't trip over or collide with anything.'

'I – uh – I don't think I can do this,' William stammered. 'I'd be bound to tread in something nasty. I'm on a ten and still rising.'

'If you can do this, you will have conquered one of your irrational fears without recourse to magical thinking.'

That's what you think, thought William. He was alternate blinking like crazy under the blindfold.

'And I know you're blinking under that blindfold, but that's OK. Once you see that dog shit doesn't harm you you'll recover something of yourself. You'll be free to walk the streets without its tyranny. I want you to take one step for me. I want you to embrace the idea of dog doo. I want you to wallow in it.'

William's feet remained rooted to the spot. He reminded himself of an elderly aunt who had Parkinson's disease and whose feet would not move when her brain told them to.

'Come on, one small step for man and all that.'

William felt her hand grab his and she jerked him forward. The grass was soft under foot. If it was grass . . .

It took William nearly an hour to traverse the small park. As Jean removed the blindfold he felt no relief. His head was pounding and he thought he was going to faint. But there she was, beaming him a cheerleader's smile. 'You did it!' she said. 'Fucking A, you did it.'

Her enthusiasm leaped the small gap between them and surged through him. He was a little shocked by her profanity but could see she was just carried away by his triumph. He smiled back, trying to cover his pride. 'I did, didn't I?' he said. 'I did it and I survived.'

William felt like he was walking on air until they hit the sidewalk again. Then his feet suddenly felt like lead. He looked down. He couldn't see his shoes any more. They had been black. Now he had two enormous brown overshoes. That's how much dog shit he'd stepped in.

'You're covered in the stuff!' chortled Jean. 'And you're still alive. Nothing terrible happened, did it?'

William wanted to say that this was terrible enough, but he felt it would be unfair to dampen Jean's enthusiasm, although that was not so great it stopped her shuffling her position around him even as she spoke, which he realized was to get upwind of him.

'Now I want you to go home and clean the shit off those shoes,' she said. 'Every last bit of it. I want you to come to me next week with those shoes looking like new.'

On the way home, William found he had a whole car of the normally crowded subway to himself. He wasn't bothered by people sharing their Walkmans with him. Even the smelliest-looking hoboes failed to include him in their requests for alms.

Outside his apartment building he removed his shoes without touching them by levering them off against the front steps of the neighbouring building. After checking no-one was about, he used an empty beer bottle he found in the basement area to lift the shoes, one by one, into the trashcan. Inside the building he removed his trousers and socks, took them down to the basement and burned them in the incinerator. Next day he went out and bought a pair of shoes identical to those he'd thrown away. When he turned up for his appointment with Jean the following week his shoes looked good as new because they were.

The problem with Jean's method of dealing with his OCD was that no sooner had William got one compulsion under control than another appeared or an existing one worsened. William was now able to walk past dog poop without crossing the road (although he vowed he was never going to go into *that* park again), but his anxiety at the sight of out-of-line pictures grew worse in direct proportion to his dog-shit improvement.

Jean attempted to exorcize this by making him sit in her consulting room with a picture slightly askew. Next session they had two pictures slightly haywire, the third, three, and for the fourth all four of the pastoral scenes were now inclined this way or that. The higgledy-piggledy effect was even greater for the fifth session when Jean turned up the heat by increasing the slant on each picture. The paintings were hanging every which way now and Jean made William sit there and take it. After ten sessions he was able to bear them all as far askew as you could get them to go. It had cost him more than a thousand dollars, but he could now have braved a large art gallery with careless staff.

The therapy was going so well that William began to imagine a time when he might be cured of his disorder altogether. But you can never write off a thing like OCD. Just when you think you've got it licked in one area, such as dog poop, it pops up somewhere else, maybe in the way pictures are hung. This time it popped up in Jean.

William first noticed it when they were sitting outside at a pavement café on a breezy but not too breezy day. As he was in dog-poop remission, he and Jean were discussing scatology in literature. William made the point that some authors seemed, well, obsessed with shit to the detriment of their works. They kept on about it even when it was irrelevant to the lives of their characters. Jean argued back that shit was never irrelevant; everyone produced it every day and not mentioning it was a big omission. She reminded him about the great satirist Jonathan Swift's scatological bent and suggested his obsession with excrement was an expression of his disgust with humankind. William, thinking she meant *his* obsession rather than Swift's, replied that he liked people. It wasn't people who disgusted him, just the excrement they produced. The discussion was just getting interesting when William realized Jean was no longer listening to him. She wasn't even looking at him, but at the ground behind him and off to one side.

'You know,' Jean murmured, 'I can see how it would get kind of annoying.'

'What?' said William. He turned to follow her gaze and lighted upon a paper napkin on the ground. 'Oh. I wish you hadn't mentioned that.'

They both stared at it for a moment then Jean shook her head, focused on William again and said, 'Now where were we?'

'Shit,' he said.

'Shit is right!' said Jean, swinging her gaze back to the napkin. 'Do you mind . . . ?'

Before he could answer she was out of her seat and making for the napkin. She was a tall, gangling woman, but she moved with surprising speed. Even so, a bit of the breeze that was around that day reached the napkin before her and just as she bent to retrieve it, jerked it out of her reach. Jean tried again and the breeze once more teased it from her grasp. The situation was repeated a couple more times and William had the unedifying experience of everyone seated at the café's tables stopping eating, drinking, conversing or shouting into their mobile phones to watch an awkward, lanky therapist chasing a paper napkin and intermittently swearing at it. She reminded William of a dancing giraffe, and indeed some of the café's other patrons were obviously under the impression that she was dancing because he heard people at the next table discussing whether they should toss her some coins. Eventually Jean got the napkin with a two-footed tackle that landed her right on top of it and returned to the table flushed with embarrassment and exertion. She then sat ignoring William's conversation and staring at the napkin with a horrified expression that told him she didn't like having physical contact with it but didn't know what else to do with it. William wouldn't have minded, after all, he knew just how she felt, except that he was paying two hundred dollars an hour for this.

Later on his way home he recalled how there had been an incident when Jean arrived at the café. William had been there first and sat with his back to the outer wall of the building, leaving Jean the seat opposite with her back to the street. But when she appeared, instead of sitting down, she asked William to vacate his seat for her and take the other one.

'I thought I told you about this,' he said. 'It's one of my things. I have to sit with my back to the wall.' He gave a nervous little laugh. 'In case of drive-by shootings, you know.'

Jean didn't laugh. 'I know that, that's why I'm asking you to move. It's part of your therapy.'

'Um, I'm not sure that I can.'

Instead of arguing further Jean grabbed his arm and hauled him physically from his chair. She thrust him into the other seat. While William sat glancing nervously over his shoulder, she studied the menu and said casually, 'You'll thank me for it one day.'

The day at the café had been a revelation to William. Afterwards other signs of what he'd observed piled up like speeding cars in freeway fog. At her office Jean was obsessive about the crockery. One day she screamed at William when he absent-mindedly picked up and drank from her coffee cup instead of his own. Another time he arrived early and caught her adjusting a picture frame with a spirit level. When he confronted her she said the client after him was excessively concerned with symmetry. But later William remembered that she'd often told him he was her last appointment of the day.

Jean began to excuse herself halfway through a session to 'wash her hands' and would disappear for ten or fifteen minutes at a time. Now when he mentioned Sheena, Jean's sympathies seemed to lean more and more towards his former girlfriend. On one memorable day Jean went off to wash her hands the moment he arrived and didn't reappear until just before it was time for him to go. It struck him as an expensive – for him – absence.

By this time William was beginning to suspect that Jean herself had OCD and even to wonder if he was helping her more than she was helping him. The only thing now, it seemed to him, that separated therapist and patient was that he was the one who paid. He considered whether maybe the time had come to call a halt to the whole thing.

Next time they spent the whole session discussing whether or not a picture was straight and then, when Jean produced a spirit level from nowhere to prove that it was, arguing about what 'straight' actually meant since it was obvious the wall was out of true and that while the picture frame was in line according to the rules of gravity, because of the wonky wall it appeared upsettingly off-beam to the obsessive eye.

William spent a tortured week agonizing about cancelling the therapy. He realized the only thing preventing him was the embarrassment of telling Jean. She had been so sympathetic and kind to him he didn't want to repay her by calling her a nut. Fortunately this wasn't necessary. When he arrived for his next appointment, the receptionist told him that all sessions were cancelled until further notice because Jean had builders in.

'There's a major problem with the walls,' the woman said.

William never went back. He would always be grateful to Jean for helping him get over his problem with shit, but if he'd wanted another OCD nut in his life, he would have stuck with Sheena.

THIRTY

_____

It was a day of magic on the island. If you had ventured into the jungle you would have noticed the silence straight away. The parakeets did not shriek and cry as was their wont but restricted the sound they made to the beat of their wings as they flew from tree to tree; the howler monkeys refrained from howling, they sat upon the ground in groups where they waited for something to happen; they didn't know what it would be, but they knew it was coming; even the black bantam pigs searched for bright orange fungi without the snuffling and grunting noises their rooting usually occasioned. Magic was in the steam that rose from the jungle floor and it was in the globules of condensed water the leaves of the tree canopy returned to it. It was in the very air and all living things knew it.

Even William, even the *gwanga* who was not attuned to the moods and nuances of his new habitat, sensed it. As he walked back to the Captain Cook from the daily degradation of the shitting beach he felt he was being followed, but when he turned to look, there was no-one there and he put it down as a flashback from the *kassa*.

Later he decided to ask Purnu for help to look for Pilua. It was during their morning reading lesson. The lessons were not going well. Purnu was intelligent but he had a disputatious nature that led him to challenge the basic principles of a written language, principles that William was finding it hard to get across because the native's knowledge of the outside world was so negligible it severely limited the vocabulary available to him for examples.

'CUH-A-TUH,' William was saying right now, indicating the letters one by one on the paper on which he'd written them. 'Now you say it.'

'CUH-A-TUH,' repeated Purnu.

'Now say it faster and you have a word.'

'C-A-T,' said Purnu. He looked puzzled. 'I is not hear any word.'

'C-A-T. Cat!' said William. 'C-A-T makes cat.'

'Cat is be word?' said Purnu. 'What is be cat?'

'You don't know cat? A small furry animal, kept as a pet?' Purnu looked even more perplexed. 'Miaow!' William imitated the sound of the animal. Purnu stared at him. He looked like he thought William was going to bite him.

'OK,' said William. 'I guess you don't have cats. All right, let's try another one. CUH-A-PUH'.

'CAP,' said Purnu right away and William allowed himself a smug smile of satisfaction.

'That's good,' he said.

'What is be so good 'bout this?' demanded Purnu with a scowl. 'What is be cap? Is be more damn animal is not be on island?' Before William could answer the man held up his hands seemingly in terror. 'No, no, you is not make noise of cap, we is not have caps here. Is be no need for tell me noise cap is make.'

'It's not an animal. It's something you wear on your head.'

'You is make with dead animal?'

'No,' said William. 'Well, yes, sometimes, I guess.'

'Is not matter,' said Purnu. 'We is not have cats or caps. I is not want for read about they things.'

William thought a moment. He wished he had a dictionary with him so he could look up other words beginning with C-A instead of having to think of them. Managua had a dictionary, he'd seen it on his plastic crate, but he didn't want to ask to borrow it in case Managua demanded to know why he wanted it. He decided to try a different tack.

'A-R together make the sound AR,' he said.

'What is be AR?' asked Purnu. 'Is be another damn word we is not have here.' William realized that was true. The word 'are' didn't figure in the natives' vocabulary because they always used the singular 'is' form of the verb 'to be'.

'It's not a word on its own. It's a blend of letters that make a sound that you can use to make other words. Let's go back to C. CUH-A-RUH. CUH-AR.'

'Car,' said Purnu. He looked annoyed now. 'What for you is teach me this? Is be more furry animal you is put on head in America? Is not be any use for me.'

William was going through all the words he could think of that began with CA. He thought of CAB, but there wouldn't be much future in trying to explain the concept of a cab to someone who not only hadn't heard of a car, but who even if he had wouldn't understand the concept of paying for a ride in one, except maybe in yams. Try that in New York! William worked his way through the alphabet and came up with 'CUH-A-NUH.'

'Can!' shrieked Purnu. 'I is can use this word. You is see, I is just say "can". Can is be plenty useful word because is mean two things. Now you is teach me Coca-Cola. Is be easy. I is know how is look on cuh-a-nuh.' He laughed at his little joke.

'Well, perhaps not today,' said William. 'You've done a lot. Maybe you should just practise saying "can" to yourself for now before we move on to what goes into it.'

'CUH-A-NUH. CAN,' muttered Purnu. 'Is be good. *Gwanga*, I is think before that you is be shit teacher, but now I is see you is not be so bad.'

'Thank you,' said William. Purnu rose to leave. 'Actually, Purnu, I wanted to ask your help.'

Purnu looked suspicious. He lowered himself to the ground again. 'What you is want?'

'I need some assistance to find Pilua.'

'Mebbe.' There was a note of caution in Purnu's voice.

'Well, will you help me?'

'Before I is answer you that, you is answer me this. Is you want my help like you is say, "Purnu, give me hand for lift this canoe" or "Purnu, you is help me carry these fish"? Or is you is want I is help you by magic?'

'What's the difference?'

'Yams.'

'Magic costs more, right?'

'No, no, no, no. First kind I is do for nothing. Is be custom, someone is need help, you is help. But not for magic. For magic you is need yams.'

'There's a problem here. I don't have any yams.'

There was a gleam in Purnu's eye that told him the conversation was going according to script. He leaned his head to one side and nodded, as though thinking it over. When he thought he'd thought long enough he said, 'OK, you is can give me another thing instead.'

'Such as?'

He pointed to William's wrist. 'Watch.'

'Er, I'm afraid not. I need it and it has sentimental value.'

'What is mean, this long word you is say?'

'Sentimental? It means it's special to me because someone I loved gave it to me.'

'You is have wife. *You?*'

'My father.'

'You is know how spell?'

'FUH-A-TUH—'

'No, senti-senti—'

'Sentimental? Yes.'

'You is teach?'

'I uh, I think we're a little way off that. It's a bit of a leap from "can" to that. But we'll get there.' An idea came to him. 'If we keep on with the lessons, of course.'

'What you is mean, if we is keep on with lessons? I is not give up. Now you is get hang of teacher business I is soon read good as Managua. I is already know "can".'

'Well, you see, when I offered to teach you, I had no idea how much time it would involve. Now that I do, I'm going to need something in return. What I'm suggesting is an exchange of services. You help me find Pilua, just normal help or magic, whatever gets the job done, I teach you to read. Is it a deal?'

Purnu studied his pubic leaf intently. A minute passed. Then another. Finally he looked up.

'But mebbe is not be possible for find Pilua. Mebbe she is be dead.'

'I know that. You just have to try every which way you can.'

'OK, is be deal.'

'Great,' said William.

'But . . .'

'But?' said William.

'But you is must throw in pocket calculator.'

With all the magic in the atmosphere, Purnu had a very busy day. After his lesson with the *gwanga*, the first person who came to see him was Lamua. His eyes lit up when she entered his hut, looking nervously over her shoulder as though anxious about being seen. He had always liked Lamua. She was a woman made for *fug-a-fug*. He thought about the handful of occasions in their youth when she had shared his bed in the *bukumatula* house. He remembered that it was good, the best *fug-a-fug* he had ever had, but he couldn't remember what it had felt like, the smell of her sweat, the soft yearning of her body as he kneeled between her tender thighs, the whisper of her sighs. No matter how hard you tried you could never get those things back; it was all so long ago.

She sat down without being asked and began speaking quietly and quickly. Like most of his consultations, it was confidential; if you wanted magic to make someone fall in love with you, you didn't want to alert a rival; if you came seeking a spell to kill someone you didn't want to let the intended victim know.

'I is need some plenty damn powerful magic from you, Purnu,' she said.

'What for you is need magic? You is not have problem with husband, I is hope? Managua is be such great man, is can read and all that.' Purnu couldn't help letting his resentment of Managua show. Long before he envied the older man his literacy he had coveted his wife. How come Managua had been the one to snare her? Why had she preferred an old man with one leg to him?

'I is need spell for make baby, that is be first.'

He gave a casual shrug. 'This I is can do. Is not be big problem. There is be more?'

She blushed. 'I is need spell for make Managua love me again.'

He raised an eyebrow. 'Managua is not love you? Beautiful woman like you? Is this man be blind? Or mebbe he is be too old now for make *fug-a-fug*?'

'He is be too busy with they damn books.'

'Mebbe you is like I is make spell so Managua is not can read any more.' Of course Purnu had already tried to accomplish this with every spell he knew without success, but Lamua didn't know that and there might be a few yams in it.

'I is not want for stop he read. When we is first know each other he is read stories for me. I is love he for the stories he is read and he is love me for I is listen they.'

'Mebbe too much read is be bad for *pwili*.' Lamua couldn't help noticing that Purnu looked a little worried as he said this. It was plenty strange, he'd never shown concern for Managua before.

She pressed on. 'And I is need spell for find pig.'

'Hunting spell, this I is can do. Is be very easy.'

'No, I is not want for hunt pig, just find.'

'You is want for find pig without you is hunt? Is plenty funny thing for want. You is mean you is want for you is walk in jungle and is not look for pig and is just trip over one?'

'How I is find is not matter, just so long as I is find.'

'Well, OK, you is not want for hunt pig but what for you is want for find? You is want for special occasion? You is maybe want spell for kill somebody, eat pig for funeral? I is have way for find pigs. I is look in bowl of water for see where is be herd of pigs in jungle.'

'No, is just be *one* pig I is want. Not any old pig. Is be one special pig. Is be pig Managua is have for pet. He is be as crazy for this damn pig as for books. Between Shakespeare and pig is be no time for me.'

'Pig is not be at you house?'

'No, Managua is know I is be angry at pig, is want for kill. Is want for slit throat and drink blood. He is take pig somewhere for hide. I is not can find.'

'All right. So, you is want spell for make baby, is want spell for make Managua show you he *pwili* again, is want spell for find special pig.'

'Yes, but you is make spell for find pig first. Managua is be so in love with damn pig he is never love me again before pig is be dead, spell or no spell, you is understand?'

'I is understand. Is be three spells.' He shook his head. 'Is be plenty yams.'

'How many?'

He named a figure. After an initial gasp of shock, Lamua went right into haggling. She pointed out he'd said a hunting spell was easy, he retaliated that the hunting spell he'd been talking about was to find a herd of pigs in the forest, not one particular pig that was being hidden by a man. Lamua replied that, when you thought about it, she was actually only asking for one spell because she was sure that with the pig out of the way Managua would love her again and that maybe no floating baby had come to her because no child would want to come where there wasn't a loving father. They went on and on for some time until she had beaten him down to a figure from which he would not budge.

'I is not have,' she said. 'I is not can take so many yams without Managua is notice. How much is be just for find pig?'

Purnu threw her a disparaging smile. 'Most of yams is be for pig. Is be most difficult spell of whole lot. No-one is ever make spell for find one special pig before. Other two is not really count for many yams.'

Lamua's chin sank to her chest. Tears trickled down her lovely cheeks.

Purnu cleared his throat. 'Mebbe there is be one way . . .'

'Yes?' said Lamua. She looked up at his face. 'No!'

'Is you not remember *bukumatula* hut, all they years ago?' He reached out and laid his hand gently on hers. 'I is still smell you sweat. I is still feel you body yearn for mine as I is kneel between you tender thighs, I is still hear whisper of you sighs . . .'

'I − I is not can. I is not say is not be nice, but that is be then. This is be now. I is be married woman.'

'Married woman who is not have *fug-a-fug* for plenty long time, unless I is be mistake.'

'But even so . . .'

'I is do all three spells. You is not give me any yams.'

'I is just not can. I be faithful wife . . .'

'I is throw in pocket calculator.'

The next person to consult Purnu was Lintoa. He lumbered into the hut, pausing only to adjust the slipping shoulder strap of his dress, and dumped his huge form onto the floor in front of the sorcerer. The latter sat and stared at him. Unlike Managua who was outraged by the dresses, Purnu found them amusing. He reached out and sampled the soft cloth just above the hem, testing it gently between thumb and forefinger. Managua was old-fashioned. Purnu appreciated the things the white men made. Lintoa ignored him, took out a powder compact from his handbag, opened it and examined himself in the mirror, adjusting his hair here and there. Finally he snapped shut the compact, dropped it into the handbag, snapped that shut too and looked at his host.

'What you is want?' asked Purnu.

'I is want for be boy.' Lintoa reached up and pulled up the shoulder strap which had fallen down again.

Purnu laughed. 'But you is be girl. Look at you! How is be possible for you is be boy?'

'This all is be so damn silly,' said Lintoa, his cheeks suffused with the flush of anger. 'I is already be boy.'

Purnu pulled a face. 'Really? I is think not. Is not can happen. You is be born girl.'

'I is be boy!' shouted Lintoa. He hauled himself to his feet, staggering over his high heels in the process and kicking one off in fury. Purnu ducked as the flash of red flew past him. Lintoa stood before him and rolled up his dress.

'Look, I is be boy! I is have *pwili*!'

It was Purnu's turn now to be angry. The she-boy was behaving outrageously. It was indecent, against every taboo to expose yourself in public like this. He grabbed the hem of the skirt and yanked it down. 'You is cover youself up. You is not behave this way in my house!'

Chagrined, Lintoa sat down again. For the second time that day Purnu observed tears in a visitor's eyes. He felt sorry for the she-boy, of course he did, but then he was used to tears in his business. People who wanted something badly enough to ask for magic were always on the brink of tears.

'What for is must be me?' The boy was sobbing now. 'What for is my *mamu* not have proper girl child?'

Purnu, for all his greed, his craft and guile, his plotting, was not without a kind pair of kidneys. He reached out and laid a fatherly hand on the boy's muscular thigh.

'I is wish I is can help, but how is be possible? I is not can change nature. You is born for be girl. But you is must not despair. One day you is be boy. Is how things is be.'

The boy reached into the top of his dress, wriggled his hand inside his bra, extracted a rag, an action that left his breasts looking somewhat lopsided, and blew his nose upon it.

'Tell me, if you is not want for be girl, what for you is wear white woman's dress?'

'Is start as joke. Miss Lucy is let we try on old dress. Tigua is ask she. Then Tigua is like so much she is not want for take off. Sussua is be bit same. Me, I is not like, but then I is look at Tigua and I is see how silly she is look and I is think, I is go wear this dress, is go show Managua and all they old mans and womans, is go show my *mamu*, how crazy whole damn she-boy custom is be.'

'Is be brave thing for do,' murmured Purnu. 'Listen, you time is come in year or two for choose. You is make fine boy then. But for now you is be girl. You is must be patient. I is not can help you.'

'You is not understand what I is want. I is want you is make big spell for work on every mans and womans on island. Is make they forget whole she-boy custom. Is make they is think boys is be boys and girls is be girls.'

Purnu whistled through his teeth. 'You is talk plenty big spell. Is cost plenty yams. Where you is get so many yams?'

Lintoa didn't answer. He picked up the shoe he'd thrown and put it back on. Once again Purnu felt a stab of pity in his kidneys. What really got him was that although the boy looked sullen and miserable, he still put the shoe back on. It was so accepting of his fate.

'Listen,' said the sorcerer, 'I is not know if I is can make this spell you is want, but I is try.'

'But the yams . . . ?'

'I is mebbe let you off some of they yams if you is do something for me. Is must do quietly. Is not tell that chattering monkey Tigua.'

'I is not say word!'

'Well, then, you is know Managua pig? I is need for find and I is need for find woman . . .'

After he'd visited Purnu, Lintoa went to Managua and asked him for some magic. He didn't ask him to change him into a boy because he knew that Purnu was the greater sorcerer and if he couldn't do it then nobody could.

'I is want love spell,' he said.

Managua tried not to smile. He could see the boy was distressed. He looked pitiful in his ridiculous white woman's dress.

'Who is be lucky person I is put spell on?' asked Managua. He'd never before been asked for a love spell by a she-boy. Even as he asked the question the complications of the situation were beginning to dawn on him.

'Is be for Kiroa,' Lintoa replied.

Purnu's daughter. Managua understood now why Lintoa had come to him. He could hardly ask the girl's father to enchant her. It would be like asking for her hand in marriage. Managua couldn't imagine two people in skirts marrying one another.

'She is sure be one plenty damn pretty girl,' he said.

Lintoa's face brightened, chasing away his customary sullen expression. 'You is think so?'

Managua nodded. It was hardly necessary for Lintoa to seek his opinion. Everyone agreed that Kiroa was the most attractive girl on the island. 'You is know when you is be on boat and is come big storm,' said Lintoa, 'and is be black clouds and sky is be dark as night?'

Again Managua nodded.

'And then sun is make hole in clouds and is be so bright you is be dazzle?'

A third time the old man nodded.

Lintoa clutched his knees and rocked from side to side. 'Is be like when Kiroa is appear.'

His big face was so illuminated by his joy that Managua was loath to return it to its normal sullen state. But there was nothing for it. He must bring the she-boy back to earth.

'There is be just one problem,' he said.

'I is know, I is know,' said Lintoa, any light extinguished in his expression. 'I is be girl.'

'Exactly. How is can two girls be in love? Where you is go take she for make *fug-a-fug*? You is be girl. You is not have place in *bukumatula* house.'

'I is can wait for that. I is can do without *fug-a-fug* until I is become boy. But is be two years till then. What I is want for you is do for me is be this. I is want for you is make Kiroa is like me. You is make she is love me but because I is be girl she is just think she is like me, you is understand?'

'Is be plenty mix up.'

'Yes, but is stop she is fall in love with somebody else so she is not marry they before I is be boy.'

Managua sighed again. 'OK, I is try, but is be one damn tricky spell. I is ask you for plenty yams for this one, Lintoa. How you is go find they?'

'You is just make spell, you is leave me for worry 'bout yams.'

Lintoa got to his feet, put his fingers through his hair to get it under control and tottered out of the hut on his high heels. He paused to haul up the troublesome straps on his already slumped shoulders. Yams were getting to be a bit of a problem.

THIRTY-ONE

As twilight gathered, Lucy slipped from her house and made her way towards the village. She wore William's spare chinos and khaki shirt, both identical to those he always wore. He'd given her his slouch hat; it would cover her face so only somebody close up would recognize her. Any of her blonde hair that showed was the same colour as William's. Only their difference in size might give her away, but the plan was for her to arrive at the *kassa* house at the very last moment, and duck into the entrance tunnel after the last man, so no-one would get a good look at her. Afterwards, everyone would be so out of their minds on *kassa*, they wouldn't notice her.

Lucy couldn't help thinking it was ironic that her special friends on the island, aside from Managua, were boys who dressed as girls. Now she was dressed as a man. She wasn't sure how convincing she was, but William said it was all a question of belief. He cited the celebrated actress, Sarah Bernhardt, who'd apparently played Hamlet with great success. Well, Lucy knew she was no actress; she could imagine herself suffering from stage fright. She'd told William of the strict taboo against women entering the *kassa* house. She hadn't said she suspected that the punishment for breaking it would be something dramatic, maybe even death. She imagined it too as an orange fungi kind of way to go, slow and painful. She wondered if the natives would let her have a green shoestring and die like Cleopatra, fast and without suffering.

She paused at the edge of the village to get herself into character. She tried to imagine she was William. It wasn't easy to put yourself into the shoes of this shy, diffident man. It took more than wearing the same clothes as he. She tried doing the winking thing he always did, but the action contained no clue as to its motive, or to what went on behind those blinking eyes.

In the outer ring of huts, the dwelling places, people were sitting around the fires outside their doorways. Lucy strode boldly through, eyes straight ahead. Every step she was waiting for the cry that would expose her but none came; if any of the natives had bothered to look up at her, it seemed they hadn't noticed anything odd and she reached the comparative safety of the inner circle. So far, so good. She positioned herself at the corner of one of the storehouses so she could peep around it for a good view of the *kassa* house.

She was much too early! The centre of the village was full of men standing around talking. There was William, identically dressed, but carrying a briefcase, chatting to Managua who was sitting cross-legged outside the *kassa* house with his spectacles on and an open book in his hand. William was there because if every-one saw him clearly just before they went into the *kassa* hut, they'd be unlikely to suspect an impostor inside. To this end he was being very sociable. He was like a politician glad-handing people at a cocktail party. He exchanged a pleasantry with Purnu, who laughed, and spoke to one or two of the men with prosthetic limbs whom he'd been interviewing the past few days. Lucy looked around anxiously. Come on, she begged that unknown god she always prayed to at such times, not that there had ever been such a time before, but at, well, tricky moments when only some super-natural intervention could assist her, Come on, make them get a move on!

Eventually one of the men got down on his hands and knees and crawled into the *kassa* house tunnel. Others followed. Soon half the men in the village centre had entered. Managua stood, put an arm around William and steered him towards the tunnel. But the American stopped and shrugged the old man off. He nodded across the clearing. Tigua, Lintoa and Sussua were approaching.

Christ, thought Lucy, if Managua had gone in and I'd made my dash they'd have caught me. She knew the people she definitely couldn't fool into believing she was William were the she-boys. They were, after all, experts on cross-dressing.

William walked over to them and the four of them walked towards the far side of the clearing. William called something back to Managua and the old man waved and sat down again with his book. He pushed his spectacles further up the bridge of his nose and resumed his reading. Lucy's heart was in her mouth. She could taste it there. Time was running out. The number of men left outside the hut was fast diminishing, no more than a dozen or so now. William was still in the clearing. He spoke animatedly to the she-boys and handed them his briefcase. This was all according to plan. Part of his role was to make sure the she-boys were out of the way by sending them on an errand to collect eggs and minoa bread for his breakfast and leave them in the briefcase outside the *kassa* house for him. The she-boys were always so delighted to be able to do you any service that they wouldn't suspect trickery. Managua looked up from his book, watching the four of them walk away. When they disappeared behind the huts he looked anxiously at the tunnel, as the last couple of men entered. He closed his book and began the heavy process of rolling over into a crawling position.

Lucy braced herself. If Managua entered the tunnel, even if she ran she wouldn't get through the tunnel before the stone was rolled across the inner opening and she'd have lost her chance. On the other hand if she appeared before Managua went in and he waited for her, all would be lost. She took a deep breath, pulled the hat further over her face and stepped into the clearing.

Managua had just got onto his knees when he saw her. The sight stopped him dead. There was the *gwanga*, but how could this be? Hadn't he just seen the American leave the other side of the clearing? How could he have got round to this side so quickly? Even stranger, a moment ago the *gwanga* hadn't been wearing his hat, and now he was. Managua was pretty sure he hadn't been carrying it either, so where had it come from? This was all plenty strange. Then he remembered the bag. That was it! The *gwanga* must have had it in there. But then, why put the hat on now, when the sun had all but disappeared and he was going into the *kassa* house anyway? There was something odd here. Even the way the white man was walking didn't look right.

Lucy's confident stride was eating up the space between her and Managua. 'Hurry!' he called out to her. 'Is be almost time for begin!'

Lucy almost called out, Go ahead, I'll catch you up! But she stopped herself just in time. Instead she made a shooing motion with her hands, hoping against hope that it conveyed the same message here and not, say, wait for me a moment, would you, then you'll be able to see I'm a woman dressed as a man. She recalled the taboo against cross-dressing except for she-boys and wondered if she'd already done enough to be force-fed orange fungi.

Managua saw the gesture, nodded and bent his head into the tunnel entrance. As he crawled along he was still puzzled. The *gwanga* had sure looked plenty different, as though he had shrunk, maybe. How could this be, unless someone had performed a shrinking spell against him? But why would anyone want to do that? He was just deciding he'd have a closer look at the *gwanga* when they were both in the hut when something slipped down his face and hit his hand. His spectacles! Why of course, he'd been reading and he'd forgotten to take them off! No wonder the *gwanga* had looked different. And smaller, too! He used the spectacles for reading only. With them on he couldn't see clearly anything more than a few feet away. Chuckling at his foolishness, he emerged into the *kassa* house.

As soon as Managua was out of sight, Lucy broke into a run and was at the entrance to the hut in seconds. She paused to adjust her hat once more.

'Hey, *gwanga*!' It came from behind her. It made her head spin.

Her legs seemed to lose the power of movement. She suspected
they might not be able to hold her up more than a second or two.
The village swayed before her eyes. She was going to faint. Hold
on, Lucy, hold on! she told herself. Slowly she turned around. She
found herself face to face with Lintoa. He stared at her and did a
double take you'd have sworn was over-the-top in a comic movie.

'Miss Lucy?'

She could think of nothing to do or say. She either went into
the *kassa* hut or she stayed out. She might never get another
chance. Everything about tonight had gone so well. Until now. She
stared into Lintoa's eyes for the briefest of moments. There was no
need to tell him to keep quiet, to not tell anyone; they both knew
what would happen if he spoke out. He would either remain silent
or he wouldn't. It would be down to him. Without a word or
gesture to him, Lucy dropped to her hands and knees and crawled
into the tunnel.

What was keeping the *gwanga*? wondered Managua. He was a
nice man, all right, but he sure had one plenty big problem with
being in the right place at the right time. He was always on the last
minute for shitting. Managua had given up waiting for him now
and went on his own as he always used to. He didn't want to get
there after everyone was gone and miss out on the daily gossip and
exchange of news and opinions that were so integral to the morning ritual. Ah! Here was the American at last, coming in through
the entrance, looking all hurried and flustered, like a worried girl
almost, late again! With no small gleam of satisfaction in his eye,
Managua shook his head to indicate there was no space near him
and the *gwanga* sat down by the entrance.

This is it, thought Lucy, sitting there cross-legged on the dirt floor
of this primitive hut on the other side of the world from where her
centre felt to be. The male animal. Around her were some couple of
hundred all-but-naked men, smelling their own particular male
sweaty smell. This is the club from which I have been excluded all my
life. This is the kind of thing they get up to, the *kassa* house, the stag
night, the rugby club; things they do without women.

The darkness inside the hut was grateful to her. She watched Purnu and another man go through the ritual of mixing the *kassa*. William had told her about his experience inside the *kassa* house, of course, so she knew what to expect. As the two men began to circle the room dishing out the *kassa* she could feel her heart drumming fit to burst her chest, beating faster and faster and so loudly she was tempted to hiss at it, Quieten down! Everyone will hear us and then the game will be up! And it would be up, she knew that. Although she was right by the entrance, if she was discovered, even if she could move the stone and get through it before anyone could catch her, where would she go? There was nowhere she could hide on the island, no way she could survive on her own.

She was relieved when it was the other man and not Purnu who approached her with the spoon bearing her glob of *kassa*. That old fox Purnu would have rumbled her, for sure.

She took the *kassa* into her mouth and let it slide, sweet and gentle, down her throat. A minute or so later she felt a tingling in her toes that spread quickly and deliciously through her body. She lay there helpless, unable to move anything, other than her eyes and tongue, and she guessed she must be imagining the tingling along her spine as mist began to rise from the fire and dim figures to appear. She heard their plaintive calling for their loved ones and had an urgent need to swallow the lump swelling in her throat.

'Tr'boa, Tr'boa', 'Lisuo, Lisuo', 'Namabua, Namabua', pleaded the voices as they searched for those who had summoned them. One after another they stepped from the flames, their shapes putting on flesh, filling out all the time.

She peered anxiously into the mist. She hadn't been completely honest with William. Although research was her prime motive for risking her life to be here, there was something else too.

After the wraiths that emerged from the fire had dispersed about the hut, one remained. A white woman of around sixty, frail beyond her years, in a faded floral dress. Lucy caught her breath. The old lady looked about her anxiously, clearly disturbed by the presence of so many other people when this was obviously not a Thursday market day with bargains to be had by way of compensation for the crowd. Lucy wanted to call out to her, but was fearful her voice would give her away. She could only wait until the woman's searching gaze finally lighted upon her. Her mother smiled and shuffled across the hut.

'Mum! I – I thought you'd never see me.'

Her mother looked about her. 'Where is this place? Who are these people?'

'It's a hut, Mum, on a little island on the other side of the world.'

'I'm glad it's not my hut. I wouldn't like having all these people in it. There's nowhere to hide.'

'Mum, I wanted to see you. I've wanted to ever since you – you—'

'Died?'

'Yes. I needed to tell you something. How I killed you.'

Her mother smiled. She brushed her thinning hair from her eyes. 'It wasn't you, love, it was the cancer. You mustn't go blaming yourself for that. There wasn't anything anybody could have done.'

Before Lucy could explain how she had erased her mother from her life a couple of decades before her actual death, the ghost of an old man walked through her mother, followed by a middle-aged woman. As another old man walked towards her, her mother neatly stepped out of his path. 'Get out of it!' she snapped at him. 'What do they think they're doing, walking through someone else's body uninvited? I don't want them in my body!'

Satisfied that no-one else was approaching and the invasions were over she turned back to Lucy and smiled. 'Don't fret about me, my love. I felt the same when my mum went, so I know what it's like. It's just guilt because they've been taken and you haven't. It'll go, you'll see. Life goes on. It has to.'

Lucy made no further attempt to confess or explain. Maybe the idea that if you could only resurrect your loved ones you would say all the things you hadn't been able to before was a delusion. She managed to swallow and to say instead, 'Loved you, Mum.'

Too late she realized she'd used the wrong tense; her mother was starting to fade. 'Lucy,' the old woman said, her voice no more than a whisper, now, 'do you remember that teacher who tried it on with you? Do you remember my growl? I saw him off, didn't I?' She suddenly laughed. 'I liked being that dog and seeing off a stranger. I liked being that dog.'

A moment later her features were as faded as her old dress and a moment after that, she was gone.

THIRTY-TWO

I it was one plenty damn nuisance, the two missing pages. and not just any old pages either. What for is must be two such important pages? Managua asked himself. But then he reminded himself that there were no unimportant pages in *Hamlet*. Every word counted. You couldn't take away a single one without diminishing the whole. Still, these were two exceptionally busy pages; plenty things happened in them. The bottom of page 618 had Claudius instructing Rosencrantz and Guildenstern to take Hamlet off to England. Then his deficient copy of the *Complete Shakespeare* skipped to page 621 and Polonius was dead! How had this happened? Not only that, Hamlet had killed him! He admitted as much to the Queen. '*For this same lord, / I do repent . . .*' But then he went on to say, '*I will bestow him, and will answer well / The death I gave him.*'

This was one big puzzler for Managua. He wasn't entirely convinced by the Queen's explanation of the killing as an accident. According to her, Hamlet heard something moving behind the arras, whatever that was, a wall, perhaps, probably made of loosely woven fibre rather than bamboo since Hamlet's sword was easily able to penetrate it. Be that as it might, Hamlet called out, '*A rat! A rat!*', thrust his sword through the wall and killed Polonius.

Well, here was a damn good one. If Hamlet thought there was a rat behind the wall at what height did he thrust his sword through it? He would surely have expected a rat to be upon the ground, but if he had stabbed at that height he would only have hit Polonius in the ankle. Would that really have been enough to kill him? And so quickly, in less than two pages? It was simply not credible. Unless of course, the sword had been dipped in deadly poison, some Danish kind of *terrada* venom, perhaps, something that was, of course, entirely possible, given that a poisoned sword was used at the end of the play by Laertes in the duel. Although that fact might equally well suggest the opposite since it was quite clear in the duel scene that the use of a poisoned weapon was considered both unfair and unusual. Then again, perhaps Polonius was lying down behind the wall, though why the old man should do that wasn't at all clear. Perhaps he was ill? Or was suddenly tired and lay down to sleep?

Managua's head was spinning from it all. He'd spent the whole morning trying to reconstruct the missing pages from what he knew. He had to do this. He couldn't rely on another, entire *Hamlet* magically appearing before he'd finished the rest of the play; he'd waited a year already and nothing had turned up yet. Even Miss Lucy hadn't managed to get him a copy although she'd written to the people from whom she ordered her magazines. She'd even written to relatives in England requesting one, but either her letter or their reply had gone astray because nothing had turned up. She said she would write again but the trouble was he didn't think he could carry on with his translation until that missing bit was taken care of. He had to know what had happened so far before he could move on to what came next. It was not easy, trying to write Shakespeare so that no-one would be able to spot the difference between his work and the Bard's. He hadn't been sure he was up to the task. But then once you got stuck in you absorbed the man's style and after two or three hours Managua felt the stuff he was producing was pretty convincing. He'd come up with a more plausible explanation for Polonius's death, too.

He tossed his pencil aside and came out of the writerly trance that he entered whenever he picked it up and that cut off all extraneous sounds. He realized that the hut was quiet, that Lamua wasn't there. He strapped on his leg and limped to the doorway where he took in the position of the sun and worked out that this was the same time his wife had been absent the last few afternoons. He wondered where she was. He knew that some of the women chose this time to collect water from the hole. Perhaps Lamua had changed her time and begun going with this group; some petty falling-out with those she went with customarily, perhaps. But then he noticed the large water pot standing by the door.

He didn't have time to speculate further about where she might be. This was his opportunity. He grabbed a cloth shoulder bag and hurriedly began to fill it with food. He was just putting in a loaf of minoa bread when he noticed something at the bottom of the old tin they kept bread in to protect it from termites. He picked it up and stared at it. One of those American things that was full of numbers. A pocket calculator. Now what was that doing here? It could only have been brought into the hut by Lamua. But how had she come by it? Presumably it must be one the village boys had dropped, or perhaps the *gwanga*. But in that case, why had Lamua hidden it in the bread tin? He stared at the calculator for a moment and then put it back where he had found it. It was one big damn puzzler, all right, but he didn't have time to think about it now. He shouldered his bag and limped off, looking this way and that, just to make sure Lamua wasn't watching him. It would be just like her to spend several days establishing this regular absence to lure him into carelessness when he took the food.

What Managua didn't know was that Lamua wasn't the only one who was trying to find the pig now. And so he wasn't concerned when he passed Lintoa as he made his way into the jungle.

Lintoa had been watching Managua's hut for a couple of hours. He'd made an excuse not to go hunting for turtle eggs with Tigua and Sussua today, saying he didn't feel well.

As Managua limped by, Lintoa bent down to fiddle with the strap of one of his slingbacks, pretending to do it up. He was actually undoing it, ready to slip the shoes off as soon as Managua entered the jungle, so that he could move more swiftly and silently as he shadowed the old man. He was also avoiding conversation with Managua. If they got talking he would have to ask Managua where he was going which would mean that if Managua was on his way to feed the pig he would have to invent some other destination and would probably end up not going near the animal at all.

As soon as Managua plunged into the forest, Lintoa stashed his shoes in the crook between two branches of a tree where he hoped nobody would notice them and followed.

It was hard to figure out where Managua was going. The route meandered and at one point actually went in a circle and crossed over itself, so that Managua was suddenly coming back towards Lintoa who had to duck behind a tree to avoid being seen. At another it went across the shitting beach. Lintoa couldn't step out into the open because if Managua should happen to turn around the game would be up; it would be obvious he was following him. So when the old man hobbled once more into the jungle, Lintoa had to sprint across the shitting beach – with predictable results, the tide hadn't been in yet – so as not to lose him.

Eventually, though, as they emerged further along the shoreline, it became apparent where they were headed. There was only one place it could be, the Captain Cook. Of course, Managua must be taking food to the *gwanga*. Lintoa heaved a sigh of frustration and turned back. To think he'd wasted the best part of the day on this when he could have been finding eggs. And he needed the eggs to exchange for yams to pay Managua and Purnu for all the magic. It was such a damn joke! Here he was, following Managua to pay for the spells and instead it had cost him yams and made him less able to pay.

And then he remembered that he'd earlier seen the *gwanga* talking to Managua, then setting off in the direction of Miss Lucy's. Of course he could have returned while Managua was in his hut and Lintoa was watching for him, but equally well he might not. The *gwanga* usually walked through the village going to and from Miss Lucy's, talking to people he saw there, asking questions to help him

get them the reward for having their feet blown off. It was unlikely
he had returned yet. Besides, if Managua had food for the
American, wouldn't he have given it to him then and there? Or
wouldn't the *gwanga* have said he'd pick it up on his way back
home? There was no need for Managua to go to the Captain
Cook. So what was he up to? Suppose he had come now precisely
because he knew the *gwanga* was out?

Lintoa turned and ran back to the hotel. There was no sign of
Managua. But he hadn't met him returning to the village which
meant he'd either walked past the hotel on his way somewhere
else, or that he'd gone into it.

It would be pointless for Lintoa to walk past the building. For
one thing, if Managua had walked on and gone into the jungle,
he'd never be able to find him now. And if he'd gone into the hotel
and came out again they would walk slap-bang into one another.
Lintoa couldn't think of a plausible reason for his being there. So
he lowered himself behind a bush where he had a good view of
the hotel entrance and steeled himself for another vigil. It didn't
last long. A few minutes later Managua came out, the bag on his
shoulder flat and empty-looking now. Obviously he'd just fed the
pig! Lintoa smiled. It was hard not to laugh out loud. Purnu sure
was going to let him off some yams for this!

He kept low as Managua limped past his bush and watched him
along the beach until he was out of sight. Then he emerged from
his hiding place and walked towards the hotel. There was just one
mystery. How had Managua concealed the pig from the *gwanga*?
Unless, of course, the *gwanga* was in on it too. Then again, the hotel
was a large building. Bigger than twenty huts maybe. What if the
pig was at the far end? Then he had a sudden inspiration. What if
it was upstairs?

He walked as softly as his huge feet would allow and stood
pondering outside the hotel entrance. He imagined walking
triumphantly into the village with the pig under his arm. How
Purnu would be impressed by that! Not only would he get plenty
of yams, his chances of a match with Kiroa would improve no end.

He'd have to find something to muzzle the pig with first, of course, or he'd end up with no arms. Maybe ask the *gwanga* for compensation, he thought and giggled at the idea. He told himself to calm down. He hadn't even caught the pig yet. Knowing where one was and having it under control were two different things. He applied himself to the muzzle. That was it! He could slip off his bra and tie it around the pig's snout. That would stop it biting until he got it to the village. 'Pig is go feel what is be like for have bra pinch all time,' he said aloud.

He stepped through the doorway of the hotel and stopped dead. There was one thing he'd forgotten. The hotel was possessed by bad spirits. Everyone knew that. He could remember Managua telling all the children about them many years ago, when he himself was only a little girl. He took a step back and was about to leave when the thought came to him that, if the story was true, why had Managua gone in there himself? Was it because he was a sorcerer and able to deal with bad spirits? Or was it because he knew there was none there? He turned again and was about to pass through the doorway once more when he heard voices. They were distant, murmuring softly, as though not seeking to advertise themselves in the still of the afternoon. It was the hottest part of the day now, when even the insects slept.

Lintoa was out of there like a shot. In three seconds flat he was behind his bush again. He was shaking and for once he cursed his clumsy bigness. The bush scarcely concealed him. If only he had been slightly built like Tigua! He listened. He could hear nothing from here. Perhaps, after all, he'd imagined the voices. Perhaps it had been nothing more than the pig squeaking its pig noises. He reassured himself that this must be so. But, even so, he would forget about carrying the pig home in triumph. What if it escaped? There was more than a chance that it would; black bantams were plenty damn good at that! And if it did, however would he find it and save his yams? No, much safer, safer all round, just to go back and tell Purnu where the pig was. And he was on the very point of doing this when the slightest movement from above caught his eye. He

looked up towards the balcony that ran along the whole of the
back of the hotel's first floor, intended for the British to sit upon
and watch the ocean, he'd been told, though why they should have
wanted to do that he had no idea. No matter, he couldn't even
think of that now. He couldn't think of anything at all. For on the
balcony stood the most beautiful girl he had ever seen. So beautiful that had she been standing next to Kiroa you would never have
even noticed the latter was there. Her skin was pale, white he
would have said, and she looked to be tall, almost as tall as him,
perhaps. Lintoa rose and was about to call out to her when his
shoulder strap slipped. For once he didn't curse it. How could he
have forgotten? How could he approach this vision in his stupid
girl's clothes? Not to mention the stink of his feet from having
crossed the shitting beach too fast and carelessly. He threw himself
behind the bush again, hoping she hadn't noticed the movement.
He waited a moment, then lifted his head and peeped through the
fronds of the shrub. The balcony was empty. The white girl, if she
had ever been there, was now gone.

THIRTY-THREE

After William left, Lucy sat on her veranda sipping wine. It was probably not the best thing to do given that she'd woken with a massive *kassa* hangover. What was worse was the nagging anxiety that accompanied it. Lintoa. It was like having been very drunk and remembering just enough to know that you have made a fool of yourself. Only this was worse. This might cost her her life.

William had said he couldn't believe any of the natives he knew would harm her but Lucy had told him he didn't understand the power of the taboo. Besides, one of his friendly natives had attacked William. He had fallen quite a distance. He could easily have been killed. Even now, as she sat here, looking at the ocean, hearing the comforting sound of the breakers falling on the shore, she didn't know if Lintoa had betrayed her or not. If he'd told, it was all up with her. Her only hope was that he obviously hadn't done it last night or she'd know about it by now. If she could talk to him she might be able to use her past kindnesses to him, the dresses, the bras, the high heels and the beers, to plead his silence.

She heard a foot on the stair of the veranda and there, as though conjured by her thought, stood Lintoa. He was breathless and appeared as anxious as she herself felt.

'Miss Lucy—' he began.

She rose from the chair. 'We'd better go inside.' She managed to make it sound businesslike. She couldn't go letting him think he had a big advantage over her.

Inside they stood facing one another. Lintoa seemed too excited to say anything. She'd never seen him like this. A great adolescent boy whose masculinity was suddenly emphasized rather than denied by the silly dress he wore.

'About last night . . .' she began.

'Miss Lucy, I is want for you is do something for me,' he said.

'If I can. Will it mean you won't tell?'

'You is must do now,' he said and shucked first one muscular shoulder and then the other out of their shoulder straps and began peeling the dress down his body.

Lucy watched in horror. It was several beats before she could speak. 'No!' she gasped. 'Not that. I will not do that. I would rather die than let someone force me to do something against my will!'

Lintoa stopped pulling down the dress and stared at her. 'Miss Lucy, why you is be cross? I is not go hurt you. I is never go hurt you.'

She backed away from him and began circling the room, always facing him, hoping that she could reach the door and duck out of it before he made his move. Not that that would solve her problems. He was powerfully built and could easily outrun her. And once it was over, he had nothing to fear, because he knew she couldn't tell Managua or anyone else or he would tell about her being in the *kassa* house.

'I'm not worried about being hurt,' she said, although of course she was. She couldn't believe she was having this conversation with Lintoa, of all people. That great galumphing innocent! She got herself calm. 'I am not afraid. I just will not be forced to do it.'

Lintoa stared at her as if she'd lost her reason. 'Force? Who is force you for do anything?' Then his eyes widened. He looked like a child who has been unfairly smacked. 'Miss Lucy! You is think I is want for make *fug-a-fug* with you? You is be crazy!' A grin spread across his big lips and then he started to laugh.

Lucy was relieved by the laughter. And a bit put out too. Was it really so incredible that he might want to make love to her? Then she remembered the taboo against the islanders having sex with outsiders and saw that it was. She didn't know that Lintoa had already mentally abandoned any adherence to that particular taboo with just one glimpse of the white girl. 'What then?' she said. 'What is it you want?'

He had the dress down to his waist and reached behind him to undo his bra. 'I is want for you is *look* at me. I is want for you is say if I is look like boy.'

He dropped the dress to the floor and kicked off his high heels. He stood there in only a pubic leaf, a well-filled pubic leaf, Lucy noticed.

'You is wait,' he ordered. He lifted his hands to grab his hair and push it up behind his head so it looked as if it was cut short.

'Well?' he said.

'Oh yes,' she said, 'you're a boy all right.'

'You is be sure?' His voice was husky now, throaty with anxiety. 'I is sorry I is frighten you. I is not mean for do that. Is be no-one else I is can ask. Is be taboo against I is dress like boy.'

'I understand. Lintoa, you have no need to worry, you're definitely a boy.'

His face relaxed. 'Is be plenty good news. I is be girl all my life so I is worry plenty damn much.'

'What's brought all this on, Lintoa?' she asked. 'Why come here and do this today?'

He thought for a minute. 'OK, Miss Lucy, I is know you secret so I is tell you mine, because I is need you help.'

He told her about what he'd seen at the Captain Cook. Lucy was baffled. How could there be a white girl on the island and neither of them know about it? But she'd been in the *kassa* house only a few hours earlier and that had changed her perspective on things around here. Ghosts did walk this island, she knew that now. She'd never quite believed it until she'd seen it for herself. But if that were so, to whom then did this ghost belong?

'What can I do for you?'

'I is go see she tonight, but I is go as boy.'

'Isn't that awfully dangerous for you, dressing as a boy, breaking the taboo? What if someone sees you?'

'No, no-one is go near Captain Cook 'cept *gwanga*. I is wait until is be dark. Is be big moon tonight. I is leave village in dress. When I is reach hotel I is take off dress and is become boy. Girl is only see me as boy. She is fall in love with boy, is not be so?'

'Hmm, maybe. You can't guarantee someone will fall in love with you.'

'Is be OK, I is get magic for that. That is not be problem. Problem is be hair.' He let it drop and it fell upon his shoulders. 'What is I can do with this damn silly hair? I is not be allow for have cut off.' Tears of frustration brimmed his eyes.

'Oh, I think we can do something about that. Wait a minute.' She found an elastic band and showed him how to tie it up. He practised.

'Now I is look like boy?'

'Nobody could think you were anything else.'

THIRTY-FOUR

Managua had only got another hour or so in on the scene he'd devised to fill the missing two pages when Lintoa burst into the hut.

'Not now,' Managua snapped after the briefest glance from his page revealed who his visitor was. 'I is be busy with one damn tricky scene.'

Lintoa stood in the doorway. He didn't say anything. Peering up over his spectacles the old man could see the she-boy was anxious. He flung down his pencil with an anger he didn't really feel. He knew he couldn't leave the she-boy in this state but he was wary of setting a precedent that allowed any fool to come in here and start wasting his precious time.

'Well?' he said, in his most thunderous tones.

'I is need you is stop spell,' said Lintoa. He walked over to Managua who gave a stage sigh and gestured to him to sit. Lintoa squatted beside the milk crate.

'Stop spell? I is not understand. What you is mean?'

'How hard is be for understand? I is ask you is make spell, now I is ask you is stop spell. I is not want for Kiroa is fall in love with me.'

'But I is think "she is be like when is come big storm and is be black clouds and sky is be dark as night and sun is make holes in clouds—"'

'OK, OK, you is stop now.' Lintoa blushed. 'I is change mind.'

'You is change mind in space of few days? What kind of lover is you be? How she is can be "so bright you is be dazzle" one day and couple more days you is not want she?'

'I is change my mind, is be all.'

'Typical woman!' Managua rolled his eyes skywards.

Lintoa flinched at the cruelty of the remark. But he knew that Managua was justifiably annoyed at being messed around so he let it pass. 'Anyway, I is not want for argue. You is just forget spell, OK?'

'No, is not be OK. I is already make spell.'

'Well, then, how is be this? You is make small alteration of spell. You is take spell off Kiroa and is put on someone else.'

'Is not be possible. Spell is already be on Kiroa. Is be plenty difficult spell for make. Is be so many other spells on she for other boys is must be plenty strong magic for defeat all they.'

'OK, OK, so you is can not change spell. Just take spell off altogether then. Stop spell.'

'This is be what I is tell you, is not be possible. Spell is work right now, even as we is speak. If you is go change you mind, is best not ask for spell in first place.'

They sat in silence for a couple of minutes. Lintoa rested his chin on his fist, his elbow on his knee.

'All right then, is be nothing I is can do 'bout Kiroa. So now I is need you is make me new spell for other girl.'

'Oh yes,' said Managua, 'and how many days is you be crazy for this girl? When you is come back and ask for spell for third girl?'

'You is be plenty funny,' said Lintoa. 'But I is not have time for listen you is make joke. I is need spell fast.'

'I is can see that,' boomed Managua with theatrical disbelief in his tone. 'You is need spell plenty damn quick before you is go off this poor girl too!'

'Managua, please, just say you is do magic.'

'OK, OK, but you is go need find turtle eggs day and night for next year for get all yams for this. Now who is be this fortunate girl?'

'I is not can tell you.'

Managua exploded. 'You is not can tell me! How in name of *fug-a-fug* is you expect I is make spell for girl if I is not know who she is be? What is I suppose for do? Send spell out there and hope is find right girl?'

'Maybe you is make spell for make girl who is see me tonight fall in love with me?'

Managua considered. 'Is be plenty damn difficult spell. I is be pretty sure no-one is pull that one off before.'

'But you is be such great sorcerer, Managua. I is know you is can do.'

'Yes and cloud in sky outside is be very like whale. Flattery is not work on me.'

But a challenge would. Managua liked the intellectual difficulty of the task and therefore he agreed to do it. He sure as hell had no other reason to. He didn't ever expect to see any yams from Lintoa.

THIRTY-FIVE

The first problem Lintoa had that evening, as he'd always known it would be, was how to get rid of Tigua. Sussua was not a problem, he would just go along with anything he said, but Tigua was such a damn nosy sow he wouldn't be happy until he knew just what Lintoa was up to. Which of course he couldn't tell him.

He met them as soon as he left his hut. Tigua came tripping over to him, eyes already narrowed in inquisition. 'Where you is be all day? We is look high and low for you after we is finish find eggs. Where you is go?'

'I is not feel so good. I is sleep.'

'Where you is sleep? Your *mamu* is say she is not see you all day.'

Lintoa made a vague gesture with one hand. It took in most of the island beyond the village. 'Oh, nowhere special. In jungle.'

'In jungle? You is damn lucky *terrada* is not get you. Managua is tell me story he is read 'bout this fella 'is go sleep in jungle and other fella is put *terrada* venom in he ear. Fella who is sleep is die. Only crazy fool is sleep in jungle.'

'I is sleep in tree.'

'Ah, so is be another funny thing is can be find in tree.'

'What you is talk about?'

'They.' Tigua lifted his right hand which Lintoa now realized had been hidden behind his back and held up Lintoa's red sling-backs. 'Shoes is grow on trees now.'

Lintoa made to snatch them back but Tigua was too fast for him and danced away with them. 'Keep they, is be too damn pinchy for me. Is why I is take they off!' Lintoa yelled after him.

'But you is need they tonight,' said Tigua. 'For go *poto*.'

Poto was the village boys' favourite sport, after making *fug-a-fug*, of course, a game similar to hockey, played with sticks and a dead rat. The way a *poto* evening worked was all the teenagers in the village would go to the *poto* ground, a jungle clearing near the village. The older boys would play the game, the younger ones keep up a supply of replacement dead rats as they tended to be got through pretty fast and the girls of all ages would sit and admire the finer points of play and the even finer points of the players. Afterwards there was noise in the jungle and in the *bukumatula* houses until dawn.

'Only way I is go *poto* is if I is play. When I is boy. I is not go in silly shoes like you.' Lintoa put on his best scowl to make it look as if he was genuinely annoyed about the shoes.

'Oh, is she be upset then?' mocked Tigua, who usually put up with Lintoa because he was in thrall to him, but occasionally rebelled against his querulousness. He flung the shoes at him, rather than to him.

'You is can keep they!' yelled Lintoa. He turned and stormed off into the jungle. Once he'd gone in deep enough to be sure he was out of sight, he doubled back to the edge of the village clearing. He hid himself behind a bush – he seemed to be doing a lot of this lately – and parted the leaves to see how Tigua had taken his exit. He was relieved to see that he and Sussua had met up with some other teenagers and were chatting away like excited monkeys as they moved off towards the *poto* ground.

Lintoa ducked into the jungle on the other side of the village and made his way through it down to the shitting beach which had been washed clean by the tide by this time of day. It was past twilight but there was a fat old moon over the ocean and it laid a silver trail across the water that gave him plenty of light to see by. And be seen by, too, so he hugged the edge of the jungle, although it was unlikely anyone would be about tonight, not with the *poto* game going on at the village, except for the *gwanga* that was, and Lintoa was confident he would always be able to spot a white man before the white man spotted him.

In no time at all Lintoa was at the Captain Cook. He had no fear of spirits now that he knew a girl his own age lived there and that Managua had played a trick on them all. He walked along the back of the hotel and stuck his head through one of the window holes. The room with the big table, where Tigua had told him the *gwanga* slept, was empty. The *gwanga* must either be in the *kassa* house or at Miss Lucy's. Satisfied there was no-one to catch him, Lintoa took a couple of steps into the jungle. He slipped off his dress and bra and tied up his hair in the way Miss Lucy had shown him with the elastic band she'd given him. Then he concealed himself behind a bush from where he could observe the balcony. Now, having successfully evaded Tigua, he had to face his other potential problem. Suppose the girl did not show? But then he looked at the moon, at the great silver blanket it had stretched out across the sea and the beach, at the way it transmuted the trees into dark animal shapes that seemed to be waiting too for something to happen and he knew she could not fail to appear. On such a night, well, on such a night, no girl with a balcony overlooking the ocean could resist the temptation to step out onto it and worship the view. Lintoa was starting to appreciate why the British might have wanted to do it.

He waited a plenty long time. The *poto* game would be half over by now, he thought, but even though he loved *poto* he had no regrets. Besides, he had no choice about it. Even if he waited all night for nothing, it was all he was able to do.

Then, just as his legs were growing stiff from sitting still for so long he heard the murmur of voices. Two people were talking, both female, he judged. Laughter, light and joyful, like the babbling of a stream between two rocks. Then the sound of feet upon concrete and there she was, no longer white now, but silver, her skin reflecting back the light of the moon just as the moon itself gave back the sun's.

She turned her head and spoke to someone inside the hotel. He couldn't hear what she was saying, but he loved the way her face came alive. He decided to risk going closer. In front of the hotel the ground was clear except for a solitary bush, which he judged was just big enough to hide him. He had a new-found confidence in his ability to conceal himself behind shrubs. Of course he could stand under the balcony but then he wouldn't be able to see her. There was no choice and Lintoa made a bolt for the bush. He got there just in time, a second before she turned her head back. He peeped through the fronds of the shrub, not daring to part them lest he be seen, and found she was staring straight at him, or rather, at his bush! He thought she must have seen him but then guessed that her attention had been drawn, on so still a night, by the bush's movement. It was swaying back and forth where he'd jumped into it, in contrast to the lack of motion all around. He held his breath and the main stem of the bush with his hand to try to stop it moving. Eventually it did and her attention wandered once more to the moon and the ocean.

'Is be so beautiful,' she murmured. There it was again, the voice like a clear stream. How he could have loved her for that voice alone! 'Is sure be one special night, *Mamu*.' The voice from indoors replied but Lintoa couldn't catch what it said. He settled himself down in the bush to watch. It was enough just to do that. To watch and listen.

And it was because he was listening so hard, with all his attention, that Lintoa heard the rustle of something close to him. He ignored it, too besotted with the silver girl to pay it any attention. But then it came again. And again. At first it annoyed him. It was an unnecessary distraction. He felt that if he was perfectly quiet he might be able to hear the girl breathe. But not over this damn rustling. He looked down and saw something move just by his foot. It was small, barely as long as his pointing finger and so narrow that at first he didn't recognize it. This was entirely understandable. He'd never seen a baby green shoestring before. But then it moved out of the shadow of a leaf and the moonlight caught it. Lintoa sat as still as he would be for ever in half a minute if he moved. If he moved it would have to be fast. He wouldn't have time for concealment; the girl would see him.

He considered the irony of his situation. It was funny, a moment or so ago he'd been sitting there looking at the girl and thinking that if he died then it wouldn't matter, because he would die the happiest he had ever been. But now, faced with the possibility of it actually happening, he was not so sure. He was even more not so sure when he felt something slither quickly across his right – or was it his left? – hand, which was resting on the ground beside him. He looked down. Another baby shoestring. He turned his head and almost passed out from shock. One, two three, four . . . shit! how many babies did these things have? He gave up counting at twenty-four. The point wasn't the number, the point was what just one of them could do to you. But then, perhaps the baby ones couldn't kill you? Maybe they were like humans and hadn't got their teeth yet. How old did they have to be to administer a fatal bite? He didn't want to find out. He felt unusually exposed and vulnerable in just his pubic leaf. He realized its disadvantage com- pared to a dress: there was a lot more skin for a snake to go at. A bead of sweat dribbled down his face and hung on his chin for the longest moment. Then it dripped, landing beside one of the baby snakes. The snake turned and looked up at him, opened its mouth and hissed. Well, that was one question taken care of. It had teeth, all right, including the two at the front that did all the damage. He didn't have time to dwell upon the thought. At the same moment as the baby snake hissed a similar but louder noise came from in front of him. Something was rustling through the fallen, dry leaves under the bush. Quick as lightning, a two-foot-long green shoestring shot out from under them, stopped, lifted its head and stared straight at Lintoa.

Lintoa's other hand, the one that didn't have any baby snakes near it, moved silent as a snake itself, scrabbling over the dusty earth. It was searching desperately for a weapon. Nothing. Lintoa inwardly muttered the universal prayer for such times, the one we all make when we're up against it. 'Please, if I is get out of this, I is promise for be good girl.'

And perhaps one of his ancestors heard, because something certainly steered his hand to the only stone within his reach. His fingers curled around it in the same instant as the snake lowered itself to the ground and began to slither towards him. With a speed a *koku-koku* would have been proud of Lintoa lifted the rock and smashed it down upon the snake's head. In a fraction of the next moment he was on his feet and jumping out of the bush. And another fraction of a moment after that the girl on the balcony gasped and said, 'Who is be there? Who you is be?'

Lintoa's response was one he would not have predicted ten minutes earlier: he ignored her. He was too busy looking at the ground, trying to make sure that no newly orphaned baby green shoestrings had pursued their *mamu*'s murderer. In the end he was satisfied it was safe to look up and get his eyes back on the girl.

When she saw his face full-on for the first time she gasped again. 'What magic place this world is be for have boy like this!'

'Is be OK. Is be only me. Only Lintoa.'

She smiled. 'Only? You is be one big boy far as I is see. I is not know. I is never see boy close up before.'

Lintoa's chest swelled even more. It was lucky he wasn't wearing his bra because the straps would never have taken the strain. Not that there'd have been any strain if he had had it on. The girl wouldn't have said that to a boy in a bra.

'And you is be one plenty pretty girl,' he said.

'You is think so? No-one is ever tell me before.'

'You is be most pretty girl on island. You is light up whole night.'

She laughed. 'You is make joke of me. Is be moon is light up everything.'

'Moon is be nothing beside you. Is be like flame beside sun; you is not even see.'

The voice came from inside the hotel again. 'I is speak with self, *Mamu*,' the girl called back. She widened her eyes to Lintoa. 'I is pretend have conversation with boy.' Gentle laughter from within.

This girl is be plenty smart, thought Lintoa. Is not just be pretty face.

The girl talked in loud whispers now. 'Is be my *mamu*. If she is find you here is be big trouble. No-one is must know of we. How you is come for be here? No-one is ever come here, especially in dark.'

'I is follow Managua here when he is bring you food. I is see you for little moment. I is must come back.'

'What for you is must come back?'

'I is must see you again. I is think you is be ghost but then I is think, What for Managua is feed ghost? so I is must return.'

'Well,' she said. 'Now you is see me again you is can go.'

'No, no, I is cannot. I is not come for just see you. I is come for tell you I is love you.'

It was hard to tell in the silver light but he could have sworn she blushed. 'No-one is ever tell me this before tonight.'

He smiled. 'Is be first time for many things tonight.'

The voice from indoors again. He couldn't catch what it was saying but he recognized its suspicious tone. The girl looked anxiously towards it, then back at him. 'You is must go now. Is be one big trouble if you is be find here.'

Lintoa's answer was to take a run towards the balcony. He grabbed the branch of a tree that grew against it and swung himself up. He vaulted the balustrade and landed beside her. Over the startled girl's shoulder he could see into the hotel. A brown-skinned woman in a grass skirt. He grasped the girl by the shoulders, pulled her to him and kissed her. He released her and before she could say a word, he sprang back over the balustrade, grabbed the tree branch and swung himself down. As his feet touched the ground the silly thought leaped into his mind that life without a dress was so much easier, although, it had to be admitted, not so safe around snakes.

He looked up and waved at the girl then turned to go.

'Wait, you is must come back!' she called.

He turned and walked back to stand beneath her. 'What you is want?'

She blushed and dissimulated. 'I — I is forget.'

'Then I is hope you is never remember, then I is must stay here until you is do.'

'I — I is only want for say, you is come again?'

'Is be one damn stupid question,' he said in a kindly way Tigua would never have recognized. 'If nest of *terradas* is not stop me then nothing is go do.'

It was late. Lintoa wanted to get back to his parents' house before they started wondering where he was. If they saw Tigua and Sussua without him, they might begin to ask questions. Worse, Tigua might.

He found the tree where he'd left his dress and bra. There was the bra, hanging on the branch, just as he'd left it. But the dress, which had been beside it had gone. He looked in the neighbouring trees. Perhaps it had been blown into one of them? But no, that was impossible, the night was so still. He searched the ground all around. Nothing.

There remained only two possibilities. Perhaps a monkey had found it. Yes, that was probably it. Most likely a howler monkey. They were always playing jokes on people. The other possibility he didn't even like to think about. That the dress had been taken by a human. Someone who had followed him here and knew he had broken the taboo.

There was nothing for it, Lintoa would just have to return home in his pubic leaf. He balled the bra in his fist. There was no point in putting it on. Dressed as a boy he had a chance that anyone who saw him would mistake him for someone else. The bra would give him away. Besides, it was late. The *poto* game would have finished hours ago. All the young people would be making *fug-a-fug*. All the men would have had too much *kassa* to notice him. And the women, well, at this time the women would be in their homes, waiting for their men to stagger home.

★ ★ ★

Kiroa stood in the doorway of the *bukumatula* house and stretched. She had almost fallen asleep while her latest boyfriend was making *fug-a-fug*. He had taken so long and had kept telling her how much he loved her. It was hard to get excited when someone did that. It had just left her feeling hungry, which of course meant she would have to return to her parents' house, food in the *bukumatula* house being taboo. Still, at least she could get some sleep at home without being woken up for more *fug-a-fug* by that silly boy.

She stretched again and yawned, closing her eyes. When she opened them she saw a ghostly figure walking between the huts. He was tall and looked strong. His muscles bulged. She couldn't help noticing his pubic leaf. 'Oh, my,' she said to herself. 'Is be one long leaf string!'

She would have called out but that would have woken the pestering boy and half the village. So she contented herself with simply watching. For now she knew who it was, this muscular hero. That silly she-boy Lintoa. Who would have thought those stupid dresses could conceal a body like this? Who would have believed such a thing? How could any girl ever look at another boy again, when she had seen this? All her life Kiroa had despised boys. She had always thought it was because boys were such pathetic, wheedling creatures, so far beneath her. Now she knew she'd been wrong; it was just that before tonight, she had never seen the right one.

THIRTY-SIX

William pushed back his chair from the mahogany table, stretched his arms and yawned. He was tired after a morning spent transcribing tapes of his interviews with amputees and cross-referencing witness statements. He got up and wandered out onto the veranda. The ocean was unusually calm, unlike his mind which was hyperactive with dates and injury assessments and locations. He needed something to take it off the work for a while. He cursed himself for not bringing a book, other than law books. He thought about borrowing one from Managua, or going to see Lucy but either course of action would mean he'd get no work done this afternoon. The thought of Lucy reminded him of the manuscript she'd given him and he went and found it under the mound of papers on the working, that is the non-sleeping, end of his table. He gathered up the bundle, returned to the veranda and sat down with his back against the wall of the hotel, selected a page at random and began to read:

As you might expect, in a matrilineal society women are more highly valued. It is through women that wealth and status are accrued. A woman passes her wealth to her children, a man leaves his property to his nearest blood relations, namely his sister's children. During his lifetime it is his duty to supply these nephews and nieces (but not, of

course, those who are the children of his brothers) with
yams and any material things they might have need of. This
takes precedence over providing for his wife's children,
since, by the natives' lights, these are not his own. When a
man is looking for a wife, the best partner is a woman who
has no sisters but four or five brothers. Her children will
be supplied with many yams and other things. On the other
hand a girl who is one of five sisters and who has only one
or perhaps no brother at all, means the children he moulds
and comes to love will grow up in poverty.

Since females are the conduit of wealth it therefore
follows that girl children are more prized than boys, for it
is girls who will continue the family line and the accumula-
tion of property. One result of this is that it is considered a
great misfortune, a tragedy almost, for a woman to have no
daughters. A woman will hang her head in shame as she
confesses to you that she has five fine strapping sons but
no girl child. Out of this has been born a desperate
emotional longing among the island women for daughters.
Here must lie the origin of the phenomenon of the so-called
she-boys. It is the custom that if a woman produces a
number of boy children but no girl, and reaches the stage
where she believes she is incapable of giving birth again,
then the last boy to be born is raised as a girl. His hair will
not be cut and as soon as he is old enough to wear clothes
he is put into a grass skirt. Instead of being raised to manly
pursuits, the she-boy is educated as a girl and expected to
wash clothes, clean the hut, sew, search for turtle eggs
and tend the garden while others of his true sex learn to
fish, to build huts and dig bamboo pits for bantam pigs.
When the she-boys reach adolescence they, like real girls,
are excluded from playing poto or entering the *kassa*
house.

Because the natives generally marry young and take no
steps to limit their families, there are few she-boys. Most

women keep on having babies until they produce a girl. Even when this does not happen, if a daughterless woman has a sister who has a number of girls, it is common for her to adopt a niece. Only if this is not possible will she resort to making her youngest son into a girl.

There is of course no economic benefit to the mother of a she-boy. The motivation is purely emotional to satisfy the maternal longing that has over the centuries evolved from practical and social considerations.

She-boys are spoken to and of as girls and treated almost exactly as if they were female. The only exception to this is that they do not appear naked before girls when the latter go swimming because it is taboo for members of one sex to display their genitals to those of the other. Likewise the she-boys do not strip off before other boys; the fiction that they are girls is here maintained and, of course, it is taboo for girls to disrobe before boys. The she-boys have a specially segregated part of the shitting beach to themselves between those set aside for men and women, so that neither can see them naked, and this may be considered as symbolic of their in-between status.

Of course there is one occasion on which boys and girls see one another naked and that is during one-to-one sex. But there is a strict taboo against homosexuality and because of this the she-boys are condemned to celibacy while all their young peers are indulging themselves freely. As they are dressed as girls and considered girls, it is taboo for them to make love to other girls. But of course they cannot make love to boys like true girls since that too would constitute homosexuality.

There are at present three she-boy adolescents in the main village. When I asked them how they felt about not being able to make *fug-a-fug* I received differing reactions from each of them. Sussua, the quiet one, blushed and giggled. Tigua, always willing to talk, shrugged and said,

'Miss Lucy, we is know from time we is be little girl this is not be for we yet. Is be something we is not concern we with.' I couldn't have said why at the time but this strong denial of any interest filled me with great sadness.

At this, Lintoa rolled his eyes and said, 'Huh, you is speak for youself. Is be damn stupid custom. I is be flesh and blood like any other boy—'

At the word *boy* there was a sharp intake of breath from Tigua which earned him a scowl from Lintoa, who went on, '– like any other boy. I is tell you when I is become boy I is go make *fug-a-fug* all day and all night for one year. Is be no-one is be able for stop me.'

I expected some comment upon this from Tigua, some reference to what he might do in the future but he merely looked at the ground and said nothing. Later of course I realized why I had felt so saddened by his acceptance of celibacy: in his case it may be permanent, because it is as plain as a pikestaff that he adores Lintoa and, with the taboos against homosexuality, not to mention Lintoa's fierce devotion to heterosexuality, how can Tigua's passion ever be consummated?

I asked him how he managed now and said I presumed that in an atmosphere of so much sexual activity they must indulge in self-pleasure, which brought such strenuous denials and guilty looks that I felt like a Victorian school-marm. Masturbation is not taboo, but is seen as a perversion. With sexual intercourse so freely available why would someone want to play with themselves? It is regarded as something only someone soft in the head would want to do, is derided, rather than condemned, and never, ever, admitted to.

When a she-boy reaches maturity, that is adulthood, which is at around the age of eighteen, he is allowed to choose his sex. Nearly all decide to revert to their natural sex as is shown by the absence of any older she-boys in the village, although I understand that until shortly before my arrival here there existed a she-boy of some eighty years old, a man who continued to wear a grass skirt and took his place among the other old women of the village, sitting and gossiping around the fire with them and greatly revered for his knowledge of herbal remedies and ancient recipes.

I will have departed the island before the present crop of older she-boys reaches choosing age. Should I ever have cause to return in later years, which is more than likely if the present work attracts the attention I expect when it is published, it will be interesting to discover what choices were made. Somehow I cannot imagine Tigua in a pubic leaf; the very idea seems somewhat indecent. And yet, equally, I cannot imagine him without Lintoa as his constant companion. It is very difficult to foresee what will become of this funny little boy.

William's cheeks were on fire as he lowered the manuscript. He was burning up with embarrassment and shame. How could he have been so stupid? So blind? How could he not have noticed what should have been so obvious to anyone with half a brain, that these three hefty girls were young men in drag?

And why hadn't Lucy told him? Why had she permitted him to be hauled around the jungle by these three transvestites? Why hadn't she corrected him when she heard him call them things like 'My dear'?

She'd allowed him to make a laughing stock of himself. He'd thought he had her confidence, but this proved him wrong. And if he didn't have it in this, where else might it be lacking? He went inside, pulled on his boots and hurried to the village. As luck would have it the first people he came across were Tigua and Lintoa who were sitting on a fallen tree trunk sewing grass skirts. Lintoa's face wore its all-too-familiar scowl.

'These stitches is be one big sow for get right,' he muttered to

Tigua, not even looking up at William. 'My fingers is be too big for damn needle.'

'You is just be damn hopeless for sew,' replied the smaller she-boy. 'You is not listen when you *mamu* is teach you, that is be truth of matter.'

William coughed. Both she-boys looked up. Lintoa's face cracked open into a smile. 'Ah, *gwanga*! I is be plenty pleased for see you. I is need good reason for stop this game.' He tossed the grass skirt to one side and brushed pieces of loose grass from his pink dress.

'You're boys,' said William. He couldn't keep a certain note of anger out of his voice.

Their heads jerked up in surprise and they stared at him for a moment before replying.

'Yes,' said Lintoa.

'No,' said Tigua.

'You're she-boys,' said William. 'You're boys who dress as girls.'

'You is see,' said Lintoa, turning to Tigua, 'I is tell you. I is be mean for be boy. This man is come here from America. He is know nothing of stupid custom. But truth is be obvious. He is can see I is be boy.'

'He is be here two weeks and is not see until now. Is call you "my dear" in jungle. Is offer for find me pink boots.'

William smarted at the memory of that day. The deference he had shown them. The delicacy with which he'd averted his eyes when they popped behind a tree to relieve themselves. How could Lucy have put him through that?

'Why didn't you tell me you were boys?' he demanded.

'You is not ask,' said Tigua. She – he – gave William his cheekiest smile. 'Besides, I is not be boy. I is be girl.'

'I don't think so,' said William.

'OK, so you is see boy wear cocktail dress like this? Boy is walk around in bra? Boy is have high-heel shoes? You is go tell me that?'

'That doesn't make you a girl!'

'If is not make me girl I is not know what is make me,' replied Tigua.

'It's what's underneath the dress that counts. You have a – a – what do you call it—' he was struggling to recall the manuscript, 'a – a *pwili*.'

'Is be small point,' said Tigua.

'Is be very small point in you case,' said Lintoa. Tigua fetched him one round the ear. Lintoa took it good-naturedly.

'I'd say it was the whole point,' said William. 'I'd say having a *pwili* made you a boy.'

'You is be right,' said Lintoa eagerly. 'I is tell she that for years. You is hear that, Tigua? *Gwanga* is say just what I is always tell you.'

William left them arguing. There was no point in blaming them for his myopia. But Lucy was a different matter. He found her bathing in a small lagoon near her house. 'Come on in, the water's lovely!' she called when she saw him. It was a tempting prospect. Through the clear water he could see she was naked. But he was too angry to accept the invitation.

'Tigua and Lintoa are boys!' he shouted from the pool side.

'I know!' she replied. The answer made him even angrier.

'But why didn't you tell me?'

She paddled slowly towards where he stood. She smiled cheekily at him. 'You didn't ask.'

'You've made such a fool of me, letting me go off in the jungle with a couple of transvestites. The goddam mosquito bites have only just stopped hurting. And afterwards, you could have tipped me off then.'

'I gave you my book. It's not my fault you didn't read it.'

William bit his lip. That much was true. 'I feel such an idiot,' he muttered.

'Think you need an anatomy lesson,' said Lucy splashing water up at him. 'Why don't you get your things off and jump in here and I'll see what I can do.'

As William began to unbutton his shirt he had a sudden realization that he was allowing Lucy to buy off his anger. He felt he was being manipulated but he could not have said how or why. When he plunged into the water he could not help but shiver, for it was unexpectedly cold.

THIRTY-SEVEN

Since William's arrival on the island there had been an outbreak not only of magic but also of secrets. Now almost everybody had at least one. Managua had always had two, about Pilua's fate and about the whereabouts of the pig. But now he had Lintoa's as well, even though Lintoa had concealed from him part of the secret, namely the identity of the object of his affection. Purnu was concealing so many secrets it was difficult for him to open his mouth without letting one escape; he was learning to read; he was sleeping with Lamua; he had made spells to help Lamua find the pig; he had enlisted Lintoa to assist with the pig search and he was searching for Pilua for the *gwanga*. Lamua was sleeping with Purnu behind her husband's back and was searching for information about the woman Pilua. Lucy was concealing the facts that she'd been inside the *kassa* house, that Lintoa had discovered and loved a mysterious white girl and that he had been out dressed – or rather undressed – as a boy. She had at least been unburdened of one secret, albeit one of omission, that she had not told William Hardt that the she-boys were not girls because his confusion over them had amused her. William knew about Lucy and the *kassa* hut and he was clandestinely teaching Purnu to read. Kiroa had not told a soul that she had seen Lintoa dressed as a boy. She hadn't revealed to anyone that she'd fallen in love with him. Only Tigua had virtually no secrets. He would tell anyone who asked that he had seen a little black dress in *Vogue* which he knew was just him. Tigua's solitary secret which he told nobody was that he loved Lintoa, but it was the one secret on the island that everybody knew.

Secrecy always breeds suspicion and the atmosphere on the island was alive with it.

Purnu was by nature suspicious; he thought he saw in others the corruption he knew to be in himself. So when he watched his daughter trailing along after the three she-boys, he immediately knew something was wrong. Normally Kiroa was at the centre of a crowd of boys, all of them after her to spend the night in the *bukumatula* house with them. She treated them with disdain. Those who professed love, she mocked. Her beauty ensured she could have any boy she wished and so, like a child who can have every toy it wants, she wanted none of them. And now, here she was hanging around with the she-boys. Purnu was an overly fond father, as widowers with daughters tend to be, and kept a close eye on Kiroa. He'd even followed her this morning to try to discover what was going on in her mind and had realized that, in spite of the taboo against same-sex love, she was besotted with Lintoa. He also noticed that the big she-boy, who usually wore a red dress, had lately changed it for a pink one and wondered why that should be. No matter, he still looked ridiculous. But that wasn't the worst of it. The thing that really galled Purnu was that Lintoa obviously had no time for his daughter. Mostly he simply ignored her, but occasionally her constant attentions irritated him and Purnu watched in dismay as he shooed her away. To think his daughter, who could have her pick of all the boys, should be rejected by a she-boy! It beggared belief. And the most humiliating thing of all was, the more Lintoa pushed her away, the more she wanted him. For a girl like Kiroa, the new experience of not being able to get what she wanted was driving her wild.

There was only one answer to how all this had come to be, and Purnu guessed at whose door to lay the blame.

Managua sat trying to work on his revision of Polonius's death scene but he couldn't concentrate. Every so often he would lift the upturned crate and finger the red dress he had concealed beneath it. Managua's great secret was not a secret any more. Lintoa had un-covered it. He had surmised as much yesterday when Lintoa would not reveal to him the object of the new spell. Why wouldn't the she-boy tell him if it was just another island girl? Besides, who was there but his own daughter who could hold a pig-fat oil lamp to Kiroa? And his discovery of the discarded red dress had confirmed his suspicions. Well, it was a stand-off. He had Lintoa's secret and Lintoa had his.

He heard footsteps and stuffed the dress under the milk crate. Purnu walked in. Managua pretended to be so caught up in his work that he hadn't noticed. Purnu walked around him and peered first over his right shoulder and then over his left, looking at Managua's writing.

The little sorcerer nodded knowingly. 'Hmm,' he said, pointing a bony forefinger at the page. 'I see you is have "can" in there.' Managua followed the skinny digit and was astonished to find it actually was pointing at the word "can". He almost dropped his pen. Purnu put his hands behind his back and took another turn around the hut, finally stopping behind Managua again and peer-ing over his other shoulder. Again the bony finger. 'I is see you is have second "can" also.'

Managua could hardly believe it. Once could have been chance, but not a second time. He turned and looked up at his diminutive rival. 'So?'

Purnu shrugged. 'Is be nothing wrong with that. Is be all right for have two "cans". "Can" is be very good word. You is *can* say two things with this one word.' Here he gave a facetious little chuckle. 'How many words you is *can* say that about?'

Managua was annoyed beyond measure. 'Here,' he challenged, thrusting the paper into Purnu's weasel face, 'you is *can* read rest if you is like.'

Purnu lifted a hand deprecatingly. 'No, no, is be all right. I is just want for read "cans". Is be enough read for now. I is have something else I is must talk with you 'bout.'

Managua was pleased to see the little man's face grow angry now and felt his own relax a little. 'You is best sit down,' he said.

Purnu squatted the other side of the milk crate. 'Is be this. You is use magic on my daughter. You is put love spell on she.'

'What is be wrong with that? I is not say is be true, but if is be true, what is be wrong?'

'You is make she fall in love with damn she-boy, that is what is be wrong! Is be your idea of joke?'

Managua adjusted his spectacles and looked at his manuscript as though all this was of little interest to him. 'You is be sure she is be in love? Perhaps she is just want advice for dress.'

'You is not mock me!' Purnu was practically snarling now. 'You is must see how she is trail after this she-boy. Is be big one, Lintoa.'

Managua turned to him. 'Yes, I is see. Who is can fail for notice? I is not want for hurt you feelings.'

This annoyed Purnu even more. He looked like he could scarcely restrain himself from striking the older man. 'Is be so ridiculous is must be spell at work. And there is be only one person beside me who is can make such spell work so well. Is must be you.'

Managua said, 'You is let me ask you question. How this she-boy is treat she? He is love she back? He is ask she go in jungle with he?'

Purnu hung his head. 'You is know is not be so. He is push she away so she is make even more fool of self.'

'Exactly,' said Managua. 'So what for Lintoa is come ask me for spell for make Kiroa love he if he is not want she?'

Purnu shook his head sadly. There was no answer to that.

THIRTY-EIGHT

From 'The Other Side of Paradise: the sexual life and customs of an unspoiled people' by L. Tibbut (unpublished manuscript)

Birth and death

The longer one spends upon the island, the more one loses one's initial patronizing attitude to the islanders' beliefs and begins to admire the advantages they offer. It is easy to feel superior to ignorance and superstition, but, to use that awful modern phrase, it works for them. They are by and large happy. Depression is generally unknown. Yes, they can be unhappy, but for a specific reason: a failed crop, a disappointing love affair, the death of a loved one; but non-specific depression is something I have yet to come across. 'Methinks I know not why I am so sad' does not exist.

In considering the cycle of birth and death it is perhaps easier to begin at the end, for from death springs life.

Considerable rituals attend funerals. As far as the islanders are concerned, death never comes purely through accident or illness, nor even old age, but as the result of magic being practised against the deceased. It might therefore be said that every death is a murder. Certainly there is always an autopsy of a kind. The corpse of the deceased is kept in his home for one complete day and no longer, a practice that probably has as its basis the practical consideration of the rapid rate of decay in the heat. While it is in the house it is visited by friends and relatives who do not hesitate to embrace it and touch it. The purpose of this seems less to do with saying farewell to the deceased, as in our society, but more as an aide-memoire, to help the mourners remember their loved one. This may partly explain why it is the women who are most keen to handle the corpse, for they will not be seeing the deceased again in the *kassa* house. Gifts of food are also brought for sustenance on the journey of the loved one's soul to Tuma, the island of the dead. At the same time there is an implicit understanding that the loved one is no longer here. His body may be, but his soul, or spirit, has already fled.

After this period of mourning, during which keening and the tearing of hair are commonplace – although not among the immediate family who must, according to custom, hide their feelings – the loved one is buried in a shallow grave. Afterwards there is a kind of party in the village in which much *kassa* is smoked and the men put on their ceremonial skirts and dance ritual funeral dances. The women never dance.

Next day the body is exhumed and examined. Owing to the heat it will now be in a considerably advanced stage of putrefaction. Again mourners will touch and fondle the body. They dissect the torso and examine the internal organs, hence their intimate acquaintance with human anatomy, even though, as we have seen, they do not always draw the right conclusions from their study of it. By this time the condition of the corpse has so deteriorated that it disintegrates on being handled. It is customary now for pieces of the corpse to be removed. Any remaining flesh is stripped away and some of the bones may be kept as souvenirs. Knuckle-bones are commonly used for necklaces or bracelets, for example, and Managua once proudly showed me a tibia that had once been part of his uncle, stroking it so fondly that I could not help but wonder

whether his attachment to it did not have something to do
with his lacking one of his own. What remains of the corpse
after this dismemberment is again buried, this time permanently. Although all of this may sound grisly, I can bear
witness that it is carried out with the utmost delicacy and
affection. The natives have none of our awe of death.
Having embraced the physical decay of the body they do not
regard the end of life as a taboo subject. How much better,
for all that it is repulsive to an outsider, is this than our
own taboos about the subject, our avoidance of the physical
side of the event and our many euphemisms during
discussion of it.

The spirit of the deceased, as we have said, is no longer
present, having already begun its journey to Tuma. I was
reading Managua's *Complete Shakespeare* the other day
and came across the quotation in *Hamlet* about death.
'From whose bourn no traveller returns', Shakespeare says
of death, except of course that in that very play Hamlet's
own father comes back as a ghost! However, generally our
own beliefs about the afterlife are suppositions cobbled
together from bits of the Bible. As a child I imagined it as
a land above the clouds where everyone wore long white
robes and listened to angels playing harps. I never felt it
sounded like much of a compensation for having to die and
leave life on earth. The natives have no need of such pipe
dreams because they have first-hand accounts of the afterlife, given to them in the *kassa* house. Instead of our own
rather sterile paradise, sitting around with the saints listening to hymns, so much less fun than temporal existence,
Tuma offers an enhanced version of normal life. Food is
plentiful without having to make a garden, fish are supplied
with no nets being cast and the men are serviced sexually
by dozens of beautiful young women. This may have all the
trappings of fantasy, but the islanders claim it as fact
because of eyewitness accounts of Tuma they say they have

received from the spirits of dead relatives in the *kassa* house. Of course these meetings with ghosts are hallucinations produced by a powerful drug, although time and again an islander has insisted to me that he learned something about himself that he had no previous knowledge of from a dead relative in the *kassa* house. How can this be? Perhaps the drug allows one to retrieve long-buried memories, it is entirely possible. At the very least, some kind of mass hysteria must be involved. Certainly it would be strange, if it is merely a hallucinogenic drug that is at work here, that everyone who imbibes it should have the same hallucinations, namely that they see dead loved ones. Why not pink dragons or castles in the air?

Anyhow, real or imagined, these visions present us with a picture of life on Tuma as being not a product of the imagination – there is nothing imagined about it, it is all simply a superior version of what is – but of desire. A perfect island life.

'And how long does it last?' I asked Managua.

'Always,' he replied. 'Is be for all time.'

'So you never grow old there?'

'Yes, you is grow old, of course, but when you is feel you is become too old you is just shake off you skin, like snake, and is find new body underneath, and is be young again.'

'And you can keep doing this?'

'For sure. You is do for ever if you is like.'

I asked if this meant that everyone who ever died was on Tuma. At this he laughed. 'Of course not! If all is stay on Tuma is not be any new babies here.'

He explained that sometimes people grow bored with Tuma. They might change their skins dozens of times and then become tired of doing the same old thing every day. So they become babies. Their spirits enter the bodies of new babies which rise up from the sea and float away from Tuma and back to this island.

'But they is have no memory of who they is once be,' explained Managua. 'Is start again from new.'

The babies float on a gentle tide towards the island. If you listen very carefully, on the right night, you can hear them calling across the sea: '*Waa waa, waa waa.*' It is, apparently, not a harsh insistent baby cry, but a plaintive one as they seek for mothers among the island's population.

Once they reach the island, the babies enter the heads of sleeping women and travel down through their bodies to the womb. That is how babies are made.

It is easy of course to dismiss all this as silly superstition. But then are our own beliefs any more? We, too, have at the heart of our most prevalent religion the idea of virgin birth. What is Jesus, viewed from another angle, other than a gifted sorcerer able to turn water into wine and raise the dead? Is that any more fantastical?

It's true that the natives' belief in non-physiological paternity is scientifically ridiculous. But this is a place where science is irrelevant. Sometimes I find the concept of Tuma so attractive, such a relief after the constant battle with the self-delusion that there is any point to life, and the idea of the floating babies so appealing, that I think, Why not? Why not just suspend disbelief and live the rest of my life as if all this were true? The idea is not without its attractions.

THIRTY-NINE

'Where you is go all time? You is be more hard for find than Managua pig.'

Lintoa shrugged. 'I is like be on own sometimes. Is be some new taboo say I is must be around you two all time?'

'You is always like be around we before.' Tigua looked up at him from under his long eyelashes, eyelashes that had never known a lover's nibbles. 'Now is be like you is avoid we. And what for you is always wear pink dress? Where is be you red? You know you is look plenty better in red.'

'I is just fancy change, is be all,' muttered Lintoa. 'You is have problem with that?'

'No, is be OK. But if you is not want for wear red dress, then you is can give me. I is always like that dress. OK?'

'Mebbe.'

'What for is "mebbe"? Is be quite simple, unless you is want for wear two dress at once. You is go fetch red dress for me now.'

Lintoa was struggling here. He couldn't get Tigua the dress because he hadn't got it. But if he told Tigua that, the next question would be, How come? Luckily, before Lintoa came up with anything – and whatever he'd have come up with was unlikely to fool the other she-boy – Tigua noticed an approaching figure. 'Oh no, is be you girlfriend again.'

'Is not we Lintoa is avoid,' murmured Sussua. 'Is be she, Kiroa.'

'Exactly,' agreed Lintoa. 'I is must hide all time for avoid she.'

Tigua said nothing but shot Lintoa a decidedly unconvinced glance. The she-boy was protesting a bit too much not to be concealing something.

Kiroa reached them. She was a tall girl, another attribute besides her beauty that was valued by the village boys. She towered over the diminutive Tigua. 'Moning,' she said.

Tigua looked around, putting on a mystified expression. 'Someone is speak?' he asked, his voice even more innocent than usual.

'I said moning,' said Kiroa.

Tigua jerked up his head. 'Ah is be you. Voice is come from so far up I is think is must be monkey in tree.'

Kiroa pulled a face, 'And what is be noise I is hear? Is be sound like snake is slither in dust. Oh, I is see now, is be little Tigua.'

'And I is see is be Kiroa. I is think for moment is be palm tree is walk and talk.'

'You is be very funny, I is not think.'

'But now I is see is Kiroa head at top. I is mistake for coconut.'

Kiroa refused the bait this time. There was no point in taking on Tigua who had suddenly developed a *terrada* tongue. She had always been so friendly to Kiroa in the past. The sorcerer's daughter could not understand why she had changed. But it was certainly best to avoid getting into another spat with her. Instead Kiroa sidled up to Lintoa. She put her hand upon his shoulder, a weight every boy on the island would have liked to feel, but Lintoa merely flinched.

'I is like pink dress,' said Kiroa. 'Is suit you.'

'Thanks,' said Lintoa shaking her off and adjusting his shoulder strap. The colour of the dress might be different from the other; its fit was just as bad.

Kiroa ignored the rebuttal. 'You know, is be very nice if you is not wear red dress for let I is wear. We is be about same height.'

'Dress is belong first Miss Lucy,' Tigua snapped. 'Is not be for giant. Lintoa is make all kind of cuts in dress for make fit. If you is must make more for make even bigger, dress is go fall pieces.'

Kiroa ignored the jibe. 'You is like for I is have red dress, Lintoa?'
She used her most wheedling voice.

Tigua all but exploded. 'I is ask for borrow dress first, sow!'

Lintoa smiled. Pretty soon they would be scratching one
another's eyes out, except, of course, that Tigua would have to sit
on Sussua's shoulders to reach Kiroa's. He almost said so but
stopped himself. Jokes about Kiroa's height were getting boring.
You could overdo a thing like that.

'Is be impossible for you is wear dress,' Lintoa said. 'Is break
taboo.'

'*What?*' said the other three girls in unison.

'Is break taboo. Answer me this, Kiroa, is you be allow for wear
man's clothes?'

'Well, no, everyone is know that.'

'Well then who is wear white womans' dress here?'

'Well, is be you and Sussua and little girl there.'

'Exactly,' said Lintoa. 'You is not see any other womans from
tribe is wear they dresses?'

'Well, no . . .'

'And what is be we three?'

'You is be she-boys.'

'Exactly. She-*boys*. Only people in tribe who is wear they dress
is be boys. So, if girl like you is wear one she is wear boys' clothes.
She is be cross-dresser. Is break taboo.'

Tigua clapped her hands. 'I is love that. You is be more smart you
is look Lintoa. You is get more smart every day. Is must be because
you is be around me all time.'

Kiroa had a finger to her lip, trying to work it out. She was so
puzzled by the logic of it she didn't even notice the three of them
had sneaked off until they were long since vanished into the
jungle.

FORTY

William woke to find everything around him hazy as though something had happened to his vision during the night. It was as though he were looking at the world through a veil. He wondered if he was going blind. Could it be an effect of the *kassa*? Who knew what damage it might be doing to his body? Although since Lucy had first kissed him, or if not him then his mosquito bites, he had experienced a hitherto unknown sense of calm, he realized he was now flexing his eyelids right-left-left-right and all the old free-floating anxiety was back. Perhaps, like cannabis, *kassa* induced paranoia? Another undoubted effect was that he could see a ghostly figure moving around the place where he was lying. He was getting flashbacks now, seeing his dad when he wasn't high on *kassa*.

'Dad?' he said.

'What?' It was a woman's voice.

'Mom?' he essayed, although he knew it couldn't be. His mother was still alive. He'd no sooner thought this than he realized he'd been on the island nearly three weeks, cut off from the outside world. What if his mother had passed away in that time and was now come from Tuma to visit him?

In an instant the haze vanished and he found himself looking at Lucy. 'It's only me,' she said.

Only, he thought, as if you could ever be only. He had stopped the alternate blinking now and as his eyes recovered from the blurring it always induced he realized the haze had been nothing more than the mosquito net over Lucy's bed. A stab of anxiety went through him. He felt the pull of the Captain Cook. That he should be there. He wasn't quite sure why this should be, apart from because that was where his work got itself done. After all, it was the place where he'd been assaulted, but perhaps, too, it was also his proper home on the island. If it were true that the dead walked the island, then he felt sure the half-built hotel was where his father would look for him.

'You must have been dreaming,' Lucy said.

'Yes, I guess I must.'

She started to climb back into bed. But William jumped out the other side. 'No,' he said. 'Not now. I thought I saw a spirit and I was right. You are a spirit, an evil one, trying to stop me working.'

She tried to look innocent. It was a fair accusation. While it was true that she wanted to go to bed with him, not just for the sex – although she needed that – but also for the indulgence of watching him afterwards while he slept, she wanted too to prevent him completing his task. She knew how important it was for an ethnographer not to impinge upon his or her subjects. An ethnographer was there to record and draw conclusions without becoming part of the picture. Even the smallest most accidental intervention could upset the balance of an isolated society. If that were so, then what catastrophe might William cause?

'Would that be such a very bad thing?' was what she said now.

'Of course it would. I'm the only hope these people have of obtaining justice and reparation. I can't let them down.'

'But are you sure justice and reparation are what's right for them? Most of them have adapted to losing limbs perfectly well. Until you stirred them up they simply accepted their injuries as the result of bad magic. Shit happens, that's how they look at it.'

'They didn't have any alternative then. Now they have me.'

Lucy was wearing a thin silk bathrobe. She grabbed some underwear and stepped into it under the robe. He felt the concealment of her body, a body his eyes had been free to roam these past few days, was an act of hostility.

'You know, you live in a very black and white world, don't you? Don't you ever think things might be a bit grey where they meet? Don't you think things aren't always so crystal clear?'

He began picking his clothes from the floor where he'd discarded them the night before and putting them on. 'What are you trying to say? You sound like Managua. He's a nice enough guy but he's pretty reactionary, too. It's in his interest to keep people as they are. It maintains his special position.'

'These people have got along for thousands, maybe millions, of years without anything more than they have now. Are they any less happy than the people back in America? You've seen what a little contact with the West can do, it's why you're here.'

'I'm here to put it right.'

'You can't put back missing limbs with money and Coca-Cola. Replacing *poto* with baseball isn't going to improve things for anyone.'

'Except the rats.' He was smiling at her. She didn't feel like making a joke out of it. She felt like crying that he couldn't see what was so obvious to her. That he couldn't put himself in the islanders' shoes. Not that they had any, of course, other than the high heels she'd given the she-boys. He was holding his hand out to her, inviting her back into bed. Her first instinct was to refuse. She didn't want to let the cross feeling evaporate without a victory. On the other hand she didn't want to go on feeling it any longer. She took his hand.

As they made love again, slowly and kindly in a conciliatory way, William thought that as long as they could do this, provided they had this, they didn't have to be on opposite sides. I'm not worried about us, he told himself. I'm definitely not worried.

Lucy was trying to lose herself in the physical pleasure of the moment, but somehow she couldn't manage it. An itch of irritation bothered her. Why did he keep squeezing her breasts in this way? First the right, then the left, two squeezes for that, then

the right again, and again, and then another two squeezes for the
left. Could he really imagine she enjoyed it? How well would she
have to know him to be able to tell him that she didn't? What if
they never got to a time like that?

His hands moved away from her breasts and she was able to concentrate better on what they were doing. Never mind, never mind,
she told herself, putting more energy into it. If she worked him
hard enough maybe he would fall asleep after and she could lie
beside him and watch him and the feeling would come back.

FORTY-ONE

After prep school William and Sandy Beach went their separate ways and William was relieved to be able to be himself again, to escape from the persona that Sandy Beach had created for him, namely that he was a rich socialite (this based on his parents owning a beach house), a wealthy wastrel who masturbated a lot. So he was alarmed when at his first freshman party at Harvard Law School he heard a voice behind him say, 'Well, hello Wanker.'

He turned and found Beach, who in the five years since their last meeting hadn't changed a bit. His freckled face, topped by an unruly shock of ginger hair, was still that of a weedy, geeky ten-year-old. The thick black frames of his spectacles gave the impression of an extraterrestrial, and not one of the cuddly kind at that.

'Don't call me that,' hissed William by way of a greeting. Even though he knew it was useless, since his natural kindliness was, as they say, written all over his face, he tried to make himself look threatening. 'Don't ever call me that.'

Sandy Beach gave him a knowing look. 'Oh pardon me, have I touched a sore point? Still at it, then? Still beating your meat, huh? Still flogging your log. Still shaking the snake. Still handling the goods. Still holding the pole.'

'Shut up,' whispered William. 'I was never that into it. You leaped to the wrong conclusion, is all. You got hold of the wrong end of the stick.'

'While you had hold of the right end of it,' said Beach, miming furious masturbation with one hand and giving William a powerful nudge in the ribs with his other elbow.

'Cut it out,' said William and this time he must have actually appeared threatening because Beach stopped masturbating and held his palms up in a fending-off motion. 'OK, OK. Jesus, some people never change. Still can't take a joke, huh?'

'I can take a joke all right,' said William. 'I just can't take the same joke over and over again any more. I think it's time we moved on.'

There was silence for a moment or two. They both looked at their drinks.

'Actually,' said Beach, 'I have moved on.'

'From what?' said William.

'From masturbation,' said Beach. 'Not that I was ever into it on your scale.'

'And where exactly did you move on from it to?'

'Women,' said Beach. 'Sex.'

'Sex?' said William. He couldn't keep the croak of incredulity out of his voice. Sandy Beach had actually found someone who'd agreed to have sex with him. 'You've had sex?' He couldn't stop it coming out as, 'You've had sex?'

Beach tried to fight off a smug smile and lost, a bit too easily, William thought. His geeky head was wobbling from false modesty. 'I was at this party, see? My first night here. Can you believe that, my first night here? Well, I'm at this party, trying to look cool, but you know feeling a little nervous when this chick—'

'Chick?' The word kind of exploded from William. He couldn't believe he'd heard Sandy Beach of all people use it.

'Girl,' said Sandy Beach. 'It means girl.'

'I know what it means, for Christ's sake,' said William.

Beach stared at him for a moment, completely baffled by this outburst. But he was too absorbed in his own story to linger long on this puzzlement. 'Yeah, well, this chick walks right up to me and asks me to dance. So I try to tell her I'm not much of a dancer but she just kind of grabs me and says, "Don't worry, just hold on to me."'

'*She* grabbed *you*?' said William.

'Yes, she grabbed me. Anyway, it's a slow record and she puts her arms around me and starts pressing herself against me. Kinda grinding her pelvis into me? I tell you if I hadn't had the most enormous hard-on to cushion me, I'd have had serious bruising.'

He took a sip of his drink and looked casually around the room.

'Well, go on,' said William. Immediately he didn't know why he'd said that, but then realized it was the sheer sensationalism of Sandy Beach having had a sexual encounter.

'Well, we did that for a bit and then we had some drinks and then she invited me back to her place, which luckily was only a very short cab ride away. Very fortunate that.'

'Extremely lucky,' said William, remembering Beach's legendary stinginess. 'Saved you having to pay too much cab fare.'

'No, no, nothing to do with the fare.' Beach looked at him puzzled. '*She* paid the fare.'

William smiled and nodded, as though to say, of course, how could I have been so stupid as to expect *you* to pay it?

'No, it was lucky because if it had been any further I might have been arrested. A coupla more miles she would have had *all* my clothes off in the back of the cab.'

'She took your clothes off in the cab?'

'Not so much took. More ripped. Well, she tried to. I don't mind telling you, it was a close call.'

'Just how drunk was this girl?' asked William.

Beach didn't appear to register the implication. 'She sure was hot for me. We got to her place and she fucked me on the doorstep. Couldn't find her key quick enough so she just pulled out the old secret weapon and plunged it in there and then.'

'Jesus!' said William.

'Then she found her key and we went inside and did it some more. Every which way. Positions you couldn't possibly imagine –

well, maybe not you. I guess you do a lot of thinking about that sort of thing with your um, hobby—'

'I told you not to mention that,' said William.

'OK, OK, I won't! Keep your hair on, man. Your secret's safe with me. I swear on my grandmother's grave I'll never mention it again.'

'Do you two know each other?'

It was a tall, dark-haired girl. A bit like Katharine Ross in *Butch Cassidy*, William thought.

'We were at prep school together,' said Sandy Beach. 'My name's Aaron Beach but everyone calls me Sandy. This is William Hardt. Better known as Wanker.'

'Wanker?' said the girl.

'It's a British term for a prodigious masturbator,' said Beach. There was a weird kind of smile on his face which William had never seen there before. At first he thought Beach was about to throw up. Then, to his horror he realized it was meant to be seductive.

'Your grandmother's grave,' William hissed at Beach out of the corner of his mouth. His anxiety level was rising. This girl was stunning and she thought he was a pervert.

'I forgot,' said Beach. 'She's not dead yet.'

'It's – uh – not true,' William said to the girl. 'It was an ugly rumour he spread because of a misunderstanding.'

'Misunderstanding! Huh!' said Beach. 'Well, what were you doing in the bathroom for an hour and a half if you weren't masturbating?'

'That's difficult to explain,' said William, trying to decide – not for the first time – whether it would be better to be considered a depraved onanist or an obsessive-compulsive nut.

'You can't explain it because it's true,' said Beach.

'I think he's right,' the girl said. 'There's something funny about your eyes and everyone knows what causes that.'

William stopped the alternate blinking and transferred the action to alternate molar grinding. It meant he couldn't answer the girl, but on the other hand it wasn't visible enough to make him look a lunatic. At least he hoped not.

Beach had his hand on the small of the girl's back. 'Can I get you a drink?' he said. 'Or would you maybe like to dance?'

As she was steered away the girl looked back over her shoulder and smiled at William but he couldn't even smile back. He was at an advanced and critical stage in the tooth grinding. He didn't want to have to start all over. He wouldn't have any enamel left on his molars if he did that.

He went upstairs to the bedroom where the hosts had put the guests' coats and took his. He folded it and put it under his jacket so as not to make himself conspicuous as he slipped through the throng downstairs to make his getaway. He noticed Beach had lost the girl and was talking to a couple of geeky-looking freshmen. His shrill tones carried across the party hubbub and the last words William heard as he exited the front door were, 'It was just lucky it was only a short cab ride. Another half a mile and I'd be in jail instead of telling you guys this ...'

A hundred yards or so along the sidewalk, William heard footsteps hurrying after him. Some instinct overrode his concentration on an elaborate crack-stepping ritual and he turned. It was the dark-haired girl. She smiled. 'Hi,' she said. 'My name is Lola. Now, tell me, why were you winking at me?'

FORTY-TWO

After the breakthrough with 'can', there was no stopping Purnu. Having grasped the principles of how reading worked he couldn't wait to add to his limited vocabulary of one word. It made things tough on William. After three weeks he was just beginning to lose his inhibitions about crapping in front of other people and to enjoy the camaraderie of the shitting beach. He was able to exchange a greeting or two with his fellow crappers without wishing to die of shame. But now Purnu had taken to lurking at the edge of the beach, watching and waiting for William to finish so he could collar him for another lesson. It put back in most of the tension involved in communal crapping that William had managed to lose. What made it worse was that as soon as he straightened up, signalling the end of his bowel evacuation, Purnu would rush over and inspect his dump, along, of course, with the usual crowd of sensation-seekers. So sometimes William rose early to be one of the first on the beach and get finished before Purnu even appeared. Purnu was too afraid of evil spirits to come into the hotel on his own, so William could get started on his work without being delayed by another reading lesson.

William wouldn't have rated himself as much of an expert on giving instruction on how to read. He'd picked up just enough from listening to his mother teaching Ruth's small daughter, the way she must have taught William himself, to know the basic principles. He also realized that the lessons would be easier and the whole process be speeded up if he did a bit of preparation. He'd taken on board that Purnu's interest had been awakened by spelling a word he knew. So during his interviews with the amputees he listened carefully for the words they used most and jotted them down in his notebook. Purnu duly learned 'pig', '*fug-a-fug*', 'bomb', 'yam' and other words in descending order of popularity.

In a matter of a week Purnu was able to read whole sentences at least competently, even if no less contentiously. One big problem was tenses, which didn't seem to exist on the island. The natives had a cavalier attitude to time. Unlike most Westerners, especially William, they did not concern themselves with ticking off how much of their time on Earth had passed or computing how much might remain. Yesterday, today and tomorrow blurred into one continuum. They didn't need any more than the present tense. Past and future didn't bother them too much.

'What is mean, "He stepped on a mine"?' objected Purnu one morning when he'd actually arrived outside the Captain Cook *before* shitting so as to make sure of nabbing William. 'What is be "stepped"?' It was one of a set of sentences William had written out the day before and given to Purnu to read for homework. They all related to everyday life on the island.

William had to think. ' "Stepped" is the past tense of "step".' This got a blank reception. 'Well, I guess another way of putting it would be to say, "He did step on a mine." '

'What is be this word "did"?'

'Um, it's the past of the verb "to do".'

'Well, why you is not just say, "He is do"?'

This was getting them nowhere. 'Um, forget "did",' he said.

'Forget "did"? But what for I is want for do that? I is come here for learn spell words. I is not come for learn word and then forget straight away. Also, is be plenty easy word. DUH-I-DUH. Did. I is not want for waste easy word like that.'

'I'm not talking about wasting it. It's just not helping anything at the moment. So let's just forget it for now.'

Purnu sighed. 'That is be whole point. I is not be sure I is *can* forget now. DUH-I-DUH. See? Is be so easy for remember, is be so hard for forget.'

So it went. But in spite of all the arguments and interruptions Purnu made startling progress and then a different problem arose. He could read but he didn't have anything *to* read. So William took to borrowing books and magazines from Lucy. He had to pretend they were for him because Purnu had sworn him to secrecy lest Managua find out. Purnu wanted to spring it on Managua when the time was right. Ripeness was all, as far as he was concerned.

So it was that, lips moving all the time – almost like someone with OCD, thought William, watching him – the sorcerer ploughed his way through out-of-date *Vogue*s and *Cosmopolitan*s, a few *New Yorker*s, a chicklit novel that Lucy had idly picked up at an airport, *Captain Corelli's Mandolin*, *Pride and Prejudice* and four copies of the *Reader's Digest* from the 1970s that Lucy had found abandoned in her house. You could say Purnu had catholic taste.

One day he trotted eagerly after William at the end of shitting but William turned to him and said, 'No lesson today.'

'No lesson?' Purnu's face fell.

William shrugged. 'There's no point. There's nothing more I can teach you. You're a reader now. You'll pick up everything else just from reading.'

'I is be reader.' Purnu said the words as if he were announcing the fact to himself. 'I is be reader.'

William patted him on the shoulder and smiled. And to think Lucy thought you couldn't improve these people's lot by taking them out of the dark ages. She should see the delight on Purnu's face! 'Well done. My first and last pupil.' He turned and walked away.

'Wait, *gwanga*!' William paused. Purnu scampered over to him. '*Gwanga*, I is not find anything 'bout Pilua yet. I is be sorry. I is still try plenty hard.'

'That's OK, I know it's not easy.'

'But even if I is not can keep deal I is pay you back different way.'

'Yes?' said William.

'I is take you fly with me.'

'Yes, right. Look forward to it,' said William and walked off towards the Captain Cook.

Sometimes, thought Purnu, watching him out of sight, disappointed by William's lack of enthusiasm, white people could be so rude. Ah well, at least the American hadn't tried to thank him for his offer. At least he'd spared him that!

FORTY-THREE

The Joe Hardt who came to William in the *kassa* house on this occasion was not the stooped and balding figure of his first visit. He was his father as William remembered him from childhood. A man in his late thirties with a halo of blond hair. He was wearing the same plaid shirt and chinos, but they looked a better fit now. His body wasn't all shrunk the way it was last time they'd met here and during the final few years of his life.

'You've changed,' said William. 'You look younger.'

'I *am* younger. It just took me some time to figure out how they do things on Tuma. I didn't know I could slough off that old body. I thought I was stuck with it from here to eternity.'

'You can stay young for ever?'

'It doesn't work quite like that. You start off young and then you get older. When you decide you're getting on a bit too much you just slough and you're young again.'

William was comforted by the idea. It might be hallucinogenically induced, of course, but here was his father telling him he could live for ever and not even have wrinkles, let alone a degenerative disease like Alzheimer's. 'You look just great, Dad,' he said.

'Well, thanks, my boy. And my mind's working properly again, I've stopped forgetting all my – my—'

'Words,' said William.

'I knew. I was just joshing with you son.'

'You had me going there. Dad – I – I can't, well, you'll appreciate I can't quite take all this in. I want to believe that you're really here and—'

'I'm really here son, take my word for it.'

William thought, yes, but a hallucination would say that, wouldn't it? 'Dad, I was going to say I want to believe that you still exist somewhere, other than my own consciousness, I really do, and that you're perfectly happy—'

He stopped. Joe Hardt didn't look perfectly happy. He looked troubled.

'Dad? What is it?'

'Son, can I ask you something? Something, well, kind of delicate?'

'Of course, Dad. If something's bothering you, I'd like to help. What is it?'

'Son, do you think you can commit adultery when you're dead?'

'I – I don't understand.'

'Well, on Tuma there's not a great deal to do. There's no work, everything's provided, and you can only lie around on beaches for a limited time without getting bored. And, well, there are these young ladies. Lots of young ladies . . .'

'I see.' William was trying not to sound like a Victorian father. He'd had enough role reversal when his father was alive and needed constant care.

Joe held out his hands in a gesture of appeal. 'What's a guy going to do? Especially when he's just sloughed and he can feel the blood beating through his veins again. It's what everyone does here. It's part of being in paradise.'

William smiled at his father's discomfiture. His own generation wouldn't have such a problem with this. 'Well then, surely it's OK. Why don't you just accept that and enjoy yourself?'

'Oh, I have, son, I have.' Joe Hardt had what could only be called a salacious grin on his face. But as quickly as it had appeared it vanished again and the troubled look returned. 'It's just that I keep thinking about your mom, back home, missing me, and I hate the idea of cheating on her. I never did it when I was alive and it doesn't seem right to when I'm dead.'

William nodded. He could see the difficulty with this one. A major contribution to his childhood lack of belief in an afterlife had been the various conundrums about how old you would be when you got there and which spouse would you team up with if you'd been married and widowed and married again. How could everyone be happy ever after in that situation?

'Listen, Dad,' he said finally. 'You can't be with Mom while she's alive, that's one thing. And I'm sure she'd want you to get the most out of your new existence. Besides, now you're dead, all bets are off. I mean, legally, Mom could get married again, which must mean that she's no longer married to you. It therefore follows you can't be cheating on her.'

Joe Hardt smiled. 'Son, you have a fine legal brain. Phew!' He wiped his brow with the back of his hand. 'That's sure a load off my mind.' Even as he said it, his body was beginning to thin.

'Dad, wait, I wanted to ask you something. Besides coming to the *kassa* hut, have you been walking around the island? Only in the hotel, where I'm staying, I heard this noise . . .'

His father interrupted him. 'Son, I don't have time for this right now. I have sort of a date back on Tuma.'

'But Dad, the other day . . .' William's voice trailed away. His father was scarcely more than mist and obviously beyond hearing. A moment or two more, and even the mist had gone.

William must have drifted off to sleep, that is if he'd ever really been awake after swallowing the *kassa*, because he was woken by a tugging at his sleeve.

It was Purnu. 'Psst!' The little sorcerer looked this way and that, making sure the other occupants of the hut were asleep. William glanced around. Several hours had slipped by while he slept. Half the night was gone. Someone had rolled away the stone that blocked the doorway. All the spirits had departed, and some of the men too. 'Come!' Purnu whispered.

Outside, he thrust his face into William's. William saw the full
moon reflected back at him from the little man's pupils, as though
the centres of his eyes had been lasered blank. 'Is you is want for
come fly with me?'

Sinatra burst into song in William's drug-addled brain. He
wanted to laugh out loud and he almost did but then he saw the
earnest expression the little man wore. He tried to focus. He had
partaken of a hallucinogenic substance. It was likely that none of
this was happening. What was he talking about, likely? *Of course* it
wasn't happening! How could it be? On the other hand, Purnu did
seem to be standing in front of him, eager for an answer, tongue
practically hanging out, like a little dog begging for a treat. Then
again, assuming this was happening, which was by no means
certain, but assuming it for the time being, then was it not likely
that the sorcerer was expecting him to say no? To not check in for
this flight? This was surely some kind of bravado on the magician's
part, challenging William to in turn challenge his supernatural
powers if he dared. William was presumably meant to act out the
charade, to acknowledge Purnu's sorcery, by making some excuse
as to why he couldn't go right now. Result, Purnu's power would
be proved without being tested. Well, William was happy to go
along with that. The trouble was, his brain was so disabled by *kassa*
he couldn't think of any good reason not to say yes.

'Fly? I, er, I don't know . . .'

'You is not worry 'bout yams. Is all be part of bargain. I is take
you fly, look for Pilua, you is teach me long word, senti . . .
senti . . .'

'Sentimental,' said William.

'Sentimental! Yes! That is be one big word. Is make Managua
look plenty damn silly when I is read that one. Now, you is want
for fly?' He looked William straight in the eye. They stared at one
another for ages. And the longer William looked, the more he
began to imagine how it would be to find oneself soaring over the
island.

It was an age before William could tear his eyes away. They felt strange, kind of achy. He had to blink hard a couple of times – not alternately – to get them back in operation. 'OK, how's it work?'

'I is put arm round you waist, like so.' Purnu's hand snaked around William and he felt the sorcerer's hand grip his belt.

'Hey, you won't drop me, will you?' He was only half joking now. While part of him was waiting for Purnu's bluff to be called, for the sorcerer to invent an excuse – adverse weather conditions, perhaps – for why it was not possible to get airborne just at this moment, another part of him was concerned that the little man was so, well, *earnest*.

'I is never drop anyone so far. Now, you is be ready?' Purnu leaned forward, one leg out behind him, coiled like a cat about to spring.

William stretched his arms out above his head the way Superman did when he was flying.

Purnu relaxed his position and let go of William. 'What for you is hold arms out? Put they away! Is not be necessary. Is only be necessary you is keep arms still. For not get in my way so I is can see.'

William dropped his arms. Purnu put his arm around his waist again and coiled himself once more.

'OK?'

'OK.'

There was a long pause. Purnu was muttering to himself. He gave a little kick with his back leg. Nothing happened.

'Shit!' said Purnu. He lifted a hand and wiped the sweat from his brow. 'OK?'

'OK,' repeated William.

Again Purnu gave the little kick. Again nothing happened.

'Shit!'

'Is something wrong?' asked William. An involuntary, *kassa*-induced giggle escaped his lips but the little man didn't notice.

'Is be too much damn *kassa* is be what is be wrong. Is make I is forget spell.' He started muttering again. William assumed a mock-serious expression and hoped Purnu wouldn't notice he was hamming. Purnu himself was a good actor, you had to hand it to him. But William had called his bluff and now he was getting himself into a lather because he was about to be exposed as a fake. The muttering stopped. 'OK?'

'OK.'

Purnu kicked off with his back leg and William felt himself lift off the ground. God, this little guy must be stronger than he looks, he thought, to lift me. Then he looked down and saw that Purnu's feet were off the ground too. It had happened! They were in the air! They were flying!

Well, almost. It wasn't exactly what you'd call flying. More lurching. They rose up about ten feet and then lurched down five. William thought they were going to hit the ground but then they lurched up again and peaked at around twenty feet up. 'Woooooooooooo!' William heard himself scream. 'Wooooooooooooooo!' It was the noise people made on roller-coasters, he told himself and then thought irrelevantly, Why do they do that?

When they got up to fifty feet they started to descend again. Perhaps descend doesn't quite do it. Plummet would be more the word. They were plummeting towards the roof of the *kassa* house. 'Heeeelp!' William screamed and closed his eyes but then his stomach started to go back down to where it should be and he opened his eyes to find they were pulling upwards again, their feet just skimming the top of the roof, sending up a cloud of leaf fragments.

'Whoa!' shouted William. He was amazed at the range of involuntary noises he was producing.

Purnu turned his head and gave William a fierce stare. The sorcerer's pupils were alarmingly dilated. 'You is please not make noise. I is need think for fly.'

They flew straight for a hundred yards or so. Rather, they flew in a straight line since 'flying straight' conveys an idea of a smooth controlled movement. It wasn't. They were wobbling and tipping from side to side. It was like bad turbulence. William didn't dare look down and he soon discovered that keeping his eyes shut made him feel sick. So he opened them and looked straight ahead. What he saw coming towards them at what seemed like several hundred miles an hour made him scream again.

'Tree!'

'Please, I is ask you is be quiet.'

'Tree!'

'Three? Three what?'

'TREE!'

Just in time Purnu swerved. Ahead William saw a couple more trees with a gap of about ten feet between them. A straight line would take them right through the middle. Except they weren't taking a straight line. They were weaving from side to side and Purnu himself was rolling laterally so that one moment William was being held beneath him and the next above.

'Fly straight!' William screamed. He shut his eyes as they were about to hit the tree. Well, he thought in the fraction of a second he had left to him, at least I'll soon be with Dad. But there was no impact, nothing happened. When he opened his eyes there was nothing before them except the red glow of the sun coming up over the horizon and nothing below them but the black expanse of the ocean. They were heading straight out over the waves. It looked like there was nothing in front of them for at least a thousand miles. William had been grinding his molars in his old right–left–left–right rhythm. He had been grinding them so hard there soon wouldn't be any enamel left on them. Like Rhoda's, he thought. But at this moment he felt he was able to stop. They were moving slower now so they were no longer buffeted by a jet stream. It was perfectly silent up here. It was a rare experience for him of calm and grace. His childhood dream had almost come true. After half a lifetime of yearning, he was Superboy. And in a place where he didn't need X-ray vision to look at women's breasts! He felt like a bird. He could fly like this for ever. But then he looked at the distant horizon and the thought hit him, That could happen! We don't appear to be flying anywhere.

'Purnu, where exactly are we going?' There was no reply. He turned and looked at the sorcerer. Purnu's eyelids were drooping. He was on autopilot.

'Purnu!' William shouted. 'Wake up!'

Purnu shook his head and opened his eyes. 'Shit!' he muttered. He leaned towards William and they banked sharply so that for a moment William thought they were going to drop into the ocean. He screamed again.

'I is be sorry,' said Purnu. 'Too much damn *kassa*. Is be hard for fly with *kassa* head.'

Oh, great, thought William. I'm being flown by a drunk. Then he thought, It's not just the pilot who's drunk, it's the whole air-craft! He began to laugh hysterically.

They were wobbling and swaying from side to side. They dipped up and down. Purnu kept widening his eyes the way drunks do when they're trying to stay awake.

'I is show you all island,' he said. William couldn't tell whether his words were blurred or if it was the slipstream whipping them out of the sorcerer's mouth so fast that they ran into one another.

The island was below them now. They zoomed in low over the breakers and the beach and were headed straight into the wall of the jungle when Purnu banked sharply and they rose steeply to just crest the top of the tree canopy.

'You're flying too low again!' William shouted.

'I is be sorry. Is not all be my fault. You is be one heavy *gwanga*. I is not allow for that.'

Terrific, thought William. He's accusing me of being excess baggage.

A moment later though they were out over the ocean again. Fingers of light from the east were clutching at the sky now, but below all was dark save for the moonlight. William could hardly make out where the ocean ended and the land began. And then, as they moved along the coast, something caught his eye, something so surprising it was almost more extraordinary than the fact that he was flying.

FORTY-FOUR

In the morning, not for the first time, William was suffering badly from the effects of *kassa* and Lucy said she would make him a huge fried breakfast because that was the best cure for a hangover. William replied, Maybe for an alcohol hangover, yes, but he wasn't sure it would work for *kassa*. But he didn't protest too strongly. For one thing his head hurt too much to argue and for another he could see that Lucy was one of those thoroughly undomesticated women who every so often get it into their heads to demonstrate what a good hausfrau they could be if only they wanted. He didn't know that making him breakfast was Lucy's compensation to him for working against him, her apology for putting what she believed before what she felt.

She set about frying a couple of huge turtle eggs, slices of minoa bread and some red fungi.

'I hope they *are* red,' William remarked, standing watching her, clad only in his underpants. 'I feel bad enough already.'

'Trust me,' Lucy replied with such an air of botanical certitude about her, thrusting out her little breasts beneath a silk dressing gown, whose blue matched that both of her eyes and this morning's clear sky, in such a pointy challenging way that William decided it would be better to suffer the fabled death throes from orange fungi than to take her on. It was still early, long before shitting time, so Lucy said it would be safe to eat together on the veranda overlooking the beach, because no-one would be around to catch them at it.

She produced a small folding card table and erected it outside, and added two cane dining chairs. From a drawer of the old side-board she took a white damask tablecloth. William wondered how she had managed to get it so clean here on the island but then realized she had almost certainly never used it since she'd been here. What occasion had she been saving it for? he wondered. From another drawer she extracted some silverware, weighty-looking knives and forks, and laid the table. William helped by adjusting the cutlery to make sure it was symmetrically correct. He did his best to smooth out the creases in the tablecloth which were recalcitrant on account of it having been folded so long. Lucy invited him to sit down.

She served his meal with a big mug of hot, sweet tea which she said would get his blood sugar up. William wasn't sure that *kassa* actually put your blood-sugar levels down but he didn't want to spoil Lucy's housewifely fun by saying so. She sat opposite him with a much more modest portion of the same food.

The idea of eating, when Lucy first mentioned it, had made William feel queasy but now the food was before him he found he was hungry. Moreover, this was the first repast he'd seen on the island that in any way resembled Western food and so he went at it with a will. He remembered how *kassa* was not unlike cannabis when smoked and recalled how the latter drug had always given him a voracious appetite. After alcohol, too, he often wanted a big breakfast next day. This increased appetite wasn't the only way his post-*kassa* state resembled a normal hangover; he could not recall whole parts of the night before. As after an evening of heavy drinking, nightmarish images drifted in and out of his weary brain.

'You know, I don't remember getting here last night,' he told Lucy. 'I can recall talking to my dad – he was young this time – but everything after that is a blur—' He stopped and shook his head as though trying to clear the fog from it.

'What?' said Lucy.

He laughed, a little unconvincingly, he knew. 'Well, it's the strangest thing, but I had this dream that I was, well, flying.'

'Perhaps you were thinking about leaving. The plane's due at the end of the week.' She appeared to be too busy mopping her egg yolk with a piece of minoa bread to look up and meet his eyes as she said this.

'No, no. You don't understand. I wasn't in a plane. I was just up in the air, above the island. I was flying.'

She looked worried. 'You're going to have to keep away from the *kassa*.'

He shrugged and took another bite of egg. The yolk dribbled down his chin and he paused to wipe it with the heavy white napkin that Lucy had provided. He was staring right through her.

'What?' she said again.

'I – I saw something, when I was flying. Something significant.'

'Yes . . . ?'

There was a long pause. His forehead pleated with the effort of trying to recall. Finally he shook his head and bent it to his breakfast once more. 'It's no good, it's gone. I can't remember what it was at all.'

'You need more sugar, that'll do the trick.' She took his empty mug and he admired the lines of her buttocks through the clinging silk as she disappeared into the house. Presumably they had made love last night, but he couldn't remember that, either, and it would be insensitive to ask. He closed his eyes and imagined Lucy's naked body below his, then above and then beside him. Were any of these memories? And if so were they from last night or from other occasions? He sighed. He guessed he would never know. He tried to cast his mind further back to where this thing that was nagging at him lay, somehow just beyond his grasp. But it was no good. The constant pounding of the waves, the roar of the surf that, now he opened his eyes to look at it, was even whiter than the tablecloth obliterated all. His eye caught a movement in the distance, a figure walking this way. He watched it as it grew closer and long before he could make out the features recognized the limping gait.

'Oh Christ!' He swivelled to see Lucy in the doorway, mug in hand, looking at the figure too. 'It's Managua, he's found us in flagrante!'

William leaped from his seat, causing a stab of pain to his temples. 'I'll make the bed and get my clothes on!'

'It doesn't matter about your clothes, stupid!' snapped Lucy. 'He mustn't see we've been eating together.'

She rushed back inside with the mug. Managua had already turned from the sea and was walking towards the house. He was maybe fifty steps away.

'The plates!' Lucy beckoned through the window. William picked up one and frisbeed it through to her. She caught it deftly. He began to pick up the other one. 'Leave it!' she called. He could see her scrubbing furiously at the other plate in the pot of water she used as a sink. 'He'll smell the food. He'll know someone has been eating breakfast. It's OK as long as he doesn't think it's you. Sit down and try not to act suspiciously.'

William lowered himself into his chair. Managua was ascending the steps to the veranda. William realized that his plate was still in front of him. Waving cheerily with one hand to Managua he surreptitiously pushed the plate across the table to the place in front of Lucy's empty chair.

'Moning, *gwanga*,' said Managua. Lucy appeared in the doorway, drying her hands on a tea towel and looking flustered.

'Hello Managua,' she said. 'What a pleasant surprise. To see you so early.'

'You is sleep here?' said the older man to William. William glanced at Lucy. He had only a split second to decide on the right reply. If he said yes, would Managua know from the evidence of the breakfast table that he had eaten here as well?

To his horror William looked down at the tablecloth and noticed there were still two forks and two knives upon it. But how could he deny he'd spent the night when he was sitting here in just his shorts?

'I is not find you at Captain Cook,' Managua said, luckily

revealing the question to have been either rhetorical or a trap before William had chance to make a disastrous wrong choice of answer. He noticed the old man was looking at him rather than the table, slowly winking first one eye and then the other and he realized that his own eyes were going frenetically right-left-left-right. William made a superhuman effort to stop and Managua's eyes ceased doing it too.

'You is not have shit with me for some time now,' the old man continued, his tone regretful. He looked down at the table, examining the plate on which the egg yolk had already hardened to a golden crust. 'Of course, if you is eat too many turtle egg, you is not can shit at all.' He brought his gaze up again, staring William straight in the eye.

'That, er, that is not his plate,' said Lucy walking from the doorway and picking it up. 'I've just been having my breakfast while William was getting ready to go to the village for his.'

Managua looked down at the table again. He began fiddling with one of the knives. Behind his back Lucy performed a frantic mime of scrubbing her mouth with her hand. William copied her and realized he had egg yolk on his chin. He reflected ruefully that while being caught with his trousers down didn't matter, ending up with egg on his face did. He licked his fingers and hastily removed it, a fraction of a second before Managua looked up. The old man had picked up the knife and was weighing it in his hand.

'Is be big knife,' he said. 'Is use for hunt?'

William looked at Lucy, who shrugged behind Managua's back. No help there, then. 'Er, yes,' he said. 'It's a um hunting knife.'

'What you is hunt?' asked Managua, holding the handle in his fist and practising a downward stabbing motion.

William couldn't think. What did people hunt, for God's sake? Bears? If Managua knew what a bear was then he was hardly likely to believe you killed them with knives in hand-to-hand combat. Deer? By throwing knives at them as they ran away? What else was there?

'Foxes,' said William desperately, then seeing Managua did not understand, added, 'it's an animal we have in America. It's a kind of wild dog.' The old man's expression didn't change and William remembered Purnu and Cuh-A-Tuh. He gave up trying to explain.

'I is not understand what for you is have knife here, on table, for hunt foxes.' Managua shot him a challenging look. 'We is have no foxes here.'

'I was thinking maybe it might be useful for killing a -um – a—' stammered William. Behind Managua's back, Lucy pointed at the egg on the plate she was holding.

'An egg!' William said triumphantly.

'An egg? What for you is need kill egg?' The old man looked at William as if he were worried he might be crazy. He looked like he was glad he was the one holding the knife.

Behind him Lucy rolled her eyes in exasperation and then began making swimming strokes with her hands.

'A turtle!' exclaimed William.

Managua examined the blade of the knife. He ran his thumb along its edge. He looked again at William. 'Is not be much good for kill turtle. Is not be sharp enough. As matter of fact is not be sharp at all. Turtle is have very thick skin.'

'Yes, exactly,' said William. 'That's just the conclusion I reached.'

'What for you is have two knives on table? You is plan attack turtle from both sides in case he is try for run away?' He was laughing openly now. 'I is can tell you is not be necessary. Turtle is move even more slow than me.'

'I er took one knife out to see if it would be any good for turtles and saw it was – as you so rightly point out – not sharp enough, so I had a look at another one,' William improvised. Managua nodded and before the old man could ask anything else, William said, 'Why were you looking for me?'

'Looking for you? I is not look for you.'

'You said you were at the Captain Cook. Why else would you go except to see me?'

Was it his imagination or was it Managua who now looked

flustered? 'Ah yes, of course. I is just be friendly, is go see if you is come for have shit with me. We is go now?'

William didn't answer. Whatever it was he had been trying to remember had just crept a little bit closer. He sensed it was almost within reach. He knew it was something to do with the Captain Cook.

'Come, we is go now, get good place for shit.'

'What? Oh, OK. Just wait a minute while I put my trousers on.' William disappeared inside. Managua gave Lucy a shrug. 'I is never understand Americans. What for is put trousers on for take off again for have shit?'

William appeared fully dressed, gave Lucy a quick kiss and set off down the steps after the already retreating Managua. As Lucy watched the two of them heading along the beach towards the sunrise she heard the older man say, not without irony, she thought, 'After shitting I is give you breakfast. After *kassa* you is be plenty hungry. Yes, I is give you one plenty big damn breakfast.'

Managua proved as good as his word and gave William a magnificent breakfast. As well as the inevitable revolting stew that seemed to make up most of the old man's diet he gave him fried turtle eggs, slices of minoa and red fungi. Thrusting a huge wooden platter full of this at William as he was trying to force down the last of a bowl of stew, he smiled and said, 'Here is be what you is not have at Miss Lucy's. Is smell so tasty I is be sure you is must long for that.'

It was all William could do not to groan as he took the platter. 'Is be plenty more turtle eggs if you desire they,' said Managua. 'But I is counsel you you is stick at two. Otherwise you is mebbe not be able for make shit tomorrow.'

Wouldn't want that, would we? thought William. Wouldn't do to disappoint my fans.

When breakfast was over, that is to say when Managua finally ceased to press food upon William and allowed him to stop eating, the old man was in a mood to chat.

'Is you ever think 'bout end of *Hamlet*?' he asked. William wasn't able to say that he had.

'Well, here is be extraordinary thing. Everybody is be dead. They is all be kill at end. Hamlet, Laertes, Claudius, Gertrude. And of course all they others is be dead already, Ophelia, Polonius, Rosencrantz and Guildenstern. Everybody is be dead 'cept Horatio and this Fortinbras and he is not really be part of play anyway, is only just get there in time for end.'

'So?' said William. He didn't know much about Shakespeare but he didn't want to offend Managua by appearing uninterested.

'So, what is happen next?' Managua folded his arms and sat back with an air of triumph.

'Well, what can happen next? Horatio and Fortinbras can talk to one another and that's about it, isn't it, if everyone else is dead.'

Managua gave him a puzzled look. 'Excuse me, but you is go in *kassa* house, I is think?'

'Yes.'

'Well then, you is know that just because Hamlet and all rest of they is be dead is be no reason for they is stop talk.' He leaned forward for emphasis. '*Is not be necessary for play is stop there. Is can carry on.*'

William considered this for a moment. 'Well, I see where you're coming from but you have to remember the scene of the action is Denmark. They don't have *kassa* there, so far as I'm aware. How would anyone be able to communicate with the dead without it?'

Managua sighed. 'I is not wish for offend you, *gwanga*, but sometimes I is wish they is send American who is know more 'bout *Hamlet*. You is not remember how play is start?'

William tried to recall. It was years since he'd read it and almost as long since he'd seen it, if indeed he had.

'OK, I is help you out. Is start with ghost of Hamlet father. He is be dead but is walk on battlement – whatever that is be but we is not worry 'bout that now – and is talk with Hamlet. Is not be mention Hamlet is visit *kassa* house.'

'Well, OK. But then, Hamlet's father is an unhappy ghost who's come back for a purpose.'

'You is go tell me Hamlet is be happy for be kill in unfair fight? You is say Gertrude is be happy for drink poison by mistake?'

'Well, no . . .'

'And Ophelia? She is kill self. You is tell me is be act of happy person? She is smile as she is drown? And Polonius. He is think is be so great for stand behind this arras and somebody is stab he? I is not know what arras is be but I is be pretty damn sure is not be something you is stand behind for wait somebody is stab you.'

'OK, they don't all die happy—'

'They is not *any* of they is die happy. You is think Rosencrantz and Guildenstern is be happy when they is give letter English king and he is execute they? Is not what they is expect at all. And Laertes is be victim of trick.'

'Yes, but what I mean is you can't compare sixteenth-century Denmark to here. They had different customs and beliefs, about death and so on.'

'Not so very different, I is think,' said Managua holding up a finger. 'People is talk with family who is die, just like we is do here. You is tell me is not happen in America but is happen here and in Denmark.' He paused to stuff some *kassa* leaves into his pipe and fire it up. He took a puff and offered it to William, who, feeling the nausea rise in him, waved it away. 'And Scotland.'

'Scotland? How did that get into this argument?'

'Is be ghost of Banquo in *Macbeth*. You is not remember that one either I is suppose?'

'Yes.'

'And these Danes is have same burial customs as we is have.'

'They do?'

'You is know how we is bury dead person and then after we is dig up and is handle bones and then is bury again?'

'Yes, I've been reading about that in Lucy's book, but I don't see the connection with *Hamlet*.'

'Yorick.'

'Yorick?'

'Even you is must remember he. He is be fellow of infinite jest.

Is be dug up and Hamlet is play with he skull. Is be just like we is do. First time I is read play I is all time expect Yorick is go show up just like father of Hamlet.'

William was silent for a moment. He supposed this was part of the universal appeal of Shakespeare. Each person coming to it found in it something different, depending on their cultural references. He recalled seeing a production of a Shakespeare play transposed to the Caribbean, and a Marxist interpretation of *King Lear*. It might not be all things to all men, but it was certainly something else to Managua.

'I don't quite understand where all this is leading you,' he said, rising from his cross-legged position to indicate he wanted to leave.

Seated on the ground as he was, Managua might have been looking up at William physically, but his expression was one of pure condescension. 'Sequel.'

'Sequel?'

'Is mean another story that is come after one story is be over. You is never hear of *Henry IV Part One*? Well, is be sequel, *Henry IV Part Two*.'

'I – uh – know what a sequel is. But surely you're not suggesting . . .'

'Sequel for *Hamlet*. Is be necessary. Is be obvious all they unhappy dead people is go come back. If I is put play on here, everyone is ask what is happen next. Is must have sequel.'

'Well, how are you going to get that?'

'Is be obvious.' Managua tapped his chest. 'I is write.'

FORTY-FIVE

On his way back to the Captain Cook, where he had plenty to do processing the information he'd gathered and checking what else was needful to be done before he left on the plane in a few days' time, William couldn't help chuckling at the idea of this crazy old guy, this literary man with an artificial leg, on a remote island in the South Pacific having the hubris to think he could write a follow-up to what was arguably the world's greatest piece of literature. He tried to imagine what it would be like, a drama in which most of the characters were already dead at the start. Insane! But then again, perhaps not here, where the lines between living and dead were blurred, where, under the influence of a powerful hallucinogen, you could see and converse with your departed loved ones. Once again, William was troubled. He was always so confused the morning after *kassa* that he felt he must have hallucinated, but while he was in the hut, he was absolutely convinced his dead father stood before him. A thought struck him that had not occurred before. His hallucination had somehow peopled the *kassa* house with the relatives of all those other people present. He had presumed this to be because before he'd ever entered the place he'd heard suggestions of what he would see there. Until now he'd only thought about the reality or not of his vision of his father, but as he plodded along the beach, being careful where he stepped because he had to traverse the shitting beach and the tide was still out, he thought of the other people he had seen. And then he thought of Managua, who had sat next to him that first time, talking with an old man. Afterwards, when he'd asked who the man was, Managua had said his father. But how was it possible for William to share another person's hallucination?

He rounded the headland and the Captain Cook came into view and something below the surface of his brain, an undertow from last night, tugged at him. His mind struggled to grasp this thing that was always just out of reach, without success, and then, in the way that often occurs, his thoughts returned to where they'd been a moment earlier. When he'd first spoken to Managua about his wife, Managua had said that now he could only see her in the *kassa* house. But whenever he'd been there with Managua the older man was only ever talking to his father. Pilua had never appeared to him. Of course it could well be that the same dead person didn't show up every time you entered the *kassa* house, it could be that sometimes Managua saw his father and sometimes his late wife. But it could also be that she never appeared for a very simple reason. *Because she wasn't dead.* William couldn't believe he hadn't thought of this before. It was like one of those cartoons, where a light bulb goes on inside a character's head. And then, his mind leaping now, that image enabled him to close his fingers around the lost memory. A light! That was what he had seen. A light shining out as he swooped down over the Captain Cook. And how could there be a light when he wasn't there? The only lights in the hotel, so far as he knew, were the oil burners the natives had given him. And William had extinguished them all before he went off last night to the *kassa* house. Naturally William could be 100 per cent certain of this since the lights were the only things he checked when he left the hotel. He had no burglar alarms, no hi-fis, no electrical devices at all, no door or window locks, no doors or windows even. He *had* to check the lights, not only because he didn't want some accident to destroy the half of the hotel that was left, or rather had been built, but also by default, for the want of anything else *to* check. There was only one conclusion

to be drawn. Someone else had been in the hotel. And now, closing
his eyes, he confirmed that the light could not have been a
moment of carelessness from him, a rare checking failure, because
it had been shining from an upstairs window and he had not ventured to the hotel's upper floor after that one occasion when he
had been struck on the head.

As he approached the hotel from the beach he thought of how
he'd lain on his mahogany bed and listened to the tapping sound
from above. What else but the sound of an artificial foot moving
about upstairs? And that other noise, that lighter skittering sound.
What else but the light step of a woman? A woman confined perhaps for years to this building, dancing maybe from an excess of
pent-up energy, easing the frustration of her imprisonment. It all
made sense now. What better place for Managua to hide his
supposed dead wife and child – the child whose existence William
suddenly realized was the reason for all this subterfuge – than the
unfinished hotel, especially once he had disseminated a rumour
that it was inhabited by evil spirits? Close enough to visit them and
take them essential supplies, but somewhere they were likely to
remain undisturbed, until the visit of an obstinate foreigner who
refused the blandishments of the *bukumatula* house.

William quickened his step. The answer to his quest had been, if
not right under, then right above, his own nose all the time he had
been here. No wonder that when Managua had guessed William
had not only stayed at Lucy's last night but had eaten there as well
he had chosen not to invoke the taboo but had enjoyed himself by
making William eat another breakfast, the very breakfast that was
now weighing so heavily in William's bowels as he tried to hurry
to the hotel. The old man hadn't wanted to discourage William
from staying at Lucy's, well away from the hotel.

Inside the hotel entrance he listened. He thought he heard the
skittering noise, but there was no tapping. What was he thinking
of? Of course there wasn't! How could there be when he had just
left Managua back at the village plotting his literary sensation? He
hastened to the stairway and when he examined it realized that

though it was precarious even Managua would still be able to ascend it, especially as there would be no concern about symmetry for a man with an artificial leg.

He went up the stairs as fast as he dared. There were a couple of near-falls but he made it to the top, even remembering not to put his weight on the creaky top step. He listened carefully, but he didn't hear the skittering sound again. Pilua and her child must have heard him. He could sense them standing motionless, holding their breath, fearful of the slightest noise that might alert him to their presence. He didn't this time make the mistake of opening the doors on the front side of the hotel that he now knew led to nothing but the precipice he'd been pushed over before. He crept along the corridor and set his hand on the handle of the first door on the beach side. He turned it slowly and as quietly as possible and then flung the door open fast. The room was a concrete shell and quite empty. But as he turned, he heard the skittering noise again. He crept noiselessly along the corridor, although even as he did so, he realized caution was unnecessary. There was no escape from any of the rooms save via this corridor and the staircase behind him that he'd come up. The balconies on the beach side were surely too high for a woman to jump from. He set his hand upon the handle of the next door and as he turned it, he heard the skittering within. Without further ado he threw open the door and found himself face to face with the source of the noise. A pair of beady black eyes stared back at him.

William was too amazed to react quickly. Not so the pig. It looked from him to the open doorway and was through it even as William tried too late to slam it shut. He heard it squealing as it shot back and forth along the corridor, its trotters on the concrete making the familiar skittering noise that had so alarmed him all those nights ago. And then, the squealing and skittering stopped and he heard a shuffle and a tap, a shuffle and a tap. Then that too ceased.

'Come, come, little Cordelia, is be no need for be afraid. Here, I is have tasty orange fungi for you. Here, you is eat.' Hearing the

seductive tone of Managua's voice, William at once understood the
reasonableness of Lamua's jealousy. The shuffle and tap resumed
and William felt the door move against him. He stood aside and
Managua walked in, the pig under his arm.

'Ah, is be as I is think. Is be you *gwanga* who is frighten my little
pet.'

'You might have told me you were keeping it here. The darn
thing kept me awake at night. I was scared out of my wits.'

Managua carefully closed the door before setting the pig on the
ground. He stroked it lovingly and the pig licked his fingers and
looked up at him with what William could only describe as
adoration. Managua put his hand in the bag that was slung over his
shoulder and fed the pig some more fungi. He turned to William.
'I is not tell because I is not want for everyone is find out. My wife
is want for kill this pig.'

'What makes you think I'd tell Lamua? I can keep a secret, you
know.'

Managua's look was steely. 'No *gwanga*, I is not think you is can.
Life on this island is be good. Even with one leg is be better
than life you Americans is have, I is think. But you is must open
you big American mouth and tell everything. And for what? For
dollars! For buy things! Things we is not need. Things we is not
want. You is open you mouth and is destroy this island. You is think
I is trust you with life of my little pig?'

What could William say to such an imputation of his integrity?
A slur that was even greater than intended since he hadn't
Managua's high regard for the pig in question, because he, unlike
the native, had seen other, larger breeds of pigs and so knew just
how runty and ugly this one was. William stood and stared at the
older man in silence, while Managua glared at him, at the same
time feeding and fondling the pig which lovingly nuzzled its silky
ears against his hand.

The silence was broken not by William thinking of an adequate
riposte – he couldn't – but by a loud creak that both men instantly
recognized as someone putting a foot upon the top step of the

ruined staircase. They heard the soft pad of footsteps along the corridor. They watched as the handle of the door began to turn. As though instinctively, Managua bent and scooped up the pig, just as the door was flung open.

'I is know I is find you here with this damn pig!' Lamua flew at Managua like a fury. She balled her fists and began beating him about the head. Simultaneously she let fly with a salvo of kicks and then screamed in pain as her naked foot made contact with his artificial leg. She paused to bend and rub it, confining herself the while to spitting out insults. 'I is catch you with you sweetheart now! I is find you is make *fug-a-fug* with you precious little sow!'

She launched herself at her husband once more, this time seizing the arm under which the pig was tucked and digging her nails into it as she attempted to loosen Managua's grip on the animal. The pig began to scream in descant to Lamua's own screams. It would have been difficult to say which screams were the most horrible, but most people would probably have gone for the pig's. Then William noticed a sudden reduction in the noise level, a halving in fact, although he couldn't at first understand why because Lamua had her back to him and he couldn't see what she was doing to Managua. He took a step or two sideways to get a better view and saw Lamua had sunk her teeth into Managua's pig-holding arm and was thus unable to vocalize. At this point the volume level went up again as Managua let out a cry or two himself, supplying the bassline that had so far been lacking in the hullabaloo. There was a great deal of pushing and shoving and for a moment or two it wasn't clear to William just what was happening and then he saw Managua had tugged his arm free of his wife's dental attentions but only at the cost of dropping the pig. The animal hit the floor running and shot out the door like a bullet. Lamua let go of Managua and was through the door almost as fast as the pig, slamming it shut after her as she went. Managua paused only for a second to rub the bite mark on his arm before he took hold of the door handle and pulled at the door. It didn't open. William went to help him. With evident irritation at having to accept assistance from a man whose character he had so recently roundly abused, Managua let go the door handle and used his hand to massage his bite wound. William found that the door, evidently warped from being left open to the elements for so many years, had stuck after being so forcefully slammed. It took William some time to manipulate it free and it was just as he was opening it that he heard someone speak. At first he thought Lamua must be talking to the pig, but as she wasn't screaming or threatening he knew it couldn't be so. He opened the door, but before he could walk through it Managua barged him aside and exited first.

William pursued Managua along the corridor to the room where all the noise was coming from. He arrived to find the old man blocking the doorway, staring at what he found there. Peering over his shoulder William saw Lamua confronting a woman of about her own age, to whom, it would seem, she had reassigned her disaffection from the pig for she was midstream in another tirade whose gist William couldn't catch. At once, he knew this woman could be none other than the elusive Pilua and realized his first instinct about the secret occupant of the hotel had been right. Of course it had! Why would the pig have needed a light? What was it going to do, sit up late and read Shakespeare?

Pilua stood motionless, calmly accepting Lamua's insults. There was a movement behind her and William saw a teenage girl, of sixteen or seventeen perhaps. She was exceptionally beautiful, but that wasn't what caused William's jaw to drop. What he saw was that her skin was the colour of this morning's breakfast table-cloth or the foaming surf he'd compared it to. She had her mother's looks, a glance at them both told him that, but no hint of her colour; the girl's skin was as white as his own.

William was too busy staring at the girl to bother looking, but if he had, he would have found there was no sign of the pig.

FORTY-SIX

To understand how Lamua came to be at the Captain Cook and what had driven her to brave its evil spirits in search of the pig it is necessary to go back a few hours. For as far back as he could remember Lintoa had wanted only one thing: to be a boy. Now he wanted something else too. He wanted Perlua. He wanted to marry the beautiful white girl he had seen on the balcony of the Captain Cook, bathing herself in the light of the moon. This second desire naturally increased the intensity of the first. He wanted Perlua on his arm as he strutted about the village in his pubic leaf for all the world to see. He couldn't see her with him tottering on high heels and clad in a cast-off, too-small, pink dress.

Lintoa was sixteen years old. It would be two years before he could choose his sex. What if some other youth discovered Perlua before then? Much as Lintoa believed her protestations of eternal love, how would they stack up when she was offered the choice between some other fine fellow bulging out of a pubic leaf and him trying not to look pretty in pink?

What was he to do? Every day he had to hide his love was torture. Every moment he was not with Perlua he was beside himself with worry that she might be spotted by someone else.

Tigua knew something was wrong, of course. He and Lintoa had been inseparable from the time they put on their first grass skirts. He could read Lintoa's face the way Managua read a book. He saw there the things hidden from everyone else.

'What is be matter with you?' he asked one day. 'Half time you is walk around as if you is be half asleep like man who is have too much *kassa*—'

'Huh!' interpolated Lintoa. That Huh! meant that the chance – being allowed into the *kassa* house to imbibe the stuff – would be a fine thing and they both understood that, though Tigua ignored the exclamation.

'—and half time you is be like pig with sore arse.'

'Nothing is be matter,' muttered Lintoa, ''cept this damn bra strap,' and he began fiddling with it so meticulously that it didn't fool Tigua for a moment.

'This is be me you is be talk with, you is remember?' said Tigua. 'I is know something is be wrong. I is can see you is not be self.'

'I is never be self since first day I is be born,' snapped Lintoa. 'Self is be boy, I is made for be girl.'

Tigua rolled his eyes. 'Oh, so we is be back there again? I is be sorry I is ask. You is just must wait, you is not can see that? Boy or girl, there is be one thing you is be and that is be stupid.'

But Lintoa was not stupid. He might not be as quick as Tigua but give him time and he wasn't so bad at figuring things out, although it has to be said he also had a tendency to be hotheaded and to not think enough before he acted.

And that was what happened now. Lintoa felt that if he waited two years to become a boy, he would lose Perlua. But even Purnu's magic could not make him a boy now, even if it were available, which of course it was not. Even the best spells could not change the traditions and taboos of the tribe, the little sorcerer had said. But that didn't mean that something else couldn't, did it? What if something happened to question all the beliefs of the tribe? Would they then still insist on what was after all a relatively unimportant thing, the age when a she-boy could choose his or her sex?

Lintoa asked himself why Managua had invented the story of his wife and child being killed, why he had hidden them away. What was he trying to conceal? He knew there was something different about Perlua, other than her great beauty, and he asked himself what it was. It didn't take even Lintoa long to figure it out. She was white. But how could this be? Her mother was brown like the rest of them. Thinking about Pilua he remembered the story of the attack upon her by the three American soldiers. He recalled hearing that they had all been white. And Pilua had given birth to a white child. Could this be a coincidence? Could a white baby have floated to her by mistake?

He thought about the argument between Miss Lucy and the men of the village when she had insisted that men's sperm makes babies. The men had laughed at the idea. But suppose it were true? Certainly white people like Miss Lucy knew plenty of stuff the islanders didn't. Suppose she'd been right about this? It would explain why Perlua was white. When you thought about it, it was the only thing that would explain it. She was white because a white man, or rather, three white men, had made her by putting their sperm into Pilua. Far from having no biological father, Perlua had three.

The more he considered the theory, the more plausible it seemed. This was surely why there was a taboo against making *fug-a-fug* with foreigners, to prevent children being born with different skin colour. No wonder Managua had hidden his daughter! If it were proved that men fathered children then everything on the island would have to change. Men would no longer have to give yams to support their sisters' children. A man would have to pass his property, such as it was, on to his wife's children, not, as at present, his sister's. All the beliefs of the islanders would be overturned. Take the floating babies. How could babies be the souls of the dead returning to life if they came not over the ocean from Tuma, but were injected into their mothers as sperm? Every tradition of birth, marriage and even death would be altered, nothing would stay the same. It would all come crashing down. And in the confusion that followed, in the abandonment of the old values, who was going to object if he took off his dress and put on a pubic leaf? Who the *fug-a-fug* would care?

Once he'd decided this, Lintoa's next problem was how to go
about revealing Pilua and Perlua's existence. His first thought was
to tell the *gwanga*, who was desperate to find Pilua because that
would make other Americans listen when he told them about the
blown-off limbs. Lintoa wasn't sure why this should be, why
Americans would be more inclined to believe a woman who said
she had been forced to make *fug-a-fug*, which was something you
couldn't see, than someone who said they had had their foot blown
off by an American bomb, which you could see, or rather, you
could not see the foot, that was the whole point, the absence of
foot was definite proof. But then, Lintoa had long ago stopped trying to make sense of the Americans, who, when you thought about
it, were as loony as the British, just as mad, only with bombs.

The problem with going to the *gwanga* was Managua, who
would see it as a betrayal of the island and its customs. It would
bring the old man's wrath down upon him. Did he really want to
be in the bad books of the island's two most powerful sorcerers?
Would not the likelihood then be of him being changed not into
a boy but into something with fins or feathers or flippers? He
mustn't forget either that Managua was, he hoped, his future father-
in-law even though, of course, he was not Perlua's father, definitely
not, other than by virtue of being married to her mother, although
of course, looked at another way, that was how all the fathers on the
island regarded themselves in relation to their children. Shit! It was all
getting so complicated it made his head hurt. Anyway, all that was by
the by. It was obvious he could not tell the *gwanga* and risk upsetting
Managua.

Then there was Purnu. Telling the little sorcerer would pay off
some of the yams he owed, too. But again he risked upsetting a
powerful magician. On the other hand, could he upset Purnu any
more than he already had? Well, yes, when Purnu discovered the
existence of a girl Lintoa preferred to the besotted Kiroa. Of
course, Purnu was going to find that out anyway, but Lintoa telling
him himself might seem like flaunting his new love. And it would
be doubly annoying to Purnu to discover Lintoa had rejected

Kiroa for a girl who was the daughter of his arch-rival (even if, actually, she wasn't!). Lintoa could feel scales growing on his body at the very thought of what the little man might do. Better not mention it to Purnu.

Another option was to tell Tigua; that would be the quickest way to broadcast it all over the island. Even people in remote hamlets miles away would know about it in minutes, Tigua was such a blabbermouth. And no blame would attach to Lintoa because Tigua was certain to steal the credit for the discovery and Lintoa's part in it would disappear as completely as a baby *koku-koku* into the mouth of a *tirobe*. But even as he thought this, Lintoa knew he couldn't do it. Something troubled him about speaking of Perlua to the other she-boy. He knew he wouldn't be able to keep the admiration from shining forth from his eyes, the enthusiasm from spilling out over his lips. He didn't want to think about how Tigua would receive the news. Yes, he would have to know about Perlua sooner or later, but Lintoa knew he couldn't be the one to tell him.

Lamua! That was it. It was so obvious, he should have thought of her first. And here a brilliant thought struck him, one that Tigua himself would have been proud of. He didn't even have to implicate himself by mentioning Pilua to Lamua. Instead he would say it was the pig. He would tell her Managua was keeping the pig at the Captain Cook. It was beautiful! Lamua would go to look for the animal and instead find Pilua. There would be such a commotion about Managua's first wife and his daughter being alive that Lamua would forget all about the pig and wouldn't even notice that it wasn't there. Lintoa wouldn't get blamed at all. Of course, Lintoa didn't know that the pig was also at the Captain Cook and that Managua might be almost as upset about him squealing on the pig, so to speak, as on his wife and daughter, but it didn't matter. He was perfectly right in thinking that the ruckus over Pilua and Perlua would completely eclipse any concern over the pig.

FORTY-SEVEN

There was consternation when the small party from the Captain Cook arrived in the village. Managua had attempted to dissuade Lamua from revealing her find to the villagers. He had even offered up the pig as a sacrifice if she would keep quiet, an offer that Lamua, in a rare moment of logic among the hysterical tongue-lashing she was giving him, pointed out wasn't worth much as he didn't any longer have the pig. As Managua in turn became furious with her, William felt obliged to step in and point out that even if Lamua kept quiet, he would not be able to but was obliged to report the existence of the woman whom the American soldiers had raped.

There was nothing for it but to make a general declaration. There was no point in Pilua and Perlua remaining at the Captain Cook.

A matter of moments after their arrival in the village centre, virtually all the villagers, save for those men and boys who were out fishing, had rushed to look at the two strange women. Initially their interest was attracted by the opportunity to see, for the first time, a white woman's breasts. Until this moment they had never actually been sure that white women *had* breasts. They knew Miss Lucy had objects on her chest that were breast-shaped (if a little pointy) but then they knew she wore one of the things that she had given the she-boys and that they had stuffed with rags to look like breasts.

There were some who maintained that Miss Lucy was a she-boy herself, and among these some who even maintained that all white
women were actually she-boys. So they were agog to see the white
breasts.

The two women stood, William thought, as if for sale at an
Ancient Roman slave market as the crowd pressed around them,
examining them minutely, especially Perlua, some of the women
even venturing to touch her breasts to make sure they were real.

'Get back! Leave they alone!' shouted Managua, arms flailing at
the milling islanders. His expression was one of such fury that the
crowd retreated and waited to see what was going to happen next.
Purnu pushed his way through the throng and marched boldly up
to his arch-rival.

He looked at Pilua and smiled. 'Pilua, I is remember you. You is
can remember me?'

Pilua looked at Managua for guidance. 'She is not remember
you,' he said. Pilua lowered her eyes.

'You is hide this woman in Captain Cook for all these years? I
is not can believe this.' Purnu whistled and shook his head,
evidently amazed. Behind him William heard Tigua whisper, 'Is not
be so hard for believe as that he is hide pig for three moons. Is be
plenty damn hard for keep pig shut up, they is be too good for
escape.'

'But what for, Managua, what for you is do this?'

Managua drew himself up. A sigh escaped him. He gazed over
Purnu's head into the distance as though there were something
interesting happening at the edge of the jungle. He made no reply.

'And this, this is be Pilua's daughter?'

This time Managua nodded. Perlua looked at him anxiously and
he shot her a comforting smile.

Purnu examined the girl, walking around her, staring intently.
Suddenly his gaze swung back to Managua, quick as a green shoestring striking, those who had witnessed such a thing – although
not, of course, striking at them or they wouldn't be here to tell the
tale – later said. 'She is be you daughter then?'

Again Managua nodded.

Purnu took another turn or two around Perlua. 'So what for she is not look like you? She is not look anything like you.'

This started a buzz of conversation among the crowd. People were shocked. It was an outrageous thing to say to a father about his child, but on the other hand, they muttered, it was undeniably true.

Managua shrugged. 'I is not live with she. I is not be around enough for mould she.'

The hubbub started up again, people nodded wisely. It was obvious, after all. You couldn't expect children to grow up to resemble you if you weren't around to shape them. Someone said that mebbe that was why she was white, that mebbe that was what happened to children who had no father to mould them, they didn't get any colour. But then other people chipped in citing cases where fathers had died and their mothers had not found a new husband and the children were still brown like everyone else and then someone else said what about Gawaloa, her children had never had a father, for who would want to marry her? yet none of her children was white.

Purnu raised a hand to silence the crowd. 'You is tell everyone they is be kill by bomb, same bomb as is take away you leg. This is be lie. What for you is make this lie?'

Managua took a deep breath, as though drawing himself up for a big speech. His face looked troubled as he struggled for words. But none came. He released his breath without uttering anything and there was a collective, disappointed sigh as the crowd did the same.

'I is tell you what for!' The voice came from the back of the crowd and everyone turned. There was a disturbance as someone pushed his way through from the back. Lintoa emerged from the mob, shoving people out of his way, his lipstick and long hair, his tight pink dress and pointed breasts at odds with the masculine determination with which he thrust his way to the front. Once there, he put his arm around Perlua, but as a boy would his girlfriend, not like girl to girl. A gasp went up from the assembly. There were angry shouts. It was a shocking thing to see, one girl fondling another.

Perlua's expression was pure fear as she looked at the lipsticked face of the creature holding her. She knew nothing of the existence of she-boys. She had never seen Lintoa like this. She didn't recognize him.

He smiled at her. 'Is be OK, is be me, Lintoa, you is soon see,' he said. Fear was replaced by confusion on her face.

Lintoa held up a hand to quell the hostile crowd. 'Listen!' The noise was too great for him to be heard. Everyone was talking and arguing. A couple of sticks flew out of the mob and narrowly missed the boy in the pink dress.

'Listen!' bellowed Lintoa, so loudly that everyone heard and stopped talking. 'You is let me bend you ears. I is come for tell you what you is want for know! I is tell you what for Managua is do this thing.'

There was a hush now. Some people continued to shout sporadic abuse at Lintoa but others told them to be quiet and let the girl talk. What harm could it do?

'You is all know how Americans is attack Pilua,' said Lintoa. 'Everybody is hear this story. Is be one more bad thing Americans is do.' One or two of the people around William glared at him. 'You is know they Americans is force Pilua make *fug-a-fug*. Is force she break taboo against do this with foreigner.

'When she is come home everyone is be plenty sorry, but they is still throw she out of village for break taboo, even though is not be she fault. She is must go live alone.

'Then she is find she is go have baby and Managua here is take pity on she. He is marry she. He is offer for share she lonely life.'

People nodded. One or two said complimentary things about the old man, but his expression did not change. He simply stared in horror at Lintoa.

'Now what is happen next, you is think? I is tell you, baby is be born and Managua is see baby is be white. Three white Americans is make *fug-a-fug* with Pilua and she is have baby that is be white. Is you see connection? No? Well, is be obvious for man like Managua, who is can read. He is understand straight away. Is mean one thing. Is be true what British missionaries is say. Is mean is be man who is make babies, not woman. Is be seed man plants in woman that is grow for make baby.'

There was complete uproar. One or two pieces of fruit came sailing over the crowd and something resembling a tomato struck Lintoa's cheek. He wiped it away, smiling now.

'Yes, is be true! Is be no other explanation! Is mean everything we is be tell is be wrong. Men is make babies! There is be no floating babies! There is be no return for souls of dead! Is be father who is must care for he children. Is must no longer rely on wife's brother for yams!'

The roar of the crowd increased. More fruit was thrown. One or two people were saying, 'Wait, let she speak!'

Purnu called, 'Listen, you fools, this is be just what British and Americans is always tell we! Mebbe they is be right.'

Lintoa was shouting now. 'This is what for they is make taboo for not make *fug-a-fug* with foreigner in first place, for stop white babies or yellow babies is be born. Is be because this is happen some time in past and is make plenty difficult questions. But now we is know what is happen, taboo is can go. And this taboo is can go now as well!' He grabbed the front of his dress and plunged his hand into his bra pulling out a rag. He wiped away his lipstick. 'All crazy taboos and laws is can go now!' His huge hands seized the top of the dress and with one mighty pull he tore it asunder. As the top fell away and the crowd gasped once more at the sight of the bra, he struggled out of that. He pulled again at the dress and tugged it off, and stood proudly smiling at Perlua, clad only in a pubic leaf. 'You is see, they old taboos and laws is be crazy! You is can see for you selves. I is be boy!'

The crowd went wild. William was fearful he might be attacked as people were screaming abuse about Americans. More fruit was thrown at Lintoa, including a coconut which fortunately missed.

Some elements in the mob surged forward as though wanting to tear him apart, while others fought to restrain them. Still others were cautioning the hecklers to be quiet, saying such things as that the she-boy had a point and that what she was saying made sense. Other people said the she-boy had gone crazy and someone else wondered what damn fool had let a she-boy have *kassa*?

'STOP!' The shout was so loud that everyone went silent. It was Managua. He drew himself to his full height, cheeks flushed with anger. 'This is not be place for such talk! You is not can listen words of one crazy she-boy!' He stooped and picked up the ruined pink dress, tossing it angrily at Lintoa. 'Put this on, stupid girl! How you is dare show youself before people like that? Cover you indecency at once!'

Such was the command in his voice that there was a hubbub of agreement from the mob, who, it had to be said, were all outraged by a she-boy baring her body like this. Lintoa knew not to argue. He caught the dress and, holding it over his loins to preserve his modesty, pushed through the crowd, taking both pats on the back and cuffs around the ear as he went, such was the division of opinion among the tribespeople. As he vanished among the outer ring of huts William saw Tigua trotting after him in his red high heels. But then the little she-boy stopped and stood rock-still, gazing after Lintoa, watching until he was swallowed up by the jungle.

FORTY-EIGHT

As the crowd showed no sign of dispersing – and why would they? nothing so exciting had happened since the American bombs started going off – Managua retreated into his hut along with Pilua and Perlua. Tigua took it upon himself to stand guard at the door to keep away the curious and admit entry only to those permitted by Managua. As one might expect of him, Tigua took a delight in this privileged position, telling people, 'No, you is have no place for come in here, you is keep you big nose outside.' Really, of course, all he wanted to do was to get a close look at Perlua. What he saw served only to increase his ferocity with gatecrashers. For there was no disputing it. The girl was beautiful. She was as near perfection as it was possible to get. What chance did poor funny little Tigua, with his turned-up nose and shapeless legs, have against her, even leaving aside the important fact that of course the she-boy wasn't actually a girl?

'You is have nothing better for do than smell other people shit?' barked Tigua at the next man who stuck his head inside the door. He pulled it out again as if he'd been struck and walked away cursing the she-boy. He didn't know not to take the insult personally; that his natural curiosity had gotten more than it deserved because he'd happened to intrude upon the she-boy's rising grief.

Of the many repercussions of the resurrection of Managua's first wife and daughter, the most pressing was where everyone was to sleep. The two women could no longer remain at the Captain Cook where they would be at the mercy of the curious. But how could Pilua live with Managua when he had another wife? Although the islanders enjoyed multiple sexual partners when single, there was a strict taboo against adultery after marriage and a second taboo against bigamy to prevent anyone using that as a method of getting around the first.

Of course it was perfectly easy to divorce someone. You simply said you didn't want to eat with them any more. You announced you were not married to them any longer and left them. But Managua had not done this. He had never divorced Pilua; instead he had faked her death. There was some debate about whether he could actually ever have been legally married to Lamua, or whether all these years the two had been living in sin. There was no doubt that they had. Everyone in the village had seen them sitting outside their hut openly tucking into the same pot of stew.

The bigamy issue was solved when Lamua and Purnu burst into the hut. Tigua tried to dissuade Lamua from entering but not very hard. One look at Lamua's face was enough to tell him that here was a woman you didn't want to get into an argument with. He'd never have believed Lamua could get herself to look so ugly, but she had; her lovely face was distorted by rage.

Tigua nevertheless saw it as his duty to try to prevent bloodshed. He would not have wanted even Perlua to be hurt. 'You is sure you is want for go in there?' he asked.

'If you is not get out of my way I is kick you out of door,' Lamua replied, which struck Tigua as pretty unequivocal.

'And if you is not let me pass you is go find youself is be frog,' said Purnu.

Although there was nothing for it but to let them in, there was no way Tigua was going to allow them to have the last word as well. 'You is tell me this first,' he said to Purnu. 'Is you go make me be frog before or after she is kick me?'

'What in name of *fug-a-fug* is that have for do with anything?' demanded Purnu. 'What difference is can make?'

'Is make plenty difference,' said Tigua. 'If she is kick me first is go hurt but is not be end of world. If you is make me frog and then she is kick me I is be one plenty dead frog. Is be splat all over place.'

'Get out of way, silly girl!' snapped Lamua and shoved Tigua aside.

'You is be this close for you is spend rest of you life croak in water hole,' rasped Purnu, holding up his thumb and forefinger a millimetre apart as he followed Lamua.

Tigua contented himself with pulling a face after them. For once he could not think of a witty riposte because as his gaze followed their passage, it fell once more upon Perlua, who stood calmly listening to something her father was telling her.

Lamua interrupted his discourse. 'You is must excuse me for interrupt,' she said. 'Is only be my own house.'

'That is be problem,' said Managua with an apologetic expression. 'I is not know what we is can do. Is not right for have two wives under same roof.'

'Is not right for have two wives at all!' spat Lamua. 'Is not matter what roofs they is be under!'

'Is be true,' murmured Pilua. 'Whole situation is be very wrong.'

Lamua's expression softened as she turned to the other woman. 'I is not blame you. I is be sorry for shout earlier. Is just be my way. Is not be you fault. Is be this – this – this—'

'Pig,' said Purnu.

'No, not pig,' said Lamua. 'You is keep out of this.'

'Sorry,' said Purnu, bowing his head like a told-off child. Managua had never seen him so meek.

'Now I is forget what I is say.'

Tigua helped her out. 'You is say "this – this – this—",' he said.

Lamua glared at Tigua. The she-boy was glad that Lamua wasn't the person who knew the frog spell. He'd have been chasing dragonflies. 'Never mind what I is say, there is not be words bad enough for this – this – this—'

'You is already say that,' said Tigua and ducked out of the door before Lamua could make a run at him.

'You is be right for be angry,' said Managua, who was now at his most stately. 'I is do you big wrong. All I is can do is say sorry. You is try for be good wife but I is not can be good husband. All they years I is be split in two. I is think of Pilua when is be my duty for think of you.' He turned to her with his hands palms upwards in a gesture of helplessness. 'Now I is not know what I is can do. I is must choose.'

'Hah!' Lamua tossed her mane of black hair. 'That is just what you is not can do. You is not have choice. I is already make.'

'You? How?'

She held out a hand to her side and found Purnu's. 'I is go live with Purnu. Now I is not be marry you, I is be free for marry he.'

'You – he – you . . . ?'

She smiled and nodded.

'You is make *fug-a-fug* with he?'

She shot a look of adolescent fondness at Purnu and then turned the smile to one of insolent defiance when she directed it back at Managua.

'Ah yes,' said the older man. 'I is see now. When you is suppose fetch water and you is not take pot. And he is give you pocket calculator. Of course.'

'He is be plenty good for *fug-a-fug*. Nice big *pwili*,' said Lamua.

'Mebbe so,' said Managua. He gave her a fatherly smile, a mixture of fondness and resignation. 'But you is like he? I is find hard for believe that.'

Purnu stepped forward. 'I is read she stories she is like. Wilbur Smith. Georgette Heyer. Stephen King.'

Managua's face clouded over. He looked as if he would explode. 'You is READ?' he shouted. 'How dare you is read stories for my wife! How you is can read at all?' For a moment it looked as though he was going to fling himself at Purnu and tear him limb from limb without even waiting until he was dead. But then he caught sight of William. '*Gwanga!* This is be you is do! You is teach this fool read.'

William nodded guiltily.

Managua shook his head sadly, still not able to take it in. William could see it was hard for the old man. Not only was Purnu a stronger sorcerer, he now claimed parity in Managua's previously unique field of excellence, not to mention he'd also snagged the woman who had been Managua's wife, even though, strictly speaking, she hadn't.

Managua approached Lamua, hands outstretched. 'Surely you is not can prefer they other writers better than Shakespeare?'

'Shakespeare is be plenty boring. All they words I is not understand. All they words *you* is not understand. All they dull stories.'

'Boring? Shakespeare? You is no longer like *Romeo and Juliet*? Is be world's most great love story. You is not remember *Othello*? How you is cry when I is read how he is strangle Desdemona?'

'Yes, I is remember. But you is see, then I is not hear John Grisham. He is be plenty better writer. Is be more modern.'

'And I is think you is love Shakespeare.'

'I is think so too. Now I is know I is love Shakespeare for you. I is not love you for Shakespeare.'

Managua nodded slowly.

'So now I is go live with Purnu. Is marry he right away.' She smiled at Managua. 'I is be sorry, but you is never love me with all you kidneys anyway.' She nodded at Pilua. 'Now I is know why.'

Managua let go her hands. She took one of Purnu's and the couple turned and walked together to the door, where Lamua paused and looked back at Managua. 'There is be one good thing for you in all this. You pig is be quite safe now.'

Managua smiled ruefully. 'Yes, if I is ever find she again.'

FORTY-NINE

Tigua found Lintoa by a pool in the jungle. He put his hands on the small of his back as he experienced a twinge in his kidneys at the sight of the big she-boy, sitting on a fallen tree trunk, half in and half out of his torn and dishevelled dress, head in hands, sobbing to himself. Tigua took off his heels, padded quietly to the log and sat down beside him. He put his arm around him.

'Stop it,' he said. 'You is cry like girl.'

'Well, that is because I is be girl.'

Tigua rested his cheek on Lintoa's shoulder and he didn't resist. Ah, the times Tigua had longed to be a dress strap upon that shoulder! 'No you is not,' he murmured. 'You is be boy. You is be fine big boy.' He choked back a sob of his own. 'Most fine boy on whole island, if anyone is ask me.'

Lintoa's sobs ceased. He sniffed loudly and pulled himself upright, dislodging Tigua's head from his shoulder. He looked into his eyes. 'You is really think so?'

'I is know so. I is see you in you pubic leaf today, remember? You is have plenty long string.'

Lintoa reached out one of his big paws and ruffled Tigua's hair. 'You is just say this for cheer me up. You is not mean.'

Tigua reached up and seized Lintoa's hand in both of his own before he could pull it away and held it against his cheek for a second or so. 'Oh yes, that is be so. I is just want for cheer you up.'

He let go the hand. Lintoa dragged it through his own hair, straightening himself up.

'Is all go wrong,' he said. 'I is want for make everything change so I is can be boy. Now everyone is hate me. They is make me stay girl for say wrong thing.'

'Everyone is not hate you. Girl Perlua is not hate you.'

'You – you is think not? Not even now she is find out I is be she-boy and she is see me in dress?'

'No. I is see look in she eyes when she is realize is be you. I is see how she eyes is walk all over you body when she is see you in you pubic leaf.'

Lintoa stood up and tried to adjust his dress, what was left of it. 'Well, is be true. I is look plenty damn good in pubic leaf.'

Tigua scooped a handful of mud from the edge of the pool and flung it at him. He ducked and it splatted against a tree beside him.

'Yes, you is look good. Is be only one thing bigger than you pubic leaf and that is be you head.'

Lintoa ignored the jibe. He looked worried again. 'But what if they is not let me be boy early? You is think Perlua is go wait for me?'

'Oh yes, she is go wait. She is wait sixteen years for boy like you, extra year or two is not make much difference. Anyway, maybe they is let you choose early. They is have meeting in *kassa* house tonight and is be one of things they is discuss.'

'Yes, but there is be many people who is hate me for what I is say today. You is think there is be any chance for me for choose early?'

Tigua shrugged. 'Is depend on what they is decide 'bout other things. If they is agree mans is make babies then mebbe everything is change. Or maybe some things and not others. Who is can say what they is decide once they is start on *kassa*?'

The little she-boy rose so wearily to his feet you'd have thought he had an artificial leg. He began to walk away, taking the path not in the direction back to the village, but deeper into the jungle.

'Where you is go?' asked Lintoa. 'You is want I is come with you?'

'No, I is like for be alone,' said Tigua. His voice was flat and did not reveal any emotion. 'I is see you later.'

'See you.' Lintoa had too much on his mind to think about Tigua. He turned back towards the village. He needed to change his dress.

FIFTY

There are some stories that begin with a pig; there are others that end with one. This story, which began with a woman in a jealous fury over her husband's pet, is one of the former; Tigua's small part in it belongs to the latter kind.

Tigua had no particular purpose in wandering into the jungle other than to get away from everyone because he imagined they would all be discussing Perlua and her luminous beauty, and from Lintoa in particular so he wouldn't see how upset he was about it. Though what a crazy idea that was! As though Lintoa had ever given a moment's thought to Tigua's feelings. He spent more time worrying about his bra straps.

Mostly what Tigua felt at the moment was alone. He didn't want to be with the rest of the islanders, including Lintoa, because none of them knew what it was like to be him. Not even Sussua, who would, in the end, for all his gushing about fashion pictures in Miss Lucy's *Vogue*, Tigua knew, turn out to be a boy, the way she-boys almost always did. No, Tigua didn't want to be with anyone on the island, but he did not want to be on his own either. A twinge in the small of his back, a feeling deep in his kidneys, made him afraid of himself.

So when he pushed aside some *adula* fronds and found a pair of frightened eyes staring back at him, Tigua was relieved. When the pig didn't move, but carried on staring right at him, Tigua knew it was no ordinary pig. Any regular pig would have screamed like a child in pain, turned its squiggly tail and run like hell. This one didn't, which could only mean it had come across humans before.

'Cordelia,' crooned Tigua softly. 'Come here girl. Come see you Aunty Tigua.' The pig didn't bat an eyelid. It was the exact opposite of the twitchy American. It simply continued to stare at Tigua. It wasn't about to blink and maybe get brained by an artificial limb the way had happened to its *mamu*.

'Is you not remember me, girl? Is you not know who I is be?'

The pig decided to risk a blink at this. It was a pretty dumb question. How could it not know Tigua? How many boys in green cocktail dresses were there on the island for *fug-a-fug*'s sake? Tigua took a step closer and held out a hand as though offering the pig a snack. The pig took a couple of steps back. It wasn't falling for that one. It wanted to *see* the snack before it got near a human.

'Come to Tigua, little one. You is come here for see you old friend. I is give you something nice for eat. I is give you plenty nice stroke. You is only must come.' All the time Tigua was speaking he was shuffling closer and closer to the pig. The pig didn't move at all. It didn't heed Tigua's exhortations to get closer because as far as the pig could see the she-boy was managing to close up the ground between them pretty well on his own.

Tigua got to what he judged was an arm's length away from the pig. Carefully he shucked his handbag to his left wrist from his right, because his right hand was the pig-grabbing one, and he was just about to fling himself at the animal when it let out a squeal that made Tigua almost jump out of his dress and then bolted, leaving only the shaking of the *adula*s where it had vanished.

Tigua pushed through the bushes in time to see the squiggle of the pig's tail vanishing into another clump a few yards ahead. In this fashion he pursued the animal until the jungle opened out into a spacious clearing. As Tigua burst through the surrounding shrubbery into the open he found before him a herd of maybe twenty pigs.

He advanced slowly towards them. He wasn't forgetting that

black bantam pigs have teeth like razors. Although they didn't usually attack unless cornered, he had no idea how they might behave en masse when confronted by a solitary she-boy. The pigs all had their heads down, eating something growing among the scrubby grass that carpeted the clearing. They looked like they'd been at it all afternoon. Not a single one appeared to be out of breath. It was going to be plenty damn hard to identify Cordelia.

'Cordelia!' called Tigua suddenly. He watched the pigs like a *koku-koku* watching a green shoestring, where a failure to spot the slightest movement can be fatal. He'd hoped to catch the pig out, but none of them paid any attention. Eventually a fat old sow, which was nearest to the she-boy, lifted its head and gave him the once-over, then it turned to the well-tusked boar that was obviously the leader of the herd because he was bigger than the rest, although that doesn't amount to much when you're talking black bantams, and – it was Tigua's impression, at least – raised a quizzical eyebrow. The boar gave a shrug of its shoulders that seemed to say, 'Come *on*, it's only a she-boy. What's it going to do, attack twenty of us with its shoe?'

The mixture of indifference and hostility the pigs gave off towards him made Tigua suddenly think of how things would be when he returned home. He would have no-one any more. You simply couldn't count Sussua, who was nice but nothing more. And he would eventually have to see Lintoa with Perlua on his arm. He walked among the pigs which just shuffled aside to let him pass, but in no way else registered his presence. He looked from one pig to another but they were all the same; none of them showed signs of ever having been exposed to Shakespeare. As he inspected the pigs, Tigua realized what they were eating. Once you got among the animals, you could see the grass carpet was patterned with tiny orange domes.

FIFTY-ONE

'There is be many possible explanations for my daughter skin colour,' said Managua. He was sitting against one side of the *kassa* house with the rest of the island men in a semicircle in front of him. Several pipes of *kassa* were being passed around and the air was thick with its scented smoke and the coughs it induced. It made William's eyes water so much he could scarcely see. He hadn't expected to be allowed in to witness the debate but when Purnu had suggested he be invited Managua had not merely assented but had positively insisted he be present.

'You is scrub she until she is be white I is suppose?' said N'roa. 'Or perhaps you is leave she out in moonlight? Everyone is know moon is suck colour from things.'

Other members of the audience instantly raised cries of protest at the interruption, shushing him with cries of 'Shut up, N'roa!' and 'Give you big mouth plenty rest, N'roa!'

'Such as what?' said Purnu, returning to Managua's original statement. He sat in the centre of the front row of the crowd, directly before Managua. 'You is have cause that is be more sensible than N'roa is suggest?'

'You is must remember she is stay indoors all she life. Is hide in Captain Cook. You is look at *gwanga*.' They all turned to stare at William. 'You is mebbe notice that when he is come here nearly one moon ago he is be white. Now he skin is be start for turn brown. Is be sun is make he brown. America is have weak sun so they Americans is be white.'

There were murmurs of assent as the men peered at William, as intently as if he were a piece of his own crap, trying to assess the depth of his suntan in the dim light.

'But there is be some Americans is be more brown than we. They is call theyselves black. Most of they soldiers is be black when they is here for plant bombs,' said Purnu.

Managua gave a dismissive wave. 'America is be big country. Is be some parts where is be more hot than here. Is make people there be black.'

This brought so many more nods and shouts of agreement you'd have thought most of those present were intimately acquainted with the geography and climate of the United States.

'This is be all plenty well,' said Purnu when the hubbub had died down. 'But all babies on island is be brown when they is be born, and that is be before sun is shine on they.'

Managua thought for a moment. 'Yes, but mebbe they is not stay brown if you is keep they out of sun.'

Purnu nodded, as though to indicate he took the point. Then he raised a finger in the air. 'But if Perlua is not be white when she is be born, what for you is hide she and she mother? What for you is pretend they is be dead?'

Managua didn't answer. He bought time by reaching for the nearest *kassa* pipe and taking a lengthy drag. William declined the offer of another pipe with a wave of his hand. He was already high on the fumes that filled the cramped hut. It occurred to him that he was possibly the world's first victim of passive *kassa*.

Finally Managua passed the pipe on. 'Is be just one possible explanation. Is be others as well. For example, perhaps someone is put spell on Perlua.' Here he stared determinedly at Purnu. 'Perhaps is be evil magic is steal she colour.'

'Who you is think is do this?' replied the little sorcerer angrily. 'I is not be able for do such thing even today. Time when this is happen I is hardly be man. I is not even be sorcerer then. You is tell me is be someone then who is can make spell I is not can do now?'

Managua shrugged. 'I is say is be possible. I is not know who is be responsible. Is happen every day, someone is fall sick, someone else is die, we is all know is be magic but is not always know who is make spell.'

Muttering broke out around the hut again. There were those who agreed this was possible. William heard them saying it was a much more plausible explanation that bad magic had taken Perlua's colour than the unlikely argument that sperm caused babies.

'OK, suppose you is be right and is be bad spell is make she is be white, what for you is hide she away? You is answer me that!'

This time there was silence as everyone waited for Managua to get out of that one. The older man smiled and looked relaxed. 'Is not be obvious for anyone who is have half brain? I is fearful some sorcerer is work against she. I is hide she and pretend she is be dead for protect she from other spells.'

'Huh!' said Purnu. 'One moment you is say she is be white because you is hide she, next you is reckon you is hide she because she is be white. You is not can have both ways.'

'You is ask for possible reasons what for she is be white. I is give you two. I is not say is be both reasons. I is say one of they is be possible. You is can pick which one.'

'Is be true,' said N'roa. 'Purnu, you is have one reason, this story 'bout sperm. But he is give two reasons. I is believe Managua. Two reasons is be better than one. He is must be right.'

Purnu rounded on him angrily. 'Fool! He is give you two reasons that is contradict each other. Is not explain anything. If one is be true, other is not can be. If other is be true, first is not can be.'

'OK,' said N'roa, 'so one of they is be wrong. Then other is be right. Is only need one correct explanation if I is not be mistake. You is only give we one explanation, this sperm thing. If is be wrong you is not have other one is be make right.' He looked around at the crowd, many of whom were calling out such things as: 'You is tell he N'roa' and 'You is speak sense for once', although one or two muttered 'What for big fool is not can hold tongue' and 'This is be what is happen when you is fill brain of idiot with *kassa*.'

Purnu shifted his body round so he was facing the crowd. He raised a hand for silence. 'This is not get we nowhere. Some of we is believe what Americans is say, is be sperm is make baby. Others is not. We is not be able for agree. So puzzler here is be, what we is go do now? We is allow woman Pilua for live in village with Managua? We is permit she is break taboo? If Managua is not accept sperm story, then surely he is must agree we is must keep all they old customs and taboo. Many years ago people is decide Pilua is break taboo when she is make *fug-a-fug* with white mans. She is therefore be unclean and is not can live in village.'

'Wait up a minute there.' They all turned to look at William. Some of their faces showed outrage at his interruption. 'I'm sorry,' he said nervously. 'Perhaps it's not my place to speak here.'

'No, no, *gwanga*,' said Purnu, 'we is like for hear what you is say. We is can ignore if we is not agree.'

'Well, the taboo is against making *fug-a-fug* with foreigners, as I understand it. But the point is that Pilua did not make *fug-a-fug*. You have only that term for when a man and woman make love. That is because in your society you don't have a concept of forced *fug-a-fug*. The taboo doesn't cover it because among yourselves it doesn't exist. It was introduced here from outside. You cannot apply your taboo to what Americans and other foreigners do against someone's will.'

There were murmurs of assent and dissent to this. While some nodded in agreement with William's speech others were arguing vehemently against him. One old man at the back called out, 'Taboo is be taboo. You is break one you is break all.'

Purnu raised a hand for silence again. 'I is think we is not can decide this here. We is must hear story of this woman first. We is must know if is be true American is force she make *fug-a-fug*.'

'I would like to hear her story too,' said William. 'If what I have been told is true then it will strengthen the argument for compensation. The American government will not want bad publicity about rape, which is our word for when a woman is forced against her will, and is counted among us a very bad thing. They are more likely to pay quietly for those who have been injured.'

This was met with a huge chorus of approval coming mainly, William noticed, from those with one leg or foot. Managua shook his head, but didn't say anything.

Purnu stood. 'This is be what we is do then, is all be agree? We is wait until we is hear Pilua story, then we is decide where she is go live. I is think we is finish for tonight. We is can now take more *kassa*.'

The cheer that met this suggestion was interrupted by N'roa. 'Wait for one moment, we is not be finish yet. Is be one more thing we is must discuss. If we is change one custom we is must change others, is not be so? What we is do 'bout she-boy Lintoa?'

'Lintoa is be disgrace!' snapped the old man at the back. 'She is must be punish for make public show of pubic leaf.'

'Is be all very well for say that, but we is must think more deep 'bout this,' said Purnu. He resented Lintoa because of the she-boy's effect upon his daughter, but on the other hand he had felt sorry for him in the past. He also guessed that if Lintoa became a boy and married Perlua it might finally convince Kiroa that she had no chance with the she-boy and encourage her to look elsewhere. And of course his crafty mind was always looking out for the main chance. If the she-boy custom were altered it would be another blow against Managua's stern defence of the old order. Purnu wanted to make sure of getting compensation for his dead wife. He knew that change would favour him. It would bring Coca-Cola and American gadgets. 'We is must remember this she-boy is not act like girl. She is have great courage for speak up before whole village. She is say what many is think but is not have guts for say. She is behave like man.'

Managua shifted himself. This was a plenty tricky one for him. His daughter was in love with the she-boy. He didn't want her to spend the next two years mooning about over someone in lipstick and a dress. He'd seen what a fool Kiroa had made of herself doing that. On the other hand Lintoa couldn't be allowed to choose his sex now when he had so openly flouted tradition. 'She is be young and we is must make allowance for this,' he said. 'But we is must not give way when young people is challenge ways of we ancestors. If we is do that, then everything is be one big damn mess. We is not give she-boy what she is want, but we is must show understanding and kindness too.'

'Just how you is do both they things?' asked Purnu.

'She-boy is have two years until she is can choose. We is not let she choose now. But we is not make she wait whole two years. We is say she is can choose mebbe half a year before then.'

There was general agreement to this. The *kassa* paste was being passed round and people were growing mellow enough to agree to anything. Two years, a year and a half, what did it really matter when you were out of your head and your dead folks were starting to appear? No-one objected to Managua's proposal. N'roa was about to open his mouth but before he could do so, there was a commotion at the tunnel entrance. A teenage boy, too young to be permitted entry to the *kassa* house, popped his head through the opening. 'You is come quick!' he yelled. 'She-boy Tigua is go die!'

FIFTY-TWO

The first thing you noticed about the village was that it was never silent. One reason William had been so keen to take the assignment on the island – apart from the enormity of the wrong done to the natives that needed to be righted – was the prospect of escaping the stresses and pressures of modern urban life, the promise of an outer peace he hoped would lead to an inner one. But in the village you swapped the background noise of planes and auto-mobiles and late-night drunks abusing one another on the sidewalk outside your apartment and hip-hop music played at deafening volumes on car radios and police sirens and your neigh-bour's too-loud TV, not for silence, but for the ever-present roar of the Pacific Ocean. It sounded to William exactly like the rush of his own blood inside his head when he put his hands over his ears to block out those city sounds and it always had the effect of making him contemplate his own mortality. But he didn't hear the ocean now. Once they were outside the *kassa* hut, all anyone could hear were the screams of someone in the throes of agony.

A small group of people were gathered around Tigua's bed. His parents, on one side, the father's arm around the mother's shoulders. The sound of the woman's sobbing was lost beneath the wail of Tigua's cries; you could only tell the mother was weeping by the rhythmic heave of her shoulders. You also knew, from the way he was biting his lip, that it was only the effort it took to contain her grief that enabled her husband to hold in his own. On the other side of the straw mattress were Lucy and Sussua. The latter wrung his hands helplessly as Lucy wiped Tigua's brow with a damp rag. As William entered Lucy looked up and shot him a glance that he knew was not one of welcome. There was a dreadful stench in the room, a mixture of vomit and excrement.

The mother stood when she saw him. 'Please, *gwanga*, you is help my girl. She is be my only daughter. I is not can live without she.'

William opened his arms and the woman fell into them. He held her tight and patted her naked back, which was slick with sweat. 'I'll do my best,' he murmured, releasing her to her husband.

'Aaargh! I is be on fire! Someone is put out this burn!' Tigua screamed. The cries cut right through you. It was like someone putting a knife into your skull.

William kneeled beside the bed, opposite Lucy. 'What can I do?' he asked.

She continued to dip the rag in a bowl of water and to wipe Tigua's brow. Tigua was threshing about on the bed. Every so often his midriff would lift up, raise itself several inches from the mattress, and hold itself there for a few seconds before collapsing onto the bed again.

'Nothing. You've already done it!' snapped Lucy. Her unexpected fury took him aback. He recoiled as though with whiplash. 'He's dying,' she said.

'Dying, but how?'

'He made himself a stew of orange fungi. It only takes a few to kill you. There isn't any antidote. They're always fatal.'

William took Tigua's hand and squeezed it. The she-boy stopped moving and peered up at him.

'Hey *gwanga*,' he said softly. 'You is come for watch me die. I is be glad for have you here.' He closed his eyes and winced as another spasm gripped him.

William noticed the front of Tigua's green dress was wet and covered in pieces of bright red vegetable matter. The red and the green together made him think incongruously of Christmas.

'Are you sure they were orange? The stuff he's thrown up looks red.'

'There's not much to choose between the colours, but if he'd only eaten red he wouldn't be in this agony. Besides, Tigua would know the difference.'

'What are you saying? It wasn't a mistake? Tigua *knew* he was eating orange fungi? He *meant* to kill himself?'

'Well, what did you think was going to happen when he found out about Lintoa and Perlua? It's all your doing! It's all because of your meddling. I warned you no good would come of it. If you hadn't come here Lintoa would never have seen the other girl!'

'He'd have seen her sooner or later, even if I'd never set foot on the island!'

'I wish you hadn't!' Even as she said it Lucy knew that this was unfair. Everything hadn't been all right on the island before William arrived. It had its bad bits like anywhere else. And it hadn't proved immune to outside influence. But Lucy was upset and angry and looking for someone to blame. She had been on the island long enough to absorb its philosophy. Nothing that happened happened by chance. There was always bad magic. Someone was responsible. It was how she had thought as a child.

Their argument was cut off by a commotion behind them and the crowd that had gathered at the entrance to the hut spilled into it as someone pushed them aside. Lintoa.

Tigua didn't see him as he made his way to the bed and kneeled beside it. The little she-boy had his eyes closed, fighting off another spasm. It was only when Lintoa took his hand between his two big paws that Tigua opened his eyes. At once the pain left his face and for the first time, he was able to smile.

'Ah, so you is get here at last,' he gasped. 'I is wonder if you is manage in time. You is be late for own funeral. I is not hold out any hope you is be on time for mine.'

Lintoa let go Tigua's hand and knuckled a tear from his own eye. Then he smoothed his palm across the other boy's brow. 'Poor little fool. What for you is do this, my poor little fool?'

'If you is not know that then I is do for nothing,' said Tigua, smiling back. 'But then, you is always be bit slow.'

With a thumb Lintoa wiped a mascara smudge from Tigua's eye socket. 'You make-up is all run. You is cry too much.'

'Aaaargh!' Tigua's body bounced up again. It was all Lucy and William could do to hold him down on the mattress. He lay there panting for several minutes until the griping had passed.

He opened his eyes and smiled at Lintoa again. 'I is look one big damn mess, huh?'

Lintoa resumed stroking his friend. 'You is look beautiful. You is always be beautiful.'

'But not so beautiful as she, not so beautiful as she.'

Lintoa didn't answer. On the island you couldn't tell someone who was dying a palliative lie. It would only come back to you later in the *kassa* house. So he simply hung his huge head. He let it drop onto Tigua's chest. He didn't mind the vomit. He let it lie there like a big sleepy dog's.

'Hey, listen,' said Tigua. 'I is want for you is have my green sling-backs. I is always love they shoes. I is know you is envy they.' With a great effort that caused sweat and mascara to run down his cheeks he lifted his head from the bundle of rags it rested upon and stared, wild-eyed, across the room. Lintoa followed his gaze. The shoes stood on the floor against the far wall, neatly side by side as though someone had just stepped out of them. 'I is want when you is wear you is think of me – oh!' Again Tigua's face contorted with pain.

'You is must not talk like this,' said Lintoa. 'You is must not die.'

'There must be something we can do,' said William to Lucy. 'Just because the natives don't know of a cure, it doesn't mean there isn't one.' He stood up. He was trying to think of movies he had seen where people had been poisoned or had taken drug overdoses. Would any of those things work on the fungi? The trouble was, he thought ruefully, from everything he'd been told, you couldn't OD on orange fungi, there was no such thing as a dose, let alone an overdose. Even one was too many. Still, they would lose nothing by trying. 'We must get the stuff out of his stomach,' he said, 'that's the first thing to do. Lucy, do you have any salt at your place?'

It was funny, Lucy thought afterwards, how she stopped herself from saying, 'Why, you know I do,' because that would have revealed that William had tasted salt at her house and implied that he had eaten there. Even at this moment the instinct for self-preservation kicked in. 'Yes, but—'

'How much?'

'A pot this big.' She showed him with her hands. 'It's at least half full.'

He turned to Lintoa. 'Lintoa, I want you to go and fetch it. I want you to run like the wind.'

'Let me go.' Everyone looked towards the entrance. It was Purnu. 'I is can fly. Is be much faster.' No-one batted an eyelid and William didn't have time to question the validity of the sorcerer's offer.

'OK, if you think so. Do you know what salt is?'

'It's in the cupboard on the kitchen wall,' said Lucy. 'It's in a white plastic container.'

'It will say salt on it,' said William, enunciating the word slowly.

'SUH-A-LUH-TUH,' said Purnu. 'I is can find.'

Whether the little sorcerer did fly to fetch the salt, whether he himself had actually flown with Purnu, whether the man could fly at all, William would not afterwards be able to say. But one thing was certain. The time until he returned seemed, as any short period of waiting always does in such life-or-death circumstances, an age. Against the harrowing soundtrack of Tigua's screams, William passed it by consulting Managua about orange fungi. The old man had limped in just after his arch-rival left – fortunately, William thought, thus avoiding a further proof, a practical example, no less, of Purnu's new-found ability to read. It would have been too much for him to have SUH-A-LUH-TUH rubbed in the wound.

'Is there no treatment?'

'People is try all sort of things, but I is never know anything is work. Everyone who is eat orange fungi is die.'

'That may be so,' said William. 'But if he's going to die anyway, it must be worth trying anything. One thing's for sure, it can't make his pain any worse.'

'You is waste you time, *gwanga*. Is be best for just comfort she until is be time for you is say you is see she in *kassa* house.'

'I'm not giving in. Tell me some of the treatments.'

Managua scratched his chin. 'Well, is be one where you is take vomit from poison person and you is wrap in palm leaf and is bury in clearing where orange fungi is grow.'

William tried not to show his dismay. 'I, uh, I don't think that's going to work, somehow.'

'You is be damn right. Is not be possible for can work. You is must do in light of full moon. Moon is not be full tonight.' He thought a moment longer. 'Of course, is be useful if we is have green shoestring. That is be best thing. That is can help.'

'That's the very poisonous snake. You think that can save her?'

'I is say help, I is not say nothing 'bout save. You is make shoe-string angry and then you is let bite she-boy. She is die plenty damn fast instead of all this suffer. One blink of you eye and is all be over.'

William stared at him in horror. 'The blink of an eye?'

'Well, maybe not blink of you eye. You is blink plenty damn fast.'

Before William had time to do more than get his eyelid movements under control, Purnu was back with the salt. William took the plastic canister and poured half the contents into a coconut bowl of water. While Lucy cradled Tigua's head in her arm, lifting it from his rag pillow, and Lintoa tenderly held open his blistered lips with his fingers, William tipped the contents down the little she-boy's throat.

Tigua spluttered and the salt water shot back out. He began coughing and they had to wait until the fit subsided. 'OK, again,' said William. He nodded to Lintoa. 'This time, get his mouth closed so it doesn't come back out.'

'OK, *gwanga*.'

Again Lucy lifted the head, Lintoa pried open the parched lips and William tipped the bowl. Tigua began gagging again as soon as the first drops hit his throat but his father held his body down and Lintoa kept his lips firmly apart until William had tipped the whole bowl into his throat and then clamped them tightly shut.

This time there was no reflux. Tigua swallowed the whole lot. They repeated the exercise, then again and again until all the salt was gone.

'Right,' said William, remembering the movies he'd seen. 'Now we have to make him sick and then we have to walk him, to get the poison through his system as fast as possible.'

He and Lintoa raised Tigua from the bed and into an upright position. Immediately Tigua opened his mouth and projectile vomited salt water and bits of fungi stew right across the room, spattering the onlookers in the doorway like shrapnel, those who'd seen shrapnel – which was a fair percentage of them given all the landmine explosions that had occurred – afterwards said.

William took Tigua under the left shoulder and Lintoa the right. The slight she-boy seemed surprisingly heavy. He was, William reflected, a dead weight. After a couple of circuits around the small hut William realized they weren't walking Tigua, they were dragging him. 'Come on, Tigua,' he urged, 'you've got to move your legs, get your circulation going, it's your only hope.'

They took a few more steps. Tigua's head lolled to one side like a rag doll's, an effect emphasized by the freakishly large appearance of his lips because his lipstick had smudged. Lintoa reached down and picked up a water pot. He tossed the water into Tigua's face, dropped the pot and then slapped his cheeks two or three times with the palm of his hand. 'Wake up, you stupid sow.' His voice was strangulated. He could hardly get the words out. Tigua opened his eyes, stared at nothing in particular and projectile vomited across the room again. His mother rushed forward with a cloth and wiped his face clean.

William and Lintoa marched around the room once more. This time Tigua's feet began to move. He was somnolent, but at least he was moving. Faster and faster they marched him around, ignoring his pleadings. 'No, no,' he begged, his voice rasping and barely audible, 'you is let me go. Just let me go.'

'I is not give you up unless I is be dead myself,' said Lintoa. 'Come on, you little sow, faster!'

On and on they went, up and down the small hut until William began to feel dizzy from the constant turning. He waved at the crowd in the doorway with his free hand. 'Get out of the way, we need more room,' and then they marched the semi-conscious she-boy outside.

There was only a sliver of moon to light their weary path around and around the clearing in the village centre but people brought torches and their flickering light hollowed out the cheeks and eye sockets of the spectators making them appear ghouls to William as he hurried up and down past them. And certainly their presence was ghoulish. Every expression was the same, amazement at this strange behaviour of the *gwanga*, sheer disbelief that anyone should bother to waste so much effort when the outcome could never be in any doubt.

They must have carried on for a couple of hours before William realized something had changed. Their burden had grown heavier. Tigua's feet had stopped moving. His head had slumped onto his chest. A trickle of snot escaped one nostril and ran down his mascara-smudged cheek.

'Stop!' he said to Lintoa.

The big she-boy hardly seemed to hear. He was scarcely more conscious than his friend. It took him a few more steps to register the instruction. They examined Tigua's face. Tenderly, as though fearful his big fingers might damage so delicate a flower as the slight Tigua, Lintoa brushed away the snot. William put his head to Tigua's chest. He felt the bra beneath the dress against his ear, a piece of limp cloth filled with a few rags, nothing like the firmness of a real breast.

'Let's get him inside, I can't hear anything!'

They laid Tigua on his bed. William was relieved to see the boy's chest rise, not very much, no more than a sparrow's breath perhaps, but still some sign of life.

'Tigua,' he said. 'Can you hear me?'

Tigua's eyes slid slowly open. His lips essayed a smile, but the effort was too much and they gave up halfway, leaving a curious little grin upon them as though, inappropriately, they were registering a rude joke.

'I is not can see. Eyes is not work no more. Where is be Lintoa?'

'Here I is be. I is not leave you. I is never leave you.' He kissed him lightly on his dried and blistered lips.

Tigua's right hand moved. His smile faded and his face contorted with effort as he managed to raise his arm. He let fall his hand on Lintoa's head and made a scratching movement through the big boy's long silky hair.

'I is must go now, Lintoa. I is not can hang on no longer. I is see you soon in *kassa* house. You is know what for I is say this?'

The tears were streaming down his face but Lintoa didn't bother to wipe them away. 'Yes. You is mean I is go be in *kassa* house soon. You is tell me I is be boy. Is be so, is be not?'

There was no reply. Tigua's eyes no longer looked at the she-boy friend she couldn't see. They stared blankly at the roof.

Lintoa knelt beside the bed with his head upon Tigua's breast while Lucy, shrugging away William's hand when he put it on her shoulder, left. Lintoa remained there while Tigua's mother fought a silent battle against the urge to keen and someone went to begin boiling water to wash the corpse. He stayed until the first light crept in through the doorway, having chased away the inadequate moon, which had been no use for an orange-fungi antidote. William kept vigil with him through all the long hours, but at last dozed off in a corner of the hut. He awoke when he heard the big she-boy move.

Lintoa walked over to where the green slingbacks stood sentinel upon the dismal scene. He bent and picked them up, gently, with one hand, taking infinite care, as though they were not just some white woman's cast-offs, but something precious, which of course they were. He separated them, holding one in each hand, tipping them this way and that, examining their workmanship, the way the uppers were connected to the soles, the manner in which the heels had been attached. He transferred the one in his left hand to his right and held them both together as a pair, face-on, as if someone were wearing them. Without warning, he gave an angry flick of his powerful wrist and the shoes shot across the hut, clattered against the far wall and dropped to the dirt floor.

'She is be one crazy little sow!' he shouted. 'Anyone is can see they is never go fit me anyway.' On his way out of the hut he paused only to kick one of the shoes with his too-big bare foot as he passed and then he was gone.

Wearily, William dragged himself to his feet. He walked across the hut and retrieved the shoes. He cradled them in his hands. They were so small. Lucy's shoes! He silently upbraided himself for selfishly thinking of her. He put his mind back on Tigua. He remembered the first time he had seen the poor girl, struggling along in these self-same shoes with his suitcase. Girl! He couldn't help smiling at himself for that, for always thinking of Tigua as a girl. Girl, boy, what did it matter? He, she, was neither now. He placed the shoes on the ground, side by side as they had been before Lintoa had disturbed them, and shuffled outside where all he could hear was the Pacific's furious roar.

FIFTY-THREE

William was desperate to see Lucy. He had only three days before the plane came. He had to talk to her, to absolve himself in her eyes from any responsibility for Tigua's death. He needed to persuade her that what he was doing was for the good of the islanders. That he was bringing them not only justice but a better life. There was no immediate opportunity. Lucy spent the whole day ensconced in the dead she-boy's family hut, along with many of the village women, helping to wash and prepare the corpse for burial, as tradition demanded of the female relatives and friends of the deceased.

Outside, Tigua's four older brothers were digging the burial pit in the centre of the village. William was struck by how matter-of-factly they went about their task. Not one of them looked sad. Not one of them shed a tear. In contrast they were surrounded by dozens of keening and shrieking women, and men who had shaved their heads and covered themselves in ashes to express their grief. How could the little she-boy's own brothers be so immune to that emotion? thought William. How could anyone not be in tears at losing someone as funny and full of life as Tigua? He didn't know, of course, that custom did not allow close relatives to show grief but required them to keep their emotions bottled and that only those unrelated to the deceased were permitted to express their feelings. When the pit was finished the four young men took axes and went off into the jungle. For the next few hours you could hear the steady beat of axe against wood and later they reappeared dragging logs that they piled up beside the pit.

William asked Managua what would happen next.

'Women is keep watch with Tigua body all night for keep away evil spirits,' the old man said. 'Next day we is bury she.'

There was obviously no point in waiting for Lucy. The walk back to the Captain Cook seemed unusually long as he trudged along the sand alone. He could not help recalling the first time he had made the journey with Tigua, the little she-boy skipping around him and getting the wrong end of the stick, thinking British tourists had wanted to come halfway round the world to shit on the island's beach.

As William curled up on the mahogany table he noticed that the tide was going out. The sound of the sea subsided and there was silence, save for the distant wail of some persistent seabird. He was so tired he fell asleep in spite of it. He didn't know it was the keening women he could hear.

Next morning while the village hummed with activity in preparation for the funeral, William asked Pilua to return to the Captain Cook with him so he could question her about the assault on her. There was, as he expected, some resistance to the idea from Managua, but Pilua overruled her husband: 'No, I is want for tell. Is be right Americans is know what they soldiers is do with me.' The old man shrugged and turned away, already, it seemed to William, half defeated by events.

Before the interview William felt a bleak nothingness. He missed the warmth of Tigua. He lacked the comfort only Lucy could bring. It seemed doubly cruel that the loss of the one meant the loss of the other. But the mood dissipated after listening to Pilua. His emotions woke again. He was moved and enraged by what she told him. Afterwards he went to see Purnu and informed him roundly that it would be a wicked distortion of the island's taboo against sleeping with foreigners if she were not allowed to live with her husband.

Purnu shrugged. 'Is be for Managua for decide. I is not oppose he if he is take she in he house. If he is say taboo is not matter, then who is I for argue?'

William could see the dollar signs flashing in Purnu's eyes. He was seizing the chance to make Managua break with tradition.

Towards mid-afternoon those not already mourning in the centre of the village began to gather there, grouped around the pit Tigua's brothers had dug. The keening and singing continued among those in the inner circle. Behind them some men danced and moaned a rough dirge. And behind the ring of dancers, those on the periphery of the mourning circle smoked *kassa* pipes and chatted, often smiling and joking as though the occasion were a festival not a funeral. William was shocked by the lack of respect among these people. He didn't know they were some of Tigua's closest relatives and that they were struggling hard to behave as was expected of them.

After an hour or so there was a sudden lull in the keening and then a gasp as the corpse emerged from Tigua's hut, borne on the shoulders of her four brothers, who were naturally all smiling. Tigua's parents followed the body, with Lucy supporting his mother. William had been wondering what the dead she-boy would be wearing. Would Tigua have reverted to her real sex, perhaps, and be clad in a pubic leaf? Or maybe the traditional grass skirt the island girls wore, perhaps in some elaborate funereal version? Or would Lintoa have given her his red dress, the one she had so coveted in life? But it was none of these. Some coconut matting had been rolled around the body, leaving exposed only the head at one end and the feet, now shorn for ever of high heels, at the other. William couldn't help thinking of a hot dog as he watched the four young men lower the package into the pit. At the last they just dropped their sister, like an object, a piece of trash, perhaps, something to be disposed of, not something that had ever been alive. The whole affair was completely without ceremony; no prayers were said, no songs sung; Tigua was simply dumped.

He found Managua standing by his side. 'Poor Tigua,' murmured William.

'What for poor Tigua? Is be nothing wrong for she, she is be on Tuma now, is be happy there. Is be rest of we who is be poor.' The old man paused to wipe away a tear. 'We is must live we lives without she. We is go miss she jokes and laughter. She is be one silly girl who is always make we smile and we is all go miss have she around all time. Is not be enough for just see she in *kassa* house. Is not be same thing at all.'

Tigua's brothers took the logs they had piled up earlier and dropped them lengthways into the pit, onto the corpse, forming a layer that eventually covered it completely, thereby protecting it from desecration by any wild animals. Even a black bantam pig would not have been able to get through such a shield. After the task was completed the young men walked away and the crowd began to disperse.

'That's it?' said William to Managua. 'That's Tigua's funeral? It's all over?'

'This part is be finish. More is happen tomorrow. Now, if you is excuse me, *gwanga*, I is waste enough time today. I is have play I is must write.' And the old man limped off. William looked around for Lucy, but she was not to be seen. She must have gone back into Tigua's family hut.

He sat around for most of the afternoon, waiting for her to emerge. A breeze got up, whistling through the palm trees and making them nod their heads as if in some crazy dance. Otherwise, all was quiet. The keening and shrieking had stopped with Tigua's interment.

In the late afternoon, Lucy appeared. William had almost dozed off and the first he knew about it was when he caught a flash of movement as her small figure dashed into the jungle, heading for the shore.

He chased after her and caught up with her on the beach. 'Lucy!' he called after her. 'Lucy, wait a minute!'

She turned and shouted, 'Go away! Leave me alone! I never want to see you again!'

She carried on running. He followed her and grabbed her arm. She spun round. 'Go away! I hate you for what you've done!'

'How can you blame me for Tigua's death? She'd have found out about Perlua sooner or later.'

'If Lintoa hadn't been looking for Pilua because of you he'd never have seen the girl. Tigua would still be alive.'

'You think Lintoa was going to stay a monk for the rest of his life? You think he was going to marry Tigua?'

A cascade of spray enveloped them both. Neither could speak. They were both soaked.

'It would all have happened differently.' Lucy was shouting to make herself heard over the crashing of the breakers. 'She'd have been a couple of years older. She'd have got used to the idea of Lintoa being with somebody else. She'd have accepted he could never be hers.'

'Maybe,' said William. He paused. Funny how both of them were speaking of Tigua as a girl now. 'Maybe she would. I don't think so.'

'You don't think so!' yelled Lucy. 'You know so much about these people, don't you? You've been here less than four weeks and you know what's best for them.'

'I'm not claiming that, but I think the money will help them. How many women here die in childbirth? How many succumb to infectious diseases? You're telling me they can't use a few tools and machines to make their lives a bit easier?'

'They're happy as they are!'

'That's because they don't know anything better. Why should they be denied what the rest of the world has? You're just patronizing them, saying you know what's best.'

'Well, I know what isn't, Coca-Cola and McDonald's.'

'That's a bit of a cliché, don't you think? Not all of America's like that. What about education? Would you deny them that?'

'Your idea of education, yes. Cable TV! I was crazy to get involved with you. Your kind are all the same. You go blundering into things you know nothing about out of some misguided desire to feel better about yourself. The people here are doing all right. Why can't you just keep your fucking nose out and leave them alone!'

She tried to turn and go but he still had hold of her arm. He seized the other and held her so they were face to face. Even the threat of the pointy tits which were practically touching him didn't put him off.

'Do you think that just because I let them alone they'd be left alone? The world's getting smaller. They've already had a nasty brush with it thanks to the US military. Better we don't leave them to wait for the next contact like that. Better we get them the money they're entitled to now so they can resist malign influences and paddle their own canoes.'

'They don't want your money. They don't need it.'

'Maybe not now, but mark my words, they soon will. And there's the little matter of justice. You can't let the US government get away with this. Suing them is the only way to stop them doing it again and again. And they should be made to pay. People were maimed and killed. A woman was raped.'

'Yes and she has a beautiful daughter whom she loves. That's her compensation. Now let me go!'

'I can't let you go. I don't ever want to let you go. I – I—' He stopped, finding himself surprised at the words that had so nearly tumbled out of his mouth. His jaw clamped as his molars ground alternately, but he forced them to stop. This was no time to get into that. 'Hey, guess what, Lucy, I think I love—'

'I hate you!'

'No you don't. You know you're only saying that. You can't tell me the last couple of weeks meant nothing to you.'

'It was a bit of sex with the only white man who's come along for a long time, that's all. It was because you were the only guy who wasn't taboo. It was nothing personal!'

'But the things you said, they weren't just about sex.'

'I said them because I thought it would help me persuade you to leave these people in peace! That's the only reason! I didn't mean a word of it! Now let go of my fucking arms!' She shook his hands off and ran off along the surf. William stood gazing after her, watching her movement stroboscopically as his eyes did their old thing.

FIFTY-FOUR

Next day, late in the afternoon, as the sun was already growing weary and thinking about heading west, Tigua's family and friends gathered around the burial pit. As William watched the proceedings he couldn't help noticing that alone of the little she-boy's intimates, Lucy wasn't there. Singing cheerfully, Tigua's brothers lifted the logs from the body. Exposed to the air for two days, the corpse was already in an advanced state of decomposition. The stench was so bad William had to fight the urge to gag. As the brothers lifted the roll of matting, he almost cried out as an arm and a leg fell from it, and then caught himself thinking that, ironically, Tigua had now joined the ranks of the island's amputees. The matting was unrolled and the corpse was more or less reassembled on the ground beside the pit. A fire had been lit nearby and someone tossed herbs onto it to take away the awful stink of rotting flesh. Managua, Tigua's father and brothers and a couple of older men produced knives and began scraping flesh from the skeleton, tossing the pieces into the fire. They went about the task in a businesslike way. Nobody spoke, not even when Tigua's father passed something to Managua. The old man examined it with a wry smile. Peering at the object William realized to his horror that it was the dead she-boy's penis. The cause of all her problems and her death! Managua tossed it contemptuously into the fire. One of the brothers who had his back to William lifted a hammer and struck something cradled in his lap. A moment later he threw what looked like brain tissue into the flames. Still not a word had passed between these busy pathologists. All you could hear was the harsh scrape of metal upon bone. The heat, the humidity and various worms, grubs and insects that scuttled from the corpse had done most of their work for them and soon a pile of gleaming white bones was all that remained of what had once been Tigua.

One of the brothers picked up a rib bone. He stood up, flourished it and said, 'Goodbye Tigua. This piece of you is remain with me always for remind me of you.'

The other brothers reached into the pile and each took a bone or two. One of them had a patella, another the humerus. Each said a few words of farewell and departed with his memento of his sister.

'Come, *gwanga*,' Managua called to William. 'You is help youself. Is be custom. You is take one of Tigua bones for remember she.'

William shook his head.

'Come, everyone is do,' Managua urged. 'What 'bout rib bone, or maybe you is want hip? Is be one left, I is think. No, well then you is take a little piece of she hand, come on, have just one knuckle.'

William didn't know if it was the smell of putrefying flesh or the idea of handling the little she-boy's body like this, but he couldn't speak for fear of vomiting. He couldn't help recalling that he'd read how serial killers often kept the bones of their victims as mementoes of their kills. 'It's – uh – OK,' he managed to say finally. 'No, really, Managua, I don't need anything to remind me of Tigua. I couldn't ever forget her.'

Managua shrugged and reached into the pile. He took out a tibia. He produced an old bit of cloth from the waist string of his pubic leaf and rubbed the bone carefully to clean it of any last vestiges of flesh. Then he used it to help lift himself from the ground and limped away, clutching it in both hands. Funny, William thought, how he had chosen the bit of Tigua that he was missing himself. He didn't know how right he was, that this was what Managua always did at funerals, that he had the best collection of tibias on the island.

There were still many bones left and other villagers, lesser friends of the deceased, stood around like vultures waiting for the immediate family and inner circle of friends to take their pick before diving in themselves, as might happen at a wedding buffet, say.

The brothers had all gone. William looked at Tigua's skull, centrepiece among the diminishing ossuary, and tried to equate its ghastly grin with the playful smile he had known. At that moment, from opposite directions, a hand reached to claim it and a woman's delicate fingers brushed against a hairy masculine paw. Tigua's mother raised her eyes and looked into Lintoa's. He pulled back his hand as though the skull's dome was red hot and he had been burned. The woman smiled. She took the skull in both her hands and lifted it before her. She leaned forward and brushed her lips against its fleshless jaw. Then she held it out to Lintoa. He raised a deprecating hand. She urged the skull towards him. He muttered something William couldn't catch and her few words of reply were lost in the sound of the fire, noisy with the crackling of burning flesh. Lintoa took the skull. Ungainly, with it held in both hands as though it were a crystal bowl, he hauled his large frame to its feet. Tucking the skull under one arm, like a cartoon Elizabethan ghost, he walked slowly from the clearing.

It was time for William to slip away himself. There was only so much misery he could stand. And he had a bag to pack.

FIFTY-FIVE

'I is go miss you, *gwanga*. I is not have any mans for talk 'bout books with.' Managua undid the straps of his artificial leg, took it off and rubbed his stump, which appeared to William to be red and raw. They were sitting side by side on William's suitcase at the landing beach, looking out to sea, waiting for one of the distant specks on the horizon to turn out not to be a seabird, but the monthly plane on which William would be leaving.

William took off his hat and mopped his brow. At another time he might have risked the old man's wrath and mentioned that he had Purnu as his confederate in literacy now. But he wasn't thinking of that. He was staring at Managua's prosthetic limb. He'd noticed the tinkling of the buckles on the strap.

'It was you, wasn't it?' he said. 'It was you who hit me over the head. You used your leg.'

Managua turned and stared at him a moment. He shrugged. 'Yes, is be me. I is use my knee. You is be plenty damn lucky. If we is ever dig you skull up I is like for see. Is must be plenty hard. My knee is kill pig.'

'You meant to *kill* me?'

'No, no, *gwanga*. I is not want for hurt you. I is just see you is go discover Pilua and I is panic.'

'You knew it would bring everything into question.'

'Exactly. I is not have time for think. I is lash out on spur of moment.'

'After you'd unstrapped your leg.'

'Sure. I is follow you up stairs. I is see you go in first room. Is think I is must stop you and is take off my leg and lean against wall. When you is look out on jungle my leg is just lash out before I is can prevent.'

'Like it had a mind of its own.'

'Is be true, *gwanga*. You is have own legs, you is not know. This is be some other fella's leg. Is not always obey my brain.'

They sat for some time without speaking. There were no breakers on the ocean, but it had a roll to it, like the breast of some enormous beast that rises and falls as it breathes. Here, thought William, the ocean is alive.

'But it would have been better if I'd been dead,' he said. 'It would have solved all your problems. The traditions would be safe.'

'Mebbe. Sometimes I is think I is be like loony British king who is tell tide for stop. I is fight battle I is can never win.'

They watched the sea in silence. When Managua looked at the American he saw he was regarding him with a strange expression. He assumed it was fear. 'You is must not blame me,' he said. 'I is not like for do such things. I is must protect my people. But is all be over now, I is know that. You is not have fear. I is just take leg off because stump is be sore. I is not go hurt you now.'

'No, no, it's not that,' said William. 'I'm not afraid of you. I just got a sense of the burden you've been carrying all these years. I can see how difficult it must have been for you. You're not the kind of man who goes around hitting people over the head.'

'You is talk true. I is only ever use leg like that one time before and that is for kill pig that is go die anyway. I is not like for do against man.'

William nodded.

'For man I is use magic. But I is try everything I is know against you, *gwanga*, and nothing is work. Drowning spell, green shoestring spell, hurricane spell, all is fail. You is have strong magic for protect you.'

William smiled. So, the old bastard had wanted him dead.

Managua saw his expression. 'Is be nothing personal, *gwanga*. I is must do for my people. I is not wish you harm for youself. I is like you. You is be man who is mebbe see *Hamlet*.'

There was the distant drone of an engine from the far distance. William put his hand on Managua's shoulder. 'Come on, old man,' he said, 'get your leg on. The plane's almost here.'

FIFTY-SIX

Two more planes had come and gone and still Lucy was on the island. Twice more the fridge had been filled with beer – and quickly emptied, mainly by Lintoa who was drowning his sorrows, and still Lucy was here. Her project was finished and she knew she should be making arrangements to leave, but a strange lassitude had overcome her. She felt like Managua's great hero, Hamlet, powerless to act. It was as if she was waiting for something, something more than the next plane, but she couldn't have told you what.

There were times when Lucy wondered if she might not be waiting for the return of William Hardt or perhaps the arrival of some other man. These were the moments when she longed for her pointy breasts to be blunted by the barrel chest of a strong man pressing down on them. Now her grief and anger had abated, she no longer blamed William for Tigua's death. It had been one of those things that happen from time to time, from an unfortunate combination of circumstances. If she'd ever discussed OCD with William he could have told her such events occur no matter how much you try to ward them off by not stepping on paving cracks or by arranging objects in a room in perfect symmetry or by ritual moving of the eyelids.

Certainly now she missed the American. She missed his vulnerable smile when he slept. She even missed his strange alternate manipulation of her breasts, never mind that it had felt like he was trying to milk a cow. But although she no longer held William responsible for the loss of the little she-boy, she was appalled at what she knew his interference would do to the island. Because of him, her book would serve only as the sad memorial of a vanished culture.

Other times, when she wondered at her inability to rouse herself and leave, Lucy considered whether she could simply be waiting for death. Wasn't that what everyone was waiting for? But if so, why here, where death would not be the end, but would merely transfer her to a superior version of the same island? What would she do there? Lotus eat for eternity?

Right now she was doing her waiting on the veranda, half sitting, half lying on a battered old cane recliner, and her waiting was almost over; her suitcase was finally packed, ready for the next day's plane, and she was looking for the last time at the ocean as the sun went down in the west and the first fingers of dusk began to claw their way over the eastern horizon. It was an extraordinary night, one such as she could not remember since she'd been on the island. There were no crashing waves. There was no spray, only the merest lacy frill of surf. The sea soughed gently and was almost silent, as silent as it could ever be.

Lucy poured herself another glass of cold white wine. She found herself tipping the bottle very gently out of respect for the unusual quiet. She didn't want to disturb it by making any sound at all. Even so she only heard the other noise after she set the bottle down again: what she at first thought was singing, somewhere out to sea, far, far away.

It had to be someone in a boat, because there was no other land within several hundred miles, and this in itself struck her as strange because the voice or rather, voices, for there were certainly more than one, surely belonged to women and they never went fishing and so rarely boarded a boat.

'*Waa, waa, waa,*' sang the voices. '*Waa, waa, waa.*' Lucy felt the hairs on her neck rise in a way they hadn't even when confronted by the dead souls in the *kassa* hut; there was something ghostly in this singing.

'*Waa, waa, waa.*' It was coming closer. She knocked back her wine and poured another glass, not caring now how much noise she made, hand trembling so much she spilled almost as much as she got into the glass. '*Waa, waa, waa.*'

Her immediate thought was to run, followed fast by a second that said, where to? Away from the sea, perhaps, far inland, stumbling in the dark in the jungle surely preferable to hearing these sounds.

'*Waa, waa, waa.*' This time it was so close she found herself squinting into the fast-dimming light over the edge of the waves, trying to make out who was making this noise. '*Waa, waa waa*' it came again and this time all her terror drained from her and she felt an immense sorrow well up in her, a pity she hadn't known she possessed beneath her sharp little breasts and jagged exterior. For surely these were not the voices of women, sirens from hell trying to lure her to disaster, but the plaintive cries of babies, calling for her help. She rose from her chair and went inside to her bedroom where she always slept with a flashlight by her bed. She switched it on and by its light made her way outside and down the veranda steps. She ran to the water's edge. She pointed the torch out to sea in the direction the sounds seemed to be coming from, convinced she would see a shipwrecked baby, miraculously saved by a buoyant crib, floating there like the infant Moses. But her circle of light revealed nothing, only that the sea had now turned black, and when she pointed the flashlight beam further out, stretching the light into an ellipse, she found nothing other than water barely corrugated by the gentlest of breezes.

'Miss Lucy! Miss Lucy!' Lucy almost dropped the flashlight because she thought that the shipwrecked baby was calling her by name. But this could not be so since the voice came not from out to sea, but from further along the shore. She turned the torch in that direction and picked out the figure of a woman trotting towards her. It was Lamua.

'Lamua!' Lucy ran towards her and flung her arms around her. 'Am I glad to see you! We've got to rouse the men, get some boats out. There's a baby, possibly more than one, out to sea somewhere. It – they – must have been shipwrecked and somehow sur—'

She stopped because Lamua had put a finger upon her lips. 'Ssh, Miss Lucy,' whispered Lamua, and Lucy noticed she was smiling and her eyes were luminous, 'you is must not frighten they.'

'Frighten who? Who's "they"?'

'Come.' Lamua took her hand and pulled her towards the house. Lucy took a look back at the ocean, over which a half-moon was now rising, coming up over the horizon like a huge white rock, but even with this extra illumination there was still nothing to see. Dumbly, she followed the native woman.

Lamua led her up the steps and into the house. 'I is come for help you. Purnu is tell me is you time too.' Lucy saw now that the other woman was trembling as she herself had trembled earlier, though obviously from excitement, not from fear. 'We is must lie down.'

'Why? What is it? Who's singing?'

Lamua ignored her and began fiddling with the buttons of Lucy's shirt. 'You is must undress,' she insisted. Lucy found herself obeying as if in a dream. She removed the shirt and then her skirt. Lamua put her fingers in the waistband of her own grass skirt and it dropped to the floor. She waved her hands at Lucy's underwear. 'Come, come, you is must be naked.'

'What is it? Tell me.' Nevertheless she obeyed. The sound of the *waa waa waa*ing was all but deafening now. It seemed to fill the house as if shipwrecked babies were all around.

'You is please lie down.' Lamua indicated the bed and Lucy lay upon it. She herself lay down on the floor.

'What are you doing down there?' said Lucy, even though she still didn't know what was going on. 'There's room for you up here.'

Lamua shrugged, rose and positioned herself on the other side of the bed, William's side, Lucy found herself thinking.

'Lamua, what's happening? Please tell me,' Lucy hissed, afraid to talk and disturb the almost musical *waa waa waa*. It was all she could do. Her body seemed powerless to resist the native woman's instructions.

'Is be floating babies,' said Lamua. 'All my life I is wait for this and is think is never go happen, and then tonight I is hear they.'

Lucy sat upright, tugged out of her torpor. 'Floating babies. You mean . . .'

'Yes, they is choose we. We is go have babies.'

Lucy pulled herself from the bed and bent to pick up her underwear. Suddenly her nakedness felt very vulnerable. She wanted to cover herself. 'Oh no,' she said, 'not me.'

Lamua rolled across the bed, reached out a hand and tore the knickers from Lucy's hand. She tossed them away across the room. 'You is have no choice,' she said. 'Is not be for you for decide. If you is can hear they spirit babies, is mean only one thing. One of they babies is choose you.'

Lucy knew of course about the spirit babies. She had written about how people grew tired of Tuma and its endless round of sex and pleasure and how after they had grown old and become young again many times they often wanted to once more try ordinary life, with all its challenges, its difficulties and its heartbreaks. She knew too that there had been two planes since William Hardt left, that she had twice filled her fridge with beer while her period just had not happened at all. If she'd been like William she might have tried to ward off the inevitable and resorted to elaborate blinking or teeth grinding or straightening things in the room, but she wasn't at all like him and so she did none of these. Besides, her limbs felt strangely heavy and her eyes would just not stay open, let alone manage any energetic blinking. She lay down beside Lamua once more, aped the native woman's position, arms by her sides, legs apart, closed her eyes, listened to the plaintive lullaby, *waa, waa waa*, and was soon asleep. She was still sleeping when the plane came next day; the islanders knew not to wake her and she slumbered on long after it had flown away.

ONE YEAR
LATER

FIFTY-SEVEN

William Hardt stood on the landing beach and watched what looked and sounded like an angry black insect make a pass overhead along the shore, bank sharply at the far end of the bay and turn back. It went to the other end of the bay and repeated the manoeuvre. Once the pilot of the chopper had taken a good look at the beach, the machine hovered right above William for a moment or two, then began to descend.

The natives scattered as the whirlwind from the chopper's blades stirred up a dust storm of sand. There were a few screams from children and teenagers. Only the adult islanders remembered choppers from the last time the Americans had been here. Considering that, it's surprising *they* weren't the ones to scream.

Right-left-left-right went William's molars. He was exceedingly nervous. It felt strange being back on the island. He'd arrived on the monthly plane three days earlier so as to check that all his compensation claimants would be ready to give evidence and to go through their testimony with them.

Managua had greeted him with an air of disappointment. The old man had evidently hoped never to see him again; that William would have heeded the pleas he and Lucy had made to leave the island alone. He had remained stone-faced even when William presented his gift. A copy of the Penguin *Hamlet*.

'You'll have the missing pages,' William prompted.

'Is not be necessary for always have everything,' was the old man's haughty reply. 'Sometimes is be better for you is be without.'

William felt this was a dig about the whole compensation issue and sidestepped it. 'Well, aren't you even going to look at those two pages?' he said. 'You must be dying to know what's in them.'

Managua flexed his shoulders in a nonchalant way that seemed to suggest he couldn't even be bothered with a full shrug. Nevertheless he began to flick through the pages of the book. He quickly found what he was looking for and studied the text intently. He turned the page. A couple of minutes elapsed.

'Well?' said William.

Managua continued reading. He turned back to the previous page, read for a minute or so and then turned the page forward again. Finally he slammed the book shut.

'Is it what you expected?' asked William.

'Is be less than I is expect. Is not answer big damn puzzler at all. I is see I is must work that one out for self.'

'But at least you have the missing scene. That's something. It must be wonderful to see it at last and find out what happens.'

'Is be interesting. But if I is be honest way Shakespeare is do death of Polonius is not impress me. I is prefer way I is do.'

He put the book under his arm and began to walk away from the landing beach. William was about to start after him when he remembered his bag. He'd almost forgotten. There was no Tigua to carry it for him this time. The sudden realization hit him hard; his heart felt heavier than the bag and only partly because, learning from experience, he'd packed it much lighter than last time. He struggled after Managua.

The older man turned and shot him an apologetic look. 'You is must not worry I is not thank you. Is be taboo for thank someone for gift. Is not be because I is not be glad for see they two pages.'

'That's OK, don't worry about it.'

'I is not worry,' said Managua. 'You is be one who is do that.'

If Managua had been disappointed by his gift, the first person William had encountered, Tr'boa, who had met him in the boat, had been equally crestfallen at William's arriving empty-handed.

After greeting William fondly his first question had been, 'You is bring dollars, *gwanga*?'

He'd looked very downcast when William had said no, that was still a long way off, that he was here to meet a US government lawyer and a doctor who were going to examine the evidence.

'Besides,' said William, 'you have all your limbs. You're not due any compensation.'

'I is know that,' said Tr'boa, 'but my uncle is lose foot and he is go buy me plenty thing. Baseball hat, computer game, dune buggy. Plenty other thing too, but I is forget what they is be.'

William's own first disappointment came from seeing Lintoa. If Lintoa had been a real woman, other women might have said bitchily – *sowily* the islanders would have put it – that she had let herself go. He was wearing the recovered red dress, the one that Tigua had so coveted, but it was now badly in need of a wash and torn around the top of the zip at the back. The hem hung down three quarters of the way around. His nail polish was chipped. An attempt at lipstick had left his mouth a grotesque scarlet gash.

'I is know what you is think,' he said as he watched William appraising him. 'You is say youself, Lintoa is look one big damn mess. Well, I is not care. I is only be girl for three moons more, then I is can choose. For talk true, I is only stay girl for respect for Tigua; no-one is much mind if I is break custom now. All customs and taboos is start for go now.'

William found that while this was an exaggeration, a bit of bravado on Lintoa's part, there was nevertheless a kernel of truth in it. Take Pilua for instance. She had, as agreed before he left, moved into Managua's house, together with Perlua. It seemed that not only had hardly anyone protested and suggested she remain an outcast, the other women had positively embraced her back into village society and made her one of their number.

When William expressed his surprise about her easy integration to Managua, over a pipe of *kassa* outside his hut that night, the old man could manage only a weary sigh. 'What you is expect, *gwanga*?

Is come for pass what I is tell you. They is see Perlua. She is be white. They is know she *mamu* is be rape by three white men. Is be hard for continue think is not be *fug-a-fug* is make babies. This is why I is beg you is not go look for Pilua.'

William knew the old man was right. Things hadn't broken up yet, but you could see the way they were going. If men made babies then everything was different. Property, what there was of it, no longer accrued to women. Why would you give yams to your sister's children any more? Why not concentrate your efforts on your own, now that you knew they *were* your own?

He could see it wasn't a big step from this kind of thinking to questioning all the customs and taboos. Once the cornerstone of belief was gone, it wouldn't be that long before the rest came tumbling down.

'First strong wind,' was how Managua put it.

William's second disappointment had been even greater. Lucy. In his mind's eye, even though she hadn't answered any of the letters he'd sent during the year since he'd left, letters that he had no way of knowing had ever been delivered, he'd hoped she'd be waiting for him at the landing beach. She wasn't there.

He knew it had been an idealized image. He didn't even know if she was still on the island. Why would she be? Her project would be finished by now. It was the first thing he asked Lintoa. The she-boy shook his big head and said, 'Sure, she is be here, same as always, but she is tell me I is must not talk with you 'bout she.'

It was the same when he spoke to Managua. The old man refused to discuss her, only saying, when William asked why she was still there, 'She is have she reason, but is not be for me for say; you is must ask she.'

Next day, after the shitting beach, where his dump attracted a record number of sightseers, apparently because it had been the object of much theory and debate during his absence and had acquired an almost legendary mystique among the natives, he hurried along the shore to Lucy's house.

It had an empty look about it. The shutters were closed and

there was no Caruso sailing out on the morning breeze, no sound at all save the mournful sighs of the waves as they flopped exhausted onto the beach after their long journey.

He went up the steps to the door and tapped gently with his knuckles. He listened. Nothing stirred within. He rapped again, louder this time. Still nothing. The third time he banged as hard as he could. The whole house shuddered. But once it had gotten over its fright it sank back into stillness. Nobody home, its silence proclaimed.

William took a turn around the veranda that ran all the way round the house. Even his footsteps had a hollow, empty ring. All the windows were shuttered. It was like when you arrived for the first weekend of the summer at the Hardts' old beach house after it had been closed up all winter. The place always seemed to be waiting for someone to come live in it.

Back at the door, William pressed his face against it. He could make out little through the gaps between the lengths of bamboo. He could see only narrow strips of the interior, which gave nothing away, so he moved from one to the next, building up a picture of a tidy, empty room, devoid of beer cans, make-up paraphernalia or any sign of recent habitation. He pressed his mouth to the gap.

'Come out, come out, wherever you are!' he called. 'Or I'll huff and I'll puff and I'll blow your house down!' The silent response to this mocked his feeble attempt at levity.

William took another turn around the porch and rapped the door once more. Nothing. He considered waiting in case Lucy had simply gone out for a short time and might soon return but then he thought, where would she go? She hadn't been in the village. Besides, the house had that closed-up empty look. There was only one conclusion. She'd abandoned her home to avoid him.

Anyway, he had work to do. He didn't have time to linger here.

Just as William hadn't confessed his OCD to Lucy, she hadn't been candid with him. She hadn't admitted to the murder of her mother. She hadn't explained the submarine drill for dealing with unexpected visitors to her childhood home. If she had, he'd have known that right now Lucy was hiding. She'd been looking for him through a gap in the shutters ever since first light. When she spotted him coming along the beach, she watched him until he was close enough for her to see his habitual worried expression and that was enough to make her want to run out to him and fold her arms around him and make him feel safe. Somehow she resisted the urge and instead fastened the door and rolled under her bed. There was no way anyone peeping in could see her there.

It was a fairly risky strategy, especially on an island where the fauna included the green shoestring. You never knew what might be lurking under a bed in these latitudes. But Lucy hadn't even thought to check and if she had, it would have been half-hearted. She cared less about the putative risk of a fatal snakebite than she did about being confronted by this man who was destroying a civilization she had journeyed halfway round the world to document and had come to love as her home. Besides, she wasn't a checker. And it wasn't as if she were without a weapon under the bed. She had the biscuit tin which held his letters, all but the first two which she'd burned because she hadn't wanted to risk having his return address. Then, after the night of the floating babies she started keeping them. It seemed only right; who knew how long Lucy would be able to stay on the island? Her baby might grow up somewhere else where they believed in physiological paternity and want to know about the American she had slept with. Of course, Lucy hadn't taken the biscuit tin under the bed because she thought it would be useful for flattening a green shoestring – her home held far better objects for the killing of snakes – but because in the event of William Hardt forcing an entry and searching the house, she didn't want him finding she had kept his correspondence.

Lucy had given the baby to Lamua to look after while William was here. As everyone who has ever tried to hide from an unwanted visitor knows, the one thing you can't stop is a baby crying. Lucy had felt some guilt about this. She said it didn't seem right to hide William's child from him. But Lamua had pointed out that the baby was nothing to do with William. It had come across from Tuma and chosen Lucy as its mother. Mostly, Lamua clung to the old beliefs and preferred not to think about Perlua being the daughter of three white Americans. Trying to reconcile Perlua and floating babies had made other islanders as confused about reproduction as William's sister Ruth had been all those years ago when she fretted about the mobility of sperm.

Lucy was comforted by Lamua's words. It was true. Her child had been born on the island, where a father was not required to make a baby. What did the baby have to do with William? So she hid herself and the baby's existence from him. She had sworn everyone to secrecy and if William heard crying coming from Purnu's hut, then Lamua could just pop out and show him her own baby boy.

Now, William had to try to put the mystery of Lucy's whereabouts out of his mind and concentrate on his work. He watched as the helicopter landed, ungainly as a heron, one wheel hitting the ground before the other. A door opened and two figures emerged, ducking under the rotor blades. One had a slouch hat he was holding tight on his head against the draught from the rotors. William could see only his mouth and that he was talking intently. The other man was plump, bareheaded and older. You could tell that from his grey beard.

The helicopter blades slowed and its engine cut out. The two men came towards William. The older man lifted his head and proffered a weak smile. The man in the hat didn't even look up at William but just carried on talking. Soon they were close enough for William to hear.

'So what am I supposed to do, turn her down? Man, she was big, and I have to admit, I like 'em big. "Come back to my place," she said. Oh, man, she was rubbing these big tits in my face and I'm telling you I about pole-vaulted outa that bar, oh yes. Anyway . . .'

At this point his downcast eyes caught sight of William's shoes and he stopped talking. He lifted his head and took off his hat, revealing a shock of red hair. He stared wide-eyed at William.

'I don't believe it! It can't be . . . I come halfway across the world and . . . it is! It really is you! Wanker!'

William flinched as he heard the word. He was too stunned to even say hello. Sandy Beach didn't notice but turned to the other man and said, 'It's what we called him at prep school. And Harvard. It's a British term for a compulsive masturbator. He had a fearsome reputation for self-abuse. None better. Wanker, I mean, William Hardt, I'd like you to meet Dr Gold.' They shook hands.

'Sandy – you – you're the lawyer representing the US army?' stuttered William. His tongue would hardly work. He didn't seem to have enough brainpower to take this one in, that the man he'd been waiting for, would have to cross swords with, was the person who'd alternately bored him and driven him mad for a considerable part of his childhood.

'That's right. Prepare to get your butt kicked, my old friend. Legally speaking, that is.' Beach could have been talking about a game of chess. An image of the chequerboard linoleum in the beach-house bathroom popped into William's brain. How he wished he could retreat into that room and do some serious lateral bending right now.

William looked anxiously at the doctor. He was desperate to explain to the man that he wasn't Sandy Beach's friend. Instead he took the man's bag from his hand, a simple gesture he hoped would point in the same direction. Then he reached out for Sandy Beach's bag, but before he could get hold of it Tr'boa was there and had grabbed it.

'Is be OK, *gwanga*,' he said to William. 'You is leave for me. I is carry.' The three white men stood and watched Tr'boa struggle up the path towards the village. As the Americans began to follow, Beach turned to William and said, 'Didn't take them long to get your number.'

William was mystified. 'What do you mean?'

'What he called you. *Gwanga*. I'm no linguist but you don't have to be a genius to figure out what that word means.'

It took William a moment to understand. When he did, he thought how typical of Beach that after only a few minutes on the island he had managed to turn what William had come to regard as the islanders' term of affection for him into his hated former nickname.

He was brought out of his reverie by Beach's weasel face thrusting itself into his own. 'Well, do you?'

'Do I what?' said William.

'I knew you weren't listening. You never hear what anybody is saying when you're doing that business with your eyes. I asked which is the best hotel on the island?'

'Well,' said William, deadpan, 'I always put up at the Captain Cook.'

FIFTY-EIGHT

'Well, this is quite something, isn't it?' said Sandy Beach. They were squatting side by side on the shitting beach. Dr Gold had modestly positioned himself some twenty feet or so away, whence came the constipated grunts of an overweight man who wasn't getting enough fibre in his diet.

It sure is, thought William. I'm on the beach with Sandy Beach!

'Who'd ever have thought it, all those years ago,' continued Beach, 'that the two of us would be together here today, sitting on a beach.'

Or rather, *shitting* on a beach, William almost said but stopped himself just in time. Only someone crass and vulgar would think that was amusing.

'Or rather, *shitting* on a beach,' said Sandy Beach.

William groaned aloud, he just couldn't help it, but the way Beach immediately echoed it you could tell he hadn't realized it was a comment upon his sense of humour but had assumed instead that it was a vocal aid to defecation, a cousin to the tennis player's grunt assist on a service.

The enthusiasm of Beach's groan said it all. You could tell from that one elongated syllable that he had taken to the idea of alfresco communal shitting with gusto. He had no embarrassment, something William put down to the fact that merely being Sandy Beach was such an embarrassment in itself the man had long ago grown a skin any turtle would be proud of. Shitting in public couldn't be any worse than being who he was.

'Wow, I sure needed that,' said Beach, pulling up his pants. He turned to inspect what he had produced and found a posse of natives also staring down at it. He had no idea they were using his dump as a control in a scientific inquiry into William's. Whatever peculiarity they had detected in the latter could now be compared to another white man's production to ascertain whether it was unique or universal in the developed world.

Beach was entirely undismayed by the examination. 'I wouldn't get too close to that, guys,' he said. 'I had a fearsome red curry day before yesterday.'

After the shitting they returned to the Captain Cook, where the three of them had slept in a line on the mahogany dining table, to collect their briefcases. Beach was in a lively mood. 'I won't be recommending your hotel to anyone, William,' he said. 'The bed was too hard and you're liable to find another guest sleeping in your soup.'

'Ha ha, that's very funny,' said Dr Gold. 'That's some sense of humour you have, Beach.'

'It's not so much that I have a great sense of humour,' said Beach, with a meaningful glance at William, 'although of course I do. It's more about a world view. You have to laugh about these things or life just gets you down.'

On their way to the village Beach treated William to the tale of his encounter with a six-foot New Zealand girl in a bar in Wellington that William had caught the tail end of him telling to Dr Gold when the helicopter landed.

'Man, she was *big*!'

'Yes,' said Dr Gold with a chuckle, 'and you like them big.'

'Hey, sorry, I forgot,' said Beach. 'I told you this already.'

'It's OK,' said Gold. 'I can stand hearing it again. Nothing like this ever happens to me in bars. I go to a bar, I get drunk, that's all that happens.'

Beach had barely resumed his story when he was interrupted

again, this time by the sight of a figure coming towards them.

'Wow!' said Beach. 'Fucking bow wow, man!'

It was Kiroa. The way her hips swung from side to side you'd have thought she was teasing the three white men, but William knew it was just her normal walk.

Kiroa stopped and said to William, 'Hello, *gwanga*, is be good for see you again. Lintoa is tell me you is come back.'

There was something in the way her lips lingered over the she-boy's name that made William suspect her affections had not changed during his absence. The hopelessness of unrequited love is always obvious to an objective observer with an unreturned passion of his own. Kiroa seemed not to notice Beach whose eyes were level with her nipples. He was slavering like a hungry dog confronted by a bone.

'It's good to see you too,' William said. She smiled, somewhat sadly, he thought, and continued on her way along the shore.

The three men stood and watched her go.

'She is BIG!' said Beach.

'And you like them big,' repeated Gold.

Beach turned to William. 'Is it true they don't have any morals? They just go into the jungle with one another and do it? I mean, you don't even have to buy them a drink first?'

'It's not quite so simple as that. They have morals all right. They're just different morals from the ones we have.'

'Hot banana!' said Beach.

As William had arranged, the amputees and other claimants were waiting in the village centre. William did a rough head count to make sure all thirty-seven were present.

There were fifty-two.

He counted again and again arrived at fifty-two. So next time he was careful to include only those people who were missing something, a leg, an arm, a hand or a foot, plus a couple who had been blinded by shrapnel and one or two like Purnu who'd lost a wife or husband. Thirty-seven. He couldn't work out where he was going wrong.

They began a long day of interviews. Dr Gold examined each claimant to make sure their injuries were consistent with landmine damage. William was surprised at the speed with which he was able to do this.

'Oh, there's not much to it, it's a knack,' said the doctor in an off-hand way. 'It comes with experience. It's an area where American expertise is second to none. You see, for decades now US-manufactured mines have been blowing off limbs all over the world. I've seen so many cases I can spot them straight away.'

A little later William saw him questioning a man and shaking his head. William didn't recognize the man as anyone he remembered interviewing himself. He looked for his name on the list of claimants and found it wasn't there.

'What's his injury?' he asked the doctor.

'Bomb is blow off all toes on this foot,' said the man, indicating his right foot. 'I is not can walk properly now.'

'Machete,' said Dr Gold.

'Machete?' said William. He thought the doctor was asking for one, the way doctors always said 'scalpel' in TV hospital dramas.

'Machete,' repeated the doctor. 'He cut off his toes himself with a machete.'

'No, no, no,' protested the man. 'Is be bomb.'

The doctor thrust his face into the man's. 'Are you trying to tell me I don't know a machete wound when I see one? Are you?'

The man shook his head. 'N-no, but—'

'No buts, please, my good man. See here, Mr Hardt, the straight line of the toe stumps? A landmine doesn't do that. It's not so precise. Not so neat. A landmine blast will leave everything uneven. You end up with frayed toe stumps. And look here, this gash above the point of severance. A blow that missed the target when he was hacking the toes off. Typical of a fraudulent claim.'

'OK,' said the man, 'is be machete that is chop off toes, but you is must still give me dollars. Is be bomb is make me lose toes.'

'How do you reckon that?' demanded the doctor.

'Well, is be like this. I is go cut coconut open with machete. I is have coconut on ground and I is hold steady against stump of tree with this foot. I is just go hit coconut when someone is step on bomb. BOOM! I is miss coconut and is chop off toes instead.'

The doctor looked at William and smiled. He looked back at the man. 'Very interesting. But I'm afraid it doesn't quite explain this.' He ran his fingers over the gash.

'Ah,' said the man. 'Ah yes, now I is remember. Is be two bombs. First bomb is go bang, I is strike foot there. Is not cut toes off. Then I is lift machete again for have another go at coconut. Just as I is strike, is be second bomb.'

'Two bombs, huh?' said the doctor. 'What bad luck.'

'I is know,' said the man. 'Is be plenty bad magic. Who is believe this is can happen?'

'Not me, I'm afraid, my friend,' said the doctor, patting him on the shoulder. 'Now run along and stop wasting my time.'

The doctor was a kindly man and this last remark was not meant as a joke. He watched, somewhat chastened, as the man hobbled away with the aid of a stick.

William understood now where his extra claimants came from. They were opportunists hoping to cash in on the anticipated bonanza. Next up was a middle-aged woman who said she was blind. She was steered towards the doctor by her hopeful-looking husband. She held her arms out in front of her to prevent herself from colliding with anything.

'Your eyes?' said Gold.

'Yes, I is not can see thanks for bomb. Blast is take away my sight.'

The doctor produced a pencil flashlight and shone it in her eyes. He switched it on, waited a moment or two, then switched it off. 'Hmm, interesting. Normal pupil dilation.'

He turned away from her and bent to his medical bag. The woman stood staring patiently into space. Quick as a flash the doctor whirled round. He had a large knife in his hand which he swung at the woman's face.

She ducked.

As she walked away without the assistance of her husband Gold smiled at William. 'Not easy to fake, blindness.'

William was getting worried that all the false claimants would damage his case. They might undermine the credibility of the genuine victims.

It was especially difficult to believe that anyone was going to get anything out of Beach. He questioned the natives remorselessly, going over and over every detail of how their injuries had occurred, tripping them up over inconsistencies and, when they got through that, expressing doubt that their lives were materially affected by what he referred to as their 'so-called disability'.

'How does having an artificial leg stop you fishing? You're in a boat floating on the water, for Christ's sake. What's it matter whether your foot is made of flesh and blood or wood or plastic?'

Or, to a woman: 'Anyone can cook with a prosthetic hand. Just wedge your spoon in it, like so—' he demonstrated with a pen, 'and stir away. What's the problem?'

By late afternoon they had worked through a quarter of the claimants. They sent the rest home until the next day. Sandy Beach stretched his arms. 'What do you do for entertainment around here?'

'There isn't any,' said William. 'Read a book.'

Beach stood up, 'Aw, come on . . .'

'OK,' said William. 'If that's too dull, there's always the *kassa* house.'

'Aha, I knew it. Slip them a few dollars and enjoy a bit of the old . . .' He went into a pelvic-thrusting pose that caused a few of the natives to gather round and stare.

'He is eat orange fungi?' asked one of them.

'It's men-only,' William explained to Beach. 'You just lie around getting stoned on a hallucinogenic drug.'

'And afterwards the sex is marvellous,' said Beach. 'I get the picture. Lead me to it. You coming, Gold?'

'No, I think I'll pass. It's not exactly sensible to toy with un-researched hallucinogenic substances. They can alter your mind.'

Maybe it'll change Beach's for the better, William thought.

FIFTY-NINE

It would have been too much, of course, to expect Sandy Beach to respect the islanders' tradition of hospitality and observe the normal etiquette of the *kassa* house.

'Can I get a beer in here?' he asked as he and William emerged from the entrance tunnel. 'Do they have lap dancing?'

Even though William explained to Beach that you were not supposed to talk in the *kassa* house, it didn't stop him. He turned to the man next to him, who happened to be Tr'boa, and said, 'How do you get laid here? I mean if you want the old—' and he thrust his lap up and down, 'how do you go about it?'

'First you is need magic,' said Tr'boa.

'Magic?' It was less a question, more a suppressed guffaw. 'Oh yeah, and where would I go to get that?'

'Purnu.' Tr'boa pointed at the little sorcerer who was at that very moment circling the hut, ladling out *kassa*. Beach licked his lips.

Out of the mist Joe Hardt emerged. He'd grown a little older since the last time William had seen him. He must be in his forties now, the way William remembered him best from his childhood. There was a sparkle in his eyes that was dimmed in later years. Something else had changed about him too. There were lines around his eyes and black circles under them that hadn't been there when he was alive at this age. His hair was all mussed up and his plaid shirt wasn't fully buttoned. He looked like someone who'd been having too many nights out.

'Dad, are you OK?' William asked. 'You look, well, kind of tired to me.'

Joe Hardt shook his head and shot his son a wry smile. 'To tell the truth, son, I'm all worn out. What am I now? In my forties? I feel worse than I did when I was alive and in my fifties. Things can get kind of hectic on Tuma, you know. What with the girls, and the *kassa* . . .'

'Dad, are you getting enough sleep there?'

'Son, sleep is the one thing I'm *not* getting enough of. Everything else I'm having too much of. I'm having too much of a good thing. I'm going to have to slough again and get back to twenty so I can stand the pace.'

'Well, take it easy,' said William. He felt his anxiety level rising. His eyelids were twitching away. But then he thought, what is there to be concerned about? What more than death can happen to Dad?

His father was peering at Sandy Beach. 'Who's that with you, son? I think it's definitely time I sloughed again, my eyes don't seem to be working too well. Why it looks like . . . it looks like . . . that little runt Sandy Beach.'

Sandy managed a stoned wave. 'It *is* me, Mr Hardt. How are you? I mean, I know you're dead and all, but that aside, how are you?'

Joe Hardt looked at his son. 'He turned out just like I always said he would, then.'

'Dad, could you mind what you say about him, please?' whispered William. 'I need to keep on friendly terms with him for my case here. I don't want to antagonize him.'

'Antagonize whom?' Beach lurched across William.

Joe Hardt rolled his eyes. 'For God's sake! If it's one thing I can't stand it's a man who can't hold his *kassa*.' He was starting to fade. 'Listen son, I think it's best I go now. I'm not sure I can be responsible for my tongue. Come and see me again real soon. Don't leave it so long next time. Oh, and don't invite your pal along.'

'Dad? Dad?' William peered into the mist, but it was no use, his father was gone. Instead, he saw something bright and green in the centre of the fire's smoke. As he watched it became firmer and cohered into a figure that stumbled towards him, tripping in the dark on the high heels it was wearing.

'Hey, *gwanga*, you is come see me at last!'

'Tigua! Is it really you?'

'You is think anybody else on Tuma is dress this way?'

'Tigua, it's . . . it's so good to see you. I – I, well, we all miss you.'

Tigua managed a brave little smile. 'I is miss you too, *gwanga*. I is can not wait for Lintoa is become boy so she is can come in *kassa* house. You is see Lintoa?'

'Yes, yes I saw him, I mean her, yesterday.'

'How is be old sow?'

'Lintoa is . . .' William thought of the dishevelled dress, the garish make-up. 'Lintoa is . . . grieving. He misses you more than he knows. He blames himself for your death.' Lintoa hadn't said any of these things, but they were all written in that lipstick gash, thought William.

Tigua's mouth crinkled into a wry smile, the kind that's only a muscle or two away from sadness. 'Is seem so stupid now, that I is kill self. I is not know what for I is do. I is see Lintoa with Perlua and I is know is never be any hope for me. I is not can imagine how I is go carry on live and so I is eat fungi.'

William nodded. 'I can understand that. It wasn't stupidity. It's called love.'

A tear rolled down Tigua's cheek. 'Damn!' he said, wiping it off. 'Is mess up my make-up.' He looked at William. 'No, I is be stupid. What I is think can happen between Lintoa and me? She is never go be mine. Is not be possible.'

'I know.' William decided to change the subject. 'How are you finding Tuma?'

'Is be OK. But I is think Tuma is be more better for mans than for womans. They is not have little black dress, so I guess I is never go wear one now. Is be one funny thing, is be womans who is make babies, is make life, but if you is ask me, is be mans who is make Tuma.' He brightened. 'But you is can stay up all night, drink beer, smoke *kassa* and you is not worry 'bout looks. You is start look old sow you is just slough.'

William was going to ask Tigua to keep an eye out for his father, make sure his old man didn't overdo the partying, but just then a harsh voice intruded from nearby. He looked up and saw the enormous figure of Mrs Beach. She was so big that two or three other wraiths were able to pass through her simultaneously.

She afforded William a little nod and smile of recognition, but that was all. She was too focused on her son, who was in a semi-collapsed state, half lying over Tr'boa. 'Man, I'm telling you, she was BIG,' he was telling the bemused native who was doing his best to push the OD'd American off.

'Aaron!' It was loud enough to wake the dead, had any of them still been asleep. Half the people in the hut, both the quick and the dead, turned to look at her. 'Aaron, this is a wonderful opportunity for me to help you, you must pay attention!' she boomed.

Beach jerked upright, like a puppet who'd just had his strings pulled. 'I'm listening, Mom, I'm listening!'

'I am going to tell you something that will change your life. It's about stuff. They don't have it here on Tuma. Not a thing. Not a single personal possession. That's what you need to know Aaron: you can't take it with you when you go.'

'Well Mom, I kind of figured that. Mm, I think there's even an old song about it.'

'Son, this isn't a laughing matter. I'm perfectly serious. I spent my whole life accumulating stuff. I couldn't bear the idea of letting any of it go. I thought I couldn't live without it, and now I find it wasn't true. I can.'

'You're not exactly living, Mom.'

'Don't be pedantic! That's simply a technicality. You're just being frivolous. This is an important message I'm bringing you. You must tell all your friends. Stuff doesn't matter. You can live – I mean, get by – without it.'

Mrs Beach went on and on in the same vein until William could stand no more of it. The serene state the *kassa* house normally induced in him was fractured. That was the trouble with the newly converted. They always became such zealots. Besides, his dad was gone and Tigua had disappeared too, presumably to escape the sheer tedium of Mrs Beach. There was no-one left for him to talk to. And he certainly didn't want to listen to a lecture on materialism from Sandy Beach's late mother.

He rolled onto his front and crawled over to the tunnel. Outside the air was cool and breezy. He had planned if he could ditch Sandy Beach to take another walk to Lucy's, but you didn't need to be a local expert to know that was too risky tonight. Reluctantly he turned in the opposite direction and the certain shelter of the Captain Cook. The wind was getting up. The palm trees were bent double. The ocean roared angrily. He hoped his father had got safely back to Tuma. Bad weather was on the way.

SIXTY

When Sandy Beach emerged from the tunnel an hour or so later he was in a bad way. His head was reeling from the *kassa*. He was only a little guy and he'd insisted on second and third portions even though Purnu had warned him to go easy on the stuff. On top of that his mother had sermonized him to within an inch of his life. Her self-righteous diatribe against possessions – which was rich, coming from her! – had only made him want to rush out and buy something, which he knew was impossible because William had earlier explained to him how the island currency was yams and he didn't have any. With shopping unavailable as an act of rebellion and therapy, he decided he wouldn't mind a darn good fuck. But where and how and with whom? And could you even get one without yams?

The circle in the centre of the village was deserted. A strong wind had gotten up and was hurling rain at him. He wasn't even sure he knew the way back to the hotel. It was right on the beach, he remembered that much, and that meant that all he had to do was turn right or left when he reached the ocean. The only problem was, where was the shore? Somehow, what with the drumbeat in his cranium and the howling of the wind, he'd managed to lose the whole Pacific Ocean.

He fell to his hands and knees with the intention of crawling back into the *kassa* house, but then remembered his mother. He was just wondering whether it might not be a better idea to die of exposure than see her again, except of course dying would mean he *would* see her again, when a head emerged from the tunnel. At first he thought it belonged to a gigantic rat and that he was hallucinating again, but it was followed by a body that turned out to be human and he realized it was the man Purnu.

'Hi!' Beach said cheerily.

Purnu stared at him in surprise. Both of them were still on all fours, nose to nose, like two dogs. 'What for you is crawl around out here?' asked Purnu. There was the same note of suspicion in his voice with which he had questioned William Hardt about trying to conceal his faeces.

'Actually, I was looking for some help,' said Beach.

'What kind of help you is look for? Is be for tell where other white man is go or for find Captain Cook? Or you is want magic?'

'That's exactly—' Sandy Beach had been about to say that Purnu had guessed just what he wanted, directions home. But the word 'magic' triggered the memory of what Tr'boa had told him. In his *kassa* stupor it seemed to him that this was what he really needed.

'Magic.'

'OK. I is can do all sorts. You is want for catch pig perhaps? No? You is have someone you is want for kill?'

Sandy Beach thought seriously about this last one. Then he realized its impossibility. 'No,' he said, a wisp of regret in his voice. 'She's already dead.'

'Love potion? Ah, this is be right one! I is can tell from you face. Who is be lucky girl?'

'I don't happen to know her name, but man, you can't mistake her. She is a custom-made fucking machine on two legs. She's built for it.'

'You is can describe?' Purnu was looking at him with a hint of distaste. Since he had learned to read his knowledge of the English language had widened exponentially. Moreover, some of the blockbuster books that came his way had taught him that while 'fuck' sounded like '*fug-a-fug*' and meant more or less the same thing, suggesting, perhaps, a common root, it was here being used as a profanity. He was affronted by Beach's lack of respect for the object of his desire.

'Well, she's BIG. I mean really big. This high.' Beach held his hand horizontally above his head. Both men looked up at it. An observer might have suggested there was a gleam of dismay in Purnu's eye now. 'She walks like this.' Beach mimed Kiroa's sexy walk. There could be no doubt of whom he was talking now. A man less out of his head would surely have noticed that Purnu was almost foaming at the mouth.

The little man fought back his anger and put on a supercilious smile. 'You is want love potion for make she is love you?'

'I want something that will make her fuck me.'

Purnu rubbed his chin thoughtfully. He considered turning the white man into a cockroach and then stamping on him but decided that might be too quick. Besides, he'd probably had too much *kassa* himself to bring it off.

'Hey,' said Beach impatiently, 'can we go somewhere out of the rain? My clothes are getting soaked.'

'What for you is need clothes? If you is have only pubic leaf water is just splash off you skin. I is not understand what for white mans is wear clothes.'

'What's to understand? It's what civilized people do. Where I come from even the bums on the street wear clothes.'

Purnu was puzzled. He knew 'bum' was a British word for 'arse' but he didn't understand why Sandy Beach was talking about arses on the street. He'd seen a picture of a New York street, but there had been no arses in it. It just didn't make sense. Then again, that was Americans for you. Nothing they did made sense. What reason was there in planting bombs to blow off people's legs? It was a puzzler.

'Listen,' said Beach again, 'can we please get out of this rain?'

'I is can make potion in my house. Come.' He led the way through the inner circle of huts, then stopped and looked back at Beach. 'You is understand that for magic you is must pay?'

'OK, but I don't have any yams. Not on me, any rate.'

'Who is say anything 'bout yams?' said Purnu, who was a fast learner. 'You is pay me dollars.'

Lamua reacted to her husband's unexpected guest with the kind of annoyance Lucy's mother might have shown. She had not long been in bed. She had her own baby and Lucy's tucked in with her, one to a breast, and had only just got them both to sleep. She complained when Purnu lit the palm-oil lamp that he had woken her. Purnu ignored her disgruntled tone. 'Sssh, you is not disturb youself. Is go back sleep.' One of the babies whimpered and she turned her attention from him to comfort it. She looked around for Kiroa, hoping for some help from Purnu's daughter, but the girl wasn't there. Out moping about after Lintoa, no doubt. In this weather!

Most people walking in on a woman trying to bed down a couple of babies would have made their excuses and left, but not Sandy Beach who, after all, had a history of not knowing when he was not welcome. He sat himself down on the floor and listened to the rain drumming on the *adula*-leaf roof. His head began to sway. It reminded him of one of his favourite heavy rock music tracks.

Eventually Lamua got the babies settled down and the little sorcerer turned and smiled apologetically at Beach and said, 'Families!'

'Too right!' said Beach, the memory of his mother still recent.

Purnu produced a pipe, stuffed in some *kassa* leaves and fired it up. Lamua coughed a noisy protest for a minute or so and then settled back down again. Like any island mother she knew that there was nothing like a bit of passively smoked *kassa* for getting a baby off to sleep. Purnu handed the pipe to Beach then went over to the bed, which was really only a bunk built against the wall, and from under it pulled out a box made of bamboo and woven fibre. He opened the lid, rummaged around inside for a moment or two and took out a small leather gourd. He removed the wooden stopper from its neck and sniffed. He pulled a face, restoppered the gourd, replaced it and took out another. He did this two or three times before he found one that produced a smile of satisfaction.

'This is be love potion for you,' he said. 'Is work plenty damn fast. You is not go be here on island longtime, you is need for work plenty quick.'

Beach took another pull on the pipe. His head was swirling. The rain was drumming inside his cranium. How could that be?

'How do you suggest I give it to the girl?' he asked.

'You is not give she. Is be *you* who is take potion.'

Beach took another drag of *kassa*. There was something here he wasn't getting. 'How is it going to make the girl fall for me if I'm the one who takes the medicine?'

'You is take potion before you is go sleep. You is close eyes and think about girl. You is dream about girl. Next day you is be attractive for girl. She is fancy you like mad.'

Perhaps if Beach had not been stoned this would not have made such perfect sense to him, but with his mind performing like a psychedelic light show at some awful Sixties nostalgia party it had a wonderful logic. Of course! Why hadn't he thought of that?

'Open mouth,' ordered Purnu. Beach leaned his head back and opened his mouth. His tongue hung out in a lascivious fashion that dispelled any lingering doubts Purnu had about what he was doing. He allowed half a dozen drops to fall onto Beach's tongue. 'Is be enough,' he said.

Beach righted his head and swallowed. The stuff was sweet as the *kassa* had been in the hut. It tasted of honey.

'Now I is show you way home,' Purnu said and he led Beach out into the tempest and down to the beach where he pointed him in the direction of the Captain Cook.

He returned to his hut chuckling to himself in spite of the fact that he had been thoroughly soaked by the storm.

'What for you is do that?' Lamua raised herself carefully to a sitting position, fearful of waking the babies.

'I is have little bit of fun, is be all,' said Purnu. 'Is teach American lesson for disrespect of my daughter.' He explained to her what Beach had said and the nature of the potion he had given him.

'Is be good,' said Lamua, smiling her most wicked smile, which let Purnu know he was forgiven for having intruded on her. 'I is look forward for see what is happen.'

What Purnu had just told her was how he had duped the white man. The potion would not make Kiroa love Beach. Or anyone else, for that matter. It would only work on Beach himself. It would make him fall hopelessly in love with the first person he saw when he woke up.

Beach staggered along the beach. 'Fuck you wind!' he screamed into the gale. 'Bring it on, you hurricane! Blow all you like, see if I give a fuck!'

His words had no effect. The wind flung them back in his face. It was whipping up the sand and flinging that at him too. His cheeks were smarting from it. His eyes were stinging. Not only that, but his legs were made of lead. He just couldn't seem to lift them any more.

He took a few steps into the jungle. By sheer luck he stumbled into an *adula* patch. The broad, glossy leaves of the *adula* shrub formed a canopy as good as any tent and were a favourite roofing material among the natives. Beach, who didn't know about green shoestrings and anyway was too far gone on *kassa* to care, slumped gratefully onto the dry ground beneath the plants and was almost instantly in a deep sleep in which he dreamed, as he mostly did, of big women.

While Managua was occupied in the *kassa* house, Lintoa had secretly met with Perlua. They had made love in their favourite trysting place, the upper floor of the Captain Cook, a coupling given an additional frisson of pleasure by the presence below of the unsuspecting Dr Gold to whose stentorian snores they had matched the rhythm of their lovemaking, giggling all the while. Afterwards they lay side by side and listened to the wind fixing to get up. Then Perlua set off home to get there before her father staggered in from the *kassa* house. Lintoa did what he always did on the occasion of such meetings. He waited half an hour, so that he would arrive in the village well after Perlua to avoid any suspicion that they might have been together, then he put on his red dress and set off back himself.

He was about halfway when the storm really got under way. The rain was torrential, and he realized he was never going to make it home tonight. It was too dangerous to proceed further. The wind was tugging up small trees and flinging them around with wild abandon, like careless boys playing with twigs for fun. He had to find shelter before one of the trees targeted him. Luckily he realized he was near the *adula* patch where he had been wont to hide his dress in his first clandestine meetings with Perlua, when he had been ashamed to let her see him in it. Now he ducked gratefully under the *adula's* sheltering roof and, after his evening of arduous sexual activity, was soon fast asleep.

SIXTY-ONE

In the morning, as a finger or two of sunlight picked its way through the few gaps between the *adula* leaves, Lintoa was first to awaken, which was only to be expected as he wasn't the one who had almost OD'd on *kassa* the night before. It took him a moment or two to remember where he was and during that time he came to realize he was not alone under the *adula*s. Something nearby in the gloom was snorting. At first he thought he'd got lucky and found himself a black bantam pig without looking and was just wondering what he could use as a weapon – could you finish one off with a high heel? how much damage would a nail file inflict? – when he noticed the outline of a body next to him. Now Sandy Beach was little, and not unendowed with porcine qualities, but even he was not so small as a dwarf pig and it wasn't long before Lintoa realized his companion was human. It took his eyes a moment or two to get accustomed to the dim light but once they did he soon ascertained that his bedfellow was the little flame-haired American who had arrived on the island a couple of days earlier.

He stood up, intending to sneak off but before he had managed to part the *adula* leaves, Beach's eyes flipped open. As soon as they found Lintoa, Beach's jaw dropped open too. He pulled himself into a sitting position. 'Jesus!' he exclaimed. 'What a place this island is, to have someone like you on it!'

Lintoa didn't know how to respond. His main worry was that Beach would ask what he was doing there or might gossip about him having passed the night outside the village, which could lead to awkward questions and perhaps even the discovery of his liaison with Perlua which was taboo for at least three reasons he could think of: that she was white, that they were both girls and that he cross-dressed as a boy when he met up with her.

'Moning,' said Lintoa, for want of anything better to say. 'Is be plenty damn better from last night.' This was true. The wind had dropped and the roar of the ocean had now diminished to the lonesome sighing of the surf.

Beach didn't say anything. He wasn't about to discuss something as mundane as the weather with the vision he beheld. He hardly had the breath to talk, let alone to waste on platitudes. When he recovered the power of speech at last, all he could manage was a slow and passionate, 'Hot banana . . .'

'I is must go,' said Lintoa. 'I is be late for shitting.' The she-boys always shat together on a section of beach between those set aside for male and female defecation. As the only other she-boy of his age now was Sussua, if Lintoa was late it would mean she'd have to shit alone with no-one to talk to. Not only that but he would be conspicuous by his absence, leading to questions about where he'd been. So he thrust aside the *adula* leaves and, carrying his high heels, which were useless anyway on sand, strode off.

Beach was overwhelmed. God, this woman! She was big. No, she was really *BIG*. She was an amazon, the kind of woman who could fuck you to within an inch of your life. But it wasn't just that. Beach was taken aback at the emotion that swelled up inside of him. It wasn't centred on the fork of his legs, as his feelings for the opposite sex invariably were; it felt to start in his stomach and move in waves into his back where it seemed to take hold of and squeeze his kidneys. He could scarcely breathe. 'No, wait!' he shouted after Lintoa. 'Don't leave me now!'

He got to his feet and tried to make his way out of the *adula* bower, but when he pushed at the leaves they only sprang back and

attacked his face. He whirled his arms around frantically, desperate
to get out but this only seemed to make the leaves mad so that they
came back at him even more strongly. His head hurt like hell from
the *kassa* and his brain was dehydrated and working on half its
cylinders. The result was, after a couple of minutes he was
exhausted and fell to his knees. It was now that he noticed that the
hem of the *adula* canopy was a few inches above the ground. He
dropped to his stomach and slithered under.

By now even Lintoa's massive figure was tiny in the distance.
Beach ran after her, but he kept stumbling in the soft sand. In the
end he had to give up and could do no more than watch as
the loveliest woman he had ever seen walked further and further
away from him.

He determined to catch her in the village but as he approached
it, having to stop and rest every couple of minutes because of his
kassa hangover, he was overtaken by William and Dr Gold who
were on their way to the shitting beach.

'Hey, what's the rush?' asked Dr Gold as Beach again tried to
run on the soft sand and fell flat on his face. 'Are you that desperate
to shit? Maybe this drug you ingested last night had an effect on
your digestion.'

Beach ignored this remark. 'Didn't you see her? The girl in the
red dress? She's gorgeous. So – so – so—'

'Big?' said William.

'Yes, big,' said Beach. 'But not just that. There's something special
about her I can't quite put my finger on.'

Try putting it between her legs, thought William. But he said
nothing about Lintoa to enlighten Beach. He figured Lintoa could
look after himself.

SIXTY-TWO

In the village centre William was surprised to see Managua among the injured islanders. 'I thought you didn't want any dollars,' he said to him.

'I is not want dollars is come in island, but if they is, then I is go *need* dollars. You is bring dollars, I is must have.' William saw that Pilua was standing beside her husband. She was staring into the distance, as though she could see right through the surrounding huts, like Superboy with his X-ray vision.

They began the questioning of the claimants with William presenting the evidence and Beach battering away at it, trying to dismiss it. William wouldn't have minded so much if Beach had acted like it was just a job. It was that he went at it with such a will that annoyed William. That wasn't the only thing; Beach's brusque insensitivity meant they were whipping through the claimants; William could see they'd be all done in a couple of days. It had been arranged in the States that he would leave the island on the helicopter with Beach and Gold. He was needed back in New York to get the case moving, he couldn't linger. But he'd hoped for a few more days and some free time to look for Lucy.

It was another long day. A whole new crowd of fraudulent claimants had turned up. One man attempted to get money for a withered arm.

'That is a congenital defect,' said Dr Gold in disbelief.

'What is mean this word con – con—,' asked the man.

'Congenital,' repeated Dr Gold. 'It means a birth defect, something you were born with. There is no way it can have been caused
by a bomb.'

'That is where you is make one big damn mistake,' said the man.
'My *mamu* is be frighten by bomb blast when she is carry me
inside she. I is be born with arm like this.'

Gold sighed. 'There is no way that can be proved. There is no
record of your mother having made a complaint at the time.'

'No, of course is not be.' The man sniffed with frustration. 'She
is only think of this yesterday.'

'She never mentioned it before? Isn't that a little strange, my
friend?'

'Nobody is ever offer dollars before. Dollars is make you is think
of they things.'

Gold dismissed the man with an impatient wave of his hand.
'Nice try!' he called after him.

The next customer squatted on the ground before him and
mouthed some words but no sound emerged from his mouth.

'What was that?' said Gold.

The man stared at him blankly.

'I said, "What are you claiming for?"' repeated Gold. Again the
man's expression didn't register any understanding. At this moment
another man pushed his way through the watching crowd.

'I is be he brother. He is be deaf,' he explained. He squatted in
front of the first man and began a series of elaborate hand signals.
The other man watched intently, then looked at Gold and shouted,
'BOMB BLAST IS MAKE ME DEAF. I IS NOT HEAR
NOTHING NO MORE. BOMB IS BLOW EARS INSIDE
OUT.'

Gold nodded. He picked up his clipboard and wrote something
on it. He looked at the man's brother. 'When did this tragic event
occur?'

More semaphore followed and again the victim watched carefully. When the brother's hands were finally still the claimant

shouted, 'WHEN I IS BE SMALL BOY. I IS NOT CAN HEAR ANYTHING SINCE.'

Gold nodded and wrote something else on the clipboard. He looked up suddenly. 'Want to take your dollars now?' he said.

'Sure thing, man!' said the man. Everyone around gasped. Gold smiled. The man slapped his forehead with the heel of his hand. His brother launched himself upon him and began slapping him around the face. 'You is be one bloody damn fool!' he shouted. 'I is tell you for let me put stick in ears but you is say, "Oh no, I is go get dollars and keep ears." '

'If you is be so smart what for you is not be one who is be deaf?' screamed his brother back. He started hitting in return and the crowd parted as the two men fell to the ground and rolled around wrestling and punching.

Gold smiled at William. 'Tricks of the trade.'

William waited until the day was almost ended and most of the villagers had grown tired of watching and listening and had drifted away to prepare their evening meal before he turned to Pilua. He thought about insisting her story be heard in private, but decided that as she would almost certainly have to testify in an American court one day, rehearsing the story before a sympathetic audience might not be a bad idea.

He sat her down beside him. Managua lowered himself stiffly the other side of her. Beach and Gold sat on the dirt opposite them. Managua shooed away curious onlookers and they mostly respected his desire for privacy and stood a little way off, close enough to hear still, but far enough away for Pilua not to be intimidated.

'OK Pilua, when you're ready, tell us what happened to you that day.'

'Which day would that be?' asked Beach. 'Date?'

'It's in the written submission you have there,' said William. 'There's no need for her to repeat it. This is not a cross-examination. It's a preliminary presentation of evidence. Now perhaps my client can begin.'

Beach shrugged, as if to say, OK, if William wanted to be tough about it, he wasn't going to bother to argue because it wouldn't make any difference in the long run anyway, so they might as well get on with it, get it over and get on to the *kassa*.

Pilua looked at Managua. He took her hand in his and William saw her squeeze it until her knuckles showed white. She looked at William and he nodded. She licked her lips and began to speak in a hushed tone, staring straight at Beach, or rather not at but through as though he wasn't there. In a way, thought William, he probably wasn't, least not for her. She was seeing something long ago.

'I is be young girl. I is have all my life before me this day when I is walk out for water. Is be very hot day. I is fall asleep so I is not go water hole same time as other girls. I is meet they come back when I is be on my way. "Hurry up," they is say, "is be *poto* game tonight."

'When I is be near water hole I is hear voices. I is not recognize they voices, so I is think is mebbe boys from outside village on way for *poto* game. I is walk into clearing around water hole and is find three American soldier is be sit there. They is take boots off and is dangle feet in water. They is each have rifle on they back. I is not know is be call rifle then. I is know now.

'When they is see me, one of they is smile. He is jump down in water and is reach out hand towards me. "Give me you pot," he is say. "I is get water for you." I is smile back, say thank you. I is pass he my pot and he is fill.'

'He spoke to you first, you claim?' snapped Beach.

Pilua lifted her eyes from the floor and stared at him. 'Is be what I is say. Is be something you is not understand?' Beach lowered his own eyes at this onslaught of dignity.

'Go on,' whispered William. The clearing was quiet now. Even the distant noise of children playing had been stilled. The villagers had lined up around the edges of the clearing to listen, keeping the respectful distance Managua had demanded of them.

'He is hold out pot for me. I is bend my knee for lower myself and is take pot. At this moment I is hear noise behind me. I is turn. One of they other two is give third one he rifle. He is undo he — he—'

'Belt,' whispered William.

'Yes, he belt. He leg clothes is drop on ground. He is show me he *pwili*. I is be too shock for think clear. Is be thing of great disgust for man is do this. I is never expect for see such thing in my whole life. I is drop pot. Pot is land in water. American in water is jump on bank and is grab my arms. He is push me on ground. One who is undress is lie on top of me. I is struggle, but other one is hold my arms, like so—' here she extended her arms above her head. It made her look suddenly young. She had the careful intensity of a child explaining something. 'One on top is enter me. Is make *fug-a-fug*. I is turn head one side so I is not have for look in he eyes. He is call me names. I is not remember words. Most of them I is never hear before. I is look in eyes of other one, not one who is hold my arms, but one who is hold they rifles. He is smile at me. I is stare in his eyes for ask him what for he is allow this for happen and in end he is not can stare back. He is turn eyes away.

'When soldier on top of me is be finish, he is get up and is dress heself. Then he is go take rifles from one who is hold them. Then that one is undress and do same as first one. That is be how is happen. One is make *fug-a-fug*, one is hold rifles and one is hold me. I is lie there and is not can believe this is be happen for me. All I is can think is one is hold rifles, one is hold me, and they is treat guns with more care.

'When third one is finish first one is start again. He is do other things against me, things I is not ever dream man is do with woman. One who is hold me is lose grip for one moment and I is try for get free. One who is do things is hit my mouth with he fist. Is knock out tooth.' Here she lifted her upper lip to reveal a gap between her teeth, although in fact there was almost no gap now, the adjoining teeth having grown together to close it, but you could tell there was a tooth missing because of their crooked alignment.

'My mouth is bleed. My nose is bleed. Every part of me is bleed. With this blood I is feel all my dignity is drain from me. All my strength is be in that blood, all my hope is be wash out of me, all my future is flow away.'

'And when it was over?' asked William. 'How did it all end?'

'When they is all finish, when they is not can think of any new things for do with me, one of they who is hold me from behind is move he hands from hold down my shoulders and is put they underneath me and is lift me up. He is lift me and I is have no strength left for resist. When I is stand up one who is speak first is jump in water hole. He is take my pot and he is fill up. He is climb out from water hole and he is lift pot on my head for I is carry. He is smile. Is be a kind smile as if nothing that is happen is happen. "There is be you water," he is say. I is lift my hands for make sure pot is be firm on my head. Then I is turn and I is walk away.'

SIXTY-THREE

That evening, after Pilua's testimony, the mood at the Captain Cook was subdued. Even Beach seemed unable to deny the simple truth of her story. The foolishness of challenging her, at least here on the island, had penetrated even his thick skin.

The three Americans sat around one end of the mahogany table which had temporarily reverted to its original intended use. It was spread with food the natives had given them: minoa bread, hard-boiled turtle eggs, cold fish stew, fresh king prawns and a variety of fruit. William, thinking of Pilua, touched hardly any of it and even Dr Gold, a large man you would have expected to put away a good portion of anything, was merely picking at the meal. Only Beach ate with voracity, tearing off a hunk of bread and stuffing it into his mouth and before he had even swallowed it thrusting in a prawn or half an egg.

William, who had never before in his life so much as contemplated violence, felt like hitting him. He thought how good it would be to haul the little runt onto the table and shove turtle eggs into his mouth until he burst. If Beach's table manners weren't enough to merit this, his insistence on talking all the while just about tipped the balance.

'You can go to court with this, my friend,' he told William, 'but where's the proof? No medical evidence. No eyewitness corroboration. Only the testimony of certain natives who saw her when she returned to the village. That may or may not prove rape and sexual assault. It certainly doesn't prove US military personnel were responsible.' He paused to push another king prawn between his lips which rendered everything he said next incomprehensible. William sighed. It didn't matter that he couldn't understand a word Beach was saying. He'd had enough experience to write the script for government lawyers like him.

He thought of the American soldiers taking it in turns to hold the guns. He imagined the tenderness the men lavished upon these same weapons; the way they caressed them as they cleaned them; he contrasted this with the brutality of their assault upon Pilua.

Perhaps sensing the tension between the two other men, Dr Gold rose from his chair and went over to his medical bag. He opened it and took out a bottle of bourbon. He held it up with a smile. 'Come on you two, I think we all need a drink,' he said.

It soon became apparent that not only could Beach not hold his *kassa*, he couldn't hold his liquor either. After a couple of glasses he began to boast of his drinking exploits, a sure sign of a man with a weak head for booze, thought William. After another two or three, Beach became lascivious, regaling them with tales of his sexual conquests. After an hour or so of this even the good-natured Dr Gold grew weary.

'If you don't mind, I think I'll turn in,' he said. 'Or rather *on*.' And he hauled himself up onto the mahogany table, rested his head on the pile of clothes he was using for a pillow, and was soon emitting the snores which the night before had been the metronome for Lintoa and Perlua's lovemaking.

'Look at him, the old fart,' said Beach with a chuckle. 'He has a wife and three kids back in Albany. Imagine ending up like that.'

William tried. It didn't seem that bad to him. He would have liked a wife and three kids back somewhere, even Albany. He would have liked the ability to be content enough to sleep soundly on a strange table.

'What do you say we go into town and find us a couple of babes?' said Beach. William had never heard anyone talk like this, at least not outside of a really bad movie. 'I think I'll pass,' he said. He wanted to check out Lucy's place again although he felt sure she wasn't there. When you thought about it, if she was hiding from him, she could have holed up anywhere on the island. What was he supposed to do, mount another expedition? With Lintoa as his guide?

Beach rose from his chair. He swayed uncertainly for a moment or two, then picked up the bourbon by the neck of the bottle. 'Suit yourself.' He staggered from the room.

William delved into his bag and took out his copy of *Hamlet*, the twin of the one he'd given to Managua, to pass the time until he figured Beach would be in the village and so not see him on his way to Lucy's. He'd taken to reading Shakespeare since his last visit to the island. He sometimes felt that if there were an answer to anything it would be here, somewhere in this great play. To be, or not to be, was that the only question? Were those the only choices life offered? To get on with it or get out? He settled himself to read the gravedigger scene and thought for the thousandth time of the exhumation of Tigua's body. How long ago that seemed now! He imagined the little she-boy's bones, picked clean, white as old driftwood, bleached by the sun and the sea. And then he thought of Lucy's pale limbs, those short legs and the arms, wrapped around him, offering shelter from his fears. He didn't even notice his thumbs holding the book, squeezing ever so slightly as he read. Right-left-left right, left-right-right-left, to the steady beat of Dr Gold's bear-like snores.

As he staggered along the shore in what he hoped was the right direction to the village, Sandy Beach was glad William hadn't come along. From what he'd seen of the guy at Harvard, Hardt would probably just have cramped his style. Besides, he still did that weird thing with his eyes that he'd done at school; how likely was that to attract a woman? Beach was in the grip of a fervour he'd been fighting all day that was now fuelled by the alcohol he continued to swig as he made his way along the strand. He wanted that big girl in the red dress. He'd had a hard-on ever since he woke up that morning, just thinking about her. He reckoned that if he didn't have her, if she didn't reciprocate his feelings, he wouldn't be able to go on living and the problem with *that* was that he'd be pitched prematurely into an eternity he'd have to share with his mother.

In addition to the girl's possible – though unlikely, he thought – reluctance to welcome his advances, there was a practical obstacle to the instant furtherance of his romance. He had no idea where the girl lived. If the natives had already gone to bed, the way red-necks did back home the moment the sun showed the slightest inclination towards the horizon, then he'd never be able to find her. On the plus side was the way she dressed. She was easily the most Westernized of the island people he'd seen so far. The rest wore grass skirts and, in the case of men, vegetable thongs. A girl who dressed like this one must be after a good time; she was unlikely to be in bed early (unless of course she'd already found her good time, something he didn't even want to think about because he knew it would burn him up with jealousy); moreover, her clothing surely indicated she would be impressed by and attracted to someone from the civilized world.

Of course what Sandy Beach wasn't counting on was magic. He had no idea that his *kassa*-induced session with Purnu the night before had enhanced his own amorous feelings. And who knows? maybe magic didn't play any part at all in his desire for Lintoa. Perhaps it was just that Lintoa was the only woman he'd seen on the island who conformed to his rigidly conservative, strictly Western taste and was also BIG, that attracted Beach. But, if so, what would you say about luck? Is luck just another name for coincidence, like magic?

Who can say? But maybe luck played its part in what happened next and so in the fate of the entire island and every one of its in-habitants. As Sandy Beach swayed along the shore who should come right towards him but the very person he sought, Lintoa. Then again, perhaps it wasn't luck; this was the very time when Lintoa sneaked out of the village every night for his tryst with

Perlua at the Captain Cook, and so it was inevitable that he would meet Sandy Beach.

When Beach saw Lintoa he about dropped the bourbon bottle. If he had, things might have ended there, but he didn't and they didn't. Eventually the two met.

Now Lintoa was looking his she-boy best. He'd seen William Hardt's dismay at his dishevelment and resolved to tidy himself up. He'd hemmed his dress and he'd fixed the zip. He'd polished a machete blade up bright as a mirror and checked that his make-up was perfect. Of course it would all be coming off the moment he reached the upstairs of the Captain Cook, but until then he would play to perfection the role life had assigned him. The upshot was that he took Beach's breath away. As the two got within speaking range, for just about the first time in his life, Sandy Beach found himself speechless.

'Y-you, you are – I mean, you are—' He wanted to say, you are so beautiful, but the words stuck in his throat because he was aware of their inadequacy.

Lintoa looked at him, puzzled. Was the white man ill? He seemed to be having trouble speaking. Perhaps Lintoa should run for help? Then he noticed the bottle in the man's hand. He had never heard of bourbon but he had seen Miss Lucy drinking from a similar bottle.

Beach took a swig of liquor and tried again. He screwed his eyes up tight and attempted to think of something witty and sophisti-cated to say. No words came. Finally he held the bottle out to the girl and said, 'Want a drink?'

Well, of course Lintoa wanted a drink. He'd seen Miss Lucy down a couple of glasses of the stuff and he knew that it was like beer only more powerful. He reached out and took the bottle from Beach. He wondered if he should say thank you or if to do so was taboo among white people. Probably, because he remembered the first time Miss Lucy had given him a beer and he'd thanked her, she'd said, 'Don't mention it.' So he didn't mention it now.

All along the beach there was the detritus of last night's storm, and right where they stood was a convenient tree that seemed to have been ripped from its roots by the wind and deposited here just for them to sit on. Sandy Beach lowered himself onto it. It seemed only polite as he was about to drink the man's bourbon that Lintoa should do so too. He took a swig expecting something cool and refreshing like beer.

It came right back up his throat and exploded out of his mouth, spraying Sandy Beach. Lintoa's eyes were watering and he was gasping for breath. His throat was on fire.

Beach wiped his face with one hand and patted Lintoa on the back with the other. 'Easy, baby, easy,' he said. After Lintoa stopped coughing, Beach stopped patting but his hand remained between the she-boy's shoulder blades, squatting there like a malevolent toad. 'I can see you're not used to bourbon, baby.' There was a gleam in Beach's eye as he said this.

Lintoa didn't pay any attention to the hand. He was too pre-occupied with the bourbon. Anything that could have that effect must be good! He took a sip, cautious this time, careful to let it slide slowly down his throat. He wasn't taking a chance on having what remained of his throat lining burned out.

The bourbon slipped down easy as coconut milk now. Its effect wasn't at all like that of beer which was cold and refreshing. He could feel its warmth spreading throughout his body. His fingers were tingling; his toes were too, and strangely the small of his back – an unexpected place when you thought about it – seemed warm as well. And then he realized why. Someone's hand was massaging him there. He turned towards the American and found the American was already turned towards him. The American had a funny smile on his face, the sort of smile you only normally saw on the shitting beach after someone had had a particularly satisfy-ing evacuation.

Lintoa was not the only one who was puzzled by Sandy Beach's behaviour. Neither of the two people sitting on the windblown tree was aware of the presence of a third person, someone who was, in a funny kind of way, appropriate to be the third corner of this love triangle. After all it was she whom Lintoa had first sought to attract by means of magic, even if he had later changed his mind. And so too had Sandy Beach, although he too had also lost interest in her because Purnu had tricked him into taking the wrong potion, if, that is, you believe in that kind of thing. As William had guessed, Kiroa was still crazy about Lintoa. Either Managua was a better magician than anyone on the island gave him credit for or the combination of Lintoa's indifference and his filling of a pubic leaf was irresistible. Whatever, the passage of more than a year had not dimmed the tall girl's affection for him. She spent most of her waking life mooning around after him and tonight had managed to track him when he went on one of his mysterious evening walks. She had suspected he would be meeting someone. She hadn't imagined it would be this short American with hair the colour of orange fungi. What in the name of *fug-a-fug* was Lintoa doing with him?

Well, right now, she could see from her hiding place behind an *adula* bush – the very same bush under which the two people she was observing had spent the previous night, as it happened – Lintoa was fending off Beach's advances. In particular he was leaning his head back to avoid Beach's tongue which was particularly large for such a little fellow. As for Lintoa, it seemed to him that Beach was trying to lick him. As licking played no part in native lovemaking, Lintoa was completely baffled by the American's behaviour. Perhaps the man was trying to lick bourbon off him? Perhaps it was some kind of American drinking custom, like banging your beer cans together and saying 'Cheers' the way Miss Lucy said the British did?

Custom or not, Lintoa had no intention of being licked and pushed Beach away.

Or rather he tried to. He forgot that Beach already had one arm around him and his hand on his back. Beach was not muscular like Lintoa, but he was wiry. The sort of fellow who clings to you in a fight and saps all the strength out of you. It was what Beach did now. He got his other arm around Lintoa, linked it to the first and held on for dear life. 'Come on, gorgeous,' he said, 'give me a kiss.'

Lintoa was horrified. How many taboos would that be break-ing? Well, there was making love with someone of the same sex, for a start, then there was the foreigner one, that made two, but that was all he could think of, which didn't seem many when he thought how disgusting this little American and his huge tongue were. There ought to be a taboo against having a tongue like that. 'No!' screamed Lintoa and turned his head away.

Beach was not to be denied. He couldn't get at Lintoa's mouth so he made do with nibbling his ear. Lintoa had no idea what this was about. All he could think of was that the man was trying to steal his earring. He had his big hooped pair on tonight. Could all this just be a ruse to take them?

No such luck. Now Beach had dropped his face to Lintoa's bosom and was ruttling around in the top of his dress like a *koku-koku* worrying at a green shoestring, his little head shaking from side to side as he tried to rip Lintoa's bra off with his teeth. Well, it wasn't that difficult. Not when you remember the bra was a very old one and had for some time now been held on by a strip of liana sewn across the back. Under the onslaught of Beach's frenzied attack it snapped and Beach's terrier head plunged into Lintoa's uplift and came up with a mouth full of rags. He spat them out and grinned at Lintoa. 'Never mind baby, I've never been a breast man and anyway, a girl can't have everything!'

Lintoa tried to push him away, but unaccustomed to bourbon as he was, his head was suddenly swimming and he had to close his eyes for a moment to avoid being sick. When he opened them again there appeared to be two of the little American. Or was that just because the damn fella was moving so fast?

Beach pressed his lips against Lintoa's. Lintoa put both hands on the American's chest and shoved him off. Beach lifted one hand and flourished it before Lintoa's eyes and then darted it up his skirt. Lintoa closed his legs instinctively and screamed. Hearing him, Kiroa leaped to her feet and cried out, 'Lintoa, I is come!'

Beach tried to prise Lintoa's knees apart. 'Stop!' cried Lintoa.

'Come on, don't be such a tease,' panted Beach. 'You're going to love this, I promise you.'

With a superhuman effort, Lintoa pushed the little man off. 'I is not be that kind of girl!' he protested.

'Oh, I wouldn't be so sure of that, my dear,' said Beach, renewing his assault on Lintoa's knees. 'Wait till you've tried it before you decide you don't like it.'

Again Lintoa managed to push him off. 'You is not understand,' he said, trying to straighten his clothes. 'I is not be any kind of girl.'

Beach stared at him for a moment, mystified. Lintoa took advantage of his stillness to pull himself to his feet. He tugged up the hem of his skirt. Beach's eyes lit up like torches. Flecks of drool appeared on his lips.

'Look!' said Lintoa. 'I is be boy!'

Kiroa, who was halfway between the *adula* bush and the two struggling figures, was stopped dead in her tracks. Lintoa's not in-considerable *pwili* was dangling a couple of inches in front of the American's eyes.

Beach stared at it for a moment. Then he shrugged. 'Nobody's perfect!' he said and made another lunge. Deftly sidestepping the attack, Lintoa swung his arm and fetched Beach a good one around the head with his handbag.

Beach fell off the log and disappeared behind it. For a moment Lintoa thought he had killed him, but then the little red head popped up. Beach was grinning wildly. 'Oh, you like to play rough, do you?' he snarled. He worked his way round Lintoa, who moved round in the opposite direction, and they were like two wrestlers looking for an opening. Without warning, Beach sprang forward and hit Lintoa with all his weight. Lintoa fell backwards over the fallen tree. When Kiroa got to them they were a furious mass of flying fists and kicking feet. She didn't know what to do. Then she spotted a thick branch that had broken from the tree. She picked it up and hefted it at the fungi-coloured hair. It didn't help her aim that she shut her eyes as she struck the blow. When she opened them she saw Lintoa had stopped struggling.

His eyes stared at her without recognition and then he collapsed.

'Oh no!' Kiroa gasped. Beach was still fighting on. He hadn't noticed there was no resistance now. Then he heard Kiroa's exclamation. He stopped moving and looked up at her. The poor girl didn't know what to say. There was only one thing she could think of to make amends for hitting Lintoa. She hit Beach too.

SIXTY-FOUR

Kiroa was surprised that when she told her father what had occurred he laughed. It did not seem in the least amusing to her that the American had attacked Lintoa, nor that she had knocked out the boy – or rather the she-boy – she loved. And she might have expected him to be concerned about her hurting the American. After all, if the Americans blew you up for no reason, what might not they do if you gave them cause, and surely striking one was cause enough?

Purnu sent some young men to bring back the victims of his daughter's solicitude for her loved one and someone else to fetch the other two Americans from the Captain Cook. By the time William and Dr Gold reached the centre of the village, all the natives were there. Lintoa was already awake. He had a black eye. Sandy Beach was still out cold. He had two black eyes.

Managua was already conducting an investigation. 'What is happen?' he asked Lintoa.

'American is go crazy. First he is try for lick me.'

'Lick you!' Managua's exclamation was echoed by everyone within hearing distance. 'What for is he want for lick you?'

'I is not know. I is be plenty damn worry, I is can tell you.'

Managua screwed up his eyes. 'You is think he is go eat you?'

Lintoa stared at him. 'What for you is ask this? He is be cannibal? He is eat someone else?'

'No, no. At least I is not think so.' He turned to William. 'This one with fungi colour hair. He is eat people?'

William fought the urge to laugh. 'I don't think so. I think the tongue thing was more a mark of, well, affection.'

'He is try for kiss Lintoa!' interjected Kiroa. 'I is see.'

'He is bite my bra,' said Lintoa.

Managua shook his head. 'First he is go eat people, then he is go eat clothes. This is be one crazy American.'

'All Americans is be crazy,' said Lintoa. Then he remembered William. 'Sorry, *gwanga*, I is not mean you.'

'That's OK,' said William.

'Although I is think you is be little bit crazy. Is be eye thing.'

'Oh yes,' agreed William. 'The eye thing.'

While all this was going on Dr Gold had been working on Sandy Beach with smelling salts. By the time Beach was conscious again, William and Managua had managed to piece together the details of his attempt on Lintoa's virtue. Several of the islanders were reduced to hysterical laughter at the idea of a man attempting to make *fug-a-fug* with a she-boy. Things became even livelier when a groggy Beach looked at Lintoa and uttered his first word since regaining consciousness: 'Darling!'

William put a finger to his lips to quieten the natives. He whispered to Purnu, 'Get them away, tell them to stop laughing. If we're clever, we can use this.'

Purnu had no idea what William had in mind but he did as he was asked anyway. He knew it was something to do with the dollars. William asked Tr'boa and a couple of his friends to help carry Beach back to the Captain Cook. 'No joking,' he said. 'I want you all to look very serious.'

Next day Beach woke with a thundering headache from all the bourbon he'd consumed and the blows he'd received from Lintoa and Kiroa. His body hurt in several places. He couldn't remember what had happened but a vague idea that it involved sex was enough to get him started on a story for the doctor.

'Boy, that big girl sure likes it rough,' he said. 'I feel like I did ten rounds with Mike Tyson.'

He was surprised when Dr Gold didn't take the bait. Gold was an old married man who lived on the sexual titbits Beach threw him.

'Let me tell you, Gold, that girl may look like butter wouldn't melt . . .' Here Beach paused. Actually, when he thought about it, Lintoa didn't look like butter wouldn't melt. She was a great big bitch of a woman. 'I mean . . . owww!' He put a hand to his head as he realized too late that he'd gotten excited and moved it. Into his befuddled brain popped an image of himself rolling around on the ground fighting. The snapshot vanished and was immediately replaced by a picture of an enormous penis dangling in front of his eyes. A vague unease, more than he usually had from a drunken blackout, permeated his mind. Just what had happened last night?

He swung his legs around and sat on the edge of the table. He heard a tapping noise and looked up to see William typing on a laptop at the far end of the table. William turned and stared at him for a moment or two, then went back to his typing. Gold was writing at his end of the table.

'Shit, my head,' said Beach. 'Reckon some of that food these abos gave us must have been oxidized. Can you get botulism from prawns?'

No-one laughed. The room was deadly silent except for the tap tap of William's fingertips and the scratch of Gold's pen. Both men kept their eyes resolutely on their work.

'What?' said Beach.

No-one answered.

'Did I embarrass myself last night?'

Gold spoke without looking up. 'Embarrass would be an understatement.'

'Hey, come on, guys, stop joshing me . . .'

William looked up and stared at him, his eyes cold and expressionless. 'You attempted to sexually assault a teenage boy.'

Beach made a weak try at a smile. 'Hey, come on, what is this?

A sexual assault on a boy? I didn't go near any boy. I had a – a – tumble with the chick in the red dress, the big one.'

'She's not a chick,' said Gold. 'She's a boy.'

Beach stared at him. Somewhere in the dark recesses of his mind he remembered that huge penis. Had someone lifted a skirt to show it to him?

'No, no, she's a girl. Lintoa, right? That's the one we're talking about.'

'Lintoa is a boy,' said William. 'You were caught last night in the middle of a violent sexual assault on a transvestite boy.'

Beach stared at William for a moment. Unforgiving, unblinking eyes met his. He turned to the other end of the table. Gold nodded.

'Holy shit!' said Beach. 'I knew there was something weird about her.' He chuckled. 'Jesus, thank God nothing happened. That could have been nasty.'

'You don't understand, my friend,' said Gold. 'It was nasty.'

'It is nasty,' said William. 'Lintoa is considering bringing a lawsuit against you.'

'B-but that's preposterous. I – I was drunk. She – he – led me on, I – I—.'

William got up and walked around the table. 'Even if Lintoa doesn't bring an action, think how it's going to stack up when the compensation cases come to court. Think what will happen to your career.'

'You can't be serious—'

'A sexual assault on a transvestite boy? How much more decadent can you get?'

Beach buried his head in his hands. The other two men looked on and said nothing. All you could hear was the surf pounding the beach as the tide began to turn outside.

Beach looked up. 'William, we go back a long way. Remember how we used to play chess? Remember that?'

'I remember you getting the whole school to call me Wanker.'

'William, it was just a joke. A bit of fun—'

'Funny how it's you who turned out to be the pervert.'

'Oh my God,' wailed Beach. 'If this gets out, I'm ruined. Totally fucking ruined.'

William walked slowly around the table. He fingered the mahogany as though he were terribly interested in it, although how could anybody have been interested in this decades-old decrepit piece of furniture, unless of course it bore some imprint, some distant memory of the first time you made love on it with someone you had lost? He found himself feeling un-characteristically vindictive towards Beach. Not on account of the childhood misery the other had inflicted upon him but because the hullabaloo last night had prevented his visiting Lucy's house. He was irked that his own essential goodness, the fact that he wasn't like Beach, was making him sacrifice any other chance of finding her too. What he had in mind would ensure the chopper would be called and have them out of here today. It would probably mean he never saw Lucy again. Still, William wasn't Beach; it had to be done.

'Of course, there is a way out,' he said.

Beach's head sprang up. 'Yes?'

'It doesn't have to come to trial. A trial would benefit no-one. It could take ten years or more before anyone sees any money. Ten years of these people hobbling around on ill-fitting artificial limbs.'

'Wait a minute, what are you saying?'

William stopped his perambulation right beside Beach. He thrust his face into his. 'You could advise the government to settle out of court. If they did that no-one need ever know about last night.'

'That's blackmail.'

William didn't reply.

Beach appealed to Gold. 'He's trying to blackmail me! Are you going to go along with that?'

Gold shrugged. 'Come on, these are people who live in abject poverty. Uncle Sam did them some real damage. They ought to be compensated. Why wouldn't any reasonable human being want that? Why should you be allowed to delay and obstruct with a load of legal technicalities? What's a few mil more or less to Uncle Sam?'

FIVE YEARS
LATER

SIXTY-FIVE

It was a fine autumn day with not a single cloud in the blue Manhattan sky although William Hardt was too preoccupied with an elaborate pavement-crack-stepping ritual to notice. In the half-decade since he'd left the island William's OCD symptoms had come to occupy an increasing role in his life. It was as though, after he'd glimpsed Eden and lost it, his old anxieties had bounced back stronger than ever. Never had William felt so alone. Carrying a torch for Lucy made new relationships difficult enough. The additional burden of his OCD meant they were doomed. With his vulnerable good looks he had no trouble getting girlfriends; keeping them once the blinking and grinding and picture straightening and idiosyncratic toast buttering kicked in was another matter. There were so many weirdos out there to be fearful of, people were looking for protection from them; they didn't want to take one under their wing.

In desperation William called Sheena. OK, it hadn't worked out before with her, but maybe he should give it another chance. At least with Sheena there wasn't the constant need for subterfuge. He could be his normal odd OCD self.

She sounded pleased to hear from him and agreed to meet for a drink. She greeted him with a big smile and an affectionate hug. Her long golden hair shone and William felt suddenly hopeful. He was eager to tell her there were good reasons they should try again:

he was more tolerant these days and he had moved to a two-bathroomed apartment.

He was about to say all this and had just cleared his throat in a portentous way when he realized Sheena was almost unaware of him. She was too busy polishing a fingermark from her wine glass to remember he was there. At once he knew it was no use. Although Sheena would tolerate his disorder more than most people, every moment he was with her he would see his own obsessiveness reflected back by her.

She finished cleaning the glass and looked up and smiled. 'You know, William, the self-help weekend really helped me. It was the beginning of me learning not to be ashamed of my OCD. Now finally I got this great boyfriend. I told him everything and he's real cool about it. Plus he's real messy and he hates it? He loves that I'm always cleaning . . .'

So now William felt alone in the busiest city in the world, isolated by his OCD, although not for much longer, at this precise moment. If you walk with your eyes on the ground in the New York rush hour it's only a matter of time before you collide with another commuter and that's what happened now.

There was a big OOOMPFFF of escaping air – as though someone had punctured a truck tyre – from both William's body and that of his collidee.

'Hey, watch it, you big—' began a shrill voice. And then, '*Gwanga?*'

William's old island name brought his eyes up from the sidewalk with a jolt. He found himself looking at a small man in a business suit who seemed to have a toilet brush instead of a head. But a familiar toilet brush, one that he knew. Then he realized he was looking at Sandy Beach and that the latter had had his appalling ginger hair cut into that extended crew cut often known as a brush cut and favoured by senior American military personnel and other psychopaths.

'Sandy. I – I'm sorry, I was miles away. I didn't recognize you at first.'

'Well, it has been nearly five years, I guess.'

'*Gwanga*. You called me *gwanga*.'

'Did I? I thought I said Wanker.'

'No, it was definitely *gwanga*. Believe me, I'd notice something like that. No-one's ever called me that except . . . on the island.' William desperately wanted to escape from Beach. He was even prepared to jettison his sidewalk-crack sequencing in favour of a quick getaway, but the tenuous thread connecting him to the island, and so, of course, to Lucy, through Beach, demanded that he cling to it.

'Well, maybe you're right,' said Beach. 'I was just back there, last week. That little guy, one who looks like a rat? He was talking about you. I guess that's why I called you *gwanga*.'

William didn't want to escape from Beach any more. He hurriedly consulted his watch. 'Listen, I don't have to be anywhere just yet. Do you have time for a coffee?'

Beach ostentatiously consulted his own wrist, which was weighed down by a heavy duty Rolex. 'Well, I'm not sure. I have a meeting in the Towers at eight thirty.'

'It's on me,' said William, recalling Beach's legendary meanness. Beach beamed at him. 'Well, I guess I can manage it.'

In a nearby deli William had an espresso while Beach nursed a supersize cappuccino in a beaker as big as his toilet-brush head. He shook so much chocolate powder over it he turned the milky foam top from white to brown. William sat waiting patiently for news of the only woman he'd ever believed he might have loved while Beach tipped up his cup and slurped out of it for a good minute. When he finally lowered it his mouth was so obscured by cappuccino foam that he looked like a toilet brush with chocolate collagen lip implants.

'What were you doing on the island?' asked William.

'I was arranging payment of the final tranche of the compensation deal,' said Beach.

'It all worked out OK?' asked William, who'd been taken off the case immediately the deal had been struck. For the past five years he'd been working on compensation cases for injured mine-workers. It was about as far from a tropical island as he could get.

'Oh, sure,' replied Beach, spooning more foam into his mouth via a wooden spatula intended for stirring and so inadequate for the task that more of the stuff ended up on the table than reached his lips. 'A couple of other compensation claims came in from other places soon afterwards that made my deal look cheap. I even got promoted.'

'That's great,' said William. 'But actually, what I meant was, did it all work out OK for the islanders?'

Beach gave a little chuckle that sprayed foam across the table. 'Yeah. It enabled them to achieve a million-year evolutionary leap in a couple of months. One minute they're headhunters, the next they have McDonald's.'

William assumed this was a joke. 'Actually,' said Beach, 'it's probably a good thing we gave them the money. They have modern technology to improve their lives. They've embraced the things America can offer. And it hasn't cost Uncle Sam a penny.'

'How do you figure that?' William was trying to appear non-chalant by allowing Beach to spout off, but he couldn't help looking furtively at the massive chronometer on Beach's wrist. The time was 8.05. Beach would soon have to be leaving for his meeting. And William would have to go with him; he was due at a meeting in the same building before nine.

'Well, all the stuff they buy comes from the US. What goes around comes around. The dollars are all finding their way back to us.'

William couldn't help thinking it sounded a bit like the theory of the circulation of yams he'd constructed for the natives in the old days. Except that the natives could always grow more yams. Where would they get more dollars?

'And . . . uh . . . how is everyone there?' he asked, examining the black sludge in the bottom of his espresso cup as though that were of more interest than any reply Sandy Beach could possibly give.

'Oh, much the same. The old guy—'

'Managua?'

'Yeah, Managua, was just as crotchety as ever, and the rest of them look mostly, well, prosperous, and of course the money's brought changes . . .'

William cleared his throat. 'There was an Englishwoman there. I don't think you met her. I suppose she's long gone?' You'd have thought he was looking for the answer in the sludge.

'You mean the one you made the old *fug-a-fug* with? You certainly kept that quiet when we were there together. But I heard all about it this time. Not that I blame you. She's a babe, considering she's so small, and all.'

'Then she's still there?'

'Yup, she's still there. Must be crazy. Who'd want to live in a place like that? Shit! Is that the time? I gotta go.' He rose and picked up his briefcase. 'Cute kid though.'

'Kid?' said William. 'What do you mean? What kid?'

'The little girl.' Beach stared at him. 'You didn't know. *You* didn't know?'

'Lucy has a child? How – how old is it? I mean she.'

'She,' said Beach. 'It's a girl. About five years old.' He raised an eyebrow. 'Very pale skin. Blue eyes. Blonde hair. Work it out.'

'B-but—'

'William, I don't have time for this now. I have a meeting about a hospital we bombed by mistake. Actually we didn't bomb it by mistake, we meant to flatten it, we just thought it was something else. You want to walk to the Towers with me?'

William rose. Lucy had a child. A five-year-old child. 'Yes, I'm coming,' he said. He left some money on the table and followed Beach out. They started walking. Beach was rabbiting on about the case he was working on. William couldn't take it in, it was just noise, along with the traffic and the distant sound of aircraft. Suddenly he stopped. 'Actually, Sandy, I've just remembered something I have to do. I, uh, I'll meet up with you some other time.'

'Oh, OK. Well, you know where to find me. Give me a call. It would be great to catch up on old times.' He looked William in

the eye, his attempt at a smile strangely amplified by the foam on
his lips. 'You know, you were the best friend I ever had in my
whole life.'

And without warning he leaned forward, flung an arm around
William, and clutched him stiffly. He held him like that for half a
minute. Then he released him, turned quickly away, strode off and
was soon swallowed up by the rush-hour crowd. William watched
him out of sight, strangely touched by this unexpected effusion
from his childhood nemesis. No matter how long you lived, it
seemed, there was no accounting for human nature. Then he
remembered what he had to do and lifted an arm to hail a passing
cab.

The cab driver was some kind of Eastern European, Ukrainian,
William guessed from the miniature Dynamo Kiev soccer shirt
hanging from his rear-view mirror and the balalaika music
emanating from his cassette deck, and he didn't speak any English.
William had to direct him street by street to his apartment. He
gestured to the cassette deck and asked the man to turn it off. The
man smiled and nodded vigorously as if he thought William was
admiring the music. He reached out a hairy hand and turned up
the volume. The music was all jangling foreign folksiness and it
tangled up William's brain. He was almost relieved when a few
minutes later an aircraft screamed so low overhead that it drowned
out the noise.

The further they went, the nearer they got to William's apartment, the emptier the streets became. It was more like early
Sunday morning, when nobody is about, than rush hour. It had the
feel of one of those days when everyone is inside watching a big
football or basketball game on TV.

Outside his apartment building William had some trouble
convincing the Ukrainian to stay. When he tried to get out of the
cab without paying, asking the man to wait for ten minutes,
the driver opened the glove compartment on his dash and pulled
out a pistol. William thought this might be a signal he should pay
the man off and look for another cab, but the street was empty and

he didn't want to waste a minute more than he had to. A few minutes lost now could cost him hours, maybe even a day or two, later. Finally he paid the fare then showed the driver more dollars, pointed to his watch and held up ten fingers and the guy seemed to get the idea. Once again William wondered how people with no English made a living driving taxi cabs around a city they didn't know.

In his apartment he grabbed a bag and tossed a few clothes into it. He tried to think what he would need on the island, what he'd wished he'd had before, and threw in the *Complete Shakespeare* that he'd taken to reading every night, maybe because it reminded him of Managua. He also tried to remember to leave out all the things that wouldn't be any use once their batteries ran out – his cell phone, his laptop, his electric shaver. As he went through his desktop he came across a pocket calculator and dropped that in the case. You had to think of these things when you didn't have yams.

He had his hand on the doorknob, ready to leave, when he caught sight of something on the coffee table. His half-finished letter to Lucy. He'd written to her every month since he left the island the first time, every month without fail, and he'd never gotten a reply. At first his letters had been careful and guarded. They had rehearsed again his arguments for the need to compensate the islanders; they had been full of irritation that Lucy couldn't see things his way. After a while it occurred to him that the unlikelihood of the letters ever reaching their destination might not be the only reason for the lack of any response. So he resolved to steer clear of contentious issues and stick to the personal, mentioning their disagreement only as the subject of regret that anything should have come between them after such a promising start.

Still silence. Most people would have given up, but not some-one with an obsessive personality. William carried on writing even though he was pretty well convinced no-one was reading what he wrote. He always had in his mind Lucy as his reader, as the person he was addressing, but he no longer believed she read a single one of his words. This set him free and he began to write purely for himself. He began to open up, to tell the Lucy who wasn't reading his words, about his life. He told her about his dad. He told her about Sandy Beach. Around about the third year he felt he knew her well enough to confess his OCD. Until now he'd never told another soul, other than health professionals or fellow sufferers or Jean who was both. He told her how he had carried around the burden of it nearly all his life. How having this secret self had kept him at one remove from the rest of the world as if he'd been a serial killer. He gave descriptions at once humorous and personal of his various rituals, the difficulty of concealing them from others and the guilt that it induced. He even told her about the check linoleum floor, the toilet bowl and the bath and apologized for the secret ritual fondling of her breasts.

'It's painful to tell you all this,' he wrote, 'but in a way, it brings me comfort too. Just like that first time we were together. Ouch!'

William went back and picked up the half-finished letter. He'd be on the island long before any postal system could get it there. He'd deliver this one himself.

He was just stepping into the elevator when one of his neighbours, a white-haired old lady who had never before spoken to him but was in the habit of merely giving him an austere nod by way of acknowledgement, came out of her apartment.

'Isn't it just terrible?' she said. 'Why would they do a thing like that? Why would anybody?'

'Why indeed?' said William, pushing his case into the elevator and stepping in after it. He shot the old lady a friendly smile as he hit the button for the ground floor. 'Some people!' he said, rolling his eyes heavenwards and giving a little shrug. 'The things they get up to!'

As the elevator doors closed the last thing he saw through the narrowing gap was the old lady staring at him with an appalled expression.

Back outside, William stood by the cab, spread his arms and attempted to mime an aircraft for the driver, who at first looked bemused and then increasingly fearful until at last his hand started to move towards the glove compartment again. Fortunately, at that moment, William heard the loud roar of an engine and pointed at the distant sky where there was another low-flying jet.

'Ah, *aeroporto*!' said the Ukrainian and started the engine. Jumping into the cab, William thought how lucky that the plane happened to be going over just at that moment. God only knew how he'd have gotten through to the Ukrainian otherwise.

At the airport, of course, all was chaos and confusion and William learned that there was no plane he could catch that day, or indeed any planes flying anywhere over the United States, other than military aircraft, and naturally he found out the reason why. In the cab back to his apartment he sat on the back seat, the swirling folk dances blasting from the speakers only adding to his confusion while the Ukrainian driver, still oblivious to the news, whistled cheerfully along. William found himself thinking selfishly that if only he'd run into Sandy Beach yesterday, he'd have now been safely on his way. From that thought his mind jumped to the image of Sandy Beach clinging to him, an act so untypical of the little runt who'd all but ruined his childhood that you might have thought he had some premonition of what was to come. Of course William was twitching away in the back of the cab to an extent that was life-threatening. He was doing the eye thing, the teeth thing and tapping his hands alternately on the bag that he clutched to his chest like a child's security blanket. The reason it was life-threatening was because he could see the Ukrainian driver watching him in his rear-view mirror rather than the road ahead and that the man was driving with one hand permanently on the glove compartment rather than the steering wheel. The reports William had been given at the airport had been confused. The death toll was horrendous. Fifty thousand people, someone had said although someone else had told him they'd gotten people out of the building. He wondered if his eye movements could make Sandy Beach one of the survivors. It was like saying Hail Marys. How many would he have to do for Beach's earthly salvation?

When he stepped out of the elevator on his floor he almost bumped into the old lady he'd met while leaving. Her remarks came back to him and suddenly made sense. She didn't speak but turned on her heel to head along the corridor away from him. He reached out a hand, 'Listen—' he began.

She spun back to face him. 'Listen to you!' she snapped. 'I should listen to you, oh yes! Go on, make another joke about it, why don't you? You sick bastard.'

The crude word sounded so odd in her refined accent that it took William's breath away. Before he could think of any response she strode off down the corridor and a moment later he heard a door slam.

In his apartment he switched on the TV and sank into an armchair in front of it. He hardly moved for the rest of the day as he watched the full horror unfold. Along with most of the rest of the world he saw the second aircraft hitting the building over and over again. At each replay, a small and diminishing part of him hoped that this time something would intervene to prevent the collision. At the same time he experienced an overwhelming guilt, an OCD sense of responsibility for what had happened, a feeling that he could somehow have prevented it. At one level, of course, he knew this was ridiculous. What connection did he have with the event or its participants? What could he have done? Been nicer to the Asian man who owned his local convenience store, perhaps, a man he wasn't even certain was a Muslim? The only possible culpability on his part was that he hadn't done enough to ward off unspecified disaster, he had neglected his various rituals and failed to find new ones that might have helped. As if to compensate for this now his body, as he sat and watched the TV, was a blinking, shaking, clenching and unclenching, teeth-grinding mess. Anyone walking in would have assumed he was having an epileptic fit.

As well as the wider sense of guilt he felt for the victims of the attack there was the specific feeling that he might have done something to save Sandy Beach. Of course to begin with he didn't know for sure that Beach was one of the casualties. In the first couple of days it was almost impossible to find out. Calls to Beach's employers were useless because their headquarters in the World Trade Center had been obliterated along with everything else. It was three days before William was able to find out for certain that Beach was listed as missing.

Here surely he had to assign himself some responsibility. He was with Beach only a few minutes before the attack, for Christ's sake! He should have been able to do something to prevent him going to work. If he hadn't been so selfish, so obsessed with his own mission of returning to the island and Lucy and the child who was more than likely his daughter, he could have saved his old school-mate. If he'd only pressed him to have a second cup of coffee! Beach would surely have called on his cell phone to postpone his meeting. The guy was such a tightwad he'd have been certain to have done that for another free coffee. But what was he thinking of? Sandy was almost certainly dead and here was William remembering his meanness, something that was no fault of his own but a result of his impoverished childhood. Jesus, the poor guy had lived in a house where he probably never got a coffee because no-one could ever find the stuff or a cup to put it in! If he, William, had been a kinder person, he might have suggested Beach call in sick and they take the day off and trawl a few bars. He might at least have appeared interested in Beach's conversation which would almost certainly have led to the latter getting on a roll talking about himself and maybe forgetting his appointment. There were dozens of things he could have done that he hadn't. Maybe it was stretching it, insane even, to suggest he could have prevented the entire attack. But he could at least have saved Sandy Beach.

This was all bad enough but what made it worse was that although he had failed to save Beach, Beach had saved him. If he hadn't met Beach he would never have learned about Lucy having a child, quite possibly – no, almost certainly – his own daughter, and would never have decided to head immediately to the island and would therefore have gone to his meeting and most likely have been killed along with the people who had turned up and were all posted missing. He felt not only the guilt that all survivors feel, but the additional burden that he owed his continued existence to one of the victims.

William's anxiety levels were not only raised by these feelings of responsibility, but also by his own imagination. He saw himself standing in his own office watching through a window an aircraft heading straight for him. He realized that these visions had little basis in reality, that they were collages of various Hollywood disaster movies, indeed the whole thing was exactly like a Hollywood disaster movie, only this time without a Bruce Willis to come to the rescue. Like William, where had Bruce Willis been when they needed him?

William's sympathy even extended to the hijackers. He suffered nightmare visions of the doomed building hurtling towards him through a cockpit window. But try as he might he could not put himself in the terrorists' shoes. Imagine setting off that morning knowing that in an hour or so you would be dead! The plan had been undeniably audacious and executed with devastating efficiency. But imagine *wanting* to die! Had any of them had second thoughts? Had they maybe seen the building rushing towards them and wanted to turn away? Probably not. They had killed the pilots of the aircraft, aircraft that some commentators suggested they knew how to fly but not how to take off or land. They never had any intention of returning safely to earth. Various TV experts had spoken of the suicide bombers' religious beliefs. They had set out that morning determined to punch a hole in the sky through to the next world. That afternoon, while William and the rest of the world were watching reruns of their attack, these nineteen men would be in paradise, each of them enjoying the ministrations of seventy-two virgins. How William envied them their belief, their total conviction. Going off on a business trip in the morning, taking lunch in another world. The President of the United States called the terrorists cowards. William couldn't agree. You could call the attacks underhand, targeting defenceless civilians without warning, but how could an attack in which you were definitely going to perish be cowardly? Sneaky, yes. Insane, mistaken, inhumane, yes, yes, yes, but lacking in courage, no.

Once William knew of the fate of Sandy Beach, he had but one thought: to get away. In one respect this was a strange ambition. For the first time in his life William was not alone. He was no longer the odd one out. The result of 9/11 was that suddenly everyone in America had OCD. Everyone was walking around looking tense and afraid. Everyone was fearful of some unspecified danger. Their tall buildings were no longer monuments to American economic superiority but vulnerable beacons that invited hijacked planes to destroy them. You could get gassed on the subway; Jesus Christ! it had already happened in Tokyo. You could be on your way home and die trapped like a rat before you got there. You could be shot at a gas station by a deranged Arab sniper. There wasn't any safety any more. Everyone was twitching this and that, counting right and left, touching both walls of the corridor now. Yes, the person without OCD was the odd one out these days. You saw the disorder especially in the leaders, the politicians. The President reacted like any other OCD sufferer, indulging in activities that had no logical connection with the terrorist threat but that he and his advisors believed would magically ward it off; he made loud noises about bombing countries that had no connection with the terrorists as well as those that did and often repeated mantras about freedom and democracy which William found rich coming from a man who had been illegally elected. When William saw TV footage of the hole that had been the World Trade Centre, the vast space now given over to dust and rubble reminded him of another patch of scorched earth he'd seen where nothing was left alive. He remembered the phrase Sandy Beach had used that last time he saw him, What goes around comes around. Except of course it never did. It only got as far as the innocent and the uninvolved like those who had died here. It never made the full circle to those who ran the show.

Seeing the craziness all around him, people buying survival kits and stores of food and flak jackets and gas masks, was like a macro version of the OCD weekend. William knew he had to get away to a place where there were no tall buildings or aircraft or televisions on which to watch tall buildings being hit by aircraft, where his country had already done its usual damage and moved on, it was to be hoped, for good, where there was a woman he had maybe loved and a daughter he had never seen. As soon as planes were allowed up in the air again, one of them had William on board, eyelids furiously working, as they raced the westering sun.

SIXTY-SIX

William's first glimpse of the island from the window of the plane took him by surprise. Although he had expected there to be an airstrip – the plane that was carrying him had wheels not floats, after all – nothing had prepared him for the stark white gash in the dark green of the island's central forest. It reminded him of the scar on a man at his health club whose chest had been opened up for heart surgery. Here it was not the only cicatrice. Other white threads emanated from it in different directions all over the island, as if the one big operation had led to the necessity of other, smaller incisions.

The plane banked sharply and began to descend towards the airstrip stretching before it. They hit the ground with an alarming bounce. The aircraft seemed to be eating up the runway much too fast. With the Twin Towers still firmly in his mind, William didn't like the speed with which the volcano at the other end of the airstrip was approaching them.

But then the Australian pilot sitting beside him hit the brakes and the plane slowed fast. It came to a halt with maybe ten feet of runway to spare.

'Well, here we are,' said William, trying to sound nonchalantly confident, as if he'd never for a moment thought they wouldn't be.

'Yeah, thank Christ,' said the pilot, taking off his baseball cap and wiping his sweating brow with the back of it. 'I'm never quite sure I'm going to make this one. It's a hell of a short runway.'

As William carried the small bag he'd hastily packed three days earlier down the plane's steps there was the noise of a car horn. It was so unexpected on the island that it was only when he saw the SUV headed along the runway towards him that William realized what the sound was. The vehicle screeched to a stop beside him.

'Hey, *gwanga*, is can really be you?' At first William didn't recognize the driver. He could tell the guy was young, mid-twenties probably, but his eyes were hidden by large mirrored Ray-Bans. And although he'd called William by his old, familiar island name, he was much bigger than anyone William had ever met here. His solid neck was piped into a barrel chest. Below that − another surprise − instead of a pubic leaf he wore black cycling shorts from which tree-trunk thighs emerged and spread themselves across the car's front seat.

'Well, you is want for ride village or you is go walk? I hope you bag is not be so heavy this time.'

'Tr'boa?' said William. 'Is it really you?'

'Ah, sorry.' Tr'boa removed the sunglasses. His face broke into the big open smile that William remembered as his first sign of welcome to the island what seemed a lifetime ago. Only now, he noticed there was a gap where Tr'boa had lost one of his incisors. 'Come on. Jump in!'

William tossed his bag into the back of the car and climbed in beside the young man. Tr'boa throttled up the engine noisily and unnecessarily and then took off, wheeling round with a squeal of rubber and roaring back up the runway.

At the far end, the one where the plane had first touched down, Tr'boa hit the brakes hard and swung the wheel so the back end of the vehicle slid round and they were at right angles to their original trajectory. A road ran across in front of them. Tr'boa put his hand on the horn and swung left into the road, narrowly missing another SUV that cut across in front of him, horn also blaring.

'Goddam!' shouted Tr'boa above the engine's abandoned roar. 'That fool is must be deaf for he is not hear my horn!'

He turned to William and smiled. 'Is be plenty more easy than landing beach, is not be so?'

'Yes,' said William, pressing his panama to his head so the slip-stream didn't carry it off. 'Lucky for me you were around when the plane came in.'

'Is be nothing for do with luck. This is be how I is make living. I is drive taxi.' The jeep was doing sixty now on a dirt road. It was bouncing William around so much he had to use his free hand, the one that wasn't holding the panama, to cling to the top of the door.

'Oh,' said William. 'But you still go fishing?'

Tr'boa turned. 'You is must be make joke. Man, what for I is go spend all day on boat for catch fish nobody is go want when I is can make more in two, three trips in car? I is must be mad for do that.'

'Look out!' screamed William. There was a double blare of horns as a pick-up truck bore down on them and Tr'boa swerved just in time to miss it, braked hard to avoid a tree that came at them out of nowhere, skidded back across the road and finally finished up in the dip off the other side of it.

'Damn fool!' he said. 'Is not look where he is go.'

William raised an eyebrow. He hadn't been so terrified since the night he'd flown with Purnu. If he ever had.

Tr'boa put the car into gear, pulled back onto the road and smiled. 'Well, is be more fun for drive car than for fish. Is not be much excitement for go fish, unless maybe you is be attack by shark and then is not really be excitement is be just plain terrify.'

Tr'boa drove more slowly now. He obviously sensed William's dismay at the near-wreck and had anyway probably done enough showing off.

'Seem to have been a few changes around here,' observed William, as he noticed one or two concrete buildings along the route and other dirt roads branching off it, the white threads he had seen from the air.

'Yes, *gwanga*, and is all be thanks for you.'

Another SUV roared past with a klaxon blare as he said this. 'You is see. We is not have cars before you is get we dollars.'

William winced. 'How come you managed to buy a vehicle?' he asked. 'You didn't get any compensation.'

'My uncle is give me some. He is lose foot. Rest is be from my wife. She is get money for loss of she *mamu* who is be kill by bomb.'

'You're married? Congratulations. Who's the lucky girl?'

Tr'boa grinned. 'Is me who is be lucky, not she, as you is know when I is tell you. Kiroa.'

'Kiroa? You netted Kiroa?'

'Sure thing. I is be plenty good fisherman for catch that one, is you not think? Now I is be taxi driver.'

The road took a couple of treacherous twists and turns which Tr'boa negotiated by much athletic wrestling with the wheel, assisted by noisy skids and swearing. When they hit a clear stretch again, William pretended to gaze casually at the jungle flashing by. He cleared his throat. 'I understand Miss Lucy is still on the island?'

'Sure thing. You is want I is take you she place?'

'No, I, er, I just wondered.' He cleared his throat again. His voice, when it came, sounded to him dry and rasping, thick with the phlegm of self-consciousness. 'Does she live alone?'

Tr'boa seemed to take a moment to think about this. 'Miss Lucy, no, course not. She is not live alone.'

William's heart sank, but then, what had he expected? It had been five years. Lucy was an attractive woman. The island had most likely had an increase in the number of Western visitors since he was last here. Then it occurred to him that Tr'boa might have taken his question too literally, that he might have been referring to Lucy's child. Before William could ask him more a tinny rendition of the *Star Wars* theme interrupted him. Tr'boa used both hands to pat the pockets of his shorts, then put his right hand back on the wheel just in time to stop the vehicle leaving the road again and with his other hand pulled a cell phone from his shorts pocket.

'Yes, I is be on way from airport now.' He turned to William. 'I is take you village or Captain Cook?'

William had intended to go to the village, but now he thought about it, the Captain Cook might be the better option. He would be alone there and could collect his thoughts. He'd come on the spur of the moment. He needed a plan of action.

'The Captain Cook.'

'OK, he is want for go Captain Cook. I is make pick up there for go shop.' He flicked the cell phone shut and tossed it onto the dashboard. 'Phones!' He rolled his eyes heavenwards. 'I is think is be better when no-one is can find you.'

They drove on in silence. William couldn't bring himself to press Tr'boa about Lucy's living arrangements. He feared bad news. He wouldn't want Tr'boa to see the look on his face when he got it. They passed what William figured must be the turn-off for the village, as there were lots of people around. At first he thought they must be tourists from the States. He assumed there had been an influx of them as the result of the airstrip making the island more accessible, although he was surprised to see so many; it still wasn't that easy to get here. The reason he thought they were Americans was that they were all so big. They lumbered along on giant sequoia legs. Their butts were so huge they had flat tops like tables. You could have stood a cocktail glass on some of them and not had to worry about it slipping off. Their arms looked tiny and out of proportion to their massive torsos and stood out from their bodies like penguin flippers, because the rolls of fat around them wouldn't allow them to hang by their sides. They had no necks at all. Their heads just rolled about on top of their torsos as they waddled along. Apart from their size, the other thing that led William to conclude they were American tourists was that they had the uniform. Women's legs were encased in floral Bermuda shorts that made their distorted lumpy thighs appear to be sacks of potatoes. Huge T-shirts hung from barrage-balloon breasts that projected a couple of feet in front of them. The thighs of the men strained against the unforgiving material of knee-length Lycra shorts.

Unspecified lumps of flesh fought one another beneath the butt area of the same garments as though they kept small but pugnacious animals down there. They too sported tent-like T-shirts. Behind them often trotted scaled-down versions of themselves, their overweight children.

They came to a family that was strung out across the road, stumbling along, chatting to one another. They ignored Tr'boa when he honked. They were all too busy munching potato chips, each of them, father, mother, son, daughter, carrying in one hand his or her own giant pack, from which the other hand absent-mindedly transferred food to the mouth. Another SUV was coming from the other direction and Tr'boa had to wait for it before he could pull out around the family. As he did so, William had a good sight of them and realized they had the honey-coloured skin and facial features of islanders. As they passed other huge people toiling along the road he saw they also had the local characteristics. But not only did these people not look like the slim, diminutive natives he remembered, they didn't even look human. It was as if some race of grotesque aliens had invaded the island during the five years he'd been away.

It was some moments before he was able to speak without his voice choking. 'Tr'boa, what happened? How come everybody got so—' he had been going to say 'fat' but then he noted the absence of anything that might pass as a neck on his companion's body and the thighs that smothered the car seat next to him, 'big,' he finished, diplomatically.

'I is not be sure. Managua is say is be because we is not eat we own foods no more, others is say is be because we is have cars and is not walk, or catch fish or chop wood or do all they things. Purnu is reckon is be evil magic. He is claim for know who is be for blame.'

'And who is that?'

Tr'boa lifted his hands off the wheel, disconcertingly. 'Ah, you is must not ask me. I is not want trouble.'

'I understand. I'm not asking what you think, just tell me, who does Purnu blame?'

'Who else is can be but Managua? They two is still fight like always. Purnu is say is must be Managua who is cast fat spell, is be one good reason.'

'Which is?'

'Managua is still be thin.'

They passed more concrete buildings, evidently houses, because they had porches around them on which people lay on beach recliners. William saw that most of these people had the same Incredible Hulk proportions. He noticed too, as they passed more people on the road, that many of them, surely a bigger proportion than he had represented, sported artificial legs.

'Tr'boa, tell me, have there been more explosions? Have more people been injured by mines since I left?' He felt his anger rising. Part of the deal he'd struck with Sandy Beach had been that US military engineers would locate and remove all the landmines.

'One or two, maybe three or four, no more. And they is be plenty long time ago, before Americans is return and dig up all bombs. Is be no more bombs left now.'

William shrugged. Maybe he'd just happened to see all the people he'd helped. It was impossible to tell because their features were so inflated there was no way he could recognize them.

It was strange to approach the Captain Cook from any other direction than from the beach, but here they were, driving up a smart new road to it. Not only the road was new. What William had always regarded as the back of the hotel, but which was now obviously the front, had been finished. Instead of the cutaway, doll's-house façade he was accustomed to, there was a whole building. A large unlit neon sign said: 'Captain Cook Hotel – the only place to stay'.

Tr'boa nodded at it. 'You is see sign? Is be one big joke. Is be really only place for stay. Is not be any other hotel on island!'

Tr'boa stopped the jeep, got out and hefted William's bag out of the back for him.

'Thanks,' said William. Then he remembered. 'Oh, sorry.'

'Is be OK,' said Tr'boa. 'I is be accustom for people offer in-appropriate thanks. We is have many more visitor now. Americans for sell we things and also for sit on beach for watch sea. And little man with hair like orange fungi is be here not long ago. Also Japanese is come for take pictures. They is be worst of all. They is all be so rude – is thank we all time. Still, what you is can do?' He shrugged.

'Well, it's great to see you again,' said William. 'I'm sure we'll meet up before long, have a longer chat. Bye now.' He turned towards the hotel.

'Hey, *gwanga*!'

William stopped and turned back to face the young man. 'You is not pay me for taxi.'

'Oh, sorry. Listen, I don't have any yams . . .'

'Yams?' Tr'boa laughed. 'Nobody is have yams no more. Nobody is grow they damn things. Is be bloody damn stupid thing for use for trade anyhow, is be most tricky plant for grow, you is must always dig with yams. You is be right all along. Dollars is be much better. Now we is all use dollars.'

A local girl was behind the reception desk. In itself this was strange. She wore a band of bright red cloth around her chest, covering her breasts, and when she stood up he saw she had on a sarong-type skirt that stretched from her waist to her ankles. It was the first time he'd ever seen an island girl in proper clothes, unless, of course, you counted Lintoa, Sussua and poor Tigua, and he didn't suppose you really could. She checked him in without batting an eyelid, just as in any other hotel anywhere else in the world, taking his details and typing them into a computer with nonchalant aplomb. William couldn't help recalling the time when Managua was the only person, the only native person, anyway, on the island who could read. This was progress. The jury might still be out on whether or not motor vehicles were a good thing for the island, but he could surely be proud that one effect of his actions had been the spread of literacy.

'Is be you first visit this island, sir?'

'No, I was here five years ago,' said William. 'The hotel was a bit different last time I stayed in it.'

The girl looked at him more closely. 'I is remember you. You is be one they is call *gwanga*, who is do funny thing with eyes. Hah! you is do now! I is be just little kid when you is be here before.'

'I guess.'

'Well, enjoy you stay.' She handed him his key and pressed a bell on the counter in front of her. A local boy of about twelve, dressed in floral-patterned knee-length beach shorts, appeared as if from nowhere and picked up his bag. William followed him up the stairs, which had been restored so there was no need for him to ascend them with any worries about symmetry. As luck would have it his room was the one in which he'd found the pig Cordelia six years ago. Now the boy put down the bag and flung open the window shutters to reveal a stunning view of the sea. The room was light and airy and it was hard to recall it had ever seemed a dark and forbidding place that smelled of pig.

William walked out onto the balcony. The sea winked at him in the late-afternoon sun. He remembered Lintoa telling him how he had first seen Perlua standing in this very spot. It all seemed so long ago.

A slight cough behind him. He turned and saw the boy still standing there. He took out a dollar and gave it to him.

The boy smiled but didn't thank him. At least some of the old customs survive, thought William.

Later he went down to the dining room for dinner. The mahogany table that had once been his bed, where he had first enjoyed the exquisite pain and pleasure of making love with Lucy, where he had also slept with poor Sandy Beach and Dr Gold, was no more. Well, of course not. It had been decrepit even five years ago. Gone too was the grand piano. There was a new bar, no longer

474   ONE BIG DAMN PUZZLER

in the shape of a ship's hull, and the violent murder of Captain Cook had been erased from the wall and replaced with a pastel shade of blue.

The only other diners were a middle-aged Japanese couple. William chose a table as far away as possible from theirs, but this didn't stop them attempting to engage him in conversation.

'You have just arrived?' asked the man.

'Yes,' he replied and applied himself to the menu. He was intrigued to see it offered a variety of 'local delicacies' including king prawns, stuffed red mushrooms (one to avoid, he felt) and roast suckling pig.

'We have been here four days,' said the Japanese man. 'It's enough. There's nothing to see here.'

'The sunset is worth photographing,' said his wife. 'And maybe the sunrise, which we hope to get tomorrow morning. But as for the rest, don't waste your film. If you want to know anything about the place, ask us. We'll be here until the day after tomorrow.'

'Thanks, but I won't need to trouble you,' said William. 'I've been here before.'

'You've been here before?' said the woman, sounding as shocked as if he'd just said he was an axe murderer. 'And you came back?'

SIXTY-SEVEN

That night William lay in bed as he once lay on the mahogany dining table, listening to the sound of the surf remind him of his own mortality. Six years on from that first time. Six years older and nothing different in his life but that. Beneath the sound of the surf he could detect a steady hum, which seemed to signify his own ever-present anxiety. It took him some time to figure out it was the hotel's generator chugging away somewhere out back.

Next morning he awoke early. It was not long past dawn. His stomach felt a little queasy. He hoped the prawns he'd eaten had been fresh. More than that, he hoped they hadn't been near any fungi of whatever hue. He got out of bed, and walked to the bathroom. He sat down on the lavatory but the plastic seat felt cold and strange. It was no use. It seemed all wrong to take a dump like this.

He pulled on some clothes and went downstairs. Although it was so early the girl from yesterday was already on the desk. She obviously kept the same long hours as hotel workers all over the world. Even here.

He handed her his key. 'You is go out already, sir?' she said.

'Yes,' he replied, perhaps because of her island speech not thinking about what he was saying. 'I think I'll take a shit on the beach.'

The girl didn't bat an eyelid. But William turned around to find the Japanese couple standing right behind him, staring at him the way you might at, say, a psychopath. 'It's an old island custom,' he said, and pushed past them and out the door leaving them jabbering excitedly in Japanese.

The dawn wasn't quite as it had been. For a start there was the hum of the hotel's generator. True, it faded as he got further away, but then, as he neared the village, he became aware of an aural undertow, suggesting there was at least another, maybe several generators there. He wondered what other changes his dollars had wrought. Still you couldn't have everything and a little noise was surely a small price to pay for the benefits electricity must have brought to the islanders' previously benighted state.

He hurried because the sun was up and he thought he might be late, but when he reached the shitting beach there were only a few figures, a dozen at most, dotted around.

They stared at him as he made his way across the sand. The first thing he noticed was that two or three of them were morbidly obese, and several of the others were seriously overweight. There was much grunting and gasping, as the men strained to produce anything, a phenomenon he certainly didn't remember from before. Then he saw one of the figures, one of the slim ones, waving to him. He made his way across the beach to him. It was Managua.

'*Gwanga*, is be true then. I is hear you is come back, but I is think that fool Tr'boa is be mistake. Welcome.'

'Thanks,' said William.

Managua frowned. 'I see you is not learn any manners while you is be away.'

'Sorry, I forgot.'

'Is be OK. Is not be worst thing you is ever do.'

William shot him a questioning glance. Managua gave a dismissive wave of his hand. 'Not now, not now. Is time for do shit.' He squatted and pulled aside his pubic leaf string. William dropped his trousers and shorts and crouched beside him. He'd forgotten how refreshing it was to lift your butt to the breeze.

They squatted for a few moments in companionable silence, aside from the hum of the distant generators and the groans of constipated fat men. It wasn't just these latter that were different though, something was missing. There were too few people. There was no sense of communal ritual.

'Did I get here too late?' asked William. 'I seemed to have missed the main event.'

'No, this is be all,' said Managua, gesturing half-heartedly with the hand that wasn't holding aside his pubic leaf string. 'People now is have American toilet in they house. Is not can be bother for come here for shit. Is be one of many old customs that is fall away. Young people is no longer want for shit properly any more.'

It was true. William looked around and saw only old people. Managua, at what, sixty-five? was perhaps the youngest one there. But then he saw a youthful, muscular figure running across the sand towards them. William realized that this was the first young man still sporting the traditional pubic leaf, rather than Western-made shorts, that he'd seen since he arrived back on the island.

'*Gwanga!*' It was Lintoa, but not as he had seen him last, wearing a red dress and sporting a black eye after his fight with Sandy Beach, the fight that had led to the US government settling with the islanders out of court. You'd never have guessed this piece of smiling, supercharged testosterone had spent most of his life as a disgruntled girl.

Lintoa squatted the other side of William from Managua. 'I is shit on this part of beach these days,' he said. 'I is be boy now.'

'Man, I'd say,' said William.

Lintoa's chest puffed out a couple more inches, if that was possible. 'Is be true. Man.'

When they had all finished shitting and William was pulling up his trousers, he felt glad that at least one tradition had vanished. Purnu and his friends not being there meant there was nobody conducting a post-mortem on his dump. It was good to be able to attend the shitting without any embarrassment. At this moment he looked up and saw, maybe thirty feet away, the Japanese couple. The man had a video camera to his eye. It was pointed directly at William.

SIXTY-EIGHT

The track back to the village from the shitting beach was overgrown, Managua explained, because these days so few people walked this way for the daily communal bowel movement.

When they entered the village, William was appalled by what he saw. The outer ring of dwelling huts had all but abandoned its circular shape. Now it was a sprawl, spreading this way and that into the jungle. The reason was many of the traditional bamboo and *adula* buildings had been demolished and in their place single-storey concrete houses had sprung up. They were bigger than the old huts and had elbowed their way into the tree line. Behind each was a small cinder-block building from which emanated the drone of a gas-driven generator. No longer could you smell the scent of frangipani and lemon blossom; the air was perfumed with the acrid sting of petrol fumes.

Even those huts that remained from his former visits had changed. Almost all of them were roofed with corrugated tin. Somewhere or other on every house, bamboo or concrete, was a satellite TV dish.

If the outer circle made a distressing sight, at least it was still there. The inner circle had mostly been demolished, the one or two buildings that were left in sorry need of attention, their *adula* roofs dried to dust and blown away, the roof beams collapsed, the walls stove in by strong winds and left unrepaired.

It was some minutes before William could speak. 'What happened to the *bukumatula* houses?'

'No-one is use they any more. Young couples these days is just move in own house together. They is not bother for marry. They is sleep together and then they is sit outside they hut and eat together in full view of everyone. You is see they stuff they faces side by side. They is have no shame.'

'And the storehouses?'

'Is not be need. Now we is have shop.' Beyond the ruin of what had once been the *bukumatula* house where William had been kept awake by an orgy of sound, Managua indicated with the sweep of his arm the other side of the central village clearing where stood a long concrete building with glass windows and doors. On its roof a plastic sign read PURNU MINI MARKET. As they approached William read handwritten signs in the windows: SPECIAL! ONE MOON ONLY! COCA-COLA PLENTY DAMN CHEAP! and DORITOS – FIVE FLAVOURS NOW IN STOCK. A smaller notice said: POLITE NOTICE FOR ALL WE CUSTOMERS. WE IS BE SORRY WE IS NOT CAN ACCEPT YAMS.

Such, thought William, are the uses of literacy. He turned and, for the first time, saw beside the *kassa* house a new building, at least three or four times the size of the former. It was perhaps twenty feet high, made of solid wood, and circular. He looked at Managua, who was smiling proudly.

'Is be New Globe Playhouse. Is be what I is do with most of my dollars.'

'You built a playhouse? You have plays here?'

'Play,' said Managua. '*Hamlet*. First performance is be in few days' time.' He appeared confused. 'You is not know? I is think you is come special for see.'

'I didn't hear about it,' William confessed.

Managua pushed open the door of the building. Inside there were ten rows of steps for seats raked around an apron stage. Everything was in polished wood, such as you never saw on the island. It would not have disgraced any small American town. William shuddered to think what the rain and the sun and the termites would make of it.

'It – it's magnificent. It will be quite something to see a play here. I look forward to it.'

'Well, you is be in for one big damn treat,' said Lintoa, the Easter Island statue breaking into a huge grin. 'I is be Hamlet.'

'You?'

'Sure thing. I is learn all play.' He galloped down the step seats and leaped on to the stage. He held up one arm and declaimed. '*Is be, or is be not, is be one big damn puzzler.* You see? I is act plenty damn good, is I not? You is go tell me you is ever hear they words is be act better?'

'No,' agreed William, 'I certainly haven't.' This was true; although he couldn't remember whether or not he'd seen Hamlet, he knew that if he had the soliloquy definitely wouldn't have sounded anything like that.

Managua shot William a serious and meaningful look. 'You is see, *gwanga*, is be one good thing is come of you dollars.'

'Yes,' said William. 'One good thing.'

'No,' said Lintoa. 'You is must not forget, now we is have hospital.'

'Hospital?'

'Yes, people with dollars is put money together for build. We is have doctor too, from America.'

'Hospital! Huh!' Managua rolled his eyes. 'Come, *gwanga*. Now you is see some of mess you is make of island, how so many tradition is be ruin by you dollars, I is show you we is keep some of we customs. Even after all you is do, I is welcome you at my home.'

'Thanks,' said William.

Managua scowled and hobbled out of the building.

Managua's hut was as before, at least on the outside. It still had an *adula*-leaf roof and although a generator hummed from behind it, William saw that the noise emanated from a shed built of bamboo and *adula* rather than cinder blocks. In front of the door was the customary fire, on which a pot – no doubt containing the foul-tasting stew the old man lived on – bubbled away. Pilua kneeled by it, chopping vegetables.

'Greetings, *gwanga*,' she said. 'I is be please for see you. We is worry 'bout you with all this bad news from America.'

William was humbled by her concern. He had all but destroyed the islanders' way of life and here was one of them showing sympathy for him. He had a desperate urge to apologize, but couldn't find the words. 'Sorry' was so inadequate it amounted to an insult. 'Pleased to see you, too,' he mumbled.

If the exterior of the hut was hardly altered, inside it had been transformed. Gone was Managua's upturned plastic milk crate and in its place stood a large wooden keyhole desk, on top of which a computer sat winking. Across the room was a huge widescreen TV on a plastic stand, complete with DVD player and video recorder. Managua picked up a remote control and pointed it at the TV. A man in historic costume appeared. It took William a moment or two to realize it was Laurence Olivier in the film of *Hamlet*.

'He is be one plenty damn bad actor,' said Managua. 'He is talk like he is need for shit plenty bad. I is show Lintoa for teach he how he is must not act.' He pressed the remote and the picture vanished. Managua spat on the hard earth floor. 'Is not even be in surround sound.'

'Who is go want for hear that guy in surround sound?' Lintoa said. 'Is be bad enough for have he talk like that just from front.' He turned to William. 'Me, I is prefer *Die Hard*. Sound is be so good in that one is make walls shake. First time I is see I is think there is be hurricane.'

'Huh!' Managua rolled his eyes.

'Bruce Willis is be one plenty fine actor,' protested Lintoa.

'Huh!' repeated Managua.

'He is make fine Laertes. He is be damn good for fight,' insisted the former she-boy.

Managua shrugged. 'Yes, he is be plenty good in duel scene, I is give you that.'

Before Lintoa could argue any more there was a commotion in the doorway and William looked round to see Perlua come in, flanked by two toddlers, naked little boys, each as white as she, and identical to one another.

Lintoa rushed over to them and picked them up, sitting one on each of his massive forearms. 'Is be my family,' he announced proudly. 'My wife, Perlua, you is know, of course.' William smiled at her. She was, if anything, more beautiful than ever. She had that serene knowingness that motherhood confers upon some women. 'And these is be my sons. They is be twins. They names is be Rosencrantz and Guildenstern, like they two in *Hamlet* because no-one is can tell which of they is be which either.'

William sat on the floor and allowed the toddlers to tumble all over him and to prod and poke and pull him. Without looking up he said, 'I understand Miss Lucy has a child now.'

'Yes,' replied Managua. 'She is have girl.'

William glanced at him. The old man was regarding him seriously. 'Does the child look like anyone?' William asked. It came out as a whisper.

'How is child go look like anyone? She is not have father for mould she. She is have some slight coincidental resemblance with she *mamu*, yes, blue eyes, yellow hair, but that is be all. What you is expect with no father?'

William pretended to be absorbed in getting his hat back from one of the children. 'Lucy isn't married, then?'

'No, she is not be marry,' said Managua. 'She is become teacher. Is teach all children read and write. We is make whole generation of Shakespeares. People is use some of they dollars for buy books for she. Books is be more cheap than DVDs.'

Eventually William extracted himself from the children and stood up. He congratulated Lintoa on his young family. He declined Pilua's offer of stew. 'I think I'll just take a walk,' he said. Managua nodded. He didn't make any move to accompany

William. He might have gotten older, but he was still no fool.

William set off along the beach. It was a fine afternoon. The tide was on the way out and he watched a stranded sea turtle lumbering back towards the surf. He'd heard tell they lived for as much as a hundred, maybe, *mebbe*, even two hundred years. Time enough to make a mistake or two and put it right again, if you didn't get caught by hunters in the meantime. There weren't any hunters out today. At one time small boys had patrolled the beach regularly, on the lookout for easy turtle meat. He imagined they were all indoors now, watching TV or playing computer games, just like American kids. He sighed. You couldn't have everything. You couldn't have a school and literacy and a playhouse and a hospital and all the benefits of civilization and still kill turtles for fun, he guessed.

As he neared Lucy's house he heard the sound of voices, children's voices, singing, he thought at first, but as he got closer, he realized it was chanting. There were maybe twenty kids squatting on the beach in front of the house, ranged in a semicircle around an adult. As he got closer the blonde hair came into focus. He could see the shape of a woman. But the breasts weren't pointy any more. Maybe age, maybe motherhood, had softened them.

'Four twos is be eight, five twos is be ten, six twos is be twelve, seven twos is be fourteen, eight twos is be . . .' the children chanted. The woman looked up. She lifted a hand to push the hair out of her eyes and then used it to shield them from the sun as she stared at him. He was too far away to see her features. She probably couldn't see him well enough yet to know who he was and run away. He was wondering whether or not to proceed – after all he hadn't planned on his possible humiliation in front of twenty little kids – when the door of the house opened and a man came out, a stocky figure in Western clothes, tan shirt and pants and a slouch hat. He walked down the steps from the house to the beach. Lucy turned to look up at him. He bent and whispered something in her ear. William thought back to his conversation with Managua. He'd asked if Lucy was married. He hadn't inquired whether she had a boyfriend. Before the conversation was over and Lucy could turn her gaze back to him, William had turned tail and fled.

He cursed himself for being so cowardly. Somewhere among those children, probably, was his daughter. He wanted to see her. He wanted to find out how his genes and Lucy's had arranged themselves in her. Lucy couldn't deny him that. As he made his way back towards the village he found himself indulging in a fantasy about Lucy, as he had done once before on this very walk, so long ago now, it seemed, only this time the narrative was negative. He imagined a custody case with him fighting for access rights to his child. But already he knew there wouldn't be much point. He couldn't, as he'd planned, stay on the island, not with Lucy living on it with another man. He wouldn't need to be allowed to see his daughter more than once every five years, he told himself grimly, the island was still so difficult to get to. He began estimating how many years of life he had left and dividing it by five. It meant he'd see his child maybe eight, or nine or, at most, ten times. After that he'd be dependent on her smuggling herself into the *kassa* house, as her mother had once done, for them to meet.

He wandered out onto the island's main road where he followed the heartbreaking procession of grotesquely fat natives. As they approached the village by this route it took on the appearance of a strip mall, so familiar in America. There were a couple of concrete-built fast-food shops, one advertising PIG BURGERS, the other boasting SOUTHERN FRIED TURTLE MEAT. There was a large queue of large natives outside each. The area was littered with polystyrene carry-out food boxes and plastic cups. William could only stand and stare at what his dollars had done. From somewhere off in the jungle he heard – as he always seemed to at these pivotal moments of self-examination – the sarcastic cackle of a howler monkey.

In the village he came again to PURNU MINI MARKET and decided to visit the little sorcerer. The glass door had a handwritten sign stuck to it: ARTIFICIAL LIMB WEARERS! PREVENT ARTHRITIS! OIL YOU METAL LEG JOINTS NOW! SPECIAL CHEAP ONE MOON ONLY!

As William pushed open the door a bell announced his presence. A second or two later what he at first took to be a large rubber beach ball bounced through a doorway at the back of the shop. William was trying to peer through the doorway to see who had kicked or thrown the ball when he noticed it had things sticking out of it and then that these things were arms and legs and a head like a rat's. It was Purnu, grown freakishly large and round. It had been easy to mistake him for a beach ball because of the tight-fitting striped T-shirt and shorts he was wearing and because, by comparison with his torso, his arms and legs were like small flippers.

'Ah, *gwanga*, I is hear you is be back. If I is know earlier I is come and watch you shit. So sorry I is miss that.' Purnu's smile, never that convincing, was even less so now because there were gaps in it where he'd evidently shed a couple of teeth.

'It's OK,' said William, 'don't mention it.' He looked around at the shelves lined with bottles of cola and potato chips. 'This is some place you have here.'

'I is invest my dollars in retail. Now everyone is buy most of they food from mini market.'

'They buy food, even when there are plenty of fish in the sea and fruit on practically every tree and vegetables grow so easily in their gardens?'

Purnu sighed. 'They things is be too much work.' William winced at the word. When he'd first come to the island the natives hadn't known the concept of it. 'Besides, everything is change now we is have satellite TV. People is want tasty things they is see there.'

He paused to serve a well-built islander who had a trolley-load of cola bottles, tinned food and several giant packs of corn crackers. William watched Purnu stuff a sheaf of dollars into the cash register. The little man looked up and smiled. 'You is see, I is make plenty dollars.'

'Tell me,' said William, 'how do they pay you for magic these days, dollars or yams?'

Purnu shrugged apologetically. 'I is not do magic any more. This is be plenty more easy for make living. With magic you is must always be out at night of full moon for catch this, or dig up that, or bury some other thing. Then you is must make spell. Shop is be plenty more simple. Stuff is come in on plane. I is pay boy for put on shelves. People is take off shelf and is give me dollars. Besides, people is not want magic no more.'

'There isn't any magic?' William could hardly stop his voice cracking with despair.

'People is not grow crops so is not need spell for protect they. Is not need sorcerer for help catch fish because is not need fish.' He waved an arm to indicate shelves loaded with Doritos and Cheerios that made fishing unnecessary. 'If they is get sick, is have hospital. What for they is need magic?'

SIXTY-NINE

In the afternoon William had Tr'boa drive him out to the hospital. When he saw it he was reminded of the Captain Cook in the old days; it was half-finished. The single-storey building was of cinder block that had not yet been rendered. A few natives stood around a whirring cement mixer, chatting in a desultory manner that suggested it would be a struggle ever to get the place built. They looked ill-suited for the job, incongruously dressed as they were in nothing but pubic leaves and hard hats.

Inside there was a desk with a reception plaque. A plump young girl sat behind it, the nipples of her large and pendulous naked breasts tickling the keys of her computer keyboard.

'I'd like to see the doctor,' William told her. 'My name's William Hardt.'

'You is have appointment?'

'No, I'd just like to talk to him for a few minutes, to get some information.'

'He is make operation for this moment, but I is go see what I is can do. You is please take seat in waiting area.' She indicated the far side of the room where there were a dozen or so chairs. Half of them were occupied by superfat natives. As he sat down William observed that every one of them was missing a foot or lower leg. When a couple of them smiled at him, he noticed they were both light a tooth or two too. There were no magazines to read and there was nothing for William to do as the minutes ticked by save watch these patient patients as they opened packet after packet of potato chips and other snack foods and crammed the contents into their mouths. The idea seemed to be to get the stuff from the pack down into your stomach without either looking at it or chewing it.

Eventually he heard footsteps. 'Mistuh Hardt!' called the receptionist. He went over to her desk. 'The doctor is see you now. You is please take door on right.' As William walked off down the corridor he noticed how quiet it had suddenly become. Glancing at his fellow attendees he saw they had all stopped rustling their paper bags and munching the contents to glare furiously at him with that look reserved the world over for queue jumpers.

He knocked on the door and an indistinct voice replied, 'Come in.' The doctor was sitting behind a desk writing on a clipboard. He was wearing a surgical gown, hat and face mask. Without looking up, he gestured to William to take the customer's chair on the other side of the desk. Finally he grunted, tossed the clipboard to one side and the eyes flicked up. There was something familiar about them.

'Hardt? Is it really you? You've come back.'

The words were so muffled by the mask it was all William could do to make them out let alone identify the speaker. The doctor reached up and pulled down the mask. William gasped. 'Dr Gold!'

'It is you. I never thought I'd see you here again, Hardt.'

'I could say the same about you. What are you doing here?'

Gold shrugged and lifted his arms to indicate the building around him. 'I work here. This is my hospital.'

'But how . . . why?'

'I heard about the fix these people were in. Things sounded so bad I couldn't ignore it. I gave up my job – which was mostly trying to stop people getting their rightful compensation from Uncle Sam – and came out here to do what I could to help.'

'I don't understand. All these people with missing legs.'

'*Without* their missing legs, you mean, my friend.'

'But the US army was supposed to clear all the mines. How come so many more people are getting injured?'

Gold smiled grimly. 'And the US kept its word. It's not mines, Hardt.'

'Not mines? But what, then?'

'Diabetes.'

'Diabetes?'

'Diabetes mellitus, to give it its full name. There's an epidemic of it. More than thirty per cent of the islanders have it.'

'Thirty per cent? But that's incredible!'

'Not when you appreciate the facts. The people in this region of the South Pacific have a genetic disposition towards diabetes. Fortunately, until now they did not have the lifestyle to activate that disposition. Then you came along and gave them all those dollars. They spent them on sugary carbonated drinks and snack foods. The result is an explosion of adult-onset diabetes.'

William shook his head. For a whole minute he was speechless. 'B-but that doesn't explain why so many of them have lost limbs.'

'When you arrived I was performing a foot amputation. Amputations are virtually the only operation I do here. Diabetes is the most common cause of amputation the world over. I would have thought you might know that.'

William put his head in his hands.

'It's ironic, isn't it?' continued Gold. 'You got them money to compensate them for losing their limbs and that money has meant that even more of them have finished up missing a foot or a leg.'

William didn't move. Gold smiled. 'But look at it this way, my friend. It's not all bad. If you hadn't got them the dollars they wouldn't have been able to afford this splendid hospital to treat their diabetes.'

Gold stood up and removed his hat and gown. He walked over to a washbasin in a corner of the room, ran some water and splashed it over his face. He picked up a towel and dried himself then turned and gazed at William who finally lifted his head from his hands.

'What have I done?' William's voice came out so harsh you'd have thought he'd just had his throat rubbed with sandpaper rather than been told a shocking piece of news.

Gold shrugged. 'You've been an American. It's our big problem. We mean so well. We want to help everyone. We think we know best and we act from the best possible motives. And then the politicians and the corporations take over for the only reason they know which is to make another buck. Result, catastrophe.'

'Is – is there nothing we can do?'

'Sure. When someone comes to me with a blackened toe because he has no circulation in it and gangrene has set in I can cut it off. And when he comes back I can remove the other four toes. And some time later I will take off the rest of the foot, and after that the lower leg and then later still the rest of the leg and then it will be almost time for him to die.'

'But the money? All the millions of dollars they have. There must be some use we can put that to.'

'Gone!' said Gold, smiling broadly now.

'Gone? What do you mean?'

'It's mostly gone. Beach was here recently to pay the last small amount. But the people have spent most of it.'

'But how could they? It was millions of dollars. What did they spend it all on?'

'Doritos and Cheerios and Oreos and Coca-Cola and Pepsi. They bought a few electronic toys and the occasional SUV, but most of it they frittered away on American snack foods and carbonated drinks. I'm doing a lot of dental work, too, even though I'm not trained for it. The sweet stuff wreaks havoc on their teeth. Diabetes and tooth decay, that's all they got out of it.'

'I can't believe it. They couldn't have spent millions on those things.'

Gold smiled. 'Oh yes, they could. It all had to be imported by air, that put up the cost. And they consume prodigious quantities of it. You've seen the size of the customers in my waiting room. Buying their food meant they also abandoned their traditional pursuits of hunting and gardening. They have chemical toilets in their huts so they don't even have to walk to the beach to take a dump any more. Lack of exercise is a good friend to diabetes.'

Tears were running down William's face. 'What have I done?' he asked again.

Gold walked around the desk and gave him a kindly pat on the shoulder. 'It's OK, my friend, the end is in sight.'

William looked up at him, a gleam of hope in his eye. 'It is?'

'Sure thing. When they run out of money they won't be able to eat any more junk.'

Gold took William to his living quarters at the rear of the hospital. He had his own cinder-block building with a terrace that overlooked the ocean. He left William there with a beer while he dealt with his patients. William sat and watched the ocean which he couldn't hear above the ear-shattering judderings of a pneumatic drill that was duetting with the regular chug-chug-chug of the hospital generator. This aural intrusion into the visual paradise before him was such an obvious metaphor for what William had done to the island that his cheeks grew hot with a shame that even the tears that slid down them failed to cool. He thought how he'd carried out his own September 11 on the island. He had done far more damage than any terrorist ever could.

Such was the horror of William's self-examination he scarcely noticed Gold arrive and settle himself on a recliner with a shot of bourbon in his hand. It was only when the doctor spoke and broke his reverie that William glanced up and saw him for the first time minus his surgical gear. The outline of the stocky man and the tan chinos and shirt he was wearing were somehow familiar. It took only another second to know why. Gold was surely the man he had seen come out of Lucy's house. This plump doctor was her mystery lover!

At first William was deeply affronted by the discovery. How could Lucy prefer this unexciting, overweight, fifty-something man to him? The idea of it was beyond belief. Then he reflected that Lucy hadn't actually preferred Gold to him. She hadn't been offered the choice. After the first year his letters had ceased any attempt at reviving their fledgling relationship. When she didn't reply William had limited himself to writing about his life. He had given up hope that Lucy would ever change her mind and so he had offered her nothing. He'd abandoned any attempt to get her back, if, that is, he told himself ruefully, he could ever have been said to have had her in the first place.

Moreover, although Dr Gold was kind of old and physically un-attractive, he might have other attributes that appealed to Lucy. Especially after William, who had been – had been proven to be – the apostle of materialism and greed. Against all her pleadings he had put his pig-headed insistence on destroying a primitive civilization before a relationship with her. Why wouldn't she prefer someone like Gold, a man prepared to devote himself to helping where William had damaged, a fatherly man who could offer her protection and security? A medical man who, you never knew, might come in handy if you ever had a nasty run-in with a green shoestring snake. Above all, Gold was a serious person, a grown-up; the results of William's naive tampering with the island made him feel like an inadequate little boy.

He didn't know how to mention the subject of Lucy to Gold. He didn't want to precipitate the inevitable confirmation of his suspicions. Instead he told the doctor about Sandy Beach and his almost certain demise in the Twin Towers.

'That's a shame,' said Dr Gold. He took a long pull on his bourbon and sat nodding to himself. Then he said, 'Actually, it's not a shame. He was a mean-spirited little shit. I feel bad that I don't feel more sorry for him, but I have to confess I don't.'

William was surprised to hear the good doctor talk like this. He tried to defend his former schoolmate. 'He wasn't all bad, you know,' he said.

Gold pursed his lips and nodded. He sat looking at the ocean, deep in thought. Finally he spoke. 'Actually, I think he was.'

It was William's turn to look at the swelling expanse of blue water. He thought about Beach as a ten-year-old boy, playing a vindictive game of chess, he thought about the nickname Beach had labelled him with and how it had blighted his schooldays, he recalled the relish with which Beach had dismissed the legitimate compensation claims of the natives. Then he remembered Beach's dysfunctional family, how he had had to pick his childhood through tottering piles of junk, his parents' misplaced pride in their short-sighted, ginger geek of a son. Mostly he remembered that last morning, a few minutes before the known world exploded, and the unlikely hug Beach had given him.

'Nobody's all bad,' he said. 'Everyone has some good in him. It's just that we never managed to find it in Beach.'

Gold turned to look at him. William continued to stare steadfastly out to sea. Out the corner of his eye he could see the doctor's expression was one of reappraisal, as though he were seeing William in a different light.

William cleared his throat. It was now or never. He had to confront his rival. The late-afternoon light off the sea was winking at him as his eyelids fluttered with an OCD grandmaster's speed. 'Lucy's still here, then.'

'Yes,' said Gold, pouring himself another bourbon. 'She's doing a wonderful job with those children. She helps with the sick too. She really is a most remarkable woman.'

'Yes,' William whispered. 'And she's very attractive too.'

'Not only that,' replied Gold, 'but she makes the best breakfasts you've ever had.'

William didn't say any more after that. He took another can of beer when Gold offered it, without taking his eyes off the ocean. After staring out to sea for half an hour, he rose, said a brief, formal goodbye, and left. It was only when he was halfway along the road back to the Captain Cook that he realized he hadn't thanked Gold for his hospitality. Why was it that however hard you tried, there were always some things you could just never get right?

*　*　*

Back in his hotel room William lay on his bed and watched satellite TV. The news channels were still showing the attack on the Twin Towers, replaying the pictures over and over. No matter how many times you saw it you couldn't help watching again. You still hoped that this time the plane would turn away at the last moment, that this time it would miss, but it never did.

SEVENTY

Next morning there was a bigger turnout for shitting. There were no more participants than there had been the day before, but Purnu appeared with a large party of spectators, all of whom had evidently moved their bowels on the chemical toilets back in their huts, or possibly not, given that their huge size indicated a Western diet and hence probably constipation and unreliable shitting times. Purnu and his friends watched the proceedings from a respectful distance until they saw William pull up his trousers and begin to walk away, at which point they all tore across the sand as fast as their vast bulks would permit and gathered round his deposit, poking it with bamboo sticks and chattering excitedly. Looking back at them William reflected that he might have been the unwitting cause of the demise of most of the island's traditions, but at least he was also responsible for the establishment of a new one.

He'd agreed to help Lintoa fish. Hardly anyone else went out in their boats to fish any more; indeed, most of the boats lay unused and rotting at the landing beach. Only Lintoa and Managua and one or two others kept up the old traditions. Now that Managua had built his playhouse and bought his few electronic goods, he didn't buy anything – save for the odd DVD, Kenneth Branagh in *Hamlet*, Mel Gibson in *Hamlet* – any more. He and Lintoa were virtually self-sufficient, but, Lintoa explained, the fishing was hard

when you were on your own. Just pushing the boat off the beach
was difficult and hauling up full nets took all his strength.

They sat in the large canoe waiting for the nets to fill. It didn't
take long now, Lintoa said, because the sea was so underfished. The
sun was hot and William took off his hat and wiped his brow.
Lintoa smiled.

'What?' asked William.

'I is just think—' Lintoa had to stop, he was giggling so much.
'I is just think of that day we is take you in jungle for find Pilua.
You is get plenty hot.'

'It wasn't that funny to me. I almost gave up. If there'd been a
plane next day, I would have done.'

'That is be whole idea,' said Lintoa.

'What do you mean?'

'Is be Miss Lucy and Managua is cook that one up. Managua is
get idea from Shakespeare. Is be Miss Lucy who is ask we she-boys
for lead you all over island.'

William stared at him.

Lintoa raised his hands like a cowboy surrendering. 'Now, now,
gwanga, you is must not get mad. Is be plenty long time ago. And
you is find Pilua anyway. And you is must admit, is mebbe better
if you is not.'

'Miss Lucy asked you to do this?'

'Sure thing. She is not want for dollars is come here. She is be
plenty keen for keep old customs. She is write book 'bout we but
she is not be sure she is go let anyone is read, because she is have
big fear they is come and change island. She is not need for
have that fear now. Island is all be change.'

William thought on that for a while. How could he blame Lucy
for what he had endured that day when she had been right to
deceive him, when she had been right all along? Thinking of the
expedition to find Pilua and the northern village, he recalled his
discussion about pink hiking boots with Tigua. 'I'm looking forward to the *kassa* house tonight,' he said. 'It will be good to see
Tigua again.'

Lintoa's face fell. 'You is have disappointment, *gwanga*. You is not see Tigua there. She is not come *kassa* house no more.'

'Not see her? Why ever not?'

Lintoa smiled. It was a subtle smile for so straightforward and open a person. It contained both fondness and regret. 'Well, you is see Tigua is never be happy for be she-boy, even on Tuma. Then one day she is think, I is not have for remain she-boy. If I is not slough no more, I is grow more and more old until I is become floating baby. Is go back island, only this time, I is be girl, *real* girl.'

William smiled. Trust Tigua to figure that one out.

'Of course,' Lintoa continued, 'Tigua is find plenty difficult for not slough. Is not like for grow old, become ugly old sow. But she is put up with that for become real girl at last.'

'You figure that's what happened, that she became a real girl?'

'Who is can doubt, *gwanga*? Who is can think Tigua is can be so unlucky twice?'

Lintoa leaned over the side of the canoe and began hauling in the net. He turned back to William. 'Come on, *gwanga*, is no time for sit and stare at sea. I is know you white mans is like for do that, but not now, net is be full. We is let any more fish is get in there we is never be able for haul net out.'

The *kassa* house was almost empty. Managua had told him one reason was that most of the island's men were now so obese they could no longer get through the tunnel. There had been an embarrassing incident when someone had become wedged halfway along it and they had had to leave him for a few days until he slimmed down enough to crawl back out. After that the larger islanders no longer attempted entry. Managua had considered rebuilding the tunnel to make it wider but decided against it because he feared that any alteration to the *kassa* house might destroy its mystery and precipitate its destruction. Besides, making entry easier was no guarantee of increased attendance. It was likely most people would choose to remain in their huts, preferring what they saw on TV to visions of their dead ancestors. They didn't need *kassa* any more to get out of their brains. They could do that with beer.

Of course Purnu wasn't there. His circumference was larger than that of the stone they rolled across the tunnel to block it off. There was no way he could have gotten in, which was a shame, according to Managua, because for all his faults – everything about him really – no-one could mix *kassa* like Purnu. The *kassa* house fraternity had one new member, though. Now that he was a man, Lintoa was allowed in and it was he who mixed up the hallucinogenic paste with Managua.

There was plenty to go round. There were only a dozen or so men in the place. It made the appearance of the spirit people a distressing experience for William. The hut was full of them, all calling out wistfully for their loved ones, their expressions desperate as they went from living person to living person in a hopeless search for their children, or former partners, or friends. 'Purnu, Purnu, what for you is desert me?' wailed one old woman. 'P'toa, P'toa, how you is can leave me here alone?' sobbed an ancient man.

From the midst of this mêlée of forlorn and wailing wraiths a small figure emerged. It pushed its way angrily through the misty shapes of abandoned spirits and made for where William and Managua reclined against the wall. What William recognized to begin with was the scowl. He'd first witnessed it twenty-five years ago when he'd foolishly beaten its owner with a back-rank mate.

Sandy Beach stood before them. His ginger brush cut was scorched. His skin was black and blistered. His eyes burned with disbelief.

'Wanker? Is that you? Did you see what they did to me? Did you see what those crazy ragheads did to your old friend? I went to work and ended up dead. They killed me.' Beach's voice, never especially easy on the ear, had a smoky rasp to it now. 'Why did they do that? I never liked them, I admit, never liked their medieval, limb-lopping ways, but was that any reason to kill me . . . ?'

Then Beach did something William had never expected to see

him do. He began to cry. White streaks meandered through his sooty mask, mapping it with his frustration and regret.

William was struggling for a way to say all the things he felt. He wanted to tell Beach how sorry he was, how highly he prized the unexpected gift of that valedictory hug; he wanted to acknowledge his guilt for not offering the extra cup of coffee that would have changed it all, to express his remorse at never having liked him and, more than anything, to apologize for being the one to survive when the other had not. But it was no use; he had never spoken like that to Beach when he was alive and he didn't have the words to do it now. And, already, it was too late, already Beach was fading, still complaining, but disappearing fast, until his black face was absorbed into the surrounding darkness of the hut.

William had no time to think about any of this. Even as he peered into the gloom, seeking the last vestiges of his former schoolfriend, another figure emerged, familiar in chinos and plaid shirt.

'Hello, son, I'm glad you came now. I almost missed seeing you again.'

Joe Hardt looked terrible. Although he'd obviously sloughed again and was technically probably only in his twenties and so younger than his appalled son, he looked worn out. His cheeks were hollow, the black rings around his eyes blacker; he had an air about him of general dishevelment. He walked like a man whose balls ached from too much action. William could not help thinking of the nineteen young men who had hijacked American aircraft to their own particular heaven. He wondered how they were faring with their seventy-two virgins apiece. Were they as exhausted as his father on Tuma? Was their paradise turning out to be an eternal punishment?

'You thought I wouldn't come back, Dad?'

'No, son, I always knew you would. You have unfinished business here, after all. I meant I was getting worried as the years slipped by that when you finally showed up I'd be gone.'

'Gone? I don't understand.'

Joe Hardt shook his head. 'I – I just can't take any more of this kind of life. It isn't really me, never has been. Oh, OK, I enjoyed the novelty of it for a while, but there has to be more to life – I mean, death – than pleasure. There's no challenge in being dead.'

'What are you saying, Dad?'

'I'm trying to tell you you won't be seeing me here any more. This is my last visit to the *kassa* house. Your return was all I was waiting for. You know, the years on Tuma flash by much faster than where you are. I'll soon be old' – he chuckled – 'especially the way I'm living. I'm not going to slough again. I'm going to grow old disgracefully one last time and then I'm going to become a floating baby.'

'But Dad, that doesn't mean I won't see you again. I – I'll still be coming back here to the island. I can see you in your new life.'

Joe Hardt looked at him. He was trying to savour every detail of his precious son, to enjoy the sight of his fine boy one last time. 'It doesn't work like that, son. When I become a floating baby, I'll lose all memory of my old life. I won't have any knowledge of ever having been Joe Hardt.'

'No, Dad, no!' William tried to lift himself up, but his body was heavy as lead. He couldn't move a muscle.

'It's not so bad, son. I've been there before, remember? When I had Alzheimer's I forgot who I was, what I'd been. It didn't matter any to me.'

'Dad, it's not just that. I couldn't bear it, not to see you again.'

Joe Hardt smiled. 'William, it's what happens when people die. You have to let go of them. You have to just carry them around as a memory. But you have to let them go.'

'But Dad—'

'At least this way we got to say goodbye properly, son. Your last sight of me wasn't an empty dried-out husk of a person with his arm up in a ridiculous unexplained gesture. You got to tell me that you loved me.'

William swallowed hard. 'I – I guess.'

'And it's not true that you'll never see me again. It's a pretty small island. Everyone knows everyone else. I'll be here. You'll see me. I'll be a little itty baby. Of course, you won't know it's me. But one day you'll look into a pair of brown eyes here and you'll maybe see something of your old man in them and think it might be me. 'Course I won't know who you are, either. I won't have any knowledge that you were ever my son but maybe I'll have some special feeling for this strange white guy looking down at me . . .'

It was probably the smoke from the fire that made William's eyes sting. 'Hey, Dad,' he said, 'don't go all sentimental on me.'

His father didn't reply. He lifted one hand, the hand that he'd died holding rigidly in the air, gave a single wave, and was gone. It was the last time William would ever see him and know it.

SEVENTY-ONE

In many ways William felt inferior to Dr Gold. This was not saying much because for most of his life William had felt inferior to most of the people he'd encountered, the exception being Sandy Beach. OK, Gold had evidently deserted his family to come here, but in every other way he was morally superior. He had given up his job to help the natives for no material benefit to himself and was without doubt making a real difference to their blighted lives. But William's attempt to help others had achieved the opposite end. Like many OCD sufferers he had spent his life feeling responsible for disasters which it was actually impossible for him to have prevented. Now his misplaced altruism had *caused* a catastrophe. He had not only destroyed the culture of a primitive race, he had also left many members of it obese and short of a limb or two and maybe a few teeth too. Moreover, Dr Gold had skills and talents that could assist the natives in the dire situation in which William's do-gooding had placed them. William had nothing to offer. They didn't need a lawyer. Look where lawyering had got them.

There was one area, though, in which William could not bow to Gold's superiority: physical attractiveness. At heart, William could not believe that a club to which he had once belonged would admit Gold as a member. The club, of course, was Lucy.

This was how William came to be standing in the dark late one evening, outside the hospital. After a couple of days of fishing, watching reruns of 9/11, providing shit samples for curious natives and mooching around the village, he found he just couldn't accept that Gold and Lucy were having a relationship. It was true that Lucy must know he was on the island and had made no attempt to get in touch with him or see him, but that didn't necessarily mean she was making the beast with two backs with somebody else. William resolved to have it out with Gold. To find out just how things stood between him and Lucy. It was no use doing nothing. He had to know.

He thought he would catch Gold when he left the hospital for his home behind it. He imagined broaching the subject over a glass or two of bourbon and had rehearsed in his mind the firm hand-shake he would give the doctor as he congratulated him on his choice, entreated him to look after Lucy and wished him luck. He didn't like to dwell on the happier outcome, that there was nothing between the medical man and the woman he loved. He was with the stoics on this one, better imagine the worst so you're never caught out by it.

He didn't want to enter the hospital because he couldn't bear the other staff to see him and possibly witness his distress if the confrontation happened there. Anyway, Gold might be conducting an operation; he could hardly interrupt that. He didn't want to risk getting into an argument with a man with a scalpel in his hand. Besides the danger of personal injury to himself he didn't want an innocent bystander to lose a limb they didn't need to, at least not yet.

Eventually the last light in the hospital was extinguished. It was getting on for midnight. The good doctor was working late, un-doing William's doings. A few moments later the door of the building opened and Gold emerged. William was about to step out of the shadows and greet him when, instead of turning to go around the building on the side where his own quarters were, Gold strode briskly in the opposite direction. Where on earth could he be going at this time of night?

William drew back into the shelter of a *boaboa* tree, folding a pair of its elephant ear leaves over him. When Gold had gone a hundred yards or so, he began to follow. Gold made straight for the beach and once there, struck out along it. With a heavy heart, William followed. OK, so he knew now where Gold was off to. There was only one place in this direction he *could* be off to. But William followed nevertheless. He had made up his mind to find out the truth tonight and he would see this thing through to the bitter end, if need be.

There was no moon, only starlight, and even that partially obscured by a few clouds, so there wasn't any danger of Gold spotting him. The soft dry sand tugged at his feet as he struggled to keep up with the doctor. Gold was going at a punishing pace. William could scarcely bear to allow himself to think what might be making the good doctor so eager. Eventually the journey ended, as William had always known it must, at Lucy's house. Gold took the steps to the veranda two at a time – which seemed to William to show an indecent haste – and rapped gently on the door.

'It's me!' he called softly, but the night was so quiet, the sea so still that even this whisper carried to William, a hundred yards away.

The door opened and light leaked briefly out. Gold ducked inside and the light drained away.

A gentle rain began to fall. William walked up to the tree line but it was difficult to find shelter in a position where he could still watch the door of the house. Water dripped from the branches of the inadequate tree he had chosen, but he didn't really care. He kept looking at his watch. Inside he imagined Gold's big lips folding over Lucy's small mouth, his beard absorbing it. Perhaps they would ration themselves to that one kiss for a while and Gold would now be drinking a beer to help him relax after his hard day. Then, as another quarter-hour ticked past, maybe Lucy approached his chair and began to massage his aching shoulders, perhaps she reached her arms around him and unbuttoned his sweat-stained shirt; it was possible that then she took his drink from him and placed it carefully on a side table.

Now they were kissing again, now the doctor had put his hands under her T-shirt and released her breasts, cupping them in his great hairy paws. By now they must surely be in bed and William wondered how out of alignment their lips might be on the downward stroke, a measurement entirely dependent upon the size of his rival's cock. He didn't even want to think about that. He wanted to try to stop himself casting his mind back to whether he'd happened to notice the then irrelevant length of the doctor's member when they'd squatted together on the shitting beach all those years ago.

From somewhere in the forest came the lonely hoot of a rope-tree owl, the bird of which the celebrated South Seas naturalist Gottfried Helmer has said, 'It has the most forlorn cry of any bird in the Southern Hemisphere; it is a solitary bird and yet it always sounds as if it does not want to be alone.' William had never read that description but hearing the bird now he knew just how it felt.

He waited and watched until the darkness began to thin into the grey beginnings of dawn. His damp hair was plastered to his face, his wet shirt stuck to his body; the contemptuous elements mocked his cuckoldry. He turned his back on the house from which no-one had emerged during his long vigil. There was no point in remaining longer. He'd had the ocular proof. He had no wish for anyone to see him looking so ridiculous.

SEVENTY-TWO

The plane came every week now. It had to, to meet the insatiable demand for snack foods and fizzy drinks. William decided he would take the next one out. He knew he couldn't stay on the island when Lucy was with someone else. He couldn't watch another man mould his child. Better the risk of Arab terrorists than that!

When he told Managua of his decision, he was touched by the way the old man's face crumpled. 'It doesn't matter,' William said.

'Of course is matter,' Managua replied. 'You is miss performance of *Hamlet*.'

So much for affection. 'I'm sorry. I'd love to have seen it, but I can't spend an extra week on the island,' William said.

'Bugger!' Managua spat angrily into the fire. They were sitting outside his hut. William hoped that none of the old man's saliva had ended up in the open pot of stew cooking over the fire. He'd already turned down the stew so many times he didn't see how he could do it again, but as an OCD sufferer still with a few hygiene issues he wasn't about to eat another man's spit. 'You is be only one who is see *Hamlet*. Is be no-one else on island, not even Miss Lucy or Dr Gold.'

William recoiled at the linking of the lovers' names. Managua was too preoccupied with his own concerns about the play to notice. 'Never mind, is not can be help. If you is must go, you is must go. I is make video of performance anyway. I is send you tape for see. You is can e-mail me you opinion.'

William smiled. 'I'll look forward to getting the tape.'

Managua picked up a coconut-shell bowl and began ladling stew into it. He held it out to William.

'Actually, I'll pass if you don't mind, I just remembered, I said I'd drop in on Lamua. Purnu said she wanted to see me.'

Managua didn't move. He was staring angrily at William.

'What?'

The old man shook his head. 'Is be best you is take next plane. You is never learn manners.'

'But I remembered. I didn't thank you.'

Managua slammed the bowl down on the ground so that half its contents flew out. 'That is be whole point. You is must not thank me when you is have stew. You is must thank me when you is not have stew. What is be so difficult 'bout that?'

Purnu's hut was similarly furnished to Managua's except that in addition to the latest electronic gadgetry there was a porcelain toilet against one wall. A waste pipe led into the ground presum- ably to a septic tank buried outside. There was no screen or curtain to conceal someone using the toilet.

Lamua, like almost everyone else apart from Managua's family, had put on a few pounds, but she was not much overweight. Her attractiveness was of the buxom kind anyway and she could carry it. After asking William in she saw him looking at the toilet.

'You is want shit?' she said. 'Please, you is help youself.'

'No, it's OK, thanks,' William said hurriedly, although, when you thought about it, the invitation wasn't so strange. It was maybe too big an evolutionary leap to go from shitting on a public beach to private bathrooms all in one go.

'You is be sure? Purnu is tell me for ask you. Is say I is must not flush after you is use.'

William couldn't help smiling at Purnu's dedication to research. He was also pleased that he hadn't been discourteous. It was

obviously the proper thing to do to thank someone for the offer
of a shit when you didn't have one but not when you did.

Now these preliminaries were out of the way he noticed that
the widescreeen TV was on and that a small boy was sitting before
it watching cartoons. Small in terms of age, that was. The kid was
the shape of a basketball. His Simpsons T-shirt was straining at the
seams.

'Is be my son, Iago,' Lamua said.

'*Iago?*' said William.

'Managua is find in Shakespeare. You is not like?'

'No, no, it's a . . . a fine name.'

'Iago, look who is come for see you. Is be man they is call
gwanga. You is remember I is tell you 'bout he?'

The boy turned reluctantly from the TV and gave William the
once-over. He returned his gaze to the screen. 'He is not be so
funny as you is say,' he muttered.

Lamua shrugged. 'Kids!' she said. 'What you is gonna do?'

While he was there Kiroa dropped in to see her stepmother. It
took him some time to realize it *was* Kiroa because half a decade
of American snack foods and sugary drinks had transformed her
into a linebacker. It made him want to cry. The ruin of her once-
beautiful face rested on several layers of chin, her formerly proud
breasts dangled dangerously around the waistband of her baggy
shorts, formidable weapons in the event of any sudden movement
on her part. She introduced him to her children, two more
basketballs he restrained himself from patting on the head for fear
of bouncing.

As he made to leave, Lamua put her hand on his arm to restrain
him and hoisted herself up onto her toes to reach up and kiss him
gently on the cheek. He put his hand up to the spot, unable quite
to believe the gesture had occurred. She must have seen his
puzzlement. 'Is be for all you is do for me,' she said. 'Without you
none of this is happen.' Although the sweep of her hand took in
the whole hut, the widescreen TV, the electronic equipment, the
exhibitionist loo, he understood it meant none of these things, but

rather the people assembled there, spherical or not. 'I is be so lonely before you is come. Now I is have family.'

William smiled ruefully. Some good he had done, then, in spite of all else.

He found Managua in the theatre, supervising the dress rehearsal. Lintoa and another young man were on stage. They each held a long stick and seemed to be beating the hell out of one another.

'Hit, hit! One plenty big hit!' shouted Lintoa, catching the other fellow a good one across the shoulder blades.

'Stop!' called Managua. He hobbled up to the stage. 'How many times I is must tell you, Lintoa? You is hit he first, *then* you is say "Hit". How you is can say "Hit" before you is hit he?'

He noticed William. 'OK,' he said to the two on the stage, 'you is can take five.' They dropped their sticks and walked off together into the wings.

William nodded in their direction. 'It's looking good. I wish I could be here. But I really do want to leave tomorrow.'

Managua studied his face with the intensity other people reserved for William's shit. 'Is be OK for miss play,' he said. 'Is not be OK for not see you child.'

'*My* child? You think I had something to do with it, then? I thought it was just another floating baby without a father.'

Managua didn't smile. 'What I is believe is not matter here. Is be what you is think that is count. Is not be good you is leave without you is see small girl.'

William looked at the scenery, a crudely drawn picture of a medieval castle, made, it appeared, not of stone, but of bamboo. He glanced at Managua. 'You're a very wise man.'

'And you is be plenty stupid one. Tomorrow after we is shit together for last time, I is take you Miss Lucy's house. Is be polite visit. You is can see child without you is be embarrass.'

'Thank you.'

Managua shook his head and smiled. 'Is be as I is say. You is be plenty stupid. You is never learn anything.'

SEVENTY-THREE

'I is not see what all fuss is be about.' Managua stared at William's dump and shook his head. 'Some people is not have enough for do, I is think.'

The sun was still skulking below the horizon and the sky had only the grey of first light as they left the beach together for the last time. They walked along the water's edge, where the sand was still damp and a little firmer. It made it easier for Managua with his artificial leg.

'You didn't get a new one?' William said.

'No, I is guess I is have attachment for this one. Is be damn useless but at least is be my leg.' William knew what he meant. 'Mebbe one day I is change. For now, I is use all money for present *Hamlet*.'

When Lucy's house came into view, William could make out two figures sitting at a table on the veranda. As they drew closer one of them bulked out into Dr Gold. Lucy sat facing him and they appeared to be in animated conversation until her head suddenly turned and looked along the shore, as though she were expecting someone. Her eyes would have met William's had he not been distracted by a movement in the doorway of the house. A small figure skipped out and William experienced a flutter of wings in his ribcage. He had thought of his child as a link to the woman he had once almost loved, a responsibility, an additional weight to be added to the burden of guilt he carried around with him, but he had never managed to visualize her. And now, here she was, all those abstracts suddenly made flesh, not an idea but a person.

As he and Managua walked from the water's edge towards the steps to the house, the head of this small figure turned to look at them. The figure flitted down the steps and pranced towards them, a pale blur in a grass skirt.

The child halted a few paces from them. She stared at William. He could not help staring back. He was looking at his own face, the same blue eyes and blonde hair, the identical vulnerable smile. The only difference between them was that one of them was frantically blinking alternately and the other was not.

It was the child who broke the spell between them. 'Hello. You is be one who is be call *gwanga*?'

'Yes.'

'I is know because you is do funny thing with you eyes everyone is tell me about.' She reached out a hand and took his. Her hand was so small it fitted into his palm and disappeared when he closed his fingers over it. 'Come, my *mamu* is wait for you.'

She led him up the steps. He was conscious of the tap of Managua's artificial leg behind him. Gold smiled. He and Lucy had plates of half-eaten food in front of them. William noticed that a fleck of yellow yolk enlivened the grey of Gold's beard.

'*Mamu*, I is bring *gwanga*.'

'Yes, dear. Let go of Mr Hardt's hand and run inside and fetch another cup, would you?' She watched as the child disappeared indoors. Then she returned her gaze to William. She looked at him boldly, confidently, in the manner, he thought, of a woman who has a new lover greeting a discarded one. 'Hello.'

His own greeting came out as a mumble mainly because he was alternately grinding his molars as a means of keeping his eyelids still. Before William could get out another word the child reappeared with the cup and saucer. Lucy indicated an empty seat with a brusque gesture. Managua was already settling himself into the fourth chair around the table. William sat down. The little girl placed the cup and saucer before him and Lucy poured him some tea. She gave Managua a glass of water.

'Actually,' said William, 'my real name is William. What are you called?'

'Perdita.' The child clambered onto Dr Gold's lap and helped herself to a piece of toast from his plate. William found he could not tear his eyes from her.

'Is be from *Winter's Tale*. Is mean one who is be lost,' said Managua. He was looking at William with a wry smile upon his face.

Lucy butted in before William could comment. 'Would you like some breakfast? There's more toast on the way inside and I can easily fry up a few eggs and red fungi.'

'No. No thanks,' said William. He felt he might be sick. He didn't think he'd ever be able to eat again.

'He is go have breakfast with me back at village,' said Managua. 'I is have plenty nice stew there.'

'Second thoughts,' said William to Lucy, 'maybe I will.'

Lucy rose without speaking. She went inside and he heard pans being moved around.

The little girl climbed down from Gold's lap and disappeared into the house. William smiled at Gold. He didn't know what to say to him. 'You lucky dog,' was what he felt. 'You bastard.' Something like that. He looked out at the sea. 'It's a pleasant place to have breakfast,' was all he could come up with.

'Yes,' said Gold. 'That's just what I always say.'

If Gold's reply was by way of staking a claim, marking his territory like some dog lifting its leg, his affable smile belied it. He picked up his knife and fork and resumed his breakfast. The plump and baggy doctor lacked the physique to provoke sexual jealousy, but it was impossible not to envy how at ease he was with the child, his comfortable familiarity with his surroundings, the ghosts of many other breakfasts he had eaten here that were summoned by the casual disappearance of every forkful of food into his beard.

'You intend to stay here – I mean, on the island – for good?' said William.

'Yes, what have I got to go back to the States for?'

A wife and children in Albany, William thought, but he didn't say it. He didn't want to embarrass Gold. You couldn't really blame anyone for deserting his family for Lucy and anyway, who was William to censure someone else for leaving their family? He'd abandoned his before he even had it.

Lucy reappeared with a plate of minoa toast, fried turtle eggs and fried red – he hoped – fungi. She set it before William. He looked at the food and felt as much like eating it as he had the greasy, bacteria-laden repasts served up so many years ago by Mrs Beach.

'Eat!' prompted Dr Gold. 'You have a long journey ahead of you today. You need a full stomach.'

The man's concern seemed genuine in spite of coming with a reminder of William's departure and his defeat in the matter of Lucy. William lifted his knife and fork and picked at a red fungus without conviction. He'd gladly have swallowed an orange one, fully accepting the inevitable consequence, could he have guaranteed it would evoke any concern in the woman who now sat across the table from him, her face impassive.

Dr Gold cleared his throat and gently pushed Perdita from his ample lap. 'Managua, I wonder if you could spare a moment on Lucy's garden? She's been trying to grow a few yams but there's a bit of a problem with worm infestation . . .'

With a weary sigh Managua used the edge of the table to raise himself from his seat. He accompanied Gold down the steps, Perdita running after them and taking the doctor's hand. 'Is be real bugger for grow yams. Sometimes I is can see what for people is prefer dollars . . .' muttered the old man. They disappeared around the side of the house.

William put down his knife and fork, now he was safe from stew. He stared across the table at Lucy. She stared back, defying him to blink first. Even as he looked at her it seemed to him that her breasts were sharpening for battle. He couldn't tell that she was reappraising this man with whom she had had what really was no more than a fling so many years ago. Of course, elsewhere, it would have amounted to more than that. In another society he would have been considered the father of her child.

'*I is bring?*' said William. '*I is bring?*'

'What?' Lucy was taken aback by his tone. He had surely come to the island to see her. What other purpose could his visit have? She had not expected to come under attack.

'You taught our child to say "*I is bring.*"'

Lucy bridled. 'I didn't teach her anything. This is her home. She speaks like all the other children here. Anyway, she's not our child. We don't go in for physiological paternity here.'

'But—'

'You're not her father. A father is someone who lives with a woman and moulds her children, not someone who deposits a dollop of sperm inside her and clears off.'

'Is that why you didn't tell me about her?'

'Yes. It was none of your business. It had nothing to do with you.'

'The child's the spitting image of me.'

'That's nothing but coincidence. There isn't a causal connection.'

'How can you believe that?'

She shrugged and looked out at the ocean. Today, with the clouds overhead, it was grey and implacable. 'It's no more ridiculous than thinking Coca-Cola can save the world.'

'I'm sorry. You were right, I was wrong. There's nothing else I can say.'

'You can't say sorry to the whole island for what you've done. It won't bring back their legs or their health or their customs. How are you going to compensate them for that?'

'I wasn't apologizing to them. I was saying sorry to you. For not taking notice of you. For getting everything so wrong.'

'Oh, that's all right then, isn't it! That's bloody well all right!'

Lucy's voice had risen and it was now so loud it brought Managua and Dr Gold scuttling round the building from the back garden with Perdita skipping beside them.

'Look, *Mamu*,' she shouted excitedly, 'Managua is find yam!'

William stood abruptly, and went down the steps to meet the child.

'Look!' she shouted, holding something up, but his eyes were too full of tears to see what it was. He seized the child in his arms, picked her up and hugged her tight. When he relaxed his grip, she stared at him with something like fear in her eyes and ran back up the stairs to her mother. William set off towards the sea.

'Good luck, my friend!' he heard Dr Gold call after him.

Fifty yards or so along the strand, a puffing Managua caught him up. William strode along without speaking. The old man was scarcely able to keep up. Finally when they'd rounded the headland and the house was out of sight, William let up a little.

Managua paused to wipe his brow. 'That Miss Lucy,' he panted. 'She is be plenty nice but sometimes she is can be plenty damn pointy too.'

William didn't comment. Irrelevantly he found himself thinking, In a few hours I'll be leaving here for ever and I still haven't seen a yam.

SEVENTY-FOUR

Lucy paused in her reading of the *Arabian Nights* when she heard the plane's engine. The children craned their heads to watch it climb higher and higher into the sky and grow smaller and smaller as it took William Hardt further and further away.

Lucy thought of the pile of well-thumbed letters in her rusty old biscuit tin. She had constructed from them the frightened boy who had alternately blinked and molar ground his way through life. She had fitted this profile to the fading memory of the man she had scarcely known.

It was all so long ago, their relationship, that the man she had briefly loved then, if that's what it was, had been subsumed in the man of the letters. She felt like one of those women who meet men on the Internet or who marry prisoners on Death Row. It was so much harder to engage with the real thing.

Maybe she should have replied to his letters. She'd chosen to become an islander because she'd wanted to record the destruction of an isolated and primitive culture by outside influences which she had so correctly predicted. It would be her next, angry, book. And she'd wanted to give practical help to ameliorate the effects of modernization. She could, for example, provide the education the island's children would need to survive in this more modern world. She could minister to the sick. But this altruism had not been her only motive, she knew. Becoming an islander meant

denying William any connection to her child, for what repercussions might not his influence have there?

She had felt sorry for him today, sitting there with his eyelids
flickering away and she hadn't even had the kindness to tell him
she'd read his letters and understood. The poor man had kept
putting a hand over his eyes to conceal the tic, or had clamped his
jaws shut and ground his molars. She felt strangely affected by
his disorder. He had found comfort in writing of it to her, but
there had been no comfort here, today.

Did she still think of him as a lover? she asked herself. Certainly
if she were to, it would be as much for his tics and rituals as in spite
of them. He had hardly changed physically. The hair was a little
thinner, there were a few lines around his eyes. But mainly he was
as she'd remembered him. Then again, she thought, looking at her
daughter, she'd had his mirror image before her every day. So why
had she let him go? Why had she not encouraged him to stay?

She'd got annoyed with him, it was as simple as that. She was still
furious for what he'd done to the island and her fury had surfaced
in their quarrel over the way Perdita spoke. Even that made her
angry when she thought of it now. How typical of an American to
be incapable of allowing the difference of others! They always
wanted everyone to be like them! They were so convinced of
being right!

Still, it wasn't fair to blame all Americans. Dr Gold wasn't like
that. He'd abandoned his country and his career to come here to
help the people. He worked tirelessly for them, putting in
fourteen-hour shifts every day at the hospital. Lucy knew she
couldn't make it on the island without him. She wasn't able to be
a complete islander yet. She wasn't ready to abandon 'I am' for 'I is
be' just now. That would take time.

Lucy looked at her daughter, now, like all the other children,
standing to watch the plane shrinking to a speck in the distant sky.
She felt suddenly sorry for her child, growing up with a mother
who had no husband, no man to mould her. And yet, Perdita was
an island child, defined not by her blonde hair but by her grass

skirt. Lucy had chosen to stay here. Her daughter could not be moulded by a man who would try to stop her saying 'I is be'. It would never have worked.

She lifted the book. 'Come, children, sit down now. Let's get on with our story.'

No-one took any notice. The children were all standing, peering at the spot where the plane had disappeared, craning their necks, searching the sky. One or two leaped up and down in excitement. Lucy couldn't work out what was going on. Then she heard an aircraft engine, faint at first, no more than the hum of a mosquito, but soon growing steadily louder, until the children were pointing at the sky and shouting.

'Look, *Mamu*,' cried Perdita. 'Plane is come back.'

Lucy looked, and sure enough, there it was. No wonder the children were so excited. It had never happened before.

SEVENTY-FIVE

'Strewth!' the Australian pilot had the joystick back as far as it would go but you could still hear the plane's undercarriage brush the top branches of the trees. A moment later they were clear and the pilot had relaxed enough to remove his baseball hat and wipe his sweating forehead with it, just as he had when he'd landed the plane before. 'That was fucken close, mate. I'm bloody glad I won't be doing that again.'

'Why not?' William asked as he peered out of the window beside him at the shrinking island below. Another minute and they'd be so far away he wouldn't be able to make out the insults his interference had inflicted upon its emerald beauty.

'Because I like fucken living too much, that's why. I've told them I'm not doing this run any more. Fucken runway's too short. Let some other poor bastard get killed taking Coke to a load of one-legged Abos. Have you seen the size of those people? You take two or three of them to the big island and it's a fucken miracle if the bloody plane can even get off the ground let alone over the fucken trees.'

They were over the coastline now. There was the village, with the New Globe Playhouse rising magnificently out of the ramshackle collection of huts and concrete-block houses around it; there was the Captain Cook, shiny white and finished now, and that SUV was probably Tr'boa's taxi. There was the shitting beach where this morning he had taken what was almost certainly his last ever alfresco dump unless he ever went back to the Long Island shore and ate another carry-out pizza. There was a solitary fishing boat, Lintoa of course, getting in the day's catch before turning superstar for the evening's performance of *Hamlet*. And there, below now, as the plane followed the shoreline, there was Lucy's house where no doubt she and his daughter, rightly named Perdita because she was surely lost to him for ever now, might look up from their recitation of two times two is be four and think of him. Not that two twos always did make four, of course. Sometimes, no matter how you computed things, the answer came out odd. He thought how right, how even, how symmetrical it would be if he and Lucy could be together. Impossible to believe now that only a few hours ago he had sat on that very porch below, eating breakfast with her and the new man in her life and Managua . . .

William clapped his hand to his forehead. 'Stop!' he cried. 'Turn the plane around, we have to go back!' What a fool he was! Why hadn't he thought before? Of course there was nothing between Lucy and Dr Gold!

'What?' said the Australian. 'Are you serious, mate?'

'I'm a fool,' William said aloud. The Australian gave him a strange, worried glance. William began laughing. The pilot looked alarmed.

'What?' he said. 'What's the matter, mate?'

'Breakfast!' shrieked William.

'Breakfast? Listen mate, we don't do breakfast on these flights. I got some biscuits somewhere . . .'

'No, not me, them!'

The pilot glanced quickly at his instruments as though afraid to take his eyes off William. He shook his head. 'Sorry, mate, I just don't get it.'

'They were eating breakfast together!' William cried.

The plane dipped and then righted itself as the Australian, looking positively scared now, stopped staring at William and concentrated his efforts on flying.

William didn't notice the man's fearful expression. He was thinking about how Dr Gold had been eating breakfast with Lucy when he and Managua arrived. They hadn't made any attempt to hide it. There had been no frisbeeing of plates through windows, no desperate whisperings about egg yolk staining facial hair. And Lucy was always so respectful of the island's traditions. She would never have offended Managua by openly flouting them. Eating breakfast with Gold could mean only one thing. There must be some other explanation of why he had spent the night in her house. It couldn't be sex. She wasn't sleeping with him!

'Turn the plane round!' William cried again.

'Now listen here, mate . . .'

'I said, turn the plane round. I want to go back!'

The pilot laughed. 'You're fucken joking, mate. There's no way I'm going back there. Whatever it is you've forgotten, you can just fucken send for it later.'

'I haven't forgotten anything, I just changed my mind.'

'Too late for that, mate, you'll just have to wait for next week's flight.'

'I can't. I'm desperate. I want to go back now.'

'No way. No way I'm doing an extra landing and take-off.' He gunned the engine to indicate that not only was he not going back, he was getting away faster.

William leaned over and grabbed the steering mechanism. He tried to turn it and the plane lurched.

'What the fuck—' The pilot smacked him in the face with his fist. William slumped back into his seat. 'Haven't you had enough of people hijacking planes lately, mate? I could have you locked up for life for trying a trick like that.'

William rubbed his cheek. 'I'm sorry. Please, won't you turn around? I really do need to be back there today.'

'No way. Nothing on fucken earth would make me chance that runway two more times. Nothing.'

'I'll give you a thousand dollars.'

'Make it two.'

'OK.'

'Cash?'

'Yes.' Of course William hadn't got anywhere near two thousand dollars on him, but he'd worry about that when they were on the ground. Purnu must have that much from all his business affairs. He'd surely lend it to William at a suitably exorbitant rate of interest. He hoped so. He couldn't imagine being able to buy this guy off with yams.

SEVENTY-SIX

> '*Is be, or is be not, is be one big damn puzzler:*
> *Is you be bigger man for put up with*
> *Clubs and bamboo pits of real damn bad luck,*
> *Or, is take blowpipes for fight herd of pigs*
> *And is by use of snakebite, end they?*'

There was complete silence, Lintoa was doing the great soliloquy so well. Those in the audience − most of them, really − who had been rustling family packs of potato chips and crunching the contents, stilled their hands. They watched enraptured, open- and empty-mouthed. No-one so much as thought of disturbing a candy wrapper. No-one popped the tab on a can of Coke. There was but a single person who was finding it hard to concentrate but it was not because he was the only one who had seen the play before, if, that is, he had. It was the presence of Lucy next to him that was making things difficult for William Hardt.

Managua turned to him and smiled with the satisfaction of an author who knows his work is going down well. There was no anxiety in his expression. What I is tell you? it said. This is be per-formance of *Hamlet* even you is not be able for forget. It was the same self-confidence he'd demonstrated upon his encounter earlier with William outside the theatre when the American was supposed to be hundreds of miles over the horizon. Any surprise was blown away by literary vanity. 'I is be glad for see you, *gwanga*,' he'd said. 'I is know all along you is not can miss this.'

William's meeting with Lucy a moment later had been more awkward. She'd stared at him, not completely surprised, which made sense, when you thought about it: anyone not preoccupied with Jacobean drama would have noticed the plane had come back. 'I didn't expect to see you again quite so soon,' she'd said brusquely. 'You stayed away rather longer last time.'

William had had difficulty composing a reply. She obviously hadn't read his letters and 'I think I love you' didn't seem an appropriate remark to someone who didn't know he'd had a relationship – albeit a somewhat one-sided one – with her for the past six years. She hadn't exactly opened the door to that kind of declaration. Fortunately just then Dr Gold showed up accompanied by a middle-aged American woman and three children of various sizes, all a few years older than Perdita. He introduced them to William as his wife and children. They'd arrived on the plane William had left – and come back – on. The doctor presented his family all round and as Gold was talking to him William overheard Mrs Gold say to Lucy, 'I hope your daughter's recovered. I understand she was real sick.'

'Yes, but she's better now, thank you,' said Lucy. 'Your husband was so kind. He sat up all night with her.'

He realized he'd missed what Gold had said. 'What?' he said.

'I said, I knew it wouldn't be long before you were back.'

'You're not surprised?' asked William.

'Why would I be? Why would you want to stay in America? Why hang around in a country full of fear and hate and littered with vulnerable tall buildings?'

William would have liked to say more to the doctor, to tell him he wanted to help him, to do as much as he could to compensate for the effects of his first efforts to help the islanders, but the performance was about to start. Inside he found that Managua had contrived to seat him between himself and Lucy. Anyone could see from their faces that they were neither of them happy about it but

there was nothing they could do; in spite of *Die Hard* being shown
on one of the satellite channels that evening, there was a good
turnout and the little theatre was crammed. Only the most
committed Bruce Willis fans and Purnu had stayed away. 'I is prefer
action hero not *inaction* hero,' the little sorcerer had told Managua,
making him wonder if his rival had now read *Hamlet* as well, since
he seemed to know so damn much about it. Lamua had stayed
away too. She had suffered too much in the creative process of the
translation to endure the performance. She preferred to babysit
Perdita and Iago instead.

> *'For die, for sleep;*
> *For sleep: mebbe for dream: yes, here is be big problem;*
> *For on that isle of Tuma what dreams you is go have*
> *When you is limp, mebbe one-legged, from this life,*
> *Is make we think . . .'*

Although William's concentration was keenly affected by the
awkwardness of the seating arrangements one of the things that
makes Shakespeare the greatest dramatist of all is his ability to lift
your mind from the close proximity of a former lover with whom
you have unresolved issues to higher – *loftier*, Managua would have
said – thoughts. So it was now. Lintoa was speaking his lines
beautifully and in the end William found himself transported by
the words as he had never been before. Certainly not the last time
he'd seen *Hamlet*, if he had seen it. Indeed, not being transported
could be why he couldn't remember if he had.

> *'. . . who is go bear heavy load,*
> *For grunt and sweat on artificial limb,*
> *Unless is not be ready yet for Tuma,*
> *That undiscovered island from where*
> *All traveller is return in kassa house –*
> *Is be one more big damn puzzler'*

Of course, another reason the words were affecting him more than before, assuming there had been a before, was that they were not the same words. It wasn't Shakespeare's work that was making him think, but Managua's transformation of *Hamlet* into something else. The original carried the bleak message that only the fear of unknown misery after death keeps us struggling through this life. But the old islander, with his *kassa*-house view of the afterlife, was asking, how can you give up on life until you've lived it? It might be hard, it might be heavy, you might have to get through it on one leg, but getting through it was what you did. Endurance was an essential part of being alive.

William's thoughts went back to the *kassa* house. Word back from Tuma, via his dad, was that a life, even an *after*life without struggle, lacked interest and that unalloyed pleasure eventually cloyed. Maybe that's what the suicide bombers were finding now, that being pampered for all eternity was not worth the price they had paid.

He thought how he'd spent his whole life being afraid and look where it had gotten him. He'd wasted huge chunks of his three and a half decades in meaningless rituals to ward off things that might never happen and one thing, death, that definitely would. His rituals hadn't stopped that one getting any closer. Did it matter if Tuma was a myth and that the dead people who returned were no more than drug-induced hallucinations? You just had to let yourself believe and get on with your life. He pulled absent-mindedly at his trousers. He was starting to get comfortable in his thoughts, but not in what he was wearing.

He heard a tinkle of laughter and realized it was Lucy. He couldn't recall having heard her laugh much before; they hadn't had a lot of time for fun. The sound was taken up by others around them and William got his focus back on the stage. It was the beginning of the last act and the audience was appreciating the topical jokes Managua had worked into the gravedigger scene. Instead of Shakespeare's lampooning of lawyers and tanners, Managua poked fun at American soldiers; he was merciless on the subject of British hotel builders; he punned concerning the water-proof qualities of the hide of the black bantam pig. Then the laughter stopped as the first gravedigger lifted up a human skull.

Lintoa obeyed the stage direction *Takes the skull* with such infinite tenderness that once more all snack foods were put on hold. A hush came over the audience. As Lintoa held up the skull, face to fleshless face, and stared into its empty sockets his voice sank almost to a whisper that you had to strain to hear.

> *'Alas, poor Yorick! I is know she . . .'*

The former she-boy's voice cracked and died. There was a long pause. No-one dared breathe. William saw the footlights reflected in small jewels upon Lintoa's cheeks. He was struggling to regain his voice after the slip. His expression took on a determined look.

'I – I is know she . . .' he managed at last, the stress falling with heavy deliberation upon the final word. William's flesh tingled as he understood what all the audience surely already knew, that Lintoa had not, after all, made a mistake but that he was holding the skull of his childhood friend, the little she-boy who had died for love of him. Tigua had always been meant to play Ophelia. Well, that was out of the question now, but Lintoa had contrived to find him this small part in the play. He swallowed and began again.

> *'I is know she, Horatio: is be fellow who is always make joke, of most excellent fancy: I is bear she upon my back plenty many damn times; and now, I is not bear for imagine this thought!'*

His fingers caressed the skull's gaping jaw.

> *'Here is hang they lips that is always long for kiss me. Where is be you jokes now? you flashes of laughter that is make whole village roar? You is not have one now for make fun of you own grin? You is must go see white lady and tell she she is can paint she face as thick as she finger, still she is end in look like this; you is make she laugh at that, old friend. . .'*

It was Lintoa's finest hour. The moment when he became an actor. Of course he had been in training for it most of his life, playing unwillingly the part of a girl. But this was something else. This was the real thing. There was not a dry eye in the house. How Tigua would have loved this! William thought, to be, if only for a moment, the star of the show.

William stole a sideways glance and saw a tear begin its slow progress down Lucy's cheek and be hastily wiped away. Another followed. Before he could stop it, his hand reached out towards hers but she recoiled from its touch as though she'd been surprised by a green shoestring.

He reached for it again.

'No, leave me alone!' she hissed.

'If I'd wanted to do that, I wouldn't have come back.'

'Ssh!' said Managua.

Onstage the funeral of Ophelia was taking place. The audience became slightly restive. It wasn't a burial service they could recognize. Ophelia's relatives were all too upset. A woman in front of William turned round to see what was happening between him and Lucy.

'Please, I know that you don't know me and I don't know you, not in one way—'

'Not in any way!' Her voice was louder this time.

'Be quiet!' snapped Managua, raising his voice too. Onstage they had moved on from the funeral to the final scene of the play, but the bit before the duel, Hamlet's teasing of the hapless Osric, failed to grip the spectators. Two or three more people in front of William and Lucy turned around to see what was going on. One man stood up to look at them and a woman in front of the man, *behind* him looking back at the two white people, told him to sit down because she couldn't see them.

William shifted uncomfortably in his seat again, pulling at his trousers. He tried to get his mind back on the play but it was no good; Shakespeare's relentless wordplay was just too hard to follow, especially when filtered through Managua. It was a relief to see

Claudius and Gertrude walk onto the stage. William tapped Lucy's arm and when she looked at him, he smiled, and mimed, 'Lucy, please—'

Lucy shrugged. It was not the gesture of hostility William took it to be. His mime had been accompanied by alternate tooth grinding and it was impossible to decipher the words he was mouthing. That said, she felt annoyed. On the whole, she'd told herself, after he'd left this morning, she didn't want him in her life, churning her feelings. She didn't want him on the island where his American ways could not but make things even worse. In front of them more and more people were turning around, craning their necks, watching the dumbshow between them, which was looking to be more interesting than what was happening onstage, where the swordfight had begun. It was pretty tame, two people hitting one another with pieces of wood. If they'd wanted to see fighting they could have stayed home with *Die Hard* where they had proper guns.

'I'm staying!' said William.

'You don't belong here!' snapped Lucy.

'*Is be hit, is be definite hit,*' said Osric.

'Sssh!' said Managua.

'I don't know what you want from me!' said Lucy. It came out as an exasperated sob, louder than anything you could hear from the stage. Even Lintoa and the young man who was playing Laertes glanced up at them.

'*Gertrude, you is must not drink.*'

'A chance to try again. You must at least grant me that. To be the husband of my daughter's mother.'

A fat woman in the row behind them tapped William on the shoulder. He turned and she flashed him a wide, almost toothless smile. 'You is think you is can say that again?' she asked. 'Is be plenty damn complicate for get in one go.'

'*Look out for queen there, ho!*'

'She doesn't need her mother to have a husband,' said Lucy. 'This is one place on earth that can get by without men. Especially men like you. You're just all wrong. We've had too much of America since you came here. You simply don't belong.'

'*Treason! treason!*'

William didn't answer. He rose from his seat.

'Sit down!' hissed Managua.

A man behind him, who was sitting next to Dr Gold and his family, prodded Managua in the back and said, 'You is be quiet. I is want for hear what he is go say.'

A woman in front said, 'You is be right. This is be too damn good for miss. Is be highlight of whole evening.'

'*Here, you taboo breaker, murderer, damn Dane,*
You is drink this red fungi stew,' interrupted Lintoa.

William didn't need silence either from the audience around him or the people on the stage because he didn't say anything. Instead he pulled off his T-shirt revealing his naked chest. He began to unbuckle his belt.

> '*You that is look pale and is tremble at this chance,*
> *That is but dumb fellas or audience for this act,*
> *If I is only have time—*'

'What the hell are you doing?' cried Lucy.

'Oh dear,' shrieked the fat woman behind him, putting her hands to her face. 'I is think he is go break taboo!'

Onstage Hamlet dropped to the floor at the very moment William dropped his trousers. Every eye in the house was upon the American rather than the fake Dane. There was a huge collective gasp. He was naked except for a pubic leaf.

There are some places in a story where you have to get on with the narrative, without pausing or digressing or figuring stuff out, where you have to keep the momentum going, to cut to the chase and run headlong to the end. And there are others where you just have to stop and explain why someone is wearing a pubic leaf. This is one of the latter.

The first thing William did when the plane landed was to hail Tr'boa's cab to take him and the Australian pilot to Purnu's Mini Market where, after a brief explanation of his predicament, the little sorcerer counted two thousand dollars into the Australian's outstretched palm.

As they watched the man depart in the cab, Purnu said, 'Is be plenty money for fly when you is only be in sky five minutes. If you is want for do again, I is take you plenty more cheap.'

After not expressing his gratitude to Purnu, William sought out Lintoa who had just returned from the morning's fishing.

'*Gwanga!* I is think you is take plane.'

'I did, but then I came back.'

'How long you is stay this time?'

'For ever. I'm not leaving again.'

The big former she-boy looked at him hard. 'What you is go do here?'

'Fish, if you'll still have me on your boat. Help Dr Gold if he'll have me at the hospital. Grow yams, once I find out what they are. Get stoned on *kassa*. Grow older. See my daughter every day. Die. Go to Tuma. Come back and see you in the *kassa* house. Grow older. Slough. Grow older, become a floating baby, start all over again. What else is there?'

'I is not know, *gwanga*. If is be anything else, I is not find.'

He helped Lintoa carry his catch back to his hut where a surprised Perlua greeted him warmly and then began the task of gutting the fish and smoking them over the fire outside. The two men sat and watched her. Lintoa fired up a *kassa* pipe and passed it to William. Then he got up, went into the hut and came out again clutching a thick wad of typescript.

'I is must go over my lines for tonight. You is please excuse me?'

'Of course.' William passed the pipe back. 'There's just one thing you can do for me.'

'Yes?' Lintoa took a hit of the *kassa*. 'Anything, if I is can.'

'Could you show me how to make a pubic leaf?'

Lintoa put down the script and weighted it with a cooking pot.

He went into the hut and emerged holding a length of liana with what looked an unfeasibly small leaf dangling from it. He thrust it at William. 'Here, you is can have my spare.'

William took it from him. He wondered if spare meant in case of accident to the one Lintoa was wearing or if he changed them to wash them. Could they even be washed or did you wear one until the autumnal moment when it fell apart and then just make a new one? He resisted the urge to sniff it.

Lintoa was smiling. 'You is not dress like American no more?'

'You got it. Nor think like one, either. Do you mind if I change in your house?'

William could hardly believe that he, who had been unable to use unfamiliar lavatories for fear of bacteria, had progressed through a slow process of shitting on a public beach to pulling on a thong that had in all probability recently encased the genitals of a primitive tribesman. He marvelled at the journey he had made since he first came to the island. He had never expected to reach this point, never dreamed he would share underwear – or was a pubic leaf technically outerwear since nothing was worn over it? – with another man. At least the leaf was not hard and scratchy as he'd expected but soft and smooth as silk. He wasn't sure, though, that he'd ever feel comfortable with the liana string bisecting his butt.

He emerged self-consciously from the hut. 'Ha!' said Lintoa. 'Now you is not be American. You is be islander.'

Perlua looked up from her fish-gutting and raised her eyebrows. 'Is suit you, *gwanga*,' she said, a smile playing on her lips, 'but I is think you is go need longer string.'

William fetched his trousers and pulled them on over the pubic leaf and put his T-shirt on again. Lintoa and Perlua looked puzzled.

'It's just for a while,' he said. 'I'd be grateful if you'd keep quiet about the pubic leaf for now.'

Onstage Horatio had kneeled to cradle the dying Hamlet's head in his arms. No-one was watching. There was too much of a hubbub at the spectacle of an American in a pubic leaf. Well, it was a surprising sight. Most of the men in the audience had gone the other way, dresswise. They'd abandoned pubic leaves for Bermuda shorts.

'*Oh, I is die, Horatio,*' said Lintoa. Nobody heard. None of them believed Lintoa was really going to die, anyway. Bruce Willis never did.

'What the hell do you think you're doing?' said Lucy for the second time.

Before William could reply he was interrupted by a loud voice from the row behind. Mrs Gold said to her husband, 'I hope you're not going to start going around in one of those things.'

'No, I want to stay here, but I won't be going the whole hog like him,' replied Gold with an amiable laugh. 'I wouldn't look good in something like that – and it doesn't really go with wielding a scalpel.'

'It kind of suits him though, doesn't it?' said Mrs Gold. She chuckled. 'But I think he's going to need a longer string.'

Managua stood up and swung round. 'BE QUIET!' he bellowed. His voice was so commanding that if anyone had still been looking at the stage they would have seen Lintoa stop speaking mid-sentence. 'We is be here for hear play,' boomed the old man, 'not you!'

Lintoa took his cue from the play's translator. '*OH I IS DIE, HORATIO!*' he shouted. He didn't sound like a dying man, but better that than not be heard at all. '*THIS GREEN SHOE-STRING VENOM PLUS RED FUNGI STEW IS DO ME IN!*'

The fat woman along the row from the Golds, who'd spoken earlier, raised an admonitory finger to Managua. 'What for you is tell she for be quiet? She is be plenty damn right. He is go need longer string. Anyone is can see that.'

'That is be plain truth,' said another fat woman next to her, revealing a mouth as equally devoid of teeth as her companion's. 'I is not be surprise if string is break any minute now from strain.'

'If we is be lucky!' said the first woman, digging her in the ribs and giggling.

Managua put his face in his hands.

'What are you doing?' cried Lucy. 'Why are you dressed like that?'

William puffed out his chest and struck himself proudly on it. He'd hoped for a Tarzan effect but the sound was more like the slap of a wet fish when you dropped one into the bottom of Lintoa's boat. Still, he was into it now. It was too late to back out. He had the attention of the whole audience. 'I is not be American no more,' he shouted. 'I is be islander now!'

'*I IS NOT CAN LIVE FOR HEAR NEWS FROM ENGLAND!*'

The fat woman and her friend burst into spontaneous applause. It wasn't at all apparent to anyone not in their immediate vicinity whether they were applauding William or the play. Lintoa lifted his head from the floor of the stage and nodded and smiled this way and that by way of appreciation as the clapping was taken up around the auditorium. Onstage, Gertrude, who had been dead for quite a few speeches now, put her hands together and clapped too. William turned and bowed.

'I is not want for be American,' William announced. 'I is want for live here.'

'You is not live at all if you is not shut up soon!' said Managua, trying to pull him down.

'No, you is be quiet and let he speak!' came a voice from right at the back that William recognized as belonging to N'roa. 'This is be better than play!'

'*HE HAS MY DYING VOICE.*'

Lucy looked sympathetically at Managua. She turned to William. 'Please, you're ruining the performance,' she said. 'What do I have to say to make you sit down?'

'Just three little words.'

'Ah, no. Don't ask me that. It would be so crazy. I can't. It was all so long ago. I – I don't even know if I loved you then.'

'I'm not talking about love,' said William. 'I don't expect that, at least not yet. That needs time. Those weren't the words I meant.'

'I don't understand.' Her eyes were pleading with him now. 'If it's not that, what is it that you want from me? What three words are you on about?'

William lowered himself into his seat. 'Bed and breakfast.' He looked at her awaiting an answer. She didn't speak. She bit her lip and glared fiercely at the stage. The audience, not convinced that the sideshow was over, kept its gaze upon her.

'SO YOU IS TELL HE WHAT IS HAPPEN HERE.'

'Well?' whispered William. He reached out tentatively and covered Lucy's hand with his own. This time she did not move. He was so nervous he could not prevent his thumb and little finger pressing her flesh in a minor right–left–left–right routine.

Lucy turned and looked at him. William shifted his gaze back to the stage where Lintoa was taking advantage of what might well prove only a hiatus in the audience disturbance to gabble out his final speech.

'Well?' said the fat woman behind.

William could have sworn he felt Lucy's thumb move beneath his, lifting slightly, and then her pinkie, not once but twice, followed by her thumb again, but then he could easily have been wrong. And if he had felt it, it didn't necessarily mean she'd read his letters after all; it could have been her fingers were merely unconsciously rebelling against the pressure from his own. Whatever, it gave him hope, but it wasn't anything you could call an answer.

'Well?' he whispered again.

The fat woman behind leaned forward and spoke loudly into Lucy's ear. 'You is better say yes, if you is ask my advice. You is not go get better offer.'

'Is be damn right,' agreed her companion, loudly. 'Specially not with they pointy breasts.'

Lucy licked her lips and everyone around her caught their breath. Lintoa lifted his great Easter Island statue head from

Horatio's arms to summon the words that in Managua's version would end the play. Everybody was waiting to hear what Lucy would answer. Even over the distant chug-chug of generators you could have heard a pin drop.

'Rest . . .'

The word came out as a harsh whisper. It wasn't very loud – Lintoa had worn out his voice shouting over the disturbance – but its very hoarseness gave you the feeling the speaker had a mortal wound, and coming out of the blue, when everyone was expecting to hear something from the Englishwoman, it was enough to remind them all that there was another drama being played out here too, down on the stage.

The audience didn't know which way to look. The white woman said nothing. She turned and stared at the *gwanga*. Her blue eyes looked into his. And then, the merest flicker of her right eyelid. So fast you could think you'd imagined it, but it was there all the same. A wink, a palpable wink. A second later, more slowly now, the same with the left. Once. Twice. And then the right again.

The two fat women behind sighed loudly. That old eye thing the American always did! Now the Englishwoman had started doing it too. As if it were catching! And now he was doing it back to her. They were both doing it! Getting faster and faster! It made you dizzy just to watch. Not that there was any point. Who could understand this crazy white mans' language? Even Managua would not be able to translate this.

The two women gave up on waiting for the white woman to speak. She was too busy with her eyes to say anything now. They got their own eyes back on the stage because there seemed to be more happening there. One by one the rest of the crowd did the same.

'Rest . . .' croaked Lintoa again, sensing that he had the audience's attention back and summoning a last effort to turn up the volume of his strained vocal cords. He paused to exchange smiles with the skull that squatted on the other side of the stage, watching patiently. No-one in the theatre made any more noise than what was left of Lintoa's old friend. Tension hung in the air thick as smoke in the *kassa* house.

'*Rest,*' said Lintoa, '*is be silence.*'

THE END

AUTHOR'S NOTE

I am hugely indebted to ethnographer Bronislaw Malinowski's classic book *The Sexual Life of Savages in North-Western Melanesia* (Routledge and Kegan Paul 1929), an account of his research among the natives of the Trobriand Islands, British New Guinea, during the years 1914-18. Although it seems incredible, even for ninety years ago when Malinowski was conducting his research, the Trobrianders had never made the connection between sexual intercourse and pregnancy. They practised free love from an early age until marriage and their society was matrilineal. Malinowski's book provided the basis of much of Lucy's descriptions of my natives' ideas and practices, principally their sexual habits, including the institution of the bachelor huts, the natives' reliance upon magic, their beliefs about birth and death, and their burial customs.

My other main source for background on the South Pacific islands was Paul Theroux's wonderfully sad travelogue *The Happy Isles of Oceania* (Hamish Hamilton 1992).

For information on OCD I have drawn upon the following books upon the subject: *Obsessive Compulsive Disorder* by Dr Frederick Toates and Dr Olga Coschug-Toates (Class Publishing 2002); *Obsessive-Compulsive Disorder* by Padmal de Silva and Stanley Rachman (OUP 1998); *Living with Fear* by Isaac M Marks, M.D. (McGraw-Hill, Inc 1978); *Understanding Obsessions and Compulsions* by Dr Frank Tallis (Sheldon Press 1992).

The edition of Shakespeare used by Managua is *The Complete Works of William Shakespeare* (Nelson Doubleday, Inc. Books Club Edition, date of publication unknown).

ONE BIG DAMN PUZZLER

John Harding

___

Observations and

Topics for discussion

John Harding reflects on the role of the island in literature . . .

The Tempest, Robinson Crusoe, Gulliver's Travels, Treasure Island, The Island of Doctor Moreau, The Mysterious Island, Pascali's Island, Captain Corelli's Mandolin, and now – a humble addition to that illustrious but far from complete list – this new novel of mine, *One Big Damn Puzzler*, why is it that so many writers choose to set their stories on islands? Well, for a start there are obvious plot benefits: the author has a tight, inward-looking community with a clear boundary between it and the outside world; there are no blurred edges, no easy escape from the intense relationships that develop amongst those who have grown up amongst one another with little knowledge of anything else. And isolation can produce the Galapagos-style evolution of a society radically different from our own, inviting satire by comparison. The conflict all writers of fiction are constantly seeking is virtually ready-made. Just toss in a stranger, or, in the case of *Corelli*, a whole army of strangers, and it's there right away. But it's not just plot that makes islands attractive; if fiction is about creating a new world readers will want to spend time in, an island gives you a physical base from which to start.

Islands play an elemental role in our psychology too. An island may represent the self. New psychotherapy patients are sometimes asked to draw a map of their own island and the results often provide startling insights. The sea is a common symbol for the unconscious and in most island novels is never very far away, so it almost becomes another character whose mood swings from calm to tempest play a major role. If most writers are drawn to islands, I find myself especially so. Only after completing *One Big Damn Puzzler*, did I realise all three of my novels were about islands. In the first, *What We Did On Our Holiday*, the hot and crowded island of Malta becomes a pressure cooker for a holidaying British family, bringing to the boil simmering conflicts about an old man's Parkinson's Disease and his son's ambivalence about fatherhood. My second book, *While the Sun Shines*, may not be set on an island, but the protagonist, Michael Cole, is a boozing, drug-taking academic whose isolation from other people is at odds with the most celebrated saying of his specialist subject, the poet John Donne, that 'No man is an island', and who tries to get off his own personal island and connect with others through his relentless sexual promiscuity. Flashback scenes in the book have an island setting, the fenland Isle of Ely, where interestingly, perhaps, both Cole and I were born.

Both these books were first person, single point of view stories and for my third I wanted to spread my wings technically and write about lots of characters as an omniscient narrator. Moreover, this was to be a book involving Obsessive Compulsive Disorder and, as a fairly obsessive personality, I wanted to tell the story at a remove from myself. Initially I was nervous about abandoning a form that had proved so successful before, but once I decided upon the Pacific island setting, it was as though a dam had burst inside me and I experienced a flood of exhilaration. Omniscience meant omnipotence. This is the thing about islands. They don't have to be on any map. You can do what you like. You can create a whole new world. I had a lot of fun imagining my own flora and fauna from poisonous mushrooms and laughing monkeys to dwarf pigs and the green shoestring, a snake whose bite was so deadly that the moment you felt it you were gone. And I peopled my world with a tribe whose prelapsarian innocence was such they had not even made the connection between sex and reproduction, and whose mixture of naiveté and wisdom was a counterpoint to our Western ways. One of the leading characters in the book is a tribesman who is translating *Hamlet* into his own tongue and so naturally I had to invent a language for him to translate it into, a new pidgin English, and so stumbled upon the title of the book as 'To be or not to be, that is the question,' became 'Is be or is be not, is be one big damn puzzler'.

On islands, normal rules don't apply. OCD sufferers are victims of magical thinking, at some level believing they can ward off bad things by certain rituals, avoiding cracks in the pavement, perhaps, or repeating a meaningless action over and over. On my island, as on Prospero's in *The Tempest*, I could have real magic, so the dead walk and talk and the living fly, and you can take a potion to make someone fall in love with you.

Of course it's a very OCD thing to want to control your environment. OCD people are control freaks, something I understood as I found it wonderful to play God in this way. Except of course, in the end, I wasn't running the show. As any novelist knows you can make up your world, you can put your brave new people in it, you can give them all the strange customs you want, you can even tell them how to speak, but then they just break free and do their own thing. They start to say things they weren't meant to, they behave as you hadn't supposed they would. The villians act a bit nicer and the good guys reveal a bit of a nasty side. The wrong people fall in love with each other and then you see it was right all along. Sometimes the ones you love best up and die on you. My island declared its independence from me. It developed a life of its own. And I got an inkling of how God feels about the human race.

When you finish writing a book and reconnect with the real world, what stays with you is the feeling of having created something out of nothing. Part of me believes my island exists, though another part of me knows I'll never be able to go there again, though I'd like to see how my people are getting along. And part of me thinks, this mad magical world is the island I drew, and worries, what does that say about me?

Suggestions for Reading Group Discussion

Given the quotation from *Hamlet* with which the author prefaces *One Big Damn Puzzler*, the book's main theme appears to be that the fear of death can be overcome by the way we look at it. How far is it possible that the idea of *Tuma* – fictional though it is – can offer comfort to readers of the book?

The Times review called *One Big Damn Puzzler* 'an allusive *tour de force*'. How many of Shakespeare's plays can you find referred to, either directly or indirectly, in the book? What other works of literature are alluded to?

Magic is an important element in *One Big Damn Puzzler*. How does the author link William's 'magical thinking', his OCD, to the islanders' beliefs about magic? Why do you think he does this?

The reader never learns how Managua overcomes the problems of his missing page and explains the death of Polonius. Ask each member of the group to write the missing scene in island pidgin. Compare and discuss them and choose which would be the most likely for Managua to have written. Alternatively, try discussing the book for fifteen minutes in the island dialect.

Although most of the action of *One Big Damn Puzzler* takes place on an unnamed island in the South Pacific, the author occasionally takes us away from it, mainly in flashbacks. What do you think is the dramatic purpose of this?

Are the effects of William's visits to the island entirely negative or are there benefits to the islanders from his intervention in their lives?

John Harding has said that the humour in his books is never there for its own sake but always contributes to the narrative. What do you think is the function of the Shitting Beach and what do the (not infrequent) mentions of excrement signify?

The islanders have not made the connection between sexual intercourse and procreation. Do you think this is an example of ignorance being bliss?

Further Reading

If you enjoyed *One Big Damn Puzzler*, you may like to explore these books with similar settings or themes:

An Outcast of the Islands by Joseph Conrad
Lord Jim by Joseph Conrad
A Prayer For Owen Meany by John Irving
Typee by Herman Melville
The Moon and Sixpence by W Somerset Maugham
The Happy Isles of Oceania by Paul Theroux
Girlfriend In A Coma by Douglas Coupland
The Beach by Alex Garland